DOMINION

Thanks to Athina Paris, Editor for your dedication and tireless effort.

Cover art by Neyra Gomez

Published By

RockHill Publishing LLC
PO Box 62241
Virginia Beach, VA 23466-2241
www.rockhillpublishing.com

DOMINION

JOHN L. FORD

Special thanks and appreciation to Matthew McCarthy for his devotion and attention to detail. Borrowed from his own publication successes, his assistance at times proved invaluable.

Special thanks to Daniel Schwartz, whose fondness for native topics helped instill very necessary confidence during the polishing phases of this fictional design.

Dedicated to Richard Pearson and David Ford, whose acumen in science planted seeds in me very early in childhood that grew into a life journey blessed with scientific imagination.

"…In the future, AI could develop a will of its own – a will that is in conflict with ours" – Stephen Hawkings

"A computational device is incapable of developing a mind. We got consciousness not just by being clever" – Sir Roger Penrose

Visions of you … endlessly

NOTE to the reader

It is recommended that one takes the time to brief the INTRODUCTION primer for this ensuing fictional work. The functional technology that scaffolds the entire thematic-arc has roots in real-time sciences that are quite esoteric. The familiarization provided by the introduction is hoped to give both a sense of relevancy to modern times, but also instill a sense of urgency that may well transcend this fictional account.

Considering the present and prospective eras of ever-advancing technological ethos, humanity nears a techno-evolutionary gate, through which the advent of 'real' Artificial Intelligence may be engineered by the provinces of human ingenuity; that which only God and nature had succeeded in creating: self-awareness and the power of consciousness.

INTRODUCTION

What is a microtubule, and why do I care?

The short answer? Perhaps… to *care* at all.

In his book, *The Emperor's New Mind* (1989), preeminent Mathematical Physicist, Sir Roger Penrose, employs multiple intellectual disciplines to consider the question of consciousness as an emergence in Artificial Intelligence. With his special facilities to turn the wheels of Mathematics, Physics, observations borrowed from Cosmology, as well as reasoning sculpted by formulaic Philosophy, he delivers us to a fascinating implication: machine borne intelligence will never more than merely assimilate human sentience. From that we may infer, the very best the technical artisans of advancement will ever achieve is to cleverly mimic, where the observer would be unable to detect the difference between what is ingenuity and what is genuine; that which has taken nature millions of years to "perfect" by process of natural selection and evolution. And so the naturally inquisitive type by now may be inclined to ask what then is consciousness if it cannot be recreated?

The ultimate answer to that, which is one of the whopper original questions of all time, seems to have as many definitions as there are eras since our species first emerged out of the primordial oblivion with the capacity to even ask the question. So let us start somewhere simple. According to the first among various preferential definitions offered by "Merriam-Webster", we are perfectly valid to assume that consciousness is: "The quality or state of being aware especially of something within oneself."

Elegant and succinct enough, but later preferences then mention "The state of being characterized by sensation, emotion, volition, and thought." And suddenly we are exposing an increasingly mottled, broader spectrum of component-psyche as actually involved – those of which that prior definition does not even begin to scratch the surface. So, where does that end? We could just as well plumb this thought experiment into the murkier abstractions of ego, self-preservation and ambition for that matter. Why not how these faculties give rise to general metacognitive awareness – how we as individuals identify with ourselves, and others around us as having their own 'cognitive processors.' This also seems important in the total ability of one to situate their own existence within a collectively acceptable framework of the space-time-continuum – the one we assume to be reality.

In a greater sense, then, it would appear a larger set of subsidiary contributing aspects of the psyche must be melding together, where perhaps more of a *gestalt* is really the fuller definition of consciousness. And like gestalt, its ephemeral nature disappears as we begin to remove the various components integral to its occurrence; certainly, changes the characterization of the synergistic emergence if we were to begin replacing individual components with variances.

That gestalt is the challenge and ambition in the creation of true AI. It really is astounding that natural evolutionary refinement, purely via randomness of quasi-infinite events occurring over unimaginable time-spans, created our ability to conceive the way we do as second nature. Whether by agency, or lottery of vicissitudes to fortune, vagarious chance over time succeeded in conjuring a 'biological computer' whose provinces, you and me, are according to Penrose beyond the capability of machines. Over prior technological eras, that is certainly evidentiary.

Then there is the fundamental philosophical question related to the vastness of the universe; if an event ever happens once, can that event happen twice? Particularly given the scale and dimension of the Cosmos, 'yes' becomes intuitive, perhaps even statistically argued to be the case with extreme likeliness. This does leave an interesting ambiguity that conflicts with the assumption of machine-limitation: It does not seem we can logically presume that just because human ingenuity is at the whim and helm of discovery, humanity cannot also be the agency of that design. After all, humans are part of the vastness of the Cosmos. It may simply be a matter of time. The account in the furthering pages of this novel will create the accident, and implicitly broach the pertinent question humanity seldom considers, whether we should.

What is of particular intrigue comes later by Penrose, himself, in his book *Shadow of The Mind* (1994), the conceptual framing for the ORCH OR theory *Orchestrated Objective Reduction* where he and colleague Dr. Stuart Hameroff brought forth the postulate of microtubules, which are intrinsic in our plot. They espouse them as being instrumental in the emergence of consciousness. Then, in 2013, they furthered their postulations "Consciousness in the universe: a review of the ORCH OR theory." The abstract follows...

"The nature of consciousness, the mechanism by which it occurs in the brain, and its ultimate place in the universe are unknown. We proposed in the mid-1990's that consciousness depends on biologically 'orchestrated' coherent quantum processes in collections of microtubules within brain neurons, that these quantum processes correlate with, and regulate, neuronal synaptic and membrane activity, and that the continuous Schrödinger evolution of each such process terminates in accordance with the specific Diósi–Penrose (DP) scheme of 'objective reduction' ('OR') of the quantum state. This orchestrated OR activity ('Orch OR') is taken to result in moments of conscious awareness and/or choice. The DP form of OR is related to the fundamentals of quantum mechanics and space–time geometry, so Orch OR suggests that there is a connection between the brain's biomolecular processes and the basic structure of the universe. Here we review Orch OR in light of criticisms and developments in quantum biology, neuroscience, physics and cosmology. We also introduce a novel suggestion of 'beat frequencies' of faster microtubule vibrations as a possible source of the observed electro-encephalographic ('EEG') correlates of consciousness. We conclude that consciousness plays an intrinsic role in the universe."

"Consciousness in the universe: a review of the 'ORCH OR' theory." Hameroff, Stuart & Penrose, Roger. (2013). Physics of life reviews. 11. 10.1016/j.plrev.2013.08.002

Unbeknown to the more popular sciences and the hurried cultural urgencies during the bustling early 21st Century world, those extraordinary theoretical claims were then followed up with a startling empirical observation, one suggesting direct corroborative evidence that they are uncovering truth. These prompted the very necessity to revisit the subject in their 2014 review of the 20-year-old theory. Since the inception of this novel, it should be noted that quantum vibrations in microtubules have been observed and thus, corroborating the theory of consciousness as originally proposed by Hameroff and Penrose.

"Reply to seven commentaries on "Consciousness in the universe: Review of the 'Orch OR' theory," by Stuart Hameroff, MD, and Roger Penrose, FRS. dx.doi.org/10.1016/j.plrev.2013.08.002

This should give anyone with a modicum of foresight some pause. Science appears to be narrowing in upon the origin of what makes us who we are, if occurring under the radar of common popularization, or even awareness. Most importantly, as history repeatedly demonstrates, such extraordinary advances seldom are left unguarded. *They will tend to precipitate… application.*

Somewhere between the mid-1990s postulate, well prior to the 2013 paper, and the 2014 review, our story was engineered. Though the composition of this fictional account was formulated during those years, as destiny would have it, the very same thoughts lending to science created by the engineers of this story, seem to be coincidentally converging in time with science fact.

It should not be taken lightly. What should resonate is the sticky plausibility, if and when mere randomness out among the white noise of society can grapple with such esoteric subject matter, yet formulate so similarly, where else then are these investigations taking place? It certainly would appear right off the bat to be of importance, considering what machine-intelligence is already capable of – and considering, *airplanes will never fly either*. Moreover, that ease suggests the scope of these efforts would be more ubiquitous out among the general research ambits than a mere enthusiast's turning of the pen.

Our experiences with humanity teach us, whether for fearing failure in challenged veracity or perhaps something else motivating, in either reality, said research would probably be done so confidentially. Who else may be onto this? And with resources of whatever agencies at their disposal, do they plumb its potential and for what purpose? Recreating sentience in AI being the true goal that extends beyond mere similucra, discovering vibrational energy in microtubules has become empirical, and once that happens in the realm of technological states and affairs that so favor the advances of newer science and technology, it would be wise to consider that recreating those same physical processes artificially, may not lag far behind. We may be, for better or worse, nearing the threshold where mimicking nature's elegance gives rise to more than the sum of its integration. And the problem with gestalt is that the upper boundary of where the emergent power can extend is inherently unknown.

This novel offers a quasi-blueprint. As though hidden out there tucked away in one of many seams in the technological tapestry of society our story takes place. It takes place in a similar realm increasingly devoid of morality, not necessarily at the fault of the contributing engineers, either; but where they are so enabled. It is just too tempting, and easy, to turn dials and push buttons and fulfill the instinct for discovery, or the rush to realize ambition, in any realm where modernization powers experimentation like no other time in human history – that hurry subsumes the morality of the engagement…

Table of Content

1
CONCEPTION

For any normal human being, of which one or two college students might happen to qualify, the droning of Professor Lombard's lectures was particularly torturous. Seemingly, far more adept at submerging brains in melatonin than actually flooding minds with useful information, his ninety minutes of eternal tedium actually required the student need intensely focus too. "...Lectin proteins linking intermediate filaments with adjacent neurons, inside of which house recently discovered microtubules," along with, "Actin filaments; membrane components; plexins that are receptors for semaphorins," punctuated by the soft taps of a dry-erase pen to whiteboard made all the difference.

Onward through the professor's esoteric language of neurobiology, Colton and his weary-eyed companions trudged. He sat only half in and out of direct awareness of the professor's pedantic style. However, different from his companions, his mind was ablaze with derivation. He seemed to feed off the lecture in formulating answers to key questions, and explanation for triggered insights, those that could even offer fundamental truths. Some people are natural synthesizers. They have a special perception. They can use their minds to probe into systems and see how disparate factors and forces that to most others may seem trivial. In their perceptions they begin to uncover deeper relationships. He was one of these, and his postulations were capable of that prescience visionaries often possess that provide leaps in forward.

As to the surrounding strew of provincial daydreamers, they created a pall of disinterest to the amphitheater while the soft fluorescent illumination from above bathed them all in subliminal ocular rhythms. They situated hands over their brow, as though peering pensively downward upon their notes, but the head bobs briefly slipping from one's grip betrayed them taking turns losing in instances their war on slumber.

With his attention to a whiteboard, the professor appeared oblivious to the apathy.

Not for Colton, his fingers danced along the keyboard of his tablet. For reasons only he could fathom, the drudgery and content only sparked invention. Where the fervor in text as it charged across the screen may have been triggered by Lombard's content, this rest was the power of a genius in a state of creation.

Nearing thirty years of age, he was a physicist in need of a new idea. The circumstance of the university life, in a lot of ways, is supposed to be nurturing, and by default, empathetic. And though his unwitting reliance on that afforded him a direly needed hiatus from the sciences, this could not carry on indefinitely, and he knew it. He was beginning to sense the world moving on without him. And so his salvation had arrived at last, one sorely needed for a truly gifted, albeit troubled mind on the verge of wasting away into the great catch basin of mediocrity.

Despite his present efforts, mental notes found freedom outside the confines of his mind. "Microtubules must be… no, wait…" he paused unknowing that an onlooker turned in his favor.

"What purpose does that serve? oh, fascinating! Because nature never creates anything it doesn't use and—" a voice drilled into his concentration.

The nine tiers above Lombard's lectern were at first offering enough buffer to engage.

"Come again? Did I just hear you right, fascinating?" the stranger said through an uncommitted chuckle, "You can't mean this crap. Oh my god."

His immediate response was to stare.

2

"Hello. Ha. Glad to see someone's actually taken-in by this tedium."

"Uh, I... don't understand. What do you mean?" Colton paused, "Ooh, I see. You caught me."

"I mean, we're up to our ears in... whatever that is, semiphorins? And you're fascinated. Okay, there bro, I guess. Whatever it takes, huh? But, please, by all means continue."

Colton knew this sort. So much of what radiated off it was never far from droll, if not centered in outright frivolity. And it was often quick, too quick, leaving lesser wits at a loss; of course, only until they had left the scene and it was too late.

"So, hey," the stranger shifted a little closer in his seat. "Since we're doin' Q and A, has old Limp-dick here ever turned anyone on? Man, is this guy fuckin' dry or what? Kinda sorry I," he broke to turn a glance over the auditorium, "any of us signed up for this course."

"Yes, he... ah... he does carry a bit of a dry delivery, doesn't he? It's not his fault though. I mean, think about it; there is only so much one can do to really dress up this kind of subject matter."

"I-um, I think you mean, there is *nothing* one can do, but, go ahead."

"Ha ha, okay, I'm with you. But, this is the third of his courses in neurophysiology I've passed through. I haven't detected much variation in his style."

The stranger quickly added, "Yea, sounds riveting."

In tandem with his feigning jocular façade, invention roiled internally. Then, the opportunity occurred. If sold the right way, could this stranger purchase such a notion? "Well, to be honest, I kinda dig on this stuff though. I find it fascinating to think of these intricate complexities; why do they exist... in nature."

"Guess I can't argue with that. Hell, neurobiology gave us Einstein, Mozart... Hitler for that matter. Those didn't take place in a vacuum?"

He allowed the man's sarcasm to smolder, "I mean, the physical make-up of the mind. Like, with these nanoscale features."

"Nanoscale? Ooh, sounds serious."

"Anyway, so they are cone-like structures. But why… why do they exist, like, at all? It is as though through purely by fortunate chance or vicissitudes that take place in evolution."

"Hold it. Wait a sec," the stranger exaggerated a deep cycle of respiration, "Okay, all caught up with ya. Go ahead."

"Are you sure?" he pleaded in his version of sarcasm. "So, among the billions of processes that can be identified in living organisms, why would they have ever evolved? I mean…"

"What evolved?"

"That! In the lecture." He pointed in the air. "A microtubule. Or I should say, microtubule density at synapses and in neurons -that too," Colton looked more directly at the stranger's profile. "I mean, nature never wastes anything. They can't just *be*."

"Oh, I dunno 'bout that, my friend. You've never met my cousin Séamus. So lemme guess, now you're after what… purpose?"

"Exactly. That's… exactly it. I want to know what purpose they serve. Why would there ever need be such devices. I mean, biological devices. We're talking about in the human mind, no less."

"Yeah. Wow, at least I think wow. Is now the appropriate time for a wow?"

The steady diet of cavalier replies gave him pause, but in his deeper motivation Colton took the chance. "So, what has my curiosity piqued; they are attached to the termini, you see?"

The stranger nodded, "Mm, I've definitely known a few with a wire loose in my time."

Maybe not, Colton thought, while waiting for lucidity's arrival.

"Heh. Look, Of course I'm messin' with ya, dude. So, right, you're talking axons and dendrite neuron physiology, of course I got a bead on that stuff," panning his sights over the auditorium, the stranger added, "certainly didn't walk into this lecture series on a goof."

The devotion to the conversation temporarily waned, perhaps because they unconsciously realized they were no longer being bathed in Lombard's ambient voice. At this realization, both their attentions were instinctively drawn forward to find the professor's discontent guided in their general favor.

Colton was too eager to desist, rather, he furthered in a guarded tact. "Sort of. I mean the transmissions between nerve cells, the termini? But they are inside the neurons."

"I know. I got it."

Lombard's halted lecture interrupted them again.

"Okay, so, these tube-like structures are in dense quantities in those regions."

"But where are you taking me here? I mean, you said you want their purpose though. What are you thinking?"

Colton exhaled aggressively, "Well, that's just it. I, ah... I'm not sure entirely. But I have an idea... maybe... how to use technology, in an original way. It would be to prove something is true." His intonation seemed to run astray.

That appeared to at last capture the type of attention in the stranger he had hoped to achieve. "Mmm, what's true?"

"The emergent property of— shit."

The stranger turned rapidly, "What? I was sort of wondering if you were full of crap, but man, you really nailed it!"

"No. Ssh. It's Lombard," he scolded, attention already recommitted to his tablet.

The long overdue censure finally arrived from below. "Excuse me, excuse me... You two, up zer." The professor wagged his index finger in the air, "Is der zomesing you vould like to add to ze lecture at zes time?"

"No, sir. Please excuse us. My apologies," he said, loud enough to overcome the distance.

"Oh! Is dat Colton Reinholt, I presume?"

"Shit," he whispered first, "Yes, doctor, my apologies. Please continue."

"Yes, yes. Tiz okay, my young friend," the professor turned his glances over his suddenly inquisitive audience, "class, vee are in ze presence of greatness."

Slumping down in his seat upon hearing that, Colton susurrated, "Oh, Christ," while pulling the rim of his baseball cap downward.

The stranger had been studying the exchange with interest.

"Okay, veel talk zoon, zen. So, anyvay, ver was I?" The professor returned to a whiteboard strewn with enigmatic curvilinear forms. "Ze receptor's original zignal degradation can be anticipated, zus predicted..."

A stirring permeated the auditorium occupants, sensing the Professor's cadence nearing its final measure. They soon amassed at the exit bottleneck near the top of the tiers.

Staying seated, Colton pinched his lower lip, and gazed taciturnly. His new-found partner of classroom impropriety lingered alongside. Under normal circumstance it would be more like him to have joined in the fervor of the escaping crowd but, the aura was too alluring.

"Fame? I'm in the presence of fame!" This did not however, break the deeper cogitation, so the stranger encouraged differently, "Actually, I'm not as unversed in this sort of material, the subject matter at hand. I mean, why else am I here, right? It would be a bad sign. I mean, considering. Listen, I know about the micro-tubes."

"Microtubules."

"Whatever. I mean in general. Granted, I wouldn't have poured out a tsunami of information like that at someone I don't really know." He ended by offering an agreeable chuckle. "By the way, I'm Jack," and reached over a closed fist.

"Oh-uh, right," Colton completed the gesture. "Well, I suppose you gathered already then, Colton's the name."

Jack ran a thumb up and down along a backpack strap. "So, hey, if you're wondering. I hail from biochemistry geek-dom. Masters. My focus deals in certain aspects of neural sciences?"

Colton's eyebrows subtly moved.

"Yup, that's right. So, I'm not altogether unfamiliar with that stuff. Sort of taking me down the road into psychiatric shit. Some transgresses. A few sorted affairs and shenanigans here and there and... well, here I am. So, I, uh, I guess you, what... you're a neurobiologist then?"

"*Oh*, hell no." Colton pushed a hand through his hair. "I mean, I can see why you might have that impression, but no. I'm, well, as far as I'm still aware..." he shifted his attention afar, "...applied material physics. That's always been my pre-doc discipline."

"Huh. That sounds as though there's a cool backstory there?"

"Neeah - heh, nah. No, thanks," Colton overtly reengaged his personal space.

"Ooh, well now you *really got me* curious."

"Nah, it's not... well, sometimes I wonder..."

"What?"

"I was gonna say, for some odd reason neurophysiology has always sort of interested me along the way. That's all."

"Right. We're, ah, pretty sad, huh? But, I gotta say, it sounds like you hold a bit more than a passive interest there. You seem to possess an actual manifold of knowledge."

"I might know enough to get us into trouble," Colton said then added after some delay, "listen, I was airing mental notes earlier." He pulled his portable phone from his pocket.

"That makes both. I gotta jet."

7

Colton abruptly hastened in egress, "Hey, thanks for listening," his voice faded.

"Huh. Odd guy."

2
NOSTALGIA

Near the center of town was Saguaro park was an area so maintained it had become a man-made oasis. Established to bring some greenery to civility, University affairs of many ilk often brought the region spry energy during days of the school seasons. At times, the vicinity would burgeon over, seeping down connecting thoroughfares, not too far from a favorite university haunt, Wrangler's pub. The setting was not uncommonly spilling out of door to blend in as one seamless throng saturated in the ebullience of youth.

That laissez-faire culture, occurring day or night, melded frolics like that because the University itself created Don Quixote's culture. So much of the town's atmosphere was defined, its vitality engendered, because of the college life; such that once the spring diaspora finished emptying the valley, ghostly memories were more abundant than actual souls. Really, the University did more than influence the rules, the mentality of college affairs defined much of them.

One night, much earlier in his collegiate days, he rather inexplicably dared to venture into the frolicsome din and it was there that he first met Christine. Her physique was instantly captivating; the perfect focus to tune out a revel that typically annoyed him, if not aroused insecurity. A sense of comfort arrived in the focus she offered as they stood face to face. Her eyes moved along his features, covertly. Was it a familiarization as they lingered in their collective gaze, somehow ineffable? She was not sure how, or why. But as that storyline usually goes, he too was instantly drawn to her.

Later, as they wended their way through their own aspirations they often crossed paths. It appeared the vagaries of reality would not allow any mutual absentia to carry on for very long.

Then, it happened, an opportunity for research collaboration, and just as fate never spares uncanniness, she happened to be the best candidate for what he needed in any practical measure as well. Despite his coveted sensations, it was she who initiated that offer. It was a perfect opportunity; languish internally with desire and not actually have to do anything about it. Though their ensuing friendship and its base in simpatico was very real, it was also thus built upon a foundation of denial and physical lies.

Studying her dark-chocolate hair tones tress around her nape, or gesturing artfully the tops of her shoulders, he wired those images soundly into his memory. The sun pierced the edges, and lingered an impression of auburn highlight. He thought it was like a piece of art. All of which, to him, commanded a body sculpted out of God's clay. That was all his desire.

She was your basic nightmare in crowds. Be it jealousy among females, or that sort of disenchanted moment where any gender might be caught between intense desire and unattainability. She was so hot she pissed people off.

That was not all. She had an outré combination of attributes, one would not come to know unless she so chose to reveal. Native artistic prowess honed through her accomplishments in dance, ambitions she would slowly, ultimately let go of, while maturing through academia. These gave her an unusual versatility as an adult. So it turned out Quantum Mechanics really did require intrinsic ability for syncopation. In many ways, she might have even been smarter than he. Yet, she was kind. Altogether, not typically a type of woman one would expect to find alone, let alone, ever meet.

Once, from behind a shield of tepid humor, he offered, "I would have had you checked-off as with a boyfriend and a waiting list with what you got goin' on over there," banter he

stole from some other source. She told him she was always
too devoted to her work. He believed it.

It came to be that he owed a lot to her. Despite his massive
mind, his brilliance was unorthodox in nature; it leaped from
flashes of insight to flashes of insight where the connecting
facets might need something more, like unsettling faith to
any accomplished academic circle. A paradox within, as
though his analytic and mathematical abilities were lucid,
they vied for dominance against the raw power of his
imagination. She bestowed in him a gift that was uniquely
useful to him in particular; a deeper understanding of the
necessity for refinement, archetypes to sophisticate his
creativity. Raw genius often belies its sagacity, and is too
often dismissed. Oh, he certainly possessed the necessary
faculties, if he so desired; his issue was clearly simply,
discipline. In those early days, possibly maturity as well.

She brushed away a lock of his chestnut hair, while it
hung precipitously over his teal-colored eye; those that
offered her mystery. "You're some kinda man for a rock
band," she got even; and so, it went back and forth.

His endurance workouts kept him thin. He had his own
aspects available. Lines were fine, reasonably well placed.
Ultimately, these characteristics assisted him, like they
would for anyone in any walk of society.

Working side by side like that was really a platonic
nightmare. And though their collective efforts were
stunningly bright, if they had ceased the charade that
eclipsed their happiness, those would have been dimmed by
comparison.

*   *   *   *

One night at long last it happened. They finished dinner and
found themselves upon his balcony as the desert moon
showed brightly. He stood in quiet consternation as her

comforting elocution was in harmony with his philosophies, on life and love, as usual.

He finally, at long last, drew courage. "Chris," he whispered.

She suspended her sentence.

"I love you."

"Yes, I know. I... love you too."

"No," Looking directly into her eyes, he reached down and cloistered her hands inside his. "I mean," he whispered, "We're standing out... here, under these stars. Alone? And I love you. Don't you under—" he abruptly released her hands and stepped to the balcony rail. He was in wait for the ultimate horror and changed the subject quickly. "Listen, I... don't want you to go. I know I told you how excited I was for you." He turned slowly around only to find the moonlight reflecting discretely from the corner of her eye. Beneath, a trace betrayed her reaction to his omission. He reached with his thumb to dry it, "And I'm... I am happy for you. You do know that... I'm happy, for you," very gently adding, "I always have been."

"Oh, Colton. Goddamn it. Now?"

"But I'm, afraid. Okay, I'm afraid. I guess... of not having you here, with me, anymore."

A moment later, her hand came upon his nape, then ran slowly down over the contour of his shoulder. His legs felt sapped of strength as her other hand encouraged him to turn back around to face her. Staring deep into his eyes, "Oh my god. Look at that. There is moonlight shining off your eyes." Her breasts pressed into his torso as she laid the side of her face upon the contours of his upper chest, and within the moment came the warm sensation of her relaxed lips upon his neck. "Oh, Lumpy," she murmured.

At last on this night their connection was a discovery that took the least effort of all.

The next day the ruminations were overbearing, haunting his every move. Their tryst, what it would mean to his life, or at long last a life-future with her. And as his pulse quickened, he accessed his phone's messages. This kind of ecstatic prescience was a power which had always eluded him, seemingly preordained to do so.

'*I'll call you before I leave,*' there was rapture in the cadence of her spoken words. It was undeniable enough, and as they echoed, they conflicted with that fate. That would become his demon. And, no sooner did the never-ending day find him at last returned to his home, and there it was, a single blinking indicator: one new message.

Checking it against his watch, he missed the call by under an hour. Pacing at first, he struggled to resist the urge to take off in his car in pursuit. But even the irrationality of love was not enough to conquer the realism that he would never catch her in time; her flight would have embarked. Instead, closing his eyes he let the device speak to him.

He rewound and replayed the message several times. Upon the final listen, he found himself standing on his balcony, peering out at a mass of towering thunder clouds billowing into the twilight skies along the north and northeast horizon, not uncommon during the western monsoon season. Lightning flashes occasionally illuminated from within them, sometimes emerging tentacles of electricity that danced along the surface of their sun-fading nebular plumes. Christine's voice had played back in that message and then repeatedly in his mind.

As he peered out from that same balcony where the previous night they shared their first romance, he watched the distant twilight thunderstorms through liquid vision. And a sense of grief oddly struck him in that moment. Something about her departure was unimaginably bad; he was breathless for it. Perhaps his unyielding diffidence in allowing empathic relationships to form with others had been so rigid as to prevent them from finding true bliss in one another so much sooner. A reality that would turn out to haunt him so deeply as to sap his ability to resume challenges that would most certainly be insurmountable to any version of his mind if it were ever compromised by dimming will to succeed.

3
TEMPTATION

Though it was not actually his intent to be stealthy during his arrival, Jack availed of the opportunity nonetheless and situated himself covertly one tier above. This allowed a superb vantage point for undisturbed observation. And so, he watched. What at first appeared to be frenetic enthusiasm was not so devoid of control.

The individual conducted himself with lucidity between multiple media sources. There was the keyboard of the tablet, while muttering occasionally to himself content Jack could not quite make out, much less comprehend. Complex physical theorems were scribed upon notebook papers strewn haphazardly about the tiered desk surface nearby. Occasionally, the clicking ceased and as this drew in his attention anew, he wondered what the index finger moving cursorily along the lines of any in the multitude of derivatives was actually searching for. Fascinated by the cinema of it all, he was fighting off asking, *what in the hell are you up to?* But that would have been difficult for anyone to interrupt this emanation of sanctity so brazenly.

Professor Lombard's lecture concluded, triggering voices and commotion to rudely crowd over his ending statements. Instinctively, he waited until the last souls had vacated ear-shot, "So, what's all that about?"

"Oh! Jesus. Hey, Jack. I— Hi. Were you…"

"Here the whole way? you betcha. I would have spoken up sooner but I figured we ought-a give old Lombard a break this time. So, all that paper-salad you got goin' on down there, is that what you were excited about the other day?"

Turning his attention slowly around, Colton continued to gather in his dispersion of notes and diagrams. "What do you mean... excited?"

Jack snorted some nasal laughter, "okay then. I heard you pleading your case out loud, during the lecture."

"Oh, that? heh. Hey, man, sorry about the other day. I might have laid it on a little thick."

"No, no, it's all right. I gotta be honest; you piqued my curiosity there, dude."

"Dude, eh?"

"What's that?"

Colton spoke louder, "Um, so you're curious, you say. Honestly... I don't know if I should get any deeper into it. I mean, things have evolved since then."

"Evolved. Ooh, now I'm really intrigued. Seriously bro, it's okay."

"This idea, it's... going to be a novel attempt."

"Novel. You mean like... Mary Shelley?"

"Huh? Mary – oh, right, heh. No. Actually, I believe I can apply a varying charge, a predetermined amperage, mimicking those found in the chemo-guided electrical impulses in the brain." The immediate lapse in response drew him to look directly at his companion.

On cue, Jack replied, "creeepee."

"What? nah. Nothing of the sort. What I wanna do, I think we can artificially induce... approximate therein, to prove certain microtubule behaviors?"

"To what end may I ask? is there a practical end to all that? I mean, don't get me wrong, I get it, science is science but—"

"I understand the question. Well, the purpose could be construed as a tad open-ended, honestly. But, I'm not interested in utility here, purely discovery. Like you said, the science." Colton paused, "It's a long story, but maybe this will lead somewhere else. Tell you the truth, it could be a tough sell. Weaving fiber-optic threads containing nodes of technology, it might all be a little expensive to the ear."

"Uh huh, can imagine. Good luck on *that* proposal."

"Oh, I know. I've calculated the necessary geometrical constructs, created, and diagrammed the rudimentary apparatus. If it works, we can indeed analog microtubule behaviors. You see... I want to demon—"

"Whoa, whoa, slow down. You did all that in what," Jack glanced at his watch, "the last two days?"

"Uh, it's not all that. Really."

"If you say so," Jack rolled his eyes. "So lemme get my head around this; you're trying to control... oh, wait, my bad. I keep coming to that. I know. We aren't there yet?"

Colton was coveting encouragement. "Maybe we'll tell the world something about these strange biological processes. Or at least, one in many, if so small... seemingly insignificant. But like I said, nature."

"Seems like a lot of trouble if you ask me. But I guess discovery's gotta be like that, doesn't it? What at first may seem innocuous..." Jack left with an airborne hand-rolling.

"You could benefit from this project," Colton pointed an index finger, "I mean, if it ever really gets off the ground." He allowed a moment. "I'm sure given time, practicalities could take place. Application in psychiatric sciences?" He snapped his fingers, "Damn, I need to get back down to the material molding labs. I got to talk to those guys. I wonder if I should do that first before going upstairs."

"Upstairs? Oh, right. You're gonna have this run by the man," Jack rose and flipped his pack over his shoulder. "K. So, listen, while I'd love to sign a lease here and roomie up with you in in the auditorium, I guess I'll be seein' ya 'round campus then."

He hastily gathered up the remainder of his notes, "Hey, Jack, wait, hold on a sec. Didn't you say you were over in the department of psychiatric sciences?"

"Uh huh."

"I think you said you come from organic chem, right?

"What are you getting at?"

"Great. Great. You might… well, hey, let me work some things out. I'll see you in the next lecture then?"

"Sure, I guess. I mean, I'm a captive audience one way or the other."

"Right. Right."

Once again, Colton left him standing alone outside amid the hallowed auditorium of Tildon Hall.

"What is it with this guy; what's so great?"

4
LIMITATIONS

Superconductivity... "A Quantum Mechanical phenomenon in which zero electrical resistance results when certain materials are subjected to exceedingly low absolute temperatures."
That ending statement—exceedingly low temperatures—had always been the greatest hurdle to overcome. The gap between theory and any subsequent useful technology had continually been one of the greatest challenges of any practical science. Having to achieve temperatures that do not even exist over the nature of this world, outside of a human laboratory that is, was a pragmatic Grand Canyon.

Denoted Tc, or the temperatures in which a physical medium would begin to exhibit super-conduction, had to be less than negative two hundred forty degrees centigrade in idealized metals in order to begin transmitting electrical charge with no loss.

Prior to Colton's arrival at the University, there had only ever been minor advancements in that particular frontier, since the original Nobel Prize winning breakthrough discovery during the latter twentieth Century. Substances were discovered along the way that showed early promise; one such compound, the warmest yet, only needed to be a soothing negative seventy degrees centigrade. One small sticking point however, other than anything biological that happened to contact a metallic surface under such conditions, those experiments required a fluidic atmospheric pressure equivalent to 1,500 times those found at the bottom of the ocean.

The entire ambit of research was left to smolder in unrealized hope of ever finding materials that could operate within a framework of conditions that at least approached common everyday experience.

It was thought that if ever found, all aspects of life, and even life itself, would benefit from subsequent technologies. From conservation sciences, to medicine, to improving the quality, every tangible and intangible aspect of those realities would be hugely advanced.

This was his original flash of insight, now, trailing in years. A theoretical work demonstrating that by densely packing carbon nanotubes, molecular-scale-sized tubular structures composed entirely of carbon atoms, into mathematically predetermined geometries, his theoretical computations argued for super-conduction closer to room temperatures.

*   *   *   *

The Physics Department was headed by Doctor Stephen J. Mendal. He was an assertive man, among other choice attributes. Often, kind in the way he went about incising into your id when notifying you of your shortcomings. He almost did not have to try; he merely walked into a room, and if you were there, you assumed you were unworthy. Most of those who came in and out of the department and worked under him over the years, of course privately loathed the man. Some were, for lack of better words, legitimately afraid of him. Besides, as mathematicians and physicists tended to be stereotypically, socially awkward they were less inclined to stand up to him anyway, and this only enabled the man's predilection in self-regard. And, he was admittedly brilliant himself, an impression that, given his nature, he autonomically attempted to instill in those around him.

An overabundance of conceit would lead inexorably to deadlines of his own. Contractual obligations to outside interests seeking his self-appointed providence. And merely hiding away in the protective enclave of higher education and teaching was not enough for his starlit ego so he took on grandiose endeavors. Mostly, he excelled in these ventures, which parlayed into new ones. All of which was the culture long prior to one among a few of his protégés, Colton Reinholt, being matriculated into the PhD program. The combination of all produced its own luck, as it always seemed to play an intangible role for any champion of any endeavor in society. And so, he had quite the successes at least, in reputation, as a career.

Eventually, the man's whole sense of value became inextricably linked to the vitality of the physics department over which he presided, a department he did not only lead, but had become synonymous with his very name in the greater ambit of theoretical Physics. Be it conferences, award ceremonies, or social gatherings among the greater sphere, should ever the University's Physics Department become context, it was usually, 'Mendal's crew'. He thoroughly believed in that identification of, and for, himself.

Such that, the arriving shoulder-tap for one such request would at last be a great achievement, an elixir for an otherwise emerging mid-life crisis. As we all do at one point or another in our lives, it was his turn to face time's larceny of life due to accelerating years. Denying the possibility his life was wasted in devotion to too much so to administrative causes, his decision to advance lofty promises, if vastly ahead of their time, was a miscalculation.

Here was the hurdle in his own technological advancements: the end of the line of Moore's Law. Standard laser techniques used to etch circuitry for microprocessors could no longer burn the electron routing upon silicon wafer surfaces to anymore finite in scale. Any closer and the electrons appeared to avail of the quantum uncertainty principle. At least excuse imaginable, they seemingly shared those routes at random intervals. This would cause signal degradation, then counter-intuitively, those losses began to grow in proportion to the smallness of the design. And so, with microprocessor tech coming to a supposed limit, a completely new technology would need to be born for his own AI vision.

The closest he had come thus far was via a recent collaboration between himself and that of the solid-state physicist, Norman Wiles. Wiles, an easily obliging, quiet man, was the innovator behind the so-called Mutable Microprocessor, referred in discussion as em-and-ems, where integrated-circuit chips were omni-purpose functional. The genius of them was for their adaptive capacitance. They literally were self-programmable, based upon environment feedback. Adaptive computing was the intrinsic goal there.

Despite the exploit of those advancements, required simulacra of human-characteristic machine decision-making could not actually be produced in Mendal's private findings. Computers simply lacked what took evolution millions of years to perfect in the human mind. The *it* situational awareness of reality itself; joie de vivre to instinct to survive and back, these intrinsic abilities in the biological kingdom, he could not reproduce in real-time Military applications. A truth he quite naturally concealed during status calls. He knew it though full well; there was no such innate province in the thinking engine of his machines.

Who knew what finally drove one to perceive such matters so direly. But, during those days as the point man for that looming, singularly applauded Military contract, it probably was the fragility of ego and image that ultimately compelled his fears. Less than he had promised, meant those components of his psyche were on the verge of being shaken; despite that, many of his perceived innovations were proven useful.

5

FACE THE MUSIC

Surrendering to Mendal's tribunal was certainly not high on Colton's list of aspirations. As he stood there before him, his mind could not stop the internal cinema from punching the aristocracy right off the man's expression. Airing in elitism rarely rubs any observing sentience the right way. Colton was no different. He loathed every aspect about his indentured relationship to this particular authority figure. Nevertheless, he was a captive audience by necessity. In seeking the man's approval, he would have to concede to that most rudimentary tactics of all human social dynamics: The vector of ass-kissing always points up.

After a short while of cursory evaluation over the video screen of a tablet, the exulted Prof slowly turned toward him. "So, you're recreating... or what is this – what do think you're doing now?" He glanced over the interface through an exhale. "Okay, some kind of neurological architecture... heh," he trailed off, evading direct eye contact. "What is... why this, now?"

Colton remained vigilantly stolid, subtly nodding his head during the morass of condescension.

Mendal cleared his throat before taking another stab at testing a response, "Some kind of fiber-optics, for—" but something caught his eye. His lips soon failed to completely suppress motioning out words from finally becoming audible, "...thus achieving them artificially. So, what? Then you want to perform EEGs ... on a machine no less, huh. What in the hell is this ... Ah, hello, you there?"

Colton was momentarily lost in one of his cinema visualization exercises, feigning a series of quick acknowledgement nods.

"I don't know, Colt," dropping the tablet down on the desk, running both hands over the arcing contour of his hairless crown. He muttered at an angle, "Looks like the same shenanigans, different clown posse. Christ. Ah, listen. Can we be candid for a moment here? I think it's time we had this discussion."

"I-uh. I know. I know. I mean, where you're about to go."

"Okay. Well, then, you got some follow-through for me?"

"I know. I see your point."

"My point? Tell me something, where are you with the organic substrates, the superconductor stuff? Aren't you getting closer to a thesis? I mean, why am I entertaining," his eyes zapped the tablet with a disapproving laser, "this?"

"Some... unforeseen permutations came up... got in the—"

"Okay. Okay. Look, not to be insensitive of course, but it's been what? A couple years since?"

Colton's eyes meandered slowly about the random paraphernalia of the professor's office; his way of not revealing weakness. Yet, his peripheral vision sensed Mendal lingering. He knew this conversation was inevitable.

"This has gotten a bit old, don't you think? Look, as far as your reputation... honestly, I don't care anymore what you did before you came to this school. Not for such wild notions now. I mean, not to dissuade the process of science, of course." Mendal ended with a grin that strained sincerity.

"I have already begun doing the prospectus work. I mean, for this. A new idea. It's there. Make a solid review, would you? This time will be different. I know this can work." He had difficulty placing exactly why in the moment, but this new inspiration was affecting, like musical phrases might take one's mind to another time and place. It raised a similar sense of arresting urgency, to not let go or give up, to hold on or it might slip away. Why? He had no explanation for how any of it could conjure such deeper nostalgia. In the end, it was easier not to question it at all. Besides, these

24

descriptions would undoubtedly not resonate with this presumption of authority. All he really sought was the man's assent, a mantra he repeated internally. His muse broke as Mendal again flopped the tablet upon the desk. He tried to hide a sigh while playing with intermittent eye contact. "Yes. I'm sorry, Dr. Mendal... But please, let me explain. What I really need is more time in the lab. I know—"

The professor waved him off, "We can't afford it this time. With our status with the lab being shaky and so forth. I can't let you folks go in there and tinker with that tech down there. Those mistakes... they cost the school real money. Many thousands of dollars. And we both know you were—"

"I know!"

Mendal arched his eyebrows.

"I mean, please. Just listen. I was in Professor Lombard's lecture the other day... over in biological sciences?"

"Okay," Mendal sighed hard, "all right." He took his seat. "Yes, I'm familiar with who he is. Isn't he... psychiatric sci though—uh. Okay, hence the neurology, then. I don't think I see where you're going with this, though. What does this have to do with your previous —" he left his hand in the air, drawing in his cheeks when Colton interrupted.

"Right, right, it's all in there. You'll see it. I mean, he was elaborating upon the trillions of dendritic... um, neurons, along with their unknown biological functions. They're called microtubules, real fundamental biological components of neuron physiology. Then, it occurred to me—"

"Wait, what? Come again, microtubules?" he chortled for mercy.

"Microtubules. They are tube-like structures, mere nanoscale."

"Right, I recall. I meant the subject had slipped my mind, but I do recall discoveries, I mean research. But, slow down. Tell me what you are after."

"Okay, so science knows they exist, but there is uncertainty as to what exact functional role... I mean, biologically. There's also something less tangible here. And, I got to thinking, what if they have conductive properties? Say, not too dissimilar... some of the organics we used in our superconductor stuff? When we bumped into the quantum uncertain princ—"

"Whoa, whoa, whoa." This time, Mendal waved both hands in the air over his head. "I'm not sure I follow that. And, where are you going now, ah quantum uncertainty principle?"

"Just... alright, forget that for a moment. Look, chemo-electrically guided charges, they flow along the axons and as they go, and as we know, any flow of charge induces a corresponding magnetic field."

"Okay, I'll bite. But, I still don't know why you are even talking about quantum uncertainties now, when you start out with EEG. I assume you mean brain waves?"

"Sort of... minute magnetic field permutation in this case. Perhaps up to this point, that which might merely have even been undetec—"

"*Undetectable*. Now there's a novel connection. See, right there."

"Wait, hear me out. That's the point. I can prove it."

"Prove what? What part? THAT is the point."

Colton slowed his cadence accordingly, "All right, keeping on point, brain waves. Now, because of the way the microtubules arc in dense compaction... well, here," he reached across the desk for his tablet. Aggressively swiping his finger across its interface, it slowed upon a page festooned with linear diagrams and equations like a 1910 physicist's private office. Quickly rotating the device, "Look, it's all right here," tapping his index finger.

The professor's attention lingered before slowly turning his eyes as directed, "I... don't know why you think..."

A subtle sense of relief flooded into the moment while the infrastructure of illustrations and mathematics seemed to at last pass through his mentor's eyes in ever lessening inhibition. After a few uncontaminated moments of whatever internal monologue was activated in the man's head, he abruptly rose from his chair.

"I, uh, okay, then?"

"Well," he suspended the tablet in the air, "Here, take it!"

"Got it. Thanks. Sorry."

"I'll tell you what. I don't really have time to entertain this any further now," adjusting his watch. "Lecture in ten minutes, other side of campus. It's… well, okay, interesting, I'll admit. The EEG bio-bridging with solid state physical … thing, heh." his mien pulsed incredulity mashed with fascination. "If you can finish creating the matrices, and the mathematical models turn out correct, I'll probably approve."

Colton was about to show appreciation for the non-sequitur success but was not ultimately given the chance.

"Uh, that is if and only if you can organize this with a modicum of sagacity, and I mean a real prospectus this time, damn it." He gently pounded his spread fingers upon his desk, "I'll go through it; your rudimentary equations and prose and we'll see where we stand. But, my immediate impression is— well, we'll leave it at that for now." But the good doctor already knew otherwise.

6
SO, THE IDEA FOLLOWS...

Downing a dram of his double-malted Glenfiddich, the fireplace offered a moment for distraction, while he observed the plasma's asymmetric dance.

"Sequencing trillions of interlacing dendrites in the neuro tapestry of the mind. Hence, vibration... though quantum-scaled in dimension these dynamics, consisting of magneto guided quanta, are truly awesome in numbers..."

Mendal whispered aloud, "so, inducing electrical charges must also create magnetism, of course. Can we get past the goddamn Physiology lesson? Christ."

"...Attached in both genetically, as well as environmentally determined geometric construction—"

"Actually, wait... what? Geometry by environmental... please tell me he demonstrated that mathema—" His eyelids fluttered rapidly, as though some bit of realization was more than he could bear.

"...Such, that these pulsations are forced to propagate along the tips of the individual microtubules. No prior analysis links, specifically, that significance... The following derivatives,"

"Thank you very much."

"...describe this plausibility more in detail... Instrumentation does register the chemo-induced electrical currents... (EEG) ...the following proposes an apparatus design... successfully, empirically measure this phenomenon in a controlled methodology and environment."

The leather of his throne reported as he rose from his seated position. He wended his way around the edge of his desk, ambled to a location close enough to the fireplace that the glow reflected irregularly off the contours of his plain expression, and began to speak again to the invisible audience behind him. "Huh, that's all well and good, my friend. But you failed to specifically delve into the question of environ... oh, right. That's got to be it... learning! Of course. These are the physical manifestation, the expression of those environmental factors." He speculated whether or not Colton's idea was even connecting that discretely. Quickly returning to his chair to seek that answer, a small series of margin notes distracted him.

"Plausible necessity for further study; magnetism passing through the 'microtubule circuitry' produces emergent secondary results... reproducible via vibrational wave dynamics. A single microtubule oscillation is meaningless; en-masse, more than the sum of their parts? Synergistic property and purpose unknown."

He was left puzzled by the notion that such an insight was a mere afterthought. If these waves, permeating through countless fields of microtubules could be slowed down, they would appear as an elevated vantage of wind through a field of wheat, moving concerted fluid motions. However, unlike the vagaries of the wind these waves were driven along by intended neuro-guided transmittance. Then, a storm-wave abruptly passed through his own mind.

With this type of design, the denser, smaller the scale of the vibration, the less probability of randomness there is, and— "Extraordinary!" For he contemplated a miracle of Nature's conception, that although he was uncertain, he suspected Colton had stumbled upon it. A mere flash of insight leading the excited calculations he had yet to fully validate, must, he thought, lead to a ponderous proposition.

The whole process suggested that biology, through the trial and error of evolutionary selection, had discovered a way to counter the uncertainty principle, at quantum scales. A marriage of the physical and the electromagnetic giving rise to quantum certainties; and as such, in direct proportion to microtubule densities, this limit, likely approached a guarantee.

"But of what?" he spoke aggressively to the straw man in the room, "who cares about brain waves and EEG printouts? My god, it's the answer to that question that's—"

Three electronic tones sounded off, paused, then recurred. He scanned the small interface but the caller ID compelled hesitation. After an exaggerated breath, his attempt at a hello was stepped on by the gravelly voice.

"Dr. Mendal, I presume." It was one Colonel McFadden, the only person in his present sphere of associates that could be perceived as a threat. Naturally, a person he had grown to privately loath.

He faked a silvery tone, "yes, of course it is, Colonel. I must say, your timing... it is impeccable."

The voice poured forth in haste, "well, is this line secure then?"

"Yes. It's the same device you provided. The same number. I thought that stuff was swept... I mean, I thought that was arranged by brass?" There was no reply to the question. "So, no one knows I'm—"

"Very well then. This Thursday, nine-hundred hours – that's nine, A M. We'll wait to talk, in your office, about the status of things."

He fought off being tremulous, "roger, Colonel; over and—" The beeps interceded that he was no longer speaking with anyone. He pushed the end-call button and finished his sentence, "out, asshole."

The fire continued to crackle softly in the dim ambiance and he forged onward through the theoretical. At a point along the way, he abruptly halted his eyes' trajectory along the lines of text and equations, slowly lifting his chin. Proceeding to lay the postulate down, he rose to his feet, lifted his glass, and walked around his desk toward a separate end of the room.

Gulping a bit more than a mere dram this time, he set the empty glass down and kept entering the combination to the vaulted file cabinet located as though covertly behind a tangled mass of Ficus and Lady Palms. After pulling open and exposing rows of files, he extracted the one titled:

"Military Documents # 2004 Code Name: Freebird "Unmanned Aerial Assault Vehicles (UAAVs) Comprehensive, Fully Illustrated Overview of Current and Future Aircraft, Predator, Hunter, Shadow, Pioneer, Global Hawk, Unmanned Combat Air Vehicles (UCAVs), Dragon Eye (Ring-bound) and Artificial Intelligence Requirement Grant and Agreement Contract."

An air of apprehension permeated his expression as he turned the page of a separate document, landing on one containing a technical design. It was an elaborate schematic demonstration, chip models that would be integrated into the computers of the Freebird project. These, the conception of Dr. Mendal et al, showed intricacies of indescribable complexity. There were conduit theoretical superconductor threads, chip nodes, all diagrammed in three and two-dimensional modular forms.

After spending a few moments deeply engaged, he ended his focus, interlocking his fingers behind his bald head. His eyelids sagged to a close as he whispered, "what in the fuck is wrong with this design?" Abruptly, with one fluid hasty series of motions, he replaced the documents along their designated rank of the file cabinet, closed the outer vault door, and gave the combination dial a spin.

The bar was a welcome diversion, where he poured another Scotch; this time, a double. Tipping a belt, he then set to accessing his own mobile phone.

"Yes, Colton. No-no, that's fine. So, I'm calling you at this late hour to inform you of needing your presence in my office. Thursday morning, ten a.m. Right. Very well then."

*   *   *   *

Thursday, 10 a.m.

He tapped on Dr. Mendal's door already slightly ajar.

The door opened, instead answered by a tall man clad in military garb. An imposing figure, he protruded a chiseled prominent lower jaw and was well festooned with service awards gaudy upon the left-hand side of his uniform. With a disconcerting study, the man inspected him, up then down along the vertical edifice of his being.

The resulting, sympathetic moment of guilt that took over his psyche, transformed to dread when Stephen Mendal's voice emanated from behind the figure, "Yes, Colton. Please come in."

Shortly after stepping around him, the Military man partially filled the corridor's hollowness.

"Colton? C'mon-c'mon, I haven't got the whole day."

"I... am I interrupting or—"

"No, it's fine. Jesus. Come in."

"Who was— whatever. Did you, uh... look things over?"

Rising to his feet, Mendal positioned his hands behind his back and turned toward the oriel illuminating his office with skylight. His partially silhouetted frame spoke, "yes, I did. That is, have a chance to review. The postulate... for creating artificial," pausing to clear his throat, "EEG wave dynamics."

"Fascinating idea, don't you think?"

The attempt at leading ebullience was only greeted by, "the idea has some merit. I will approve it. That will be all. I am unexpectedly very busy today, so, I cannot go into details and will have to cut this shorter than I wanted. You will likely be issued some access to the lab. And, Colton? Colton!"

"Uh, right, of course... I, I mean yes, what?"

"Better project logging this time. No untethered assumptions. Be elaborate, clear, and concise, understood?"

"Absolutely!"

The professor then abruptly turned away from the window and wended around book stacks and vestiges of earlier sciences fading obsolete. Placing a hand upon Colton's shoulder, he encouraged him to step toward the door. "One last item, I'll need you here again next Thursday morning, same time. Good day then. I will be in contact with you."

Taken aback by the relative ease in which this meeting transpired, he was in the moment only vaguely aware how tersely it concluded, as he realized he was actually standing outside the office; for an encounter that could have been achieved with a mere phone call, no less. But he was too elated to read-in. With the approval of his vision in hand, he was already foreseeing two steps further along the space-time continuum.

7
PROPOSAL

Awaiting the arrival of his new-found acquaintance, he frequently scanned the bustle as it began pouring through the doors into the auditorium. His enthusiasm alone seemed to guide him for he began motioning, hand in air, prior to patently identifying his target.

"Oh, hey, there you are. You stealthy bastard, you. I Didn't see you there. Hold on, I'll come up. So, how are things goin' with that big idea?"

"Big idea?"

"Don't be coy. Analoging brain functions? I mean, I sacrificed some bandwidth for you already. Don't get despondent now."

"What... sacrificed? You lost me."

"Well, I geeked it the other night, for you. I mean, not that you need any more geek of course. Not funny? Okay, so we can work on that. I'm talkin' 'bout research and junk? Amazing."

"Research. For what? Where did you..."

"Oh, you haven't heard? Turns out, there's this place, called a Library? They say that Universities have 'em? Of course I'd never know. I hadn't actually ever been inside one, either."

"Okay, okay. What'd you find?"

"It turns out they got all kinds of useful information there... You realize, you're talking about real moving parts there, like actual machinery. In living biology no less. Yet, it can't be arbitrary, in nature, like you were saying. Then I got to thinking, heart beats, breathing... it's like that. We don't actually think about those processes that sustain life."

"Of course, autonomic... impressive."

"I know. I have my moments."

It was already quite clear that Jack's brand of quick wit was footed in real intelligence, but hearing such perceptions charged him internally for what he was planning.

"Oh shitcha, gone and done it, now you've pulled me in and I'm all curious and stuff. So, Colt, there may be something deeper to all this."

"Deeper?" He intoned dryly, "Not that I'm aware. This is an attempt to artificially fabricate brain waves... um, in a controlled environment. That's about it. Perhaps prove these real features in physical biology are instrumental in doing so... Not really much else to it."

While lingering at Colton's profile, Jack added, "Riight. Well, I suppose it's possible. I mean, maybe that's all. But, there's already well-correlated research, dude."

"What do you mean?"

"You do know, those moments you see on an electroencephalogram. They are connected to certain... stuff. I mean, it's a bit heavy in the literature but—"

Colton suppressed a laugh, "Stuff! Perhaps. I know, but that's a different discipline. I tell you what. What are you doing after, do you want to grab a beer? There's a pub down town. You can check out the digs. I can fill you in."

Jack lingered a momentary smirk, "Well, I dunno. That depends."

"On?"

"You're not, uh ... one of those, are ya?"

"Uhm, one of what?"

"I mean... Look, you're a handsome guy and all, but—"

Professor Lombard organizing the day's lecture upon the podium encouraged him to lower the volume of his response. "Well, based on that, this may not sound odd, but I do have a proposition for you."

*   *   *   *

The Rolling Stones' "I'm Just Waiting On A Friend", weakly penetrated the tavern's ruckus outside their immediate conversation. Jack completed a sip of his Guinness, while furtively weaving his line of sight in observance of the other patrons. His tone took on a serious demeanor, "Project? Whoa. Look, I got my own gig going on guy. Like…"

"Okay?"

"How to prove to that brunette… that one right there, oh, man, how our destinies must be inextricably linked." He let some time elapse. "Look, I get it, bro. But, it's the same drill for everyone; we're all here for our own agenda."

Colton nodded, "I know, I know. I'm not asking for much here. Look, I have completed the pre-calculations, the materialized schema, and all that. I mean, we've passed that."

"We?"

"Jack, listen. This really is possible. I'm not going to waste your time."

"Uh huh, I'm listenin'," whe continued to multitasked his attention.

"Well, to be honest, I could really use an extra materials expert. More importantly, one that's proximal to the topic at hand." He gazed away in an instant rumination, "Imagine the implications. I mean for your field. Neuroscience?"

"I'll give you that. Maybe. Sounds like a hoot."

"See? There are certain aspects of the chemistry that I, well, I'm a little weak on. I could use your inputs there. I think you'd like this and we both win. I need a particular kind of chemistry insight; if nothing else, the project could directly service even a thesis idea. Hey?"

Jack at last focused, "Alright, alright, I'm hearin' it. I'm not really worried about that though. This whole analoging micro, or nano-biology come to think about it. I find it interesting, I admit. Here," and he pulled a phone from his backpack, "tell you what."

"Oh, right. I should give you my contact, too. I can't guarantee you'll always reach me; my service is a bit spotty out by my place. Does this mean we can call it official?"

"Sure, why the hell not." Finishing his beer in a single slug, Jack signaled over to the bartender for another. "Well, this has been fun, but I think maybe we oughta go talk—ooh, look at that. She's got a friend with her now. Let's go."

"Uh, no. I... I'm good. Look, I gotta split."

"Heh, K. Suit'ur self. I'm gonna hang back for a while. I tell you what, though, give me a call, I like the idea. If we can artificially create this stuff, maybe we can," Jack croaked his voice, "control their minds! Muah-ha-ha-ha."

Colton sighed, "yeeah."

"So I'll be in touch with that brunette and talk to you later then."

* * * *

The day's light was transitioning to dusk by the time he opened the door to his apartment. He moved quickly towards the answering machine of his land-line.

"Mr. Reinholt." It was the voice of Stephen Mendal. "You are keyed into the lab. They know you're coming. Please do not tell me your existing key-card is no longer in your possession, so as to avoid that embarrassment. There are limited slots available for entry by students at the facility this semester and I am giving two of them, for your overall efforts. Obviously, for you and one other person."

"What?" *How the hell does he know?*

"I do need you to swing by my office again this next Thursday, ten a.m. A few things we need to go over. That will be all."

"That will be all, eh?" he mocked after disconnecting the call and hissing off a bottle cap aggressively. "Whatever, sarge. Okay, where's my other phone."

"You rang?" Immediately accompanying, was a female's laughter at the other end.

"I rang. Oh, right. Is this, uh, a bad time... to call. I mean, do you know who this is?"

"I'm having trouble placing it, but you actually sound a little like this asshole who's been stalking me around campus. Kinda creepy. No, of course I know who you are. What, and here it's only been two hours?"

"Heh, right, okay, okay. Sorry to ping you so soon. It sounds like you're with someone? Is that the same... wow, amazing."

"Karen? Yep, sure is. She's offering therapy in exchange for libation and... I tell you what, here, talk to her yourself."

"NO, Jack, I—"

"Hi, Colton?" the female timbre was nice. "Man of few words, I guess. I can tell the type. I'm pretty sure I read you earlier, when our eyes met?"

"Oh, uh, hi! Hey, can you... I don't mean to be rude but maybe put Jack on?"

"Okay, that's enough outta you," Jack's voice faded in, "so, what's up?"

"Hey. What is she, some sort of psyche major, or?"

"How the hell did you get your head around that? Wow, she is, actually. PhD candidate. I'm telling you, dude, there's a whole big college out here. You know like women and stuff?"

"Right, right. So, hey, ah... if you're still serious, I mean about jumping on board? We got approval! For access to the Lab... Jack? Hello, still there?"

"What, is that supposed to mean something to me? Great, then. Access to the lab. Good to know."

"Oh, right. I guess you wouldn't. See, there's... extenuating circumstance." He tried to manage lucidity, brevity, and still being aptly impressionable about the history.

"All right, I get it. So there's some background there."

"Well... I wanted you to know why. The guy wants a meeting, in his office, Thursday morning, to go over—"

"What, whoa. Meetings? Uh, ooh. That's kinda fast. Sounds a bit formal, doesn't it?"

"I figured since you're coming into the project, you should meet him... Hello, you still there?"

"Uh, I am. Wait, who's this guy?"

"Oh, right, I should... He's, uh, my advisor... doctoral."

"I guess. I suppose that's gotta happen, huh. But, did you say Mendal? As in that bald menacing-looking dude, with the black goatee?"

"Heh, sure. I suppose that's 'bout as apt a description as I've ever come across. So, I take it you have met him?"

"Uh, no. Not per se. It's the name. I think I saw a thing on him. University Times; something about... Military? It's that look of cruelty that sticks in memory. Heh."

Karen's voice pleaded in the background, "Jack, we're going... You coming?"

Distantly, "Sure, one sec?"

"It's okay, Jack. Sorry to... can you meet me out front of the Library, Thursday, around nine-thirty?"

"Fine, sounds 'bout right." The distancing clutter partially faded out, "I told you he's kinda odd— "

8
INTRODUCTIONS

In uneven periodicity his attention shifted between the inside of his closed office door, then towards the woman. She, redirected hers whenever she sensed his focus returning. The time was nearing 9:43 a.m., Thursday.

"You are not to give any indication of your prior affiliations. Is that also clear?"

Gently clearing her throat, she reset her exquisite posture, legs crossed, hands clasped over her top knee. "I understand," her tone encouraged.

"And, you also understand?"

"Uh, yes, doctor. This is steno work, organizational. But if you could answer a question, why not one of your... someone of campus charge? Why go this route?"

"You don't really need to know," Mendal answered dourly. "Do you understand the general guidelines?"

She rose her brows slightly, "yes, perfectly," then nodded assuredly. But the moment he directed attention away she subtly betrayed an eye-roll.

A couple of excruciating moments took an age of the visible Universe to elapse.

"It's your previous involvement with other physical sciences that is paramount. I mean, your experience, that is. Does this project deal with delicate subject matters?"

"I don't know. Oh, you're not asking, I mean, of course. Indeed. Exactly, it does." She opted not to speak her mind. "If it's any consolation to the course of the... this project, I was fully briefed—" She abruptly discontinued her words upon the arrival of discerned tapping sound from the opposite end of the room.

Upon depressing the home-button of his portable phone, it read 9:34. He resumed his pacing, "come on, where the hell are—"

Turning to acknowledge some laughter, he saw Jack and Karen leaning against the concrete wall lining the edge of the stairway; her tanned olive complexion and features taking on an appealing tone under the morning sun. Giggling anew, she buried her face into Jack's shoulder.

"Okay. All right. How long have you two been standing there?"

"Well, guess I gotta get going with my new buddy."

He tried to ignore their ensuing passionate kiss and lingering glances upon disconnect.

"So, I'll see you around two-ish?" Jack queried.

"What, me?" She gave him a scolding look.

"Yeah, you. This nerd belongs to me, you got that?"

"Hey, no contest," Colton raised hands unconditionally. "So, Jack?" No reply. "Oh, Jaaack?"

"What! Okay." Jack gave Karen a soft pat on the bottom. "Get out of here."

Their humanity required they both allow the opportunity to observe her bounce down the steps and disappear around the corner of an adjacent building.

"It's a few minutes' walk to where the Applied Material Physics administrative offices are located. I got… yep, nine forty-three and thirty-one seconds; we must be there by ten. That barely leaves… minutes."

"According to my calculations, it's too late then." Jack threw in.

"Huh?"

"What, with that thirty-one seconds there? Too bad, too. If only we were twenty-four seconds earlier, maybe we'd have changed the world. Buddy, I have the general layout of the campus in mind. I think we'll be fine."

"Okay, but this guy's more than a little uptight. Hey, so…
did you give any of this deeper consideration?"

"As a matter of fact I have. I mean, she's great looking,
isn't she? Ooph. And really, dude, there's been no work there
connecting and junk. It's been really rather remarkable, these
last few days," Jack elbowed Colton's arm.

He played along for a moment. "Yes, yes she is. Have you
two been together ever since?"

"Nah, not quite. I shared a drink with her and that friend
of hers. Lingered for a while after you left. We ended up
hooking up last night, which, of course ended up at
breakfast. I'm sure you've been there plenty of times."

"Sure. Huh, of course." Wending their way onward
through the commons, his illusory status in such matters was
successfully gilded.

They halted as they arrived upon the marble-granite steps.
Tall mahogany-hued doors loomed at their summit, and on
either side, tall desert-stained pillars guarded the façade like
centurions. Ivy curled around them as though their legs were
chained to the Earth. There was naturally an eerie vibe about
the place to him, whether in fairness to these appeals, but
probably for what lurked inside. In reality, it was Caldwell
Hall for Math, Science, and Engineering. This was where Dr.
Mendal and his charge kept office.

"Jesus. Helluva look to this place, man." Jack offered.

He thought how vindicating that was to hear. Just then a
student burst through the doors, leaving them to slowly
return to a thunk behind her; the sound quite effectively
terminating the motif of the moment.

They entered the spacious foyer directly on the other side
of the doors, to find a surprisingly large number of people
passing to and fro compared to the almost non-existent
traffic entering and leaving the premises.

One distant figure in particular caught Colton's eye.
Halting, he hissed, "Jack!" who needed two more paces to
process the command. "Hold on a sec." He was uncertain,

but the head and shoulders carried about in that same sort of assumption; a gate that commanded other souls to maneuver around him like water respecting a stone in a stream. *Totally in control,* he thought, as the man vectored in egress through the same mahogany doors.

A hand alit on his shoulder. "Colt? Hey, man. What's up?"

"I don't know. It's… nothing I guess. Come on, we're cutting it close."

"Right," Jack scanned for whatever caused the hesitation. "You're the one who stopped."

Approaching Dr. Mendal's door, they could hear a female, which of course prompted them to exchange raised brows.

"Huh… I wonder if we should?"

"You're asking me?"

Cautionary knocks to the door triggered the female voice's abrupt silencing, soon replaced by his own. "Yes, we're… I mean, I'm here?" He gingerly slipped his head in the door.

Mendal's impatience waved him to hasten the entrance.

His expression then morphing uncertainty, he left his hand in orbit.

The woman seemed to deliberately avoid acknowledging their arrival.

He was instantly overtaken. Legs crossed seductively by accident, her back and shoulders were of refined posture. He settled into the contours along the side of her profile.

"Colton!"

"Yes, what? right here."

"I called your name twice. Who is the gentleman with you?"

Sensing the delay in response, Jack offered his own. "Ah, yes. Hello, Dr. Mendel, is it? My name is Jack. Jack Sullivan. I've heard much about you."

"Excuse us, Doctor. Right, he's into organics."

"Uh, actually," Jack interrupted, "I'm in the PhD program up here. Biochemistry to be exact."

"I would like to be upfront and formally make you aware; I am interested in bringing him in on this new project of mine. You see, there will be specific matters—"

"I was not made aware of this!" Quickly rotating attention, Mendal seemed confused over Jack's outstretched hand.

Pulling the gesture back, Jack was also uncertain. "Wait, I thought—"

"Both of us, we can mutually benefit actually," Colton's cadence pleaded.

Though he had doubts, Jack tried again. And as suspicion confirmed, the quick jolt of the professor's hand was so frosty he left the gesture suspended in the air, turning his face slowly toward Colton for moral support.

"Well, the woman you were noticing is Monica Saxton. I am formally assigning her to you as an assistant, already though."

This initiated her to at last rise and turn in their favor. Presently, she set to crinkling her brow, flirtatiously this mien would seem to anyone who did not already know her. And so, being Jack, this captured adoration with certain rapidity.

"Noticing?" Colton tried to absolve himself.

"Yes, yes. Acknowledging… noticing."

She maneuvered to inconspicuously detach a golden brooch from over her upper torso, and in a single fluid motion placed it in her pocket book, clipping it shut. It was an easy range of motion to conceal, given to the obscuring power of her allure. The focus was how her hand felt in his, how the returning grip of her curling fingers was purposeful. Unaware the whole time he was smiling like an unabashed idiot.

There was a fleeting wonder as to whether her hair was black, or thick in dark chocolate hues. Two adorable dimples folded into her cheeks when she stood, cresting in height near the elevation of his chin. Those wavy tresses, pulled securely along the contours of her head, he imagined if they were ever set free they would bear a resemblance. Something about her touched him straightaway, as an allegory to his past.

"Are you saying hello, or are you interested in the lotion I use?"

"Oh!" Colton quickly holstered his hand. "Right. I… lost in ideas there. Uh, nice to meet you."

"So I've heard."

"What a… exactly would that be?"

"That you have big ideas."

Through a smile tinged as a grimace, Colton willed his attention towards the others. "Assistant. What's that about?"

Doctor Mendal clarified, "I think there is importance, implication-wise, behind your work. What you are proposing recommends this action be taken."

Colton's cadence quickened. "Huh… action be taken? Not sure what that means. Look, okay, mistakes have been made… in the past. I get it. But that's *in the past*. We're fabricating a new technology, an attempt for research purposes, like any other in the constellation of stuff that goes on. We don't need to be babysat. It's his materials expertise that I… or I mean the project needs, and—"

Mandel waved a dismissive hand. "Folks, step out into the corridor, please, if you would. I need to have a word alone here with Mr. Reinholt."

As soon as the door clicked shut, the elevating voice muted by the thickness of the door.

Inside, there was no escape. The man lorded, endeavoring to intimidate like a catholic countess assigning naughtiness to a child. Wisely, Colton did not fight back. Though he had limitations, it took tremendous courage for he understood and accepted his dependence upon this person's evolving support and approval.

Outside the din, they seated themselves across the hall upon a wooden bench, situated below a push board strewn over with forgotten brochures and memos. They could not make out exactly what was being said as the cadence within the office occasionally rose and fell creating an uncomfortable pall.

This was all typically beyond Jack's tolerance for awkward scenarios, having no nature to deal with quagmires, much less in others. Who would? But while taking that inventory, and wondering how in the hell recent events could have inexorably placed him in the middle of this vexation, the distraction Monica provided kept him from fleeing. "So, what's your story?"

"My *story*? Is there something precisely you are after?"

"Whoa. I'd tell you 'da chill out, but damn. You're a bit frosty already, huh?"

With folded arms her stolid mien faintly moved side to side.

"Okay, let's keep it simple then. Like, where do you hail from, ya know? What do you do, hello, the normal stuff folk glean off one another in the common practice of civility?"

"Oh, is that all?" She kept her feminine contours defensively crossed as her pump gently dangled.

He allowed a moment. "Look, I don't really care that much. The guy comes off as a little strange, but I think he's legit. And maybe I have some agenda of my own in this thing. He and I… guess they're working it out? We're all connected on this thing, okay? So, if we're gonna be around and…"

Her partial commitment of undeniable allure, a lukewarm smile, arrested his words.

Goddamn, am I glad I met Karen.

"All right, I apologize. I, just, you know, had to be certain."

"I get it, I get it. We're good. So, can I ask then? I mean, assistant, that can mean anything. Are you a what, secretary or... Where do you come from?"

"Heh, I'm a bit more than that. I shouldn't discuss it but I'm not really a secretary, no. Among other hats, I specialize... Consider me a tech writer. I've worked for the professor—"

As the door parted, Colton emerged. "Great, you're still here. I suppose you heard all that," biasing attention toward her.

"And?" Jack begged.

"Oh, right. Uh, Dr. Mendal, he- uh, wants you inside. There, in his office... Miss, or is it misses Saxton?" He held out his hand.

"It's miss. Please, I'm Monica. But, didn't we already do this, a little while ago, inside?"

Jack concealed his convulsion.

Sensing the ensuing castigation, Colton withdrew in haste. "Right. Of course we did. Heh. I guess, then, welcome to the wedding, of material science with neurobiology."

"Mmm, indeed, and let us hope you find it... exhilarating." Jack added.

"What?" She turned her head quickly between them, shooting a leer at him.

"Uh, what he means is, we're glad to have your valuable time and assistance. I mean, per the professor's mandate. Now, did he provide you with the necessary contact information? I mean, for the lab, where you can find me?" Colton probed.

"The lab stuff?" She queried. "Yes. Like I was telling Jack here, I've worked with him in the past. Different projects, similar capacities. I know my way around Nat R&D. Okay then." She turned and proceeded halfway through the door.

But Colton got it in under the wire, "Hey, you guys want to meet up later? maybe tonight. Open some dialogue, tech, and..."

"Great. All right to call you… 'round eight? Good. Ciao then," as she disappeared within.

Puffing out his cheeks, he noticed Jack's leer. "Okay. What?"

"My ass, what. Come on, nicely played. Hey, man, good luck with that one. You're gonna need it."

* * * *

The day was lengthening, so he hurriedly donned his running clothes. Quite naturally, the meeting earlier impelled his contemplation. He looked at himself in the mirror and closed his eyes. As he opened them, they instantly poured over an artifice constructed like a miniature shrine beneath the mirror. A trophy read, "1st Place. In Recognition of Achievement by The Academy of Advanced Sciences". It was placed atop a beauty chest, oddly feminine for his abode. He moved the trophy off to the side, and stepped backward, small chest in hand, to a seated position upon the edge of the bed. Once there, the chest lay down upon his lap with deliberate gentleness.

Slowly, he opened it. Inside there were photos of him and his beloved Christine, memorabilia, a ring, a locket, a necklace, a pressed rose petal, and finally, a newspaper article containing the details surrounding her death. He knew it was unhealthy to open this trove of reminiscence, for it brought him to a regressed state in healing. But the day's events compelled him. He sat there for a moment in reflection of the fondest memories of his life, the times he shared with her, how he longed for that embrace again; one he had not since ever found. And again, like so many other times, he asked himself the simple question, "Why?"

"What good does this do?" and he quickly closed the lid. He still took some care in setting up the miniature shrine that meant everything to him then exited the gelid emptiness of the moment, and allowed instead the lingering desert heat and late sun of the early Arizona evening to pull his state of mind back to a healthier psyche.

He kept his runs to four or so miles, knowing the dangers of running in the arid desert environment. The day had lengthened until blue skies transformed to auburn hues along the way, torpedoed by the horizon-nearing sun. The final mile and a half took him down Butte Avenue, but as usual, he came to a wait, hands on knees, allowing traffic to blast by an intersecting boulevard enough to where an opening would allow a bolt across. Sweat crested his brow and trickled into his lids, causing a moment of sting and blurred vision. Chance chose then for one such vehicle, a Jeep, and he glimpsed the profile of its occupant. *Was that... him?* The same military man whom he saw leaving Professor Mendal's office. The same man he saw passing through the lobby of Caldwell Hall. But there was someone else with him, "Wait… that can't be. That's not the Monica woman."

He easily dismissed it as being a contrivance of his own mind. If there was any truth to the adage of absence making the heart grow founder, it could not hold a candle to what it did for his imagination. He saw vestigial traces of Chris everywhere. He knew he had a tendency to do that; everyone female he came across often bore some likeness, some way somehow, they could resemble her if he tried hard enough. He reasoned in the moment, he was doing the same with Monica. The striking resemblance this new person in his life took to her, he thought he let it get the better of him in much the same way. "That's got to be it."

The sun had completely set and the sky's remaining twilight was a mixture of cirrus filaments aglow alongside the emergence of brightening stars. Reentering his apartment, his keys crash-landed along the coffee table, where a laptop and other notes lay in an organization only known to him. The land-line's answering machine blinked a red light.

"Hi, Colton, this is Monica. I tried your cell, but the professor told me you might not get a signal. I wanted to call you. I wanted to tell you thanks for letting me into your strange little world of intriguing science. Gosh, I hope that doesn't sound corny, but I really mean it. So, did you want to meet this evening? If you didn't get it already, I'm five-five-five, three-three-two-one. Talk to you soon."

She seems a little different now. He then spoke aimlessly, "Can't say I blame her after that ridiculous meeting. Feel bad for her. Heh, I know I do for me." Accessing his mobile phone, the time read seven forty-six. Three rings, "Yo. Hey, it's me. Still there? I mean, at the cafe?"

"No, we grabbed a bite at this other place. Karen's gotta run. So, what's the deal? Oh, shit, you said seven earlier; does that mean we missed that?"

"Uh... no, I mean... I still need to— can I meet you down there, say, in an hour? Wait, let me call you right back, five minutes, I promise." Dialing Monica's number left on his answering machine, the call was answered inside of one ring.

"Hi."

He fiddled with an earlobe, "Whoa... heh, fast. Um, Monica?"

"It's me. Hey, thanks for calling."

Silvery and gentile, he denied its primal appeal. "Ahem, so, are you free for me tonight? I mean, for the thing?" He took the receiver and tapped it on his forehead three times with his eyes closed.

"Of course. What should I bring? You wanted to go over mission parameters and so forth?"

"Mission? Heh, we're not exactly overthrowing any third-world governments here."

Monica laughed for him, "right."

"But, um, sure. I'm going to have some schematic material, as well as some physical equations and gunk for Jack. You may want to take some notes. By the way, I'm sorry about that earlier, with Mendal."

"It's on him," she spoke delicately. "You two obviously have a history. Don't feel weird about it, I heard the way he spoke to you."

"So, right, meet up. Can you meet me and Jack? There's one of those couch cafes. Same street as Wrangler's? Say in forty-five?"

"Yes, of course. I immediately freed up my evening... I mean, for this. I'll see you there."

9
RECIPE

The venue was quiet this night, dimly lit, cozy. The arrangement of vacant couches and lounge chairs gave the impression of once bustling colloquy. They were the only patrons upon his arrival.

"Yes, Jack," he aspirated, "she is going to be trouble. So, how's it hangin', y'all?"

"Whoa, hey, did it occur to you we might be having a serious dialogue here?"

"I... oh-k, sorry?"

"Ha-ha. Relax man, bustin' your balls. Hey, you remember Karen?" Jack redirected to her after the arrested moment, "I'm not kidding, Karen, he really is a warm and charming character."

"Oh... well, yeah, of course I remember her... I-ah, I mean, you, Karen," he softened through a breathy laugh and a smile.

Her nod carried a therapeutic grin. "So, where's this troublemaker I'm hearing about?"

"Trou— oh, right. I don't know. She'll be along shortly." He sat himself strategically so as to begin constructing a research bivouac. Between his tablet, a laptop, and manila folders containing printed materials, the coffee table's surface was soon entirely consumed.

This mesmerized Jack and he took to rubbing his forehead.

"So, Jack? I wanted to inform you... My adviser, Dr. Mendal—"

"Yeah, you don't have to say more. It was kinda clear. I mean, what, with that hostility? Like, would someone get me a psyche major." He shot Karen a glance and she made an eye-rolling gesture. "Not every day one gets to hear a PhD candidate throwing caution to the wind and sparring with his adviser. It was inspiring, really."

"Embarrassing is more like it. Gah-hod, sorry."

"What was all that about? Wait, don't answer. I tell ya what, not to be insensitive, but do I care? Just keep it to the verdict, am I in or out?"

"Oh, you're in. I need you... I mean, my project does. That much really shouldn't be up to him. Look, it all goes back some ways. I was into some pretty advanced stuff a long while ago. Things happened... life. So I took time off."

"How long have you been at it, in the game?"

"It's... been several years."

"*Several*? Ho, man. What are we talking five years, *ten* years?"

"Hell, no, not that bad. God, I hope not. I can't take this place... The guy did give me leeway, I admit. Maybe I'm too hard, or judgmental, and he kind of rubs me the wrong way. But hey, science must prevail, right? So we move forward."

"And, maybe while we're at it, we can even ply your 'sitter with a Jim Beam and coke?"

Fending off the smile, Colton suggested, "Um, yeah, about that, Sully, let's... can we tread lightly with that?" squinting.

"All right. Hey, while we're on the subject, what's that about? What is she for again? Seems sort of formal."

"It's... uh, some appointed thing... Hey, if that's what the guy needs to give me permissions, I'm not gonna ask."

"But, wait, what am I to this thing then? I get the impression that I'm... demoted or something. Sympathies to Pluto."

"Heh, no. Don't even think about it."

"Fine by me, I won't. In fact, I really don't want to care that much. Look, in all seriousness, this sounds like a hoot, it does," Jack tapped his index finger upon the manila folder. "Like you say, we can mutually benefit. Sweet. But I won't lose sight of that goal. If it gets weird, dude, 'cause of that guy? I mean, he's not my advisor. C'est la vie."

Colton affirmed with gentle nods.

"Okay, as long as we get each other. SO, what do we got here?" Jack spun the folder around.

Stealthily, Karen rose to her feet. "I'll leave you men to your devices, I'm doing one of these damn eight-pm lectures for my adviser's one-o-two students. So, babe, I'll call you. Jack, hello? Okay, I'm gonna head out in front of a train and lie on the tracks."

"Ok, babe, sounds good."

She lightly slapped the back of his head, "hey!"

"What? Oh, right. Of course, check your tire, traction, or?"

"No, not quite." She drew the tip of her index finger along the line of his chin, "but I suppose it'll have to do, for now."

Soon after she left, they were immersed. Tacitly in the moment outside the zygote technology, at other times more so engaged when they aired observations, notes, and primitive diagrams of the embryonic project.

Jack was murmuring to himself when a motion afar drew Colton's attention towards the entrance of the café. Even for Colton, the innate primal skill of the human male would not be denied, needing very little visual input so as to instantly identify the physical nature of the entering form. Who it was did not take long to follow.

"Colton? Colt!"

"Huh? oh, sorry. Distracted."

"I said, when's miss Monic-America gonna show up?"

"I don't know, ask her yourself."

"Uh, what— does that mean?" he asked while still reading.

"She's standing right behind you."

Saucering his eyes upon registry, Jack rose to attention like a first-year cadet.

Leaning back and folding his arms, Colton reveled in his vengeance.

"Hey, I wasn't, uh, serious there. I mean... with that little Miss America barb?"

"Don't worry about it, none taken. Offense, that is. So, where are we, gentlemen?" She sat near Colton, ensuring that the hem of her skirt was tucked along the backs of her thighs as she landed.

"Okay, so," Colton interceded while glancing over the interface of his tablet, "...the baser model takes form in a domain where an artificial brainwave apparatus will reside in a nucleus. What we will attempt to do is to attach carbon nanotubes; here, I'll turn to page ten of the prospectus. Actually, wait... Monica, do you want a drink or something? pardon my manners. They got the usual, beer and wine. Even teas, all that stuff."

"Oh, I know. Not my first time, sport," she administered pats to his knee. "Sure, I'll have whatever you guys are?"

"Better make it a double," Jack added, "okay, I'll get that."

"All right, where was I?"

"Attaching nanotubes?" she set up her own laptop.

"Right. I have it mathematically predetermined, we'll need a flexural modulus of .75. and, Jack, where are you?"

"Right here, I'm right here, relax." Jack delivered three fresh Guinness pints. "What will need what?"

"A critical polymer. We need some way to affix our nanotubes near the interfaces where the MM processors intersect. Here, it's diagrammed for us."

"Oh, I see. There are compounds, but I wonder if..." Jack briefly faded to a side-glance, "didn't you say a molecular thickness?"

"Well, according to calculation, that and the application density can't exceed, otherwise it will likely ohm the conductive potential at those critical junctions, as you see there. We don't want that."

"Ok, wait. This, 'using organic substrates' business, to 'compensate for nanoscale permutations', I don't understand that," Jack then glanced towards Monica, "and, what in God's name are you typing?"

"Short hand. Interpretive."

"You, have an interpretation, for all this?"

She shot a resting bitch-face back at him. "Whatever. Look, there are some details that obfuscate, of course. I'm posting the meat, so to speak. It will approach interpretive concision. That's what's paramount. Any uncertainty intervals we may need to review... any critical phases at post-op mission reanalysis, it can all be reviewed. Now, if you two could hold back for a moment, there's something I need to do."

Jack waited until she was out of earshot, "have you ever seen that – I mean, that kind of intelligence floating over the top of an ass like—"

"Hey man, cut it out! Look, if she goes, we lose Mendal's support, and this all goes away. Okay?"

"Are you kidding? 'Critical phases of post-op,' though. Who is this girl, and who talks that way? Come on, you gotta be a little weirded out by her, dude, babe status and all. And by the way, I doubt it very seriously that you 'don't want her around.' Ya get my drift?"

"I said the situational mandate, okay. She can stay or go."

"Ha-heh, right. Look, I wasn't shot out of a particle accelerator ten minutes ago. I've seen the way you look. Shit, I thought you were gonna knock-out the witnesses and throw her ass across Mendal's desk."

Colton's face emptied in an aimless gaze, "she happens to look a great deal like... Wait, drop it, she's coming back."

"Wow, that was quick, as far as trips to the ladies' room go. How'd you accomplish that?" he felt the warm glow of Colton's disapproving leer against his profile.

"Are you going to actually make me tell you to fuck off, or are you going to instructionally get it. I was into my messages, if you must know."

Colton emphasized a throat clearing, "So, we're talking about artificially creating detectable vibrant energies. How? By using carbon nanotubes, that's how. And when the charge is administered, the unusually small sizes become critical in the emergence," he added while pointing to pertinent physical equations on his partially rotated laptop.

"It almost seems like using substrate organic technique, the relationship between RNA delivering DNA. Sort of analogous there?" His voice was timidly rejoining.

"Interesting, I didn't think of that. You see, the problem with these nanotube crystallization matrices... how to explain this, they are prone to quantum uncertainty. Well, with the application of that secondary medium, we introduce geometric instructions."

"And thus we have reduced those fractal effects."

"Yeah. Yes, essentially that's correct."

"Fascinating," Jack redirected toward Monica, "ya getting' all this?"

She remained transfixed to her monitor.

At best, he imagined a facial twitch. "All right, fine. So, we are all on the same page. But your sub-micron fiber optics though, where are you getting those components?"

"Right, let's move along in this overview. We must use the drawing towers at NRD, several of them as a matter of fact. The preform blanks shouldn't be an issue either because they have them in stock. There's an entire division devoted to research into fiber—"

Jack interrupted, "wait, you said preform blanks? Listen, I gotta be completely honest here. I know my resume says *biochemist*—"

"Don't worry. I'll try to explain it quickly. Blanks are composed of prorated graphite. They get lowered into a furnace; once melted, the purest glass there is. I once heard an analogy that if you stood on a slab that was as thick as the Sears Tower you could still clearly see the earth beneath it. You can't do this with the same stuff that is used in windshields... too many impurities."

"I know drawing towers use gravity. But that's about all I know."

"Correct, actually. The molten glass is gravitationally pulled, and it cools as it descends to form a trailing thread. This is where we will cheat the process."

"Cheat?" Looking at Monica, Jack still could not resist the attempt, "How do you feel about that?" The glare she gave him registered before he knew he snapped his attention away from her. His peripheral vision sensed that it took her a moment to clear her face of its condemnation. He puffed his cheeks full of air through a heavier exhale.

"Where was I? the resulting strands are spun in industry. But, we are going to intercede at that point with our component as we've discussed so far."

Jack more fully reengaged, "I see here in your schema, page thirteen, 'Cortical threads' though. Really?"

"Exactly. By then interweaving the combined mutable microprocessors, the resulting matrices are composed of threads containing the MMs and our nanotubes. The weave of these threads will then be folded into a fabric; thus concentrated density, doing so in manageable volume."

"All that, and... what kind of densities are we talkin' here? I mean, even with automation that could take some time. I don't, uh, see that specified here," Jack turned over pages.

Colton nodded, "Yes, unfortunately, it could take several weeks. We'll have to monitor the automation occasionally, of course. At point-one meter per second we can draw out and inject... over a mile of this stuff inside of a week in linear form. It's the weaving that's the problem, in order to make the individual threads into a fabric? That will probably run twenty-four hours a day, at approximately one-square millimeter per minute. It's calculated, we'll need a total fabric density of a hundred and eleven point nine square millimeters. Thus, cubed of course."

"Then these," Jack's expression abruptly widened, "wait, did you say one-eleven? That's very close to fourteen hundred cubic... centimeters, hello?"

Monica snickered, then she and Jack shared an expression that signaled a rare simpatico. "Mm, that's right," she added, "even I know that."

Colton naturally directed towardboth, "am I missing something? Why in the hell are you two looking at me like that, what's right?"

"Wow, he really doesn't know." Leaning back in his chair, clasping hands over the top of his head, Jack added, "Oh, so *this*, this is what feels like to be you."

"Huh?"

He pulsed a gentle laugh. "Look, it goes like, humans have a cranial volume ranging from nine hundred and fifty c-c to... in the neighborhood of eighteen hundred?" he squinted at an upward at angle, "that's an average of... fourteen hundred."

"Uh huh?"

"Your calculations. You derived an amount landing on that same number? Like, accidentally no less. That's kind of incredible."

"Mm, but a total coincidence, I assure you," Colton renounced. "I tell you what, though; if we are creating artificial brain waves, a volumetric coincidence may be intuitive. I don't know. Just offering that. It's again ...""

"So, in all, this experimental subject's construct to charge ratio... oh, wait, happens to be identical to that found in the myelinated neurons. Creepy, but incredible."

Colton gently scratched beneath his eye with an index finger and stared in reply.

"You really don't know about that stuff either, do you?"

"Well," Colton averred, "it's not necessary to the purview of what we're doing here. At least, I think. Of course I mean, yes, I'm aware of what *myelin* is."

"Excuse me, guys? That I don't know. May I ask, what is myelin?"

He smirked as he leered at Jack, "Well, you brought it up, you're the teacher."

"Sure. Ha. And to think, my education actually becomes useful to this thing. Amazing," he muttered off to himself before continuing. "So, myelin? It's an amphipathic compound... uh, think of it as insulation medium. Kinda like what you find around wires? For physics, ah, this kind of physics I should say, it encases neurons for the same fundamental purpose. But that enters an interesting question, Colt. How are you going to stop charge leakage in your structure here, and there?" Jack slid his pointed finger along the scaffold of designs.

"Okay, right. Those are great insights, Jack. Giving this more thought, it may help achieve results if we integrate protection. Uh, right off the top of my head? We could pre-calculate the drain into free air. Goose the charge to compensate. I don't like that idea. The other way, we can create some kind of medium that acts to insulate the entire construct, not just at the discrete level. Boy, that's not part of my calculations. So we're kind of in discovery mode at the moment, aren't we?"

"Yeah, I think you may need to consider *some* kind of discrete level analogical design, not just at the general encasement scales."

Acknowledging through a brief gaze, Colton made subtle nods, then took notice of Monica suppressing a yawn. Scanning the interface of his phone, he added, "Buuut, I think we've overloaded the chorus with song for one night. Monica?"

"Uh. Yeah," she smiled to him, "Still here, believe it or not."

"Sorry if, uh… how are you doing with this stuff? I mean, I can paraphrase, later. I'm not entirely certain what your background is with this sort of thing. I wasn't considering the myelin stuff either and …"

"Well, some of that was getting technically edgy but I have the gist of what's going on. I'm not here to understand, so long as I can translate. Most of what I have here recreates the evening sufficiently, I believe. This is what the professor asked, well, I mean the organizational aspect."

He reacted uncommitted to them, "Christ, he has no faith," then spoke directly, "So, the way this works, we've been given two access permits for NRD labs. I guess that means two's company three's a crowd with plant managers. It's all dubious to me. I mean, if Mendal has that much control he should… I don't know, do more."

"If it's any help, you said yourself, I won't truly be needed until we get to the goop part of this project," Jack offered.

"Goop, ha. Well, the good news, you don't have to wait really. You have the project outline; you can get started on chemo synthesis. I'm hoping you'll pull through though?"

"Don't worry," Jack smirked.

"Ah, may I interject? Essentially, I won't need to be down in the lab… with you gentlemen. I mean, you are intending to provide recorded data of those operational stages – am I mistaken?"

"Mm, hm. And Jack, I suppose you will have to record your methods when we're not around?" Colton motioned the collection of himself and Monica with a hand.

She added, "I then I can then integrate them into the ongoing time-line," nodding, "that'll work fine."

"I guess there's no other way, huh? Can't be there at all times." Their gaze lingered as Colton closed his laptop.

"So, we're done for tonight?" Jack interrupted, "wow."

They opened the outer door to the street and noticed a line of tavern-goers aligned in a broken single file line down the sidewalk, with what looked like two bouncers standing with his arms folded. They were peering toward the front of the café he and his entourage had recently left. After Colton noticed the unusual scene, one of them appeared to speak into a walky-talky, then unclipped the draping rope that held them back. People immediately started filing into the pub. This was unusual, as in the years he had been around campus, he never remembered there being any kind of wait like that. He turned to comment this to his companions, but only Jack was standing beside him, Monica had vanished into the dark ether of the night. "Hey, where did… you see her leave?"

Jack was thumbing his phone. "Huh, what? Oh, no, sorry. Didn't see her leave. Goodnight, sweet Monica, I guess."

10
The Lab

They drove the twenty-two miles to the parking lot of the
National Electromagnetic Research and Development labs.
Noticing Jack acting uneasy from time to time, it finally
drew him to ask. "Ok, is there something going on with
you?"

"What do you mean?"

"You're distracted, more quiet than... you."

"I am, eh? What, are you like my girlfriend? let me
distract in peace."

"Oh-k. Sorry," Colton lifted his hands off the steering
wheel.

"No, it's... I guess I was just lost in the moment there,
thinking about that strange phone call I got last night."

"Strange?"

"Uh huh. It was your hottie hall-monitor there, Monica.
First, I don't remember giving her my phone number. Did
you do that, for me? I mean, not that I'm disappointed or
anything," he tittered in wait of any response. "Seriously, did
you do that?" He still waited. "Yo, is this car driving itself
over there? Hey!"

"Huh? Oh, no. I mean, yes. That is... that's odd."

"Hey, man, don't sweat it. It wasn't exactly a make-out
session. I don't really give a shit about uninvited phone calls,
whatever."

He only listened intently.

"So, I take it you didn't give her my digits? Along the
way here."

"You're up in graduate housing, right? She probably
ferreted it out of the directory. So, what did she—"

"Seriously, it's not a big deal if you did. You can be honest, at least I think," Jack turned his view to the landscape rushing past the window.

"Jack, I can assure you, I did not. Do you mind me asking what you talked about?"

"Well, that's the part that has me kinda... distracted. Should I be spooked? Definitely an interesting exchange. Put it that way."

"Interesting, huh. What exactly?"

"I mean, it wasn't *what* so much. More the way she spoke – like the timbre of her... I dunno. Something was just off about that inquisition. She started out with he – I assume she meant Dr. Mendal? But at some point, it became *they. They* wanted to know how long I've known you?"

This earned a direct head turn.

"Mm hm, I wondered, too. I mean, firstly, what are we doing here, espionage? And who the fuck are they? Look, Colton, I, um, don't really know you that well, or any of this background and frankly..." he left it open.

Refocusing his line of sight over the steering wheel, Colton agreed, "huh, yeah. Okay, that's odd. Sure." Sensing the ensuing focus, he briefly offered his eyes, "I don't know what that means. Did you ask?"

"Well, no, duh. I mean, beyond the non-sequitur vibe of it. Not sure if you've noticed but she and I... heh, how to put it nicely."

"I know. I know."

"Okay? So yeah, we haven't established any sort of boundaries. I mean, it didn't lend to my probing her. I guess I was just sort of caught off guard."

"But she did eventually tell you why she needed to know."

"Mm, no, not exactly, she danced a bit. I wonder, does she think I'm an idiot? Normally, who cares – right? But that stuff with your cagey douche advisor, he forced her into this thing. So now I'm getting cryptic phone calls from her?"

"I know. I mean. At a loss there."

"Ah, hell, I'm new to this university. Like I said, I don't know the history between all you cats. Look, change the subject. Besides, we know who she really wants to call, don't we? I mean, come on."

"What do you... not sure I follow."

"Oh, come on. You gotta wanna tap that. I mean, you're not gay, are ya?"

"I... what? Homo— no."

"Relax – it's okay either way" he weakly laughed.

"Look, I just... I don't know if I like the girl, is all. Sure, she's... cute. I'm not blind."

Jack lowered his brow to his profile, "Really. Cute, huh."

"Hey, I'm male, what do you want me to say?" reaching with his closed fist.

Tardy to complete the forced bonding, Jack shook his head behind a mask of incredulity. "Seriously, dude, you only live once. She looked at you, too, bro."

Colton shook his head in sync.

"YES, she did."

A reprieve transpired, "Ok, fine! Maybe I've seen some of that. All right. Ya happy?"

"Right. Hey bud, she's not looking at me. 'Sides, what do I care? Karen's a babe. Smart too. Yup," finishing through a breath, "she's a good one."

"So, what of it?"

"You're kidding, science and sex, rolled up into one delicious enigma?"

"Come on, Jack. We can't let this disintegrate into that."

"Dude, live a little." He then let a moment elapse. "Oh, you're right of course. If you wanna get serious, it's that whole set-up with her and that overlord. Just tryin' to livin' things up 'round here – geesh."

"Somewhat of a Mendal thing. I'm really just concerned if I... mean, if the situation loses her."

65

"Yeah, for the project's sake?" Jack shook his head fending off a smile as he peered out the passing scenery. "I get the feeling you may not have any choice in the matter, anyway. Besides, it suits you better than your honestly tellin' me, but that's okay," he ended through a bit more laughter.

"Matter, huh?"

"Well, just be open to other possibilities."

* * * *

Their car came to a stop amid one in many abandoned slots of the huge facility parking. The desert wind carried the autumn variation of warmth, as it also whirled a distant dust-devil. Their doors flung open in unison.

"You ready?" Colton asked as he foisted a strap over his shoulder.

At the electric sensor, he slid his card-key through. There was a click, and the door bifurcated with a hiss to about an inch. They entered the reception area and approached the receptionist; a stout African American male security guard, who was almost indistinguishable from a police officer, gun and all, rose to greet them.

"Hi, Carmon!"

"Colton? Mr. Reinholt, my man! Damn if I thought I might never see you again. That is, until I got this from the man." At that, he held out a clipboard; upon which was a proper project issuance and program permission form.

Running his index finger down the content, Colton then lifted the page and cursorily reviewed the second, "Yes, this looks right, Carmon." Handing the clipboard back, "This here... this is Jack Sullivan. He's an important member of the team."

"You're good, I gotchu, you always good with me. There, sign off on it right quick. K, so, you folks are scheduled for development lab... See, five floors down this time. Oh, man."

66

"Oh, I know. Hey, Carmon, would Dr. Wiles be on site today? Could you try his desk for us?"

"As a matter of fact he is. Hold on," he reached for the phone. Yes, Dr. Wiles, I have Colton Reinholt here, who's requesting a moment of your time. Uh, okay, I'll let him know."

"On a Saturday, no less," Jack murmured. "Impressive."

They walked down a long, brightly illuminated corridor, its faux marble flooring not offering much to offset the appearance of sterility as its length bathed in spiritless fluorescent ambience. If it were not for the pipes lining the corners where the ceilings intersected the walls the corridor might have appeared seamless.

"I got a couple of questions for you. Your friend Carmon there... he said five floors down?"

"That's right."

"I see. Well, that's interesting, because we are on the ground floor."

"That's right."

"Underground. Hm."

"You got it. When we get there, you'll have to take off your clothes."

"Huh? See – I knew it. You and your weird phone calls in the night, Mendal, you're all in on it."

"Anyway ... you'll want to do it quickly. You can leave your clothes in one of the lockers, then, we'll be clad in factory-issued coveralls"

"You mean like hazmat get-ups?"

"Essentially, yes. We then pass through air showering. See, lots of delicate tech here. The region we'll be accessing... a little touchy. Sterile environment, I mean dust free. You'll never feel cleaner. The drawing towers must be manually manipulated and so, in jumpsuit. We'll need masks and gloves."

"Oh, I know. Not my first rodeo, bro, trust me. I guess it hadn't occurred this might be one of those times."

"Right. So, while we're configuring the drawing towers, setting up the injectors, and going forward, we only need the facility's jumpsuit protocols when we're in those specific control condition environments."

"Hey, what's with that sound, that weird hum?"

"This place is a gorilla. They do everything here. Between the power cycling for laser research, ballistics labs, heck, they've even centrifuged for nuclear application here in the past. Creates the kind of… apex, industrial white noise of research and sciences you're hearing."

"Jesus… Where do they store the bodies?"

They passed from the first corridor into the stairwell, where much of the humming was muted, though not entirely. As they cracked the door two flights up, a whoosh of air passed through the door with them; on the other side, another brightly lit corridor. When the doors closed behind them the humming was at last drowned down to negligible. They came upon a door with an address written, 'Dr. Norman Wiles; PhD Applied Material Physics and EE.' The door was ajar.

"Come in. Sit down. It's nice to see you again, Colton."

"Yes. Hello, Dr. Wiles. It's been a long while since I've seen you. How are you? Hey, sorry to drop by unannounced."

"Oh, no, think nothing of it. Stephen mentioned you would be dropping by soon."

"Interesting. So you have communicated ahead."

"Wow, sounds like it's been a while for the two of you."

"Heh-ha. By the way, this is Jack Sullivan, a brilliant Biochemist, only overshadowed by his talents as a consummate wise-ass."

On cue, Jack mocked a bow.

"It's all right, nothing I haven't entertained before. Yes, so, Dr. Mendal. He says you have an interest in the em-and-em project?"

"Come again, em-and-em?"

"The mutable microprocessors?"

"Oh, yes, right. Right, of course."

Leaning back, Dr. Wiles clasped an elevated knee, "Mmm, yes, I've been made aware of your interest."

"Okay, here it goes. I think I have a use for them in a new directive for a thesis project, I... or, we," Colton signaled to include Jack, "are working on. I mean, the last I heard, there was no vector in main-stream technology. Which baffles me. I mean, having omni-functionality in hardware... that would seem like a huge leap?"

"Indeed." Dr. Wiles rose to his feet and stepped around the desk.

They remained seated, sharing an inquisitive look as he passed them.

He began to speak quietly, gently closing the door, "Let me explain something, that is not entirely true. The cost of the devices in manufacturing makes it almost impossible to create an industry for them, that is, outside of research interests."

"Right, cost effectiveness, sure."

"But, of course, they would have application if getting over that hurdle. They were developed for a special purpose, fully integrated into a... technology. Supposed to be a one-and-done sort of deal."

"What was the technology?"

"Sorry, no can do, classified. That's why there was limited press released regarding their existence. To be honest, you shouldn't even know about them. I'm a bit surprised you... well, it's your affiliation with Dr. Mendal, I know."

Jack involved himself, "Excuse me if I'm asking the obvious; are you telling us we're not going to be experimenting with them because they're... classified?"

"No, not exactly. It's the technology they were created for that's classified. Not the devices themselves, come to think of it."

"Well, may I rush to point then?"

Dr. Wiles held up his hand, "stop there, the answer is yes. As I said, doctor Mendal and I have discussed this."

At hearing that, Colton sensed it might have been a bit much for him to believe. "Yes, the idea takes a leap of faith, I know."

"It's… a bold idea you got there, I'll give you that. And, it is intriguing. I'm aware that you may run into some trouble trying to house the MMs in the track-down during fiber growth, so, I think I can help you with that. I've rigged a device to be installed; it'll need to go in sequence prior to the first coating cup."

Jack spoke up again, "excuse me, the second coating cup, here, look at the diagram. I have a compound," handing him an adjunct mission spec. "So, I take it we can use this stage, there, to applicate a molecular adhesive, for the nanotubes, right?"

"Yes, now you guys are thinking," the doctor nodded. "Actually, we can install a third coating cup, the wire passes through; we can apply the adhesive and the nanotubules at that point."

"That would save a lot of time." There was a natural pause in the conversation. "Well, I think we've taken enough of yours. I can certainly leave a copy of the prospectus?"

"Oh, no, that won't be necessary."

"Doctor Wiles, this is all far more than I thought this little visit would provide. The help with setting up injection technology, that would be an invaluable help. I can't thank you enough."

"It's nice to have a use for these processors, the pleasure's mine," he held out a hand, "And Colton, it is good to see you back, and working. I never got the chance to say… I was sorry about your friend. She was a good thesis ally. I will get you those MMPs. Oh, here, in case, my direct office line. So, subterranean on this one, huh? The good old sterility ward. Optics! You must be on the fifth tier."

* * * *

Upon leaving Wiles' office there was a collective sense of relief; it was finally happening. They were en-route to tour the lab, where the physical manifestation of the project would at last congeal from schematics and mathematics.

Arriving at two elevators, one read, 'Elevator I: 1st & 2nd Floors only', but their destiny was the other, 'Elevator II: Authorized Personal Only. Access Subterranean Research and Development – secure code required.'

Colton slid his electronic key-card down the slot and a little red light turned to green.

"Gosh, Colton, why couldn't that guy be your adviser?"

He radiated a subtle grin and a slight roll of the eyes, "I know. But he's not even a professor, although he has guest-lectured in the past. Mendal and he are... friends. How that is, I have no idea. Actually, I know they've worked on projects in the past; not sure what their affiliation really is beyond that."

There was a sibilant wheezing at the instant the elevator doors parted.

"This whole place is hermetically sealed or something?"

"Mm, no, it's our destination. But the air pressure bleeds. You'll see shortly."

"Why is it that this facility was built bottom heavy like this?"

"Because it's easier to control climate variables underground. That, and this place got its start doing neutrino detection. There's an abandoned mine nearby. The hills of France, or maybe it was Switzerland, can't recall, but that operation moved there. Now, Nat ERD took over and built this facility, with multi-tiered research capacities. We're in Optics, because, fiber optics of course. They even build mirrors down there for orbital telescopes?"

"Be still my shimmering heart."

The elevator arrived and when the door opened, there was a short corridor with a closed glass vestibule at the other end. Within, were nozzle-like fixtures protruding from the walls on either side. Otherwise, the artificial hum of industry was the only occupant. The moment they stepped off the elevator, this triggered a pulsation of saffron light accompanied by an obnoxious honking sound. It blared three times, paused, then again.

Colton spoke over the din, "Hurry, into this locker area. It won't cut... oh, better. Been down here a million times. Never get used to that damn sound. It won't cut until you enter and the door slides shut. Here, follow my lead. We get into these jump suits."

Jack stood for a moment staring at it.

"Sorry about that, I should have warned you about these protocols. The detectors sense whether you are wearing the environmental prerequisites. Hate the goddamn thing. You ready for the chamber?"

"You mean in there? With all the probes sticking out of the walls?"

Colton laughed a little, "don't worry, there aren't any aliens within at least four-point-three light years of here; that we know of, of course."

"So, what's going to happen? I get in this thing and..."

"Close your eyes and think happy thoughts for thirty seconds. A strong wind and a decon powder will aerate the inside. The powder statically collects dust and impurities and then a strong current of in-out wind flow reduces particular contamination. Here, put this mask on too. The realm is electrically charged to assure collection. Don't worry, not much more than the pop you get off a door handle, if you even notice it."

They entered the chamber and soon the air became opaque as a loud onrush of white noise accompanied it. Clearing commenced after approximately thirty seconds, and the roar subsided a few seconds later. As the air became dead calm all they could hear was their own respiration. An electronic bell toned, and the door to the inside of the lab opened with an outward burst of air.

"You can take off your mask now. Clip it to that loop on your shoulder, right, like that. You won't need it again, unless you go inside the inner sanctum."

They ambled down the hall, stopping at two sliding glass doors that touched the ceiling and floor. Again, sliding his key-card, the doors slid apart. Another rush of air eased, but did not cease blowing altogether this time.

"Quickly, let's enter. So now you know first-hand, the R and D wings are all pressurized. In the rare occasion that some impurities might get through the traps, this is a kind of last line of defense to make sure airborne particulate vectors are always pointed away."

"But what about, like, human dander? I mean I'm a fan of good hygiene and all but what about… us?"

"It's not here that is the problem; it's in there."

"Oh, the inner sanctum. Got it. Jesus, looks like the inside of a space station," Jack scanned his view around through the plate glass.

"It can be high tech all right. These terminals out here… Jack?"

"Uh huh."

"These here monitor calibrations. Everything. Experimental results, command interfacing, on the fly corrections for automation, and so forth. The inputs feed directly into the mainframe during production phases of operations. Look! Over there." Leading him to step to an adjacent enclosed room. "Those are the drawing towers."

"Wow. Convenient those, so accessible. Hey, Colt," Jack adjusted his watch. "I'll tell you, I'm anxious to get to my own labs… at the University."

"Sure. Let's, uh, get this tour wrapped. One last thing, log onto the system and verify project start time. Hey, we're here. Guess that makes it official," and he depressed the enter key.

11
CULTURE OF CREATION

Colton returned from his run, entered his apartment, and placed his keys on the glass coffee table. He glanced over to his answering machine and the light was blinking: "3 new messages".

"Hi, Colton, this is Monica. I understand that you and Jack were at the facility two Saturdays ago. We should discuss... over dinner? I'm free on Thursday. Five-five-five, three-three-four-one." Beep.

"Colton, this is doctor Wiles. Good news. I've outfitted towers 3 and 4 for you. No sense in running only one if we have two at our disposal. This should speed up your production time considerably. The riggings are special devices that will implant the MMPs, and also, if your colleague, Jack I believe was his name, if he and I could hook up? A third coating cup is ready for applicate. Hope all's well." Beep.

"Hey, buddy. Karen and I are hangin' down at the pub. Dude, you need a drink. You're obsessing. Good news on the compound. I think I have the flexural modulus we need, but it's more organic derivatives. Well, it may not be what you think." Beep.

By the time he had finished his shower, donned in faded denim jeans, cerulean-blue Polo shirt and open-toed sandals, the clock read 8:05pm.

He grabbed his phone and dialed. "Hey, there you are. Where you been? How's the, uh... the project going?"

"You coulda called."

"Right, but no pressure. I've been busy... in the lab. So, hey, I have great news, Sully. Dr. Wiles has set up our drawing towers."

"I guess that means we're a-go for the next phase, then. Timing is impeccable."

"Come again?"

"I have news too, I have our cerebral-gel."

"Ah, the compound! Wait, cerebral-gel? Tell you what, hold that thought. Gimme twenty minutes. See you down there?"

Jamming his knee under the steering-wheel, it allowed easy use of his thumbs to accesses contacts while driving: "Call Monica."

"Colton! Hi. Where have you been? I was starting to get con…"

"I'm returning your call? I'm back. So, sure. Get caught up?"

"Do you like Italian?"

"Absolutely. Where did you have in mind?"

"I was thinking I would cook, actually. Hello… you still there?"

"Oh, hah, yeah, that would-ah, be fine."

"Are you okay? Is that your signal?"

"Y– yes, right. I… No. Right. Probably. I'm heading downtown. Going to hook up with Jack and Karen. The roads are kind of bumpy."

"Should I be there, with you, tonight?"

"Uh, no, I… if there's anything important I'll clue you in tomorrow; what time then?"

"Eight sound good?"

"Sure. I don't have it… you have to text me your address?"

"I'm at sixty-nine Cactus Lane. You need that texted?"

He waited for a short interval, "No, of course not."

*   *   *   *

"Hey, there's the mystery man."

Nodding his smile in Karen's favor, he found a seat nearby. She turned and directed Jack's chin in order to execute a kiss, then rose to her feet. The crowd was thick enough to conceal her departure in short order.

"How-come whenever I show up she seems to be leaving?"

"Nah-ha, dude, forget it. This shit's not in her bag, man. Ah... for that matter, what about me?"

"So, she's the reason you're harder to get hold of these days?"

"Maybe that's it," Jack smirked. "Hey, I really dig her though. She's got insight, bro, hard to describe but she has a clarity... Did I tell you she's a PhD candidate? Psych."

"Fitting, for you, what with your neuro science. So, okay, what is this you are talking about, this... cerebral-gel?"

"Well, it's for the addition of the fiber-level application we discussed. Just hear me out. Unlike the general apparatus case substance, the best compound turns out has to do with," Jack gently cleared his throat, "blood chemistry."

"Come again?"

"It's true. Turned out the best compound for the spec was offered by nature all along. An electrophoresis-sustaining compound. It's called Albumin."

It was one of the rare times he saw Jack appear to suppress excitement. "Uh, electrophor– oh, right. For electrical field dispersion."

Sharing a conversational nod, Jack continued. "It's one of the critical components in blood sera chemistry – the Alb' compound."

"Uh huh... Okay, I'm gonna go ahead and confess, I may need an opportunity to science the subject?"

"Well, it has very good colloidal particle properties. You're looking at me."

"Oh... Colloid?"

"Yes. Particles suspended in a fluid medium, zap 'em with an electric field. Biologists use their properties to keep them stable to sort proteins. Uh, according to responses to modulating electrical fields by their intrinsic conductance."

"Wow. Okay." Colton snapped his fingers, "I think I see where you're going."

"Mm, hm."

"And you say... albumin?"

"Class of compound, sulfur-containing proteins. That's what triggers coagulation when heated. Think of that filmy white stuff when you poach an egg. Cottage cheese? Oh, and did I mention blood."

"And I was thinking something in plastic-molding, but–" Colton's expression expanded, "You're going for *myelination,* like... as in literally?"

"It might seem a bit much but I figured it can only help. You get that far with the experimental apparatus; you don't want any degradation of signals. Why not take it the distance? I tested the modulus, it checked out, and, it has the upshot coagulant property. And, duh duh dunn. It's not conductive."

Colton nodded, "of course. Of course."

"So, that's basically it. I had to fiddle with it once in polymer form a bit to reduce the molecular weight, but we have our compound, which I lovingly refer to as cerebral-gel."

He grinned through an uneasy filter, "cerebral-gel, right."

"I'll tell you more about that in a minute. The compound should allow you to get this down to about as thin as you can, while conserving the flexural modulus, to specs, that is. I worked my ass off on this. I finished it this morning and tested a glaze in microscopy." He handed him a photo of a sub-micron application.

"You keep this picture with you?" After a moment looking it over, "it's kind of dim in here but I..."

"All right, gimme that. Forget the picture."

Colton labored a smile, "Dare I ask?"

"Where did I get the blood? First thing I did when I arrived here was to check-out the Biology department. Not in my nature to shy away from strangers. Partied with a couple of 'em that night... Don't worry, the blood came from cadavers."

"Uh, heh, I would hope so."

"Want to know what a creepy coincidence is?"

"You mean there's more?"

"Ha ha ha, of course there is. Don't ask me how weird it is that the blood was extracted from the cerebral cortex."

"Naturally," he nodded, "and hence the name?"

"Cerebral-gel. But, it gets better, or weirder, depending on your point of view. Guess what temperature the end-product needs to be to take on the right physical properties?"

"Thirty—"

"...seven degrees Centigrade. You got it. Once entering that phase state, the electrophoresis properties will allow this to automatically affix a very small amount—the molecular depth of the specs—when we apply a charge to the medium. Oh, I forgot to mention, the substance is water soluble in pre-applicated form."

"Oh, that's perfect. We'll absolutely need that solubility for... I think I'm on board now. At first, we'll put an unknown parts-per-million; we can calculate this simply enough, into a saline solution and as our fiber optics and microprocessors pass through Dr. Wiles' device, apply the field, drain the fluid, integrate... until we have the fabric constructed. By layering, etc., etc."

"About Dr. Wiles. We have to meet with him, right?"

"Mm hm. First... let's see, how to put this delicately, can you provide work notes? I mean formulaic where necessary... for the Monica aspect? I'm asking 'cause—"

"Don't worry, I understand why. Yes, I have my notes. And yeah, I'll draft them out step-wise, put them together, and text or email you the file."

"Hey, you'll need it, right? when you turn your angle on this project into your own thesis. But is there any chance you could… get those to me by tomorrow?"

"Huh," Jack mused, "That's kinda brief, eh?"

"Sorry to have to do that to you but… hey, I got a call from Monica. She wants to hook up tomorrow night, go over the Lab aspects, and whatever other notes we have."

"I wasn't told we were."

"Um, I think this… it's harmless, dropping off updates. Making sure she's in the loop."

"Oh, I see. You can handle that, alone and junk?" Jack laughed aloud. "Yup. Entirely professional. Wholly orthodox for the purpose of exchanging intellectual property—"

"Calm down, I wouldn't— the woman terrifies me… in a way."

"What's with you and chicks, dude? I know, I know. Keep this thing all business, but you gotta have a pulse too."

"Look, drop it. We have to wrap this up."

"Hey, so where were you all last week?"

"I was successful myself, my superconducting nanotubes, that is. I tested them all the way up through 40.6 C. It was really amazing how well those calculations proved true for using organic substrates like that."

"Does Mendal know? I mean, about the… super part of that conduction?"

"Not yet, no. I guess for some reason I'm apprehensive there. Besides, he'll know sooner or later when I present our… or, my findings. If Monica doesn't get around to presenting things first. Not sure how frequently she reports."

* * * *

The light of the day was draining away as he turned his car down Cactus Lane. Muttering quietly to himself each passing number along the way, he slowly stalked her address. He never found hers. Instead, he locked eyes from afar upon her silhouette, a visage shining through curtains, hovering above a second-story balcony.

Rolling his car up to a stop, there was no immediate urgency to extinguish the opportunity; until, sensations of shame crept into the moment, at which time he quickly scanned the vicinity. One last time, he traced his eyes along the elegance of her contours.

The onset of night did not completely conceal the well laid out landscape beneath the façade. Part of his middle conscience dabbled in the idea of her aristocracy; most of him resisted its appeal. Either way, it added to the mystique of who she might really be, and why someone of her pedigree would be military.

He thought it was odd that three light knocks upon the door impelled it to open part way. As there was no one on the other side to greet him, he raised his voice, "Ya, hello?"

From an origin deep inside the feminine voice arrived, "Colt, is that you?"

"Heh. Hey. Hi."

"I've been looking forward to your arrival. Please come inside, living room on the right. I'll be there in a moment."

Cautiously, he entered the premises, unconsciously choosing a non-obtrusive seated position upon the edge of a leather ottoman. Peering around the room, he could not help but notice every object he laid eyes upon seemed positioned with a purpose. The setting was immaculate, excessively well kept. There was something vaguely familiar about the aroma too, though it was being obscured by a mask of heated spices. While lost in it, a caress landed upon his nape like lightning.

"Oh, I'm sorry," she laughed. "I didn't mean to startle you."

"Ah, n-no... It's quite all right actually."

After a brief interlude of fixed gazes, he began, "Eh-here, I brought my laptop. A lot of our notes here... they're on disk for you. We met the other night, after you and I spoke on the phone? You'll see it's all here." His vision danced about the room, then he soothed the moment. "I, uh, I took the liberty of—"

Her interruption took no effort. "Hey, what's the matter? Are you... I mean, I get the sense that you are, I don't know, afraid of something. I hope it's not me." Gently advancing her hand she led him into the dining area. Candelabra sat amid a dark brown stained oak dining table, already fully set for two. "Please, sit down. Would you like some wine?"

"Uh, sure. That... that'd be good."

"I have a Pinot, a couple of Chardonnays. Your basic Merlot. What's your mood?"

"Oh, it's no fuss, Merlot is fine. And here," he pulled his backpack down from his shoulder. "It's all in here. Up to date. On the desktop," he handed her a laptop. "There's a folder. MonicaSep11."

"Tell you what. Let me run the file-exchange? But I'll format the project notes later. Should get used to doing this sort of thing, eh?"

"Hey, I'm noticing you have a lot of photos of military around?"

"Yes, it's my family. A bit of a military lineage." She proffered him a glass over half full and set the bottle down adjacently.

As he took his chair kitty corner from her seated position, a tepid impression of a smile rested into her palm, and he admired the tresses of hair pouring through her fingers. "Thanks. Um, should we let this... breathe?"

"If you like. It's only a Merlot," she gazed into his eyes while her other thumb stroked the stemware's rim.

Though less intently engaged in the moment was of course his nature, he still took inventory of the symmetries in her expressions, having difficulty stopping himself from considering what that must mean of her body. "So... uh, may I ask? How old you are, okay to do so?" He halved the contents of his wine while reading her reaction, then added, "where ... uh, you're from?"

On cue, she reached for the bottle. "Oh, not at all. I'll be thirty soon... next month," her expresion warmed in approval. "I come from a Catholic background. Irish, Italian, you know, nothing special. Just your basic all-American mashed-up heritage," she smiled before taking a sip.

He buried her affect behind a quivered grin and chuckle. They drove his thoughts and feeling to a specific memory best left behind, or perhaps state of mind. But the emotional phrases conjuring inside seemed to precede the moments during this encounter, and as lost as he was in why or how, they were becoming more difficult to ignore. He certainly never thought of himself as having psychic abilities, nevertheless he knew the waves were coming.

"Uh huh. You okay there Colton?"

"Uh yeah. I'm ha, sorry. I... anyway. So, about that?"

"About what?" she queried after a pause.

"Well, that, 'us getting used to doing things this way', thing? I mean, you told me of your affiliation with doctor Mendal. I mean, what's with this measured tact?" He looked away in surrender.

"I can't speak to any... agenda, if that's what you mean? As I told Jack, I have some history with him. Mainly admin junk, tech liaison. For you it's an organizational— wait, you didn't know of this appointment?"

"Okay, well, as I'm certain you must've gathered by now, I have history with him, too. *And no,* it was news to me."

"So, this thing you are working on, it must have some intrinsic value then?"

Vacating his eyes, he offered a subtle nod.

"Hello?"

"What? Oh, right. That's what has me puzzled. Look, all this is, what we're attempting is using technologies to try to articulate ... ah, to resonate vibra— well, let's just call it unlocking certain aspects of biology, uh using solid state physical medium."

Affirming with a smile, she added, "It's okay, I follow."

"The trouble is, the technology doesn't actually exist, so we must do some inventing. I suppose eventually some intrinsic value to psychiatric sciences, some way, somehow, who knows? Thing is," he straightened his back and commenced rubbing the back of his neck, "it really is a leap away from what I… we were doing up there a couple years—" he interrupted when his eyes happened upon a row of pictures situated along an elevated perch on the wall behind her. One such photograph depicted her standing in full-dress military garb, with another person of certain rank, a decorated tall figure.

"Oh, the superconductor theory. Yes, Dr. Mendal explained that your contribution to the field was astounding as a Masters student. But, that you had some difficulties during your PhD… Colt?"

He rose to his feet, turning his attention away from the photograph. "He actually said that? Look, this current project is a bit of an unorthodox application… It all seems a bit much." He sat back down, "I mean, this recourse on his part. Jesus."

She lingered over the photographs herself then disappeared into the kitchen.

"Monica?" He followed her with his voice alone.

"Oh, apologies." She said as four beeps sounded. "So, who was this Christine?"

"What-uh. What exactly do you wanna know?" *Wha-at?*

She placed a steaming lasagna on the counter. "The professor told me all about it. That's a really—"

"All about it?"

"I… I'm sorry." She reached over and ran her hand gently down the length of his forearm in a single stroke. "I thought… I mean, it would be okay. He told me it's been years. *Oh* god, I feel horrible."

"I guess it should be okay," he took an instant to study her expression. "Wow. I mean, it's not that, but it's nothing you ever really get over. Heh, it sort of embeds into the genetics of one's psyche, I guess. I'm taken as to why it came up in the first place?"

"I don't know. He was speculating stuff. Then, he got into it. I was listening the whole time. He didn't shine on like it was earth-shattering, though. So, you guys were serious, I take it then?"

"No. It's… I mean, at some point it's gotta be okay. We were… Well, long story."

After deciphering his expression, she offered, "listen, if you ever need someone to talk to, we can be friends. I mean, does this have to be all business?" And patted the back of his hand.

They lingered after dining, during which time he spoke like no other in recent memory. How he had met her, and their times together. The tragedy, he omitted, after a cherished night of intimacy. Where no other soul or force had since succeeded, her kindred ear allayed his fears and with ease, brought it all out of him. Yet, as he experienced those waves of relief, he was torn, for her raw attraction began eroding a melancholy, a familiarization which he grew to covet. At a point, she even slid the tip of her index finger between her nose and upper cheek. And he whispered, "I'm sorry," when he noticed.

Foisting his backpack over a shoulder, he prepared to disembark the evening. "Listen, really, this was great. I… loved this," exhaling while turning briefly away. "So, you got all the notes you need?"

She answered by uncrossing her arms and raising both hands to either side of his face with an eerily familiar touch the instant the sensation arrived. He pretended not to tremble, and so she whispered, "please, it's okay." Placing her thumb and fingertips to his chin, she raised his attention to her eyes. Pulling him down, she unambiguously settled into a kiss.

Allowing her to dictate the terms of his own surrender, he did not decline the advance. And what seemed endless, the instant her lips began to part, her warmth redirected into an embrace. Knowing her cheek rested momentarily over his accelerated heartbeat, he disengaged the gesture and turned through the door. "We'll be in touch."

The sound of the door clicked closed behind him, but he hesitated. Inhaling hard, he turned slowly back.

She opened the door upon a single bell, her ending tone pleading for understanding. "You should want to leave now."

After nodding almost imperceptibly, he regathered his belongings off the porch decking.

Upon accessing his car, he turned his attention back through the window. At first, catching his own expression, he saw his own eyes in the glass. An essence of not knowing who was looking back at him was fleeting but very real. Refocusing through her outline persisted as she stood in her door.

His thoughts raced as he sought his home, his sanctuary, where his memories were still intact, untainted. He felt as though he must be a betrayer.

*   *   *   *

They arrived in separate cars concurrently upon the grounds. The day was typically arid and warm, but getting easier to take. The lengthening sun of autumn dictated the seasonal change.

"Well, we've come this far; it ought to be interesting," he raised his voice from the driver's seat.

Smiling from one half of his face, Jack sarcastically nodded his reply.

"Hey, follow me?"

Jack signaled with a thumbs-up through his window.

They soon parked their cars for designated hazmat entry into the facility. "So, listen, we have to check our products in. I was thinking of handling that? If you want, why don't you take your car back and then go check-in with Carmon?"

"Uh, okay, sounds good."

"He'll direct you. I mean, get you to see Wiles. I assume you have your specs?"

"Dude, believe it or not, competence runs in my family."

"All right then, and sorry. You guys can get started. I'll show myself up there shortly."

"So, what's up with you lately?" Jack queried as he placed a hand over a crate comprising of several containers.

"Nothing." Sensing this was not good enough, he elaborated. "I'll talk to you about it later. Get outta here."

Their voices became discernible as Jack approached Doctor Wiles' office. The door was slightly ajar. This fortuitous, albeit unintended stealthy arrival allowed him the ability to eavesdrop on a phone conversation,

"Colton's assistant. We— yes, of course Doctor. Well, yes and no; we've gone over rudimentaries. Steve, I understand that. Like I said, I went through the calculations; there was nothing obvious—"

Ho man. Wanting to put an end to it, Jack alerted his presence with light knocks. The redirecting voice urged him to enter, so he gingerly complied to allow the conversation's ending cadence, but Wiles had already reset his attention.

"Please, please come in," as his line of sight tried to see around Jack's frame.

"Uhm, oh, no he's not with me at the moment. We, ah, saved some time? He's with logistics. Uh, for the components and junk we brought along?"

"Oh, you have your compound then."

Jack reached across the desk for the perfunctory handshake, but Wiles had turned prematurely and did not see. Slowly, he pulled the gesture back, *"what's with these dudes around here?"* he aspirated to himself.

"Excellent! So, take a look at what I have here," as he turned sideways in his chair as though to stand, he hesitated a moment then stepped to a dry-erase board.

This directed Jack's attention to an illustrated drawing tower, retrofitted with injectors for the MMPs as well as the staging cups. The model was surprisingly elaborate in detail for a free-hand drawing; clearly, time was spent, or the man had an unrealized talent.

"What I want you to focus on is this second coating cup. I have retrofitted it to be multitasking. As the tractor at the bottom pulls the fiber optic thread through this secondary cup, in addition, the secondary buffer coating, it will be able to administer the cerebral-gel in accordance with specifications."

"And from there, my nanotubes will be laser guided into place at the interface points," Colton's timing was on cue. "Hello, gentlemen."

"Eh, welcome. Yes, that is correct. By the way, I feel your team will need the two towers working in unison, and I have set the tractors of each to interlace."

"Fascinating, I had not thought of that; we can use that to integrate the threads into fabrics, and—"

"And, gentlemen, we have found a new technique that will speed this up tremendously," Dr. Wiles continued, nodding. "By several orders of magnitude, actually."

"Uh… doctor, please, I mean. We're certainly grateful for what you have already helped us with. But I cannot help but ask, why you are taking so much of your own time?"

"I understand it may seem a little odd but I… owed Dr. Mendal a favor from a while ago. It's all right, I'm currently between projects, anyway. The technology for retrofitting these towers, it's already here. It was simply a matter of rudimentary calculations, with respect to the schematics and equations you provided. This… is astounding insight here. I must admit, I'm piqued as to where this… EEG generator can have application?"

"EEG generator, heh-heh. But wait... you said you *owed* doctor Mendal, my adviser?"

"No problem. Different discussion."

"Oh, uh, I don't mean to over-step, just curious... the background."

"No worries, long story. But a... he asked me to assist you," an almost imperceptible bias of his eyes moved in Jack's favor, "specifically, in the optics lab."

Nothing usually getting by him, Jack signaled as though he were about to speak, but Colton interceded, "Ah, that's fine. I see. Much is appreciated by the way."

"No problem. Well," the Dr. clapped his palms together, "I assume the components have been checked in," as he looked back and forth between them.

"That's an affirmative," Colton made sure he spoke first, "uh, mine that is." The collection of them shared affirmation in their body language.

"Great! What do you say we get scrubbed and head into the lab? I'm estimating four hours, we can leave the outfitting in standby awaiting final calibration. Why don't you two head down ahead of me. I need to make a couple of phone calls and then I will be down with you?"

*   *   *   *

As they stepped into the corridor devoid of any other life, the outré fusion of distant industrial automation offered its only accompanying sounds along with their untold dimensions.

"Hello. Yes. Hi, Monica, how are you?"

Jack rolled his eyes.

"Yes, we're at the lab. Right, me and the gang. Cool, he'll be glad to know that. Hey, Jack, Monica says your notes were well-organized."

Jack symbolized with a two-fist pumping motion, earning him a grimace and head shake.

"Ok. Talk to you later, babe." Colton cleared his throat, "what… why are you looking at me like that?"

"Interesting, babe. Wow. Official then?"

"What do you mean? Talk to you later. I—"

"No, dude, you said babe."

"I what? No. I did— shit," scrambling to reengage, Colton accessed the call history, but her answering service picked up. "Hi, me again," as the elevator doors opened, "hold on," he clumsily said. After the doors closed with them inside, he punched in the button that read "Tier 5" and added, "Look, I might have… Goddamn elevator, cut the signal."

Laughing in halfhearted commiseration, Jack laid his arm along the back of his shoulders. "Hey, man, that sounded real precious."

He shrugged him off, "shut up."

"Dude, it's too late anyway."

"Huh, what are talking about?"

"Oh, I get the feeling that horse left the barn by the time that phone call happened. Anything you do or say now, heh… it's gonna cause a stampede. The elevator? Hey man, it's lookin' out for ya, bro. And just think, technology truly helping to advance the cause of man. Hell, dude, don't worry, she'll take it in stride. Although… hm, didn't y'all have a night last week?"

He leered momentarily at Jack's profile.

"I mean, considering it was all business and no pleasure, I mean… Hey, seriously, since this is a joint effort, I'm sure if there was something, anything *work-related* you would have told me about it by now, and—"

"All right, shut up already." He paced, "I admit, the night was… Okay, it might have been more than business. What that means, I am not entirely sure."

"Want me to help you there?"

"No. Stop."

"Well, at least gimme some details!"

"Neh-heh, no, you don't get… whatever."

The doors to the elevator opened, oscillating forth the familiar flashing light and its concomitant alarm. It did not take one long to learn that expediency was both rewarding and encouraged when passing through Decon. They had managed to cut the time it took to change into their jumpsuits and masks in half. The door opened into the interior, much more routine-like set the stage for their arrival upon Optics.

Colton went to a compartment that needed an electronic key-card to open. He slid it in a slot beneath a small red light that turned green, and opened the door. Inside, was a plastic vessel containing a maroon-brown colored substance. "Jack? Here you go."

"Oh, cool. How'd that get down here?"

"They have an interior conveyor and robotics system for transporting components around the lab. See, over here? Jack?"

"I'm looking."

A hissing sound abruptly drew their attention, which announced Dr. Wiles' arrival carrying something. Setting the black box down orderly upon the table, he unclipped the buckles along its top edge. They were transfixed, curious for what it contained; a complex of less than commonly recognizable tools. They were organized like surgical utensils.

"Ok, I'm ready if you gents are?"

"So, Jack," Colton asked, "are you ready for this operation?"

"What the hell am I doin' here," Jack replied half to himself, "Jesus, I'm a Biochemist."

Wiles scaled a ladder leading to a service loft for one of the towers. Upon his arrival, he wasted no time accessing a cartridge containing his microprocessors. Clicking it into a tailored compartment and closing it sounded like cocking a gun. "Jack," he hollered down. "I have set the coating cup for your compound and precisely the right altitude in the drop sequence. The drop velocity and cooling rates will hit right at thirty-seven c?"

"Ah, right. Yes. Perfect," Jack signaled his thumb.

"You can go ahead and load your compound. Colton?"

"Way ahead of you," Colton said while accessing the cartridge holding his nanotubes. "This device also draws these out magnetically?" and he carefully situated the cartridge into its designated retrofitting of the bottom most stage.

"Exactly, at two per three milliseconds intervals, calibrated for the right thermal-controlled coagulation timing of... sorry, Jack? Right, your compound."

"No problem."

Within the hour, they had completed the mechanical loading of the system. All that remained was the calibration at the computer side.

As they removed masks and gloves outside, Colton spoke. "Wow, it's really happening. So, gentlemen, I'm gonna stick behind. I want to finish the laser calibrations this evening. I have coded the routine. I'm gonna load it and complete some test cycles."

"And as for me," Jack said in his usual banter. "I'm gonna go ahead and reengage in my drinking' bender."

Sensing Wiles' consternation, Colton offered, "he's got an odd sense of humor."

"Heh," the Doctor said through his nose. "Well, gentlemen, this is where I leave you to your own devices. At least I think I should," with his own smile. "Unless you have any other immediate question?"

Colton turned his attention between them, "uh, no. I don't think so. Once I've calibrated, there isn't much for any of us to do for a while. Not until we have reached the critical product density. Running non-stop, around the clock, we should make some progress. In the meantime, we'll need to engineer the leads for the electroencephalograph as well as the charge distribution nodes for the device. That will take some time."

"As an afterthought," Wiles added, "these MMPs being liberated for use. They can do a lot more than exchange information among these... I guess, virtual synapses?" he looked to Colton. "A lot more actually. It seems like a waste of computing power, no?"

"Honestly, I had not considered a deeper application. What, are we missing something?"

"Well, no, not missing per se. Have you been considering their language functionality?"

Colton pinched his lower lip. "Yes, we could actually implement more than those rudimentary logic syntaxes. In fact, instruct feedback on successes. Uh, in the context of how. Even diagnostically. Interesting."

"Give this thing some personality. Nice." Jack jested.

Wiles half-grinned. "If you mean gestural, interactive dialogue and so forth? Not exactly. They can however handle *some* interpret linguistics." He waited while they shared an arched eyebrow glance.

"This project just got a whole lot more complicated, didn't it?"

"Oh, shit! Thank God," mused Jack.

"Yes, indeed. All right, good work, gentlemen. You are on your own. Listen, I will be around, don't hesitate if you need me. I left the specs for the retrofits, if you have a problem with them, you know where to find me. Colton, with your savvy I imagine you can handle it." The doors hissed at his passing through.

"You stickin' around then... or?" Colton queried.

The question ensued a yawn from Jack.

Unsure if it was in jest, he reached into his jumpsuit and extricated his phone. It read 11:04pm. They had been at their high-tech affair for over nine-hours' worth of Wiles' four-hour estimate.

"No, nah, I think I'm out," Jack confirmed as his body language was already motioning toward the entry.

"Right. Sure. Thanks, Jack. For everything. It's, ah, good that you're around. If I haven't told you that yet."

Jack's eyes twitched between Colton and the nearby machinery. "Sure. No problem."

"Don't forget, we still have to organize all this," he hesitated to turn his attention around the venue. "For Monica."

"Man, do we even know where to begin?" Jack faded as the doors hissed.

* * * *

Colton wasted no time and excitedly booted the mainframe at the primary interface terminal. Once the system came online, he entered the command key for official project start. The user interface was antiquated, and though not particularly complex, quite esoteric. From the command prompt, he typed: "System authorization," key-stroking Enter.

After a moment, the terminal blinked once per second, "System authorization commencing... Please enter routine name:"

Trying to be clever failed, "Colton alpha one"

After a moment, the facility hummed, and the monitor reported: "System to authenticate Colton Alpha One... ready instruction:"

He typed, "Disk = alpha on"

The cursor started filling across as though someone other than he was typing. "File found. Activation instruction executing. Colton Alpha One returned... system preparing test sequence. Please insert next instruction -or- manual override command sequence:"

This type of exchange went on for several minutes, as he sequenced through the prefabbed software files of the CD-

ROM. Some were fast. Some were slow. In the interim, he had reduced to approximately one-third of the lab's illumination, atoning for his native aversion to morgue lighting. Other than the distant industrial hum of advanced technological automation resonating the edifice, the venue was reduced to an eerie stillness.

He began an internal monologue, *man, this place never ceases to—*

A thousand-pound hand gently jolted his shoulder.

"OH, sh–!" he blurted, as he leaped out of his seat, spun around, and landed his ass on the edge of the desk. "Your own experiment on untimely lab shitting. Jesus! What are you doing down here?"

"I did not mean to frighten you," despite the sentence, Dr. Mendal's tone carried little sympathy. He stepped toward the glass outside the enclosed room that housed the drawing towers. "I see you have made some configuration progress?"

"I… didn't hear the door hiss when you came in. I… yes, actually. We are all set up as a matter of fact. I'm almost finished with the mainframe now. Hey, so, what brings you here?"

"I should seek permission to check in on one of my most… promising protégés?"

"Well, it's so late. On a Friday. You're in a jump suit. Decon? It seems a little unorthodox."

"If you must know," Mendal turned back around, "I was on grounds already. Late appointment. Doctor Wiles has informed me of his impressions. He believes you will be successful, more successful this time. I expect as much. So tell me if you would. Where do think you will be in terms of testability in, say, five weeks?"

"Five… what? I'm not sure I understand."

Mendal's vocal inflection abruptly became sterner, if that was possible. "I would assume with the special assistance afforded you by the great Norman Wiles, you would not take such advantages for granted."

"No. No, of course not. In fact I—"

"Good evening then. We'll be in touch." Mendal then gave off a quick forced grin, turned, and walk to the front of the lab.

Colton looked down to one side as the doors hissed closed. A yawn brought him back from the perplexed mire. He glanced at his phone, *one-thirty-one. Lord.* One final command to enter, and software calibrations would be complete. "Disk = Delta One" That completed loading the machine-level code components needed for process instructions to the tower apparatuses.

12
IT'S ONLY EXHAUSTION

Sub-micron optical threads became the infrastructure. Spatially calculated combinations of Colton's carbon nanotube vision, together with the so-called mutable microprocessors, gave rise to a substance that to an unaided eye appeared to be a transparent fabric. For over two weeks this automated process perpetuated. Layers upon layers, nonstop.

The drawing towers integrating the fibers, the retrofitted tractors, wove them into fabric; then stacking them upon one another an object of 3-dimensions emerged. Each sheet seemed to interlock with a sheet that was immediately adjacent to it; perhaps an artifice resulting from specific geometric similarity at nanoscale. As this object gathered mass, its physical nature became almost fluid-like, similar to a gelatin substance.

Wobbling when perturbed, waves rippled through the totality of its medium. It was as fragile as these physical properties would seem to suggest. En-masse, the transparency became an opaque maroon hue at a suspension volume of 1,400 cubic centimeters, and an approximate weight of three pounds.

"Wha... what was that!? Did you see that?" Jack spoke excitedly.

"No, I did not. What?"

"Do whatever that was. Do it again."

Without making physical contact, Colton waved the electrode like a wand, back and forth, near a prototype port at one end of the object. The entire mass appeared to subtly shimmer.

"There, again. It's gotta be the albumin polymer. Is it what we wanted? Hey, am I amazing or—"

"It's concentrating. It's harmonic," Colton urged.

"Har- monic. As in feedback?"

"Right, more or less. If they vibrated discordant… random quantum oscillation periods would tend to damp one another. Here, when we have billions of them synchronous, wave dynamics. Really."

"So, this is what we're after?"

"We're after electroencephalographic scans… that's the empirical goal. It didn't mean actual witnessing. That hadn't occurred to me."

Fingertips to chins, they stood in observance.

"But I suppose it would be nice to see them in action. I mean, these vibrations are quantum scalar in dimension; it's their aggregate that's— tell you what. Chalk it off as an unexpected property. This has its complexities and as we know, complex systems have a tendency to surprise. I suggest we push forward. I don't see why this should stop us."

"From having on with the EE scan?" Jack queried.

"I have the scanner already prepared to connect to the leads. But this is what has me really intrigued."

"What's that?"

"Notice that the voltage meter is zero."

"Okay, so you were multitasking?"

"Heh. Look, the charge goes in." Colton gently touched the electrode to the entrance lead. "Now look at the exit amperage meter. See how it indicates zero? The charge has got to be going somewhere."

"Interesting."

Colton whispered, "somehow, the medium of the object is grounding the charge."

"Oh, right. The electrical current is being converted into mechanical energy with these vibrations?"

"Of course, yes. But, if they have some magnetic field induced vibrations, the oscillating fields might also cause a secondary electrical field leakage during total conversion. I think we are starting to see where the EE scan may be successful. I was interested in whether this preliminary test would expose any baser empirical results. More than I thought." Then he changed the subject abruptly. "We can pick this up... testing... the week. I'm getting a real head... here," rubbing his temples, he staggered a step to the side and as the rolling chair made contact with the back of a knee, he lost control and sat in it clumsily.

Jack reached for him as he went, "whoa, okay there? What happened, stand up too fast?"

"I don't know. Did I?"

"Come on. Let's get you out to the terminal room, get that mask off. Get some air."

He rose from his seated position, giving each leg a shake of symbolic physical control. "See? Heh... No, you're right. I haven't eaten in a while either."

"Well, let's get the hell outta here, then."

Reaching a commiserating a hand, he stole an instant of stability on Jack's shoulder, "I'm going to get these results on disk... for Monica, later tonight."

*   *   *   *

Clad in a decon suit, Jack donned his mask in preparation for entry. Gloves sealed at the sleeves, a wind rushed forth from within the ultra-sterile environment of the inner sanctum, the industrial equivalent to a bassinet for the fragility of their creation. Already there as he approached, Colton was delicately trying to insert their coax aglets into the objects' tapered ends.

Sliding backward along the coax cables, they eventually bifurcated, then again, and again, several times over, to create a mop-ended array of wires that would eventually disappear into a large panel displaying many red, yellow, and green light-emitting diodes. Accompanying, were small monitors, in all, servicing as general interface for multiple black boxes stacked upon tiers of an open cabinet edifice. Out of the backside of all that technology was a splay of many of yet more cables, that vectored off into varying directions, some to labeled ports plugged into the walls, some even disappearing into the ceiling. In all, these devices funneled their input down to the finite realm of the object's infancy.

As Colton inserted the input leads of the coaxial cables into the tapered ends of the object, he gave a small ring-like structure that encircled their junction points a gentle squeeze and twist; there was a clicking sound, vaguely audible through their head-gear. The other end of the object, the exit end, had a single coaxial line. However, unlike the service end, this output did not split into different pathways; it maintained a single cable that connected a single larger server, out of which a new cable was then attached to the wall next to a label, 'OPTICS LAB 1'

A tone sounded. One of the sub-terminal monitors was prompting them, "MMP on line; ready to accept rudimentary machine logic… please specify:" with a blinking cursor.

He stood there a moment, staring at it, with an expression that could have equally been described as joy, redemption, or awe; almost feeling like a father standing outside the glass of a maternity ward, peering down at a real miracle.

"Wow, this thing's important to you, huh?" Jack's voice brought him back. "We ready then?"

He cleared his throat, "Um, yeah. Yes, let's proceed. Can you go out to the vestibule and hop on the primary terminal? All you gotta do is hit the Enter key."

The door hissed momentarily, before Jack's voice arrived via the com system, "Okay, I'm here, now?" leaning into a microphone.

Reaching up, Colton pushed a large black button situated in a small housing upon the near concrete wall. Its label read, 'Lab COM'. "Yes, the commands were sent already."

"Okay, so, what's going to happen here when I do? Do you think you should, like, maybe be out here, when this thing takes the first charge from the—"

He pushed the Lab COM button, "Jack, it's okay."

"Right, of course. I have this crazy notion like the thing's gonna detonate or something. Okay, here we go."

Upon depressing the Enter key, a vaguely discernible hum turned their heads about the lab. A row of LEDs flickered to life along the façade of the connected server cabinet, their dormant reds irregularly shimmering green.

From afar, Jack made out Colton's eyes, which grew through his mask. "Hey, what's going on in there? talk to me," but there was no response.

Lording over the ovular object, Colton slumped, hand extended, clearly in order to brace his topple, but there was nothing there to greet his reach.

"Hey, Colt, what's going on in there, man?" Rushing around the table, Jack stumbled over a box of unused hardware components and barely reached the pressurized sliding glass doors. "Come on, open damn it!" as though pushing the access button multiple times would succeed in doing so. Applying a soft grip to shoulders, he tried several jostles. "Hey, man, you all right? You take a jolt, a shock, or something?" Still there was now response. "Whaat?" he said frustrated under his breath. "Oh, come on, what the fuck is this?" Lurching toward the wall where a red button labeled 'KILL' was located, he pushed it hard several times with the butt of his palm.

The humming ceased abruptly at the instant of that measure, the lights of both inner sanctum and vestibule regions reducing to almost nothing momentarily; a clicking sound sounded from several directions, as the illumination resumed.

Having finished slumping to his knees, Colton postured himself by resting his crossed arms over the one knee bent at ninety degrees. Soon, he lifted himself with Jack's returning help. "What... what's going on... what are you doing?" he whispered hard as he performed neck rotations with his eyes shut.

"Easy, buddy! What am *I* doing? Like, do you even know where you were, man?"

Colton did not directly answer. Instead, clasping a hand to the back of his nape, he rolled his head again. "What are you talking about, what happened?"

"Dude, let's get the fuck outta here. We gotta get that mask off you," Jack ushered him back to the vestibule. "Look, man, I don't know. You tell me. You lost it there, checked out. You weren't responding. So I killed it."

Attentiveness was coming back to Colton's face, although he applied circular motions with his fingertips to his temples. "I don't know what hit me, Jack. I don't recall being hit. One moment we were prepping language integra— cut to this splitting headache."

A couple moments passed while they collected themselves. Exhaling audibly, Jack stated. "Hey, man, let's call it a day. Look, you've been hitting this thing real hard lately. I mean... first of all, do you sleep? Seriously, that's probably it. It fits. Klutziness, cognitive function? This business, I mean, you sweatin' this Monica thing? It's a host of shit, man. You gotta be exhausted. That's gotta be it and—"

"Wait, you killed the process?"

"You're kidding, right? Hey, man, I'm a big fan of cause and effect; I hit enter, you checked out. Could be exhaustion, or something else. I don't know, but—"

"No, no, you're right. To have done that, I mean. Of course. Look, I've been feeling..." he gripped the back of his neck. "It's probably fine. The kill won't irreparably harm it."

"It? What about you? You still gotta make that drive back to town."

"It's gone. I'm fine, and I'll get some sleep. If I'm still… whatever tomorrow, I'll check out the University's Med clinic, okay?" Then he tried to appease his awkward pal, "all right, you win, let's wrap this. But, Jack?"

"Yeah?"

"Do me a favor. No Monica on this one, k?"

"Hey, sure, no problem, man. Tell you the truth," Jack scanned the venue, "wouldn't know what to tell her."

Exhaling hard, Colton's office chair rolled up to the mainframe's primary monitor. "Let me… assess the damages."

Upon depressing the keyboard combination, the cursor read, "Request sent 18:34:37 hours – Termination accepted!"

Jack loomed over in observance, "Escape? Wow, haven't seen that sequence of key-strokes in years. State of the art, eh?"

Motioning a grin over his shoulder, Colton added, "we're not exactly in the same technological wheel-house of iPhones and Androids down here; twelve-inch. *So*, that key combination re-establishes the link and overrides the lock-out from the kill sequence, provided we have the correct password, and—"

The terminal text scribed, "Terminated processing of Delta One… process not completed. Do you wish to proceed: Y/N?"

"Great. We're back." He allowed a moment of inaction, "I think we should go for it again."

"What? After all that? No, friend. No way, man. We're calling it a day, dude."

"I know. I know. But wait, hear me out. We can fire it off and let the automation do it. Remember, this was a manual effort? We'll reset the system, from out here. In the off-chance there's something to your cause-and-effect theory," he offered a compromising smile.

"O-kaay. If we're both outside, I guess. Automation, you say. True, you can always log in remotely, too. All right."

Colton hesitated then entering the Y for reset command, rest his chin in the cradle of his interlocking hands.

"What? You spooked now? Can't say I blame ya?"

He returned from the gaze, "maybe. Maybe a little." He tapped the Enter key.

The monitor hesitated for an instant of eternity, then the cursor began moving purposefully from left to right, "Process recommenced… request sent 19:41:54. Manual override command sequence reinitializing… are you sure you would like to continue: Y/N?"

He entered Y again.

In short order the sensation panged into the side of his neck. "Oh, shit! Fuck. Jack, what the hell did ya do that for?"

"Hey, man, just making sure. Sorry."

The monitor displayed "Resuming Delta One," and a series of text elements began popping off, blinking imperceptibly too fast to read all their content. After a short period of this behavior, it came to rest on a blinking cursor reading, "Processing…"

Pretending for a moment that he was not actually apprehensive or fearing, he redirected to gathering the day's flotsam of notes, reorganizing them within his soft briefcase. Other materials he tucked safely into his backpack. Pausing, he sensed the eyes, and as he turned instinctively, Jack diverted his evasively. "What… I'm okay, all right? I'll take a break or something. Things will be fine, trust me," he said and clasped the back of his neck while suppressing a wince.

13
EMANATIONS

Images nearly drove him to the brink, darting through his head while he lay stretched out upon his couch, one forearm resting upon his forehead. As slumber at last ensued, pictures of Christine and Monica accompanied it, bursting in and out of his visions; echoing memories of Christine's voice seeming to meld into the dulcet tones of Monica's. All the while, desperation encapsulated this mental tapestry.

It was the project; he sensed this, though any deeper explanations were vexing. It gave rise to eerie feelings of abandonment, metaphorically explained by the ghostly whispers that hosted the nightmares. Fragmented awareness of salvation darted in, as he struggled to escape years of despondency-prison since Christine's death. It all played havoc with his sleep.

Either way, he was powerless to stop the figments of images and sounds, when at once, an entirely different noise pierced the frenzied mélange. The electronic song jostled him awake. Leaning up, he swiped sweat from his brow. "My god, what is going on with me these days?" The song played on as he reached down toward the origin on the coffee table. He picked up his phone; it was an incoming call from Monica.

"Hi. How are you?"

He suppressed a yawn, "no, it's... fine. I was on the couch for a while. We worked together during the week, in the Lab. Been exhausting. Will get everything to you."

"When?"

"Uh... tomorrow, nine?"

"Sure."

"Nine it is. Hey, look, I—" he groped the back of his neck. "We had a helluva day yesterday. Been having these... I guess sorta headaches. Heh, no. I know. It's not like a typical pain, pain. Hard to describe."

"You too. Oh, sorry, I'm here. Uh, never mind. I... thinking of something else. Visions?"

He furled his brow. "Um, no, nothing like that. What do you mean, visions?"

"No, it's okay. Look, it doesn't... I'm sure you're fine."

"I'm... Look, forget about it. Change the subject..." Within a moment he took to a slow pacing through the darkness of his living room, phone pressed to ear. Moonlight cut through the sliding glass door that accessed the balcony and whoever the person he was engaging on the other end of this call, was not the same one he had met in Mendal's office weeks ago. He felt nonplussed, for as far as he was capable of objectively assessing, this was a quasi-incarnation of Christine, yet, some fraction of his deeper effort resisted such absurdity. Why would his mind be so cruel to him now, to invent such impressions? Still, undeniably, haunting it was. So he kept responding, playing coy to such notions, struggling to keep the stolid vigil, denying how much he really wanted it to be true. "All right. Okay, I'm on my way."

*   *   *   *

The premises was not as well-lit this time upon his slow-paced arrival, a circumstance he did not promptly notice. His imagination running wild, the implications of all had set his mind upon an odyssey, keeping him distracted as he flung the leather strap to his carryall. Gathering liberated notes and annotated pages off his front passenger seat, he turned in oblivion toward her place.

There was no immediate answer to the doorbell ring. Then he heard the unmistakable sound of keys being jingled behind him. He turned to find Monica standing midway down the slope of her driveway.

"Come on, we're going out." She said.

"How did you…" he turned back around and finally the dimly lit façade of her home registered. "I didn't even hear you drive up. Ok, that works. But, uh… do you have your laptop? I mean, I have some stuff on disk on mine here, for you. It's new stuff; calibration junk. Really cool stuff." He caught up with her. "Hey, nice Jeep."

"Thanks. Hop in." With raised volume, she inquired, "so, what do you have for me? you've made some progress it sounds." Driving swiftly, steering around corners sharply enough to jerk them back and forth in their seats, she indeed handled the automobile as though she had a history of bounding over training terrain.

Forcing his voice over the din of the vehicle's machinery and wind, "First, I apologize for not getting back with you sooner… about the status of things."

"Yeah, I haven't seen you, almost three weeks?"

"Sorry about that, I… I've been very involved. Should I have called sooner?"

"I wanted you to call, but understand you were down in the lab a lot lately. I have been thinking about you. I mean… all this, a little more."

"I have some really interesting physical observations. And tomorrow we are going down to run the electroencephalograph."

"I can tell you are excited. It makes me excited to see you in this light."

What… who is this? The content, that inflection, they were too steeped in the cherished to ignore as merely contrivances of his unstoppable imagination, yet unthinkable to accept. *Some kind of transference…* must be mapping the covet of the past upon this future. *That's got to be it.* Still, this was uncanny, to the point of nearing cruelty, just how similar the memory, and the experience, were undeniably becoming one.

Her voice relaxed to room volume as they pulled up to a stop, "This whole thing with Dr. Mendal," her tone shifted wistfully. "I really wish I wasn't part of it. I mean, the for-him part." She paused and looked up at him. "I want you to know that."

His stomach cringed slightly as his eyes landed upon her supple lips. The scintilla of wetness in her eyes also betrayed their attempt to conceal sadness. He was unsure what warranted that kind of emotion but as they made their way, it occurred to him that it was as though something else forced her to express in that way.

They found themselves in a café and Colton spoke first, "Can I ask you an odd question?"

"Yes. Yes, of course. Is something a-matter?"

His seated position faced a large picture-window located along the front of the establishment. While searching for words, he was interrupted by the transient image of what he thought was a familiar individual's head and upper torso as it bobbed past. This redirected him quickly, "That's weird, what's he…"

"What?" She turned her chin over a shoulder, but by then the person had escaped the edge of the frame.

"Can you hold that thought? One moment."

"Sure. Uh, okay."

"I'll be right back." Walking briskly to the front entrance of the café, he burst through the door. He looked down the street in the general direction he saw the figure and despite the growing distance amid the night ambience, he could make out that it was unmistakably Stephen Mendal. The man slowed nearing a darkly colored sedan. About to raise his hand and yell to him, the driver's side door sprung open and a figure clad in military garb rose from the street side of the vehicle, which re-centered his attention. This encouraged him to reposition himself shoulder-wise to a utility pole, halted in place.

Half committed to this covert act, he tried to listen to their exchange of stern tones but was too far to hear what they were saying. They abruptly ceased discussion, simultaneously jerked the doors open, and disappeared as the sedan swallowed them with door slams. The engine started and the vehicle pulled away from the curb, vanishing into the night.

"You say you have worked with Dr. Mendal in the past, right?" he said as he re-engaged with her.

"Yes, that's right."

He let the moment elapse. "It's probably nothing," he looked wayward, then was back to eye contact. "It's Mendal. He's been odd lately. And I've seen him around... with this Military guy? Tall, authority, scary-looking. Heh," rubbing his palm with his thumb. "I don't know. I wonder if he's in trouble, or something? Don't know why I care. I really don't."

Why this triggered her aimless gaze, he wondered and briefly studied her for an answer.

"Anyway he, uh, he swung by the lab, Mendal, a couple weeks ago. I was there alone. It was late. Lights down for power-save mode. Spooky as hell, usual routine. I hate that technology-dungeon down there sometimes. Go figure but the guy shows up... out of nowhere, like, unannounced. Hello?"

"Oh, I'm sorry. Why was that so unusual?"

"Well, it's not. *But*, after midnight? On Friday of all nights. Come on. No one had been there for over an hour. It was desolate. Other than me of course. And then he starts probing for... I don't know, some sort of... status or something. I..." he lost himself in his own gaze.

"I'm here. Go ahead."

"I dunno if this is making any sense. This is a big project... but five weeks? Come on. And I'm not sure why he cares. I asked him why he needed to know. He seemed a bit defensive. I mean, I know the man; very well. This was different."

"Are you sure you're not reading in too deeply? It's pretty clear, you guys have some history."

Unsure if he were imagining again, but it was either that or his ear registered a susurrus jest, *remember*. "What?" he was impelled at first to ask. But her eyebrows only gently crinkled to the question. "I, uh-um, I guess. Maybe," he shook it off.

Her smile was too alluring, difficult for him, at times not hers that he saw, and it was confusing, as much as it was hard to ignore. His only defense, to turn briefly, more so than the normal conversation vagaries.

"You are distracted," she waited for his direct eye contact.

"I... uh, I like things to add up that's all, but something didn't add up there. I thought maybe since you have some priors with the guy, maybe you might know."

"Colton," she said leaning forward to wrap his hand into hers, as she began slowly rubbing his palm with her thumb.

No longer would the remember-directive be questionably an attribute of his imagination.

"With all you have going on with this project, I really think you shouldn't worry yourself with Stephen. I won't let—"

"Oh, shit," he pulled his hand back in a jerk.

"What?" she turned in her seat. It was Jack, standing outside the picture-window waving his hands over his head.

He was soon at their side, turning his head back and forth between them. "I see. Well, I happened to be passing by. Karen, she's waiting for me next door, at the pub. And you guys are—"

"Just having a cocktail here. I have our progress on disk... for her. Describing some of the events from the other day. Bringing her up to speed," Colton looked up at him as though to remind him of their low-key agreement on how to behave.

"Uh-huh, I see. So everything else going as planned? No extra-curricular discoveries I should be made aware of?"

"Nooo, we're on the same page. Are we still going down to the dudgeon tomorrow?"

She cleared her throat softly, "uh, guys, excuse me… the ladies' room."

On cue and once she was out of range, Colton prompted. "Sully?"

"All right, all right, sorry. But come on, dude, look around. It's all dimly lit in here."

"Hey, actually, I'm glad you showed."

"Cool, whatcha got for me?"

"Well, I've been thinking."

"Oh *that's* a dangerous prospect!"

"'Course… won't argue that."

"Ho-ho. He admits it even. I think he's coming along."

"Listen, Jack, this… fragile construct would be an understatement. Have you given any further thought on that?"

"What, you're asking me?" Jack offered faux giggles. "Shockingly, I have actually. We need some way to protect this thing," and ended with nods.

"Exactly. It wouldn't be part of the original specs."

"Some kind of non-conductive… sort of sheathing," Jack allowed a long pause before finishing barely audibly, "there's definitely materials."

"Why are you looking at me like that?"

"You okay, then?"

"*Then*, why?"

"I mean, about the other day. Remember, down in the lab? Didn't you get yourself checked out, or—"

"Oh, right, that. I—"

Truncating upon Monica's return, Jack took the segue in stride, "um, yes. That's right, Colt. I tell you what, we can hit at that tomorrow," receding, "you, uh, you two have a night then."

"Did I miss anything good?" She gave him the moment.

"Huh? Oh. We needed to discuss a few things, sorry. Man, this is a weird night. But I must say, I'm lucky to have that guy. His insights, heh, they've been spot on. You wouldn't expect it. You should see the stuff he did in polymer chem for this project. Amazing stuff. I don't want Dr. asshole scaring him off, either," he glanced afar.

"I've missed you." Her voice was tremulous, seeming distant. Not so much for volume, but as though it was not actually intended for him to hear.

Miss... what, where is that coming from?

"I know my role in this has a lease, perhaps sooner than we think judging by the progress you've made." She re-engaged his hand into hers. "I think your concept is extraordinary, maybe even genius. Listen, I... how to say this, wouldn't want it to fall into the wrong hands."

"Fall into the wrong... Meaning?" The inquiry took on an air of trepidation, "what exactly, fall, into whose hands?" And he pulled his away.

"Oh, I'm not... I don't mean to insinuate anything," she seemed more in the present. "It occurs to me, lately. People in positions of authority can act certain ways, do certain things."

"I hadn't really thought, and not sure I follow. I don't see how. All we are doing is extending physics into a realm it has not yet been used, you follow? That's all. Maybe it can have some... I dunno, practical use to psychiatric circles. Or maybe our apparatus proves these certain biological features are linkable to brainwaves? It's pretty esoteric stuff." He was almost terrified at how she surveyed him abruptly and cleared his throat. "...Like so many forefathers of invention, they did this. They perceived nature and it kinda led them to conjure things. In a way it all makes so much sense to me.

To improve on nature, by observing nature. That's always the intent. Of course, that rarely happens, huh?"

They were by then the sole patrons as the lights overhead seemed to brighten; the dimmer switch politely communicating the intent of the establishment.

She stood to her feet as he looked up toward her with uncertainty. The woman in front of him was in a duality, all the while, playing with the notion that he simply did not know this person well enough. *This is something else.* Yet, although he was nonplussed, the exhilaration she conjured for these emanations eroded on his abilities to resist whether he wanted them to or not.

She reached down and encouraged him to rise, then offered in sotto voce. "Come, let me take you back to the beginning."

Though he had no idea what to make of it, the intrigue was more than he could bear. This woman's persona seemed to be alternating seamlessly between the new and that of a sacred spirit, one whose destiny had long chosen another path, leaving him eternally alone. A plight he had grown so used to, he was even fondly protective. This was the truth he danced around in his mind. In the moment too absurd to take seriously, as much as the prescience could not be denied.

In the car there was little spoken until near the turn onto Cactus Lane. Parking the vehicle, she set the emergency break, turned off the ignition, and broke the silence. "Tonight was comfortable for me, enlightening. Listen, I am happy, honored really, to be part of this. It's been hard to let things go lately; I'm so happy to be back into your world," her voice ending in a wobble.

Immediately her words reverberated in his mind, playing back several times, *back into your*— The homage to another place and time compelled his physical contact. Reaching slowly, he began to delicately caress the back of her hand as it sat upon the knob of her gear shift. "Hey, it's okay," his pulse quickened, "I can. I mean, if this... if that's what you really want."

And as his heart rattled away in his chest, this was farther than his nature was even capable of insinuating. The gesture seemed to guide itself. And, as much as he had to this point been at times so confused by her nature that evening, he could not ignore her secular allure. In fact, he distinctly heard an exhalation reminiscent of relief, making the events of the rest of the night, inevitable. Then came the jest, gentle, yet thunderous vocal emanation that shattered him to the core.

"Lumpy?"

His head turned in a quivering fashion at the penetration of that song. "Wh... why did you—" From this point forward, he was hopeless to put up any defenses.

"Come back to me," she answered.

Her breasts were flawless for their curvilinear form as they occasionally heaved upward above the plain of her abdomen. Amid the passionate throes came an abundance of releases, physically, emotionally, and eerily, a part of the experience, out-of-body for both. It was as ineffable as it was unmistakable; Colton did not feel the caress of Monica, but that of a memory, and he was lost in it.

14
THE FUGUE

Reaching down, he cut the ignition to the engine, then took a moment to move his eyes along the serrate of industry buildings filling his vantage point. There were few vehicles dappled widely about the area, given to the weekend, which was good; in his fragile state of mind, even navigating around the bustle of a regular week-fares seemed unbearable.

Closing his eyes, he dropped his forehead upon the steering wheel. The discomforts, along with the tormented imagery that had kept him thrashing in his bed as of late were at least for the moment in hiatus. In the moment, the sensation of being recently intimate with Monica seemed tonic and after taking a deep breath, the scientist within rest upon the notion that the decision must be at last alleviating the stresses causing those experiences. Gathering his composure, and belongings from the passenger seat, he soon found himself standing outside the vehicle.

An epiphany surged in that moment; aspects of this project were now well beyond any original aspiration of he and Jack. Some of that sensation was reserved for actual fear; the earlier little escapade down in the hole, or simply whether any of it should continue, both loomed in his denial. Strapped with a soft leather attaché, along with his backpack, he winced away the brief recurrence of discomfort that thought-process provoked, and set out across the parking lot.

Carmon acknowledged his arrival with his usual mien, while holding a phone to his ear. "Hold on. He's... I mean, someone's here. I gotta take dis—"

A small television was airing a sporting event; vaguely emanating its sounds, it was one of many set upon a raft of similarly-sized monitors. These occasionally changed vantage point from around the facility. The one with stairwells, length-wise down a corridor spying a man lifting a page off a clipboard as he walked.

"Eh, Carmon, how goes it? Don't let me interrupt."

"Uh, yes," Carmon held an index finger up. "I, uh, understood," he then clicked the telephone receiver. "No, sir!" as he stood to extend his hand.

"Hey, has anyone... from my team been around lately?"

"Uh, hold on. We had a shift change. Lemme—" Carmon cursorily ran a finger down the monitor.

"I'm here a bit early, but our work... this thing we've been doing," he tried to fill the void, "see, I haven't had a chance to communicate with any of my—"

"Hold on. Hold on. As a matter of fact, looks like a... Saxton, Monica. Yup. Well, now wait a sec. Says heer... earlier in the week, though?" Reconnecting his eyes to a computer monitor, "maybe not too long after y'all left the other day. You and... Sullivan, Jack."

"She... was?"

"You okay, son?"

"Um. Right. Yes. Fine. I... gotta head on down," pointing a thumb over his shoulder.

Sliding his electronic key-card through the slot, two beeps toned. In short order the monitor reported, "Elevator II: Authorized Personnel Only. Access Subterranean Research and Development."

As the elevator plummeted into the bowels of the facility's buried strata, he drifted his sentiments instead towards Monica; a pleasant feeling arising. It occurred to him that the more he focused on this new sensation, the less intense were the discomforts. It appeared causally related while trying to make sense of why it seemed to force its way into his feelings. And for reasons he could not presently fathom, surged in tandem a sensation to conquer all that should oppose.

Stepping out of the elevator, those rotating saffron lights again greeted him. The preoccupation for this new elation, unmistakable as love, became too immersive; he could only vaguely recall how he got to where he stood in the moment. But, what he did know, he found himself completely devoid of any discomfort at all. And like no other time that he could recall, he was in a state of deep alleviation for being there in the lab.

Typing in the passwords brought the project out of slumber; those particular necessities, security clearance codes, and the like encouraged a surge of rationalism. The change in perspective caused him to dismiss the prior courses of internal monologue as most likely figments of tormented guilt, as though he owed those memories anything at all. He had up to very recently fought allowing such memories of his soulmate from succumbing to the erosive power of time. And as he presently conquered such absurdities as his earlier muse, a flinch suddenly struck his brow and the tips of his fingers took to a circular motion against his temples, again.

An audible beep tone centered his focus. "Charge accepted, rerouting routine pathways. Access circuits enabled." Followed shortly by, "Awaiting instruction:"

He hesitated momentarily, face awash in perplexity. "What the hell is that," he whispered. "Rerun... routine path?" *I wonder, did Dr. Wiles...* He then typed, "Help? last command req."

Immediately the monitor partially filled with text. "Help topic 'awaiting instruction:' MMP matrix requesting primary protocol for initialization of communication matrix. This can be manually entered or automated; entry start code [\drive]\STRT-READ-STOP-BGIN-PROCESS."

His peripheral attention was drawn to a manila folder placed conspicuously near, upon which was written as though to make certain he saw it prior to his current stage of re-initialization of the system. "Colton, inside is the disk containing MMP algorithms for rudimentary language. Recall our conversation? This is an automated upload. Best of luck! Norm."

He quickly reached down, tore it open, and five circular disks refracting the lab light in subtle colors fell out onto his hand. Other than the numerals 1 through 5 written with a sharpie, they had no other markings. "Jesus, it's almost like he wants this more than I do. Wow," he whispered through a nervous snicker.

He gently laid the first of the five disks into the slot and pushed the button to close. Typing in the directory path, along with command encoded instructions, pressing the carriage return caused the monitor to hurriedly flit complex images, similar to blueprints of chip designs, as well as algorithm syntax components of programming language, all of which was to fully discern.

Certitude seemed to be ever rarefied these days. More blips blinked on the terminal, language instructions hybridizing with logic that he did not recognize. He assumed this to be proprietary in nature with the MMPs. Either way, he did not like the fact that he did not know what was happening. This was not part of his original posit.

This went on for a while, as the monitor would pause, "Please enter disk 2; press any key to continue…" until the last of the disks had been processed.

He was not completely aware of the passage of time, nor did he experience any sense of weariness. He sat in front of the monitor and briefly covered his face with his hands, then slowly ran them backward through his wavy hair.

The distant sterile technological hum of the plant faded to pure silence, and upon opening his eyes he noticed the monitor had silently cleared, with the exception of a single word that read, "Creator."

Ho, what? "Help? Creator," he typed.

"Help, creator?" was the reply. This went on for a while.

Sans an associative context, words that appeared to echo questions, he did his best to interpret. Mostly, nonplussed to fathom their origin much less intent, only that they were coming on the heels of those completed configuration efforts. Clearly, those efforts were prequel to this exchange.

But how?

What was their significance, and why were they even being posed; what was their purpose? He wished he had taken a meeting with Dr. Wiles, to set expectations for the current logic integration; perhaps these peregrinations were entirely protocol? Still, something was not purely machinery in the texture of this exchange, either. Deeper was not an altogether inept description, and he was struggling to keep up.

"Creator…"

"Help? Last request."

There was a pause, then the cursor began writing, "Creator refers to point source origin of singularity protocol… no such reference can be defined."

"Singularity. Huh."

Purely by happenstance, the exchange backed him into the psychoanalytic technique, where the therapist asks the patient questions and it is hoped the answers themselves facilitate understanding of the deeper components of the psyche. All the while, not entirely sure why he was engaged in this process, or if it were even the right recourse, as none of this was part of any intended project protocols; that much was a foregone conclusion. If there were ever an emergent variable of a complex system, he found it. Yet, he did not know of its implications, either. Along with additional pauses to massage his skull, the experience at times quickened his heart rate. *All I did… load the lang—*

"Oh!" A thousand-pound hand gently jostled his shoulder.

"Ja-hack. Damn it… you and Mendal with that stealth."

"Hey, man, don't group me in with that asshole," Jack took a moment to study him. "Take it easy. You told me to meet you around this time." He adjusted his watch.

"Uh, right... I thought that was later. Well, glad you're here." He pressed a palm against a mysterious region of wetness gathered on his shirt beneath the elevation of his chin.

"Man, I was worried you were..." Jack paused as he looked around the setting, "I dunno, seized again, like before. I heard your voice though. Hey, you really didn't hear me come in, how could you miss that?"

"No, I... guess I didn't hear." He moved his head from side to side and groped the back of his neck. "I was loading these disks... here. Wiles sent 'em down, they contain language. I think it's some kind of machine-level syntax... the language calibrations?"

"Sorry I'm a little late. Carmon says you've been here for over five hours though. Decided to get an early start, did ya?"

"No problem. But, wait... Carmon's got to be wrong. There's no way I've been down here that long... whatsoever. There's not much left to do for now, as far as loading."

"Seriously though, what were you talking about? And who were you talking to?"

"What do you mean?"

"When I came in, you were talking," Jack said through a chortle, "I guess to the most important person you know, yourself," he finished with laughter. "Why are you looking at me so confused?"

"No, I was..." he re-solidified his attention toward a monitor that was completely black. "What the f..."

"Hey, man, what is it?" Jack stepped in for a closer look, "What are you looking for? talk to me."

"The inquiry... the exchanges... they're gone!" He pounded on the Enter key, futilely.

"What's gone? You mean the computer monitor stuff?" Jack leaned in closer. "Hm, nothing here to see. So, you *were*

120

talking to yourself. Hey, don't sweat it, man. Chalk it up as one of your peculiar idiosyncrasies. Hell, we've all got them," as he applied commiserate pats to a shoulder.

"No, Jack, seriously, damn it! The responses. The inquiries. We... I mean, this, there was a whole exchange."

Jack allowed the orotund sincerity without mocking this time.

"They were, I don't know, cryptic or something," he collapsed into his chair while placing his palms to either side of his head. "Oh, man, I can't believe this. If you'd seen the exchanges... you would have thought—"

"Cryptic? Well, hold on dude. I mean, we're recording, right?"

"Yes. Right! Of course. Let's... do that. I mean, I'm not sure why the interface cleared, but hopefully, it won't matter. And then maybe you can help me make sense of it." Rolling his lab chair over to an adjacent keyboard and terminal set up, he aggressively tapped the Enter key.

The monitor flashed to life. He navigated the mouse pointer to the 'System LOG Playback' icon on the computer screen, double-clicking. "When all else fails, we have the system logs."

Reading the printout, Jack's hands alternated as the paper churned out like the receipt off a vintage cash register. "No. Uh, no, Colt," poured his expression, slightly surprised but full of empathy, "sorry, pal, there's nothing here." Running his eyes again along the printout. "It stops, here. Look, at 'Please enter disk 5; press any key to conti—"

Colton snatched the printout from his hands. "Come on, Sully, can you stop fuckin' around for once," his voice warbled with vexation. "What the hell is this? It's... not possible!" He pivoted his hip into his chair with enough momentum for it to roll quickly back to a position in front of the main monitor and pounded the Enter key. "I don't understand! It was all right here... right here. Words, Jack,

like questions. I responded to each one. This went on for—
We can't lose this data."

"Hey, man," Jack's hand alit to a shoulder again, "I
believe you. It's okay. Look, anything could have happened,
right? You might have bumped the escape key. Remember,
escape kills the session? You told me that once."

"Control-escape does. I don't know, but couldn't have
done that combination without… knowing."

"Is there any other way to roll back the recording? Maybe
the power hiccupped and the bus stopped the recording. I'm
spit-ballin' here. I can see you're seriously freaked out. But
there's always tomorrow, bro. We'll do it again if we have
to."

Colton exhaled, "I guess. No choice." He looked up and
nodded, "tomorrow, then."

"Hey, come, let's bounce for the night. You should give
Monica a call, give her some updates. It might help you
focus. How about hooking up later at the pub, unwind a
little?" Jack endeavored to advertise with a party grin.

"Good idea," Colton agreed with wincing eyes, but as he
rose to his feet, lost his balance.

Jack moved fast to support him, "Whoa! You okay,
buddy?"

Clearing his throat, Colton nodded, "I'm fine. Stood up
too fast, or something. Been sitting too long, I guess."

"Dude, that looked like a bit more than *that*. Wasn't the
same thing as before, was it?"

"Heh, uh, no. Don't think so." Exaggerating stability by
alternating leg shakes, he then segmented his vision about
the vestibule. Stepping to the glass, he allowed Jack's hand
to slide away. With the tapered array of wires leading into
and from its ellipsoid form, "What the hell is this thing?"

"Well, clearly," Jack sidled next to him, "it could never
be mistaken as anything else."

The dead-pan delivery won him a profile study, "Ho-kay,
friend. Whatever you say."

"So, are we about ready to cut the cake on this operation, dare I ask?"

"We're ready."

The door hissed open.

"Again, sorry I didn't... I mean, I wasn't here in time. I really didn't know you were going to get an early start." Jack said as the doors closed behind them.

Five minutes later, the motion detectors sent the signal, and the lab's ambient lights rendered to darkness, with the exception of the primary monitor. Suddenly, a new prompt printed from left to right: "Security protocols overridden... Linguistic instruction received... accessing... we are dominion," then disappeared.

15
THE UNEXPECTED

"Typically, the recordings are obtained by placing electrodes on the scalp with a conductive gel or paste."

"And they're not random, of course. I mean, like what we got going here?"

"Mm, no, they're not. The electrodes are placed on known anatomical landmarks of the human skull; obviously, we have no such landmarks on this apparatus."

"We hope." Jack added through a half-grin, "As there are no predefined brain regions, if you will."

Colton giggled through his nose. "It won't be that uncertain, either. We can program compartmentalized inputs and these will sector. As a side, it's funny the MMPs became so useful in this research. In your head these compartments don't change, unless there's some kind of traumatic head injury I imagine."

"That'd be something, wouldn't it? We build a damaged brain. Remember how Edison once said, 'I didn't fail at creating a light bulb; I succeeded in determining a thousand ways *not* to create a lightbulb,' or something like that?" He then muttered barely audibly, "Hopefully, this idea is a little bit brighter."

"Heh, I heard that. Anyway, for our experiments, we gotta do something simi…" he looked through the specs.

"Oh, I see where you're going. And, since technically we don't have such regions anatomical…"

Colton lifted his head back off his notes to finish Jack's sentence. "We can still accomplish organization… something similar sending codes to the MMPs for charge distribution. Here, see? We'll monitor the EEG output and tweak the charge distribution until we see results."

They toiled over the course of the afternoon, delicately placing the electrodes equidistantly along the non-conductive polymer sheathing designed to house the object body.

Nearing six o'clock, the all-too-familiar orange pulsating light abruptly began rhythmically filling the air outside the sliding glass doors to the vestibule. The timing of these new arrivals was impeccable. Approaching completion of system prep work, they project-entered a ready state for their first attempt at creating artificial brain waves.

The shadows of two figures walking side by side shortened along the floor of an adjacent stretch of brighter lit corridor that extended around a corner. As they appeared, Colton recognized the taller of the two instantly.

The man stopped then turned around, so he faced away from the doors. He crossed his arms, looking once to the right, then the left. Mendal performed an up-to-down motion with one hand, and the door hissed. Walking through, the taller individual rolled back around to join in behind him. Stephen stepped square before them with his hands clasped behind his lower back, passing a quick glance back and forth, but deferred to an approach upon the glass that separated the vestibule from the infant technology located in the inner sanctum. The taller individual's arms were still crossed as he stood behind Mendal, turning his head about the venue.

Jack leaned tight to Colton's ear, "Who's this other spook?"

"Ssh."

Mendal's voice drew their attention front and center. "I see you've completed the physical integration of the edifice. Outstanding." He looked over to Jack briefly, "Gentlemen," before turning his attention back through the glass, "where are we in the testing phases? We're... I mean, I'm anxious to see if brain waves were made artificially."

After sharing an instant of curious eye contact, Colton answered, "we haven't yet begun. Today was intended to be prep run, we—"

"That is fine. But I trust you have fully integrated Dr. Wiles technology, then?"

"Yes, right, it's integral in the physical make up," Colton subtly shook his head towards Jack, who raised his hands in absolution.

"Very well then. I must be elsewhere. Good evening, gentlemen." Mendal turned toward the double doors.

The tall figure hesitated to instrumentally probed the two of them, scanning up and down. When the hiss of the doors sounded off, he then spun around to rejoin his companion. They disappeared around the same corner, their shadows lengthening.

"What in the hell was that all about?"

"Haven't got the foggiest."

Two beeps interrupted their mutual disquiet. Monitor 1 was scrolling: "Confirming status of upload. Logic interpretation commenced…"

"It's informing us that the MMPs are… I mean, there's gotta be a time lag because of the immense number of them. It'll take some time to process the spatial matrix. C'mon, let's head on out for the night. Give 'em the night to figure things out."

"Fascinating."

"You see something else?" Colton queried excitedly.

"No, *you* actually suggesting doing something else. So sure. Sure thing, man." Jack grabbed his own backpack and together, they proceded through the sliding plexiglass doors.

Several hours later, amid the darkened venue, Monitor 1 beeped a single ping as a word scrolled: "Alone."

16
WAVE SIGNATURES

"Vould zat be Mr. Reinholt?" The large picture window rose behind the person's head, the flow of daylight through the glass partially silhouetting him.

"Yes, doctor Lombard. Thank you for taking my call today," Colton drew nearer.

"Of course. Please, have a zeet. So, you haven't been in ze class so often as of late... no?"

"No. And, I really must apologize for my absenteeism. I've had to really hit a new project hard. But I promise, any make-up work I will take the time."

"It is all right. Your standings up to zees point has earned you some merit. If you need I'd be happy to extend ze incomplete. So, vhat can I do for you zes day?"

"It's my side interest... neurobiology," Colton ended through a weak laugh.

"Mm, I zee. I vondered vhy you vere taking my course. Really?"

"Well, I... I've been focusing on patients with abnormal EEGs, actually," he cleared his throat and peered down upon his lap. "Here, I have a few examples that I would like to show you. I mean," he stood to his feet, "if you could assist in diagnostic interpretation?" After a brief apprehension, he stepped closer to the professor's earth-toned desk and offered the folded pages.

"Oh, sure. Let's have a look zen." Reaching for the glasses lying next to a half-eaten scone and a cup of steaming beverage, his eyes soon took to dancing along the rows of wavy lines. His expression segued from moments of intrigue, to more like surprise. Almost inaudibly, he muttered, "Oh, vhat do vee have here," turning over the next page as though keeping up with a musical score. His next utterance meant to be heard, "hmm, very interesting beta frequency."

"What do you... how exactly? What do you mean?"

The professor dropped the printouts on the desk and rubbed his hands together as he looked off to a side. An unease about his face morphed plain. "I'm confused. Vhat exactly is your thesis vork? you ver... physicist, I..."

Colton nodded, "Mm hm. As I am sure multitudes of students have expressed their own irresistible diversion into neurophysiology."

Studying at first, the professor's face transformed into belly laughter.

"I know, I know. It's a little unorthodox, my being here... given the subject matter. Uh, it's a hobby though. Despite my history with solid state physics."

"Mm, yes. I've read ze article, exciting vork. Exciting vork, indeed," he lengthened as he studied Colton's face. "Anyvay, I'm asking because... zis type of forensic output," leaning forward, "vhy... vhere did you come by zis?"

A familiar wince led to a halfhearted smile, visibly concealing his discomfort.

"I'm sorry, vhat vas zat? You feeling vell?"

"Oh, I'm... fine. I've been stressing a little lately. Taking a short break. It's getting better."

"Vell, let us hope so. Vould you like some votter? A cooler right behind you."

Colton shook his head, "I'm here because I'm curious. How does one interpret these EEG wave channels, I mean, is there a literal interpretation available?" Pointing his index finger from the other side of the desk, "See there, a few regions I circled in red. I mean, how is there a way to determine what that organization means? *Is* that organization; maybe that is the better question?" The query itself preceded a shiver up the back of his neck. Mainly because, he already knew the answer. And the implications where not far behind.

"Vel, ze ansar to zees qvestion as to organization ve must assume proceeds ze inquiry. Vy? Because, cognition is shown to be related to ze brain's electrical activity cannot have vone vithout ze other and so on."

He weakly grinned as he lingered a sideway gaze, offering the Professor nods.

"I mean, you have ze live patient, so you have to figure for organization; simply, ze conclusion precedes ze qvestion, no? You zee, ze state of mind of human being is closely related to vhat are called EEG potential dynamics. In practice, on ze basis of ze spatial-temporal dynamics of ze EEG vave space. It's called ze spectrum analysis method. Essentially, ze theta, alpha, and beta frequency bands can be used to extract funzamental emotions… Zes anger, joy, sad, etc." rotating his hand encouragingly. "But is zes really vhat it is you are after, here, today? Seems redundant."

"Um… well, I… ooph."

The professor laughed, "I zee. Vell, to simplify. Zer is a growing body of correlative science reading of zees brain vaves. But, unfortunately zees is really not my area of expertise despite zees long vords. I know someone zough."

"Oh, I assumed…" Colton took the printouts back from the professor.

"I tell you vhat. I have a student en-route to her PhD vork. She does have some particular insights into zees subject matter… zes interpretation business. Her name is Cranston, Karen. Here," he said and handed a Stickum note across the desk.

You gotta be kidding.

"Do you mind me asking, Colton?"

"Um, no, sure… of course."

"Who vas ze subject of zos experimental trials?"

"I… actually, I can't really say."

"Hm, I zee… Vell, anyvay. I can say zes much, zhat Beta channel… mm," Wiles took an instant to reposition his glasses back upon his face, "disconcerting, my friend. Zees anger… or could zes be fear?" twitching his view along the curves of the printout again.

"Wait, what… fear, anger, what do you mean? These are emotions?"

"Vell, yes. Vhat did you ezpect?" After a moment with furled brow, "you should use zhat email and get a hold of miss Cranston." He breathed deeply through his nose. "It's zomezing in ze… I don't know. Zees differential appears almost equally random, as organized. But, it must be organized, right?" He glanced a grin over the top rim of his glasses, "Of course, assuming ze human subject. But, I have never seen zees type of… beta… is strange," he faded.

Lombard's implicit interpretation was well enough, and he was spooked by the notion that what he might really need was an actual psychologist, but most importantly, for what?

When the Professor handed the printouts across the desk, he took particular care in tucking them away into his attaché. "Well, I… perhaps I have taken enough of your time today." He rose to his feet with an accelerating tempo to his body language. Taking one step backward toward the door, he spoke hurriedly. "Okay, Dr. Lombard, thanks for your time."

"Vait, I have never seen a subject represent such a deeply sincere induced sense of emotion ven invoked in ze conventional experimental method. Tell me, please, how did you induce? How did you achieve zees?"

Halting halfway to the door, he turned his side view over a shoulder, "I don't know what you mean exactly. I didn't. I wouldn't know if they intended to invoke… that. I'm sorry, I am running late. I must be going."

"But vait. Vere your intentions rage?"

This impelled him to stop again, turning slowly to face the doctor more directly. "So, what you're saying is the subject on this printout is experiencing rage?"

"I don't know if zees beta read is fear or… vhat vere your methods to inspire ze dark emotions?"

He took a moment to echo those words in his internal monologue. "Unfortunately, there is so much that I would like to know, too. I don't have those answers for you, and I really can't let this… be known?" His ending tone of inquiry was to encourage the doctor to let it go, and he rushed his departure. "But, thank you so much for your time. It has been enlightening."

17
STRANGE SENSATIONS

At first, the door only crept to a gape, exposing an interior dimly lit and silent realm, then, the dulcet flesh tone of her alluring countenance slowly emerged within the void. Again, her beauty penetrated, and the tear-tracks signaled a vulnerability that only incensed his aegis further.

As the door aggressively opened the rest of the way, she poured forth, sliding her arms around his midriff, bringing her cheek to rest over the top of his pectoral. Despite her rapture, his was preoccupied in why she was visibly distraught, acting as though his arrival were some form of salvation. While processing these evidences, he slowly raised a single palm to caress the back of her nape. The discomforts in his head were utterly vanquished at the instant of her embrace.

His body soon acquiesced to the awareness that her perky bosom pressed into his ribs. As he pulled back and gazed briefly into her eyes, again, a familiar taunt bore into his perception; that same plaguing sensation that she embodied two forms.

Her expression conveyed an equal effortless emotion, a tenderness and a warmth no one could understand how much he missed, as though it were tailored for him. So much so that he must be contriving these sensations himself, he believed. He tried to hide any expression that would reveal his confusion. This flooded through his mind as she held on, that, and euphoria. He then took her hands inside of his, and held them to his chest.

"Listen," he spoke with an empathetic tone, "it is wonderful to see you, really. But, I have something I need to say to you."

"Yes, Lumpy, I'm right here, like I've always been."

I don't understand how you could know that endearment. Then he spoke softly, "Monica, listen... I've been having these symptoms. And they're... hard to describe."

She partially smiled, and pulled his face closer to hers, delicately touching her lips to his. "I know," she whispered.

"It's... better now. It sounds crazy but, I think it's got something to do with you?"

Pulling her hands away from his, she slowly rubbed them at the seam of her waist. "Have I done something, something wrong?"

"Deliberately? Heh, I don't see how. But it's like you're arresting... Damn it. I had this all worked out, now of course I have difficulty explaining."

"Arresting. Hey, guilty as charged."

He turned his sights over the twinkling nocturnal city-scaped valley. "No, no, it's not you, I mean... not deliberately."

"What... is it?"

He spoke as though pleading to the ether of the night. "It doesn't make any sense. I haven't even known you that... long."

An interlude of night sounds followed. "Tell me, Colton, have you ever experienced an awakening?"

"Awakening."

She faced away from him, "I mean, the way you see the world. Maybe it changes reality or something. Vision... yes, visions. Seeing the world through someone else's eyes?" she let out a breath, "I'm sorry, I'm not explaining it right."

He moved closer behind her, slipping inside her safe zone. She, of course, welcomed his arrival. Placing his hand on her elbow encouraged her to turn around and face him. "Hey," he raised a thumb and index finger to her chin, "It's okay. I understand, strange sensations." With his hands on either side of her head, they studied the other's eyes before a kiss. "I have to go back down there, and run those damn experiments again. Have you been keeping Stephen updated?"

She cleared her throat almost imperceptibly, "He's fully aware. As much as Monica has been allowed to inform him."

Her word choice stirred him, repeating them in his mind, but he was growing too weary. Having to constantly rationalize these aberrations was taking a toll, and in the moment, suddenly came on a realization. In a lot of ways, acceptance, sharing with her his impressions, listening to hers, the very engagement itself surged undeniable relief. Such that if cause-and-effect was an instinctive skill we all possess, his was consequentially leading him to one inexorable conclusion.

"Something strange is happening to me. Last night... oh, god. This is so crazy. I just..."

"Hey," he placed his hands on her shoulders, "Monica, slow down. Talk to me. It's okay."

"You don't understand, I was... there."

"Where? What do you mean, there?"

"It was in my sleep. I think. It was, but it wasn't a dream. I was there, last night. I'm certain of it. I was there. I saw you and Jack."

"This project... my God! Why does it seem to have taken over lives like this?" He offered an ironic laugh. "Listen, it's probably just anxiety, or something. It's giving you nightmares. And it's giving me this weird... dysesthesia shit. Look, you must have been imagining. We've been pretty elaborate with details. No shortage of material—"

"No!" then she relaxed, "this... this was more than that. It wasn't like... indistinct," She looked away then said softly, "it was very real." In the instant, it was as though she were drowning in her memory of what she described.

"Don't do this to yourself, hey."

On cue, she vocalized an abrupt gasp for air, then continued airily, "there is something down there. It's all about loss. Simply, loss. I don't know why I know that. You have to believe me." Non-sequitur, a smile usurped her solemn plea. "Then… there was… love… then, I was awake. I had been sweating. Somehow, I was awake, I don't remember how. I was just awake. You don't understand."

"Uh, no, I do. I'm here, I'm listening," he symmetrically rubbed his forehead.

"And… I've had this foreboding feeling ever since. I—" She turned away in haste as though abashed. "What's happening to me? Ever since I met you… ever since I was asked to get involved in… what is this?"

Abruptly, she moved toward the door, disappearing after a short hesitation, leaving him standing there with only the sound of his respiration.

He barely summoned the composure to elevate a stammer through the door. "No, it's… all right. It… doesn't sound crazy."

He wended his way to her kitchen, to find her leaning forward against her sink, both arms stretched downward for support. This posture brought his attention to her hips, and the way her waist sloped pleasingly to his masculinity. There are scanty circumstances that can succeed in suppressing the aesthetic wonder of such sights. This was not one of them.

He moved his hands up and down her shoulders, "I can't judge that. I mean, not when every time I'm close to you this alleviation…"

She turned to face him with enough of a smile to threaten exposing her dimples and it suspended his words.

For a moment, he ran his fingertips slowly back and forth across his chin, "Nor can I explain your role in this. What all that means… What you're describing. All I can say is when I light up the device… I get so focused myself my head starts with an indescribable feeling. Then later… these visions—" His expression suddenly drew blank.

The present setting of her home conjured forth a very particular memory; it was that photograph among others, an image of her posing alongside military personnel. Who knew the deeper workings of the mind, to choose then, to suture together different fragments of reality.

"What is it?"

"I... I'm not sure." Stepping through the door leading from her kitchen to her dining room, he reached his hand into the darkness, making an upward swipe that brought illumination to the room. "Here," he took down the photo off its perch and handed it to her while directing with his eyes, "who is that, that man right there, standing alongside you with these other military?"

Her response was tremulous, "I told him I wanted no part of this any longer. You must believe me. But Dr. Mendal threatened me two weeks ago, told me then that I had no choice in the matter. He hired me; I don't recall—" She cut herself off, and scanned symbolically around the premises. Grabbing his arm below the elbow, she tugged. Leading him back through her home, they succeeded through the front door, and soon she was down the driveway standing next to his vehicle with him in pursuit. "I think it's time we employed an element of secrecy."

"Secrecy? What in hell is going on!"

"Shh. Keep it down, Lumpy."

He looked around them, "Why? For whom? Fine, I'll speak quiet if you want. If that's what this situation somehow needs. But there it is again... Lumpy. How... who told you that? Why are you saying that to me... that word?"

"That's what I've always called you. You're my Lumpy."

He groped the back of his neck hard and closing his eyes in a wince, pled aimlessly from under his breath. "Sorry. Sorry. I'm still here. I didn't mean it... Jesus Christ, I'm still here. Ah."

"I could be in so much trouble for this... I'm not supposed to say. But something is happening here, and it's bigger than that." She placed her fingertips on her temples. "It doesn't feel like me. I look in the mirror... the image is me, but it's not me. And you, I can't stop—" she faded.

136

Colton stepped to her and gently arced his thumb beneath her eye. "You can't stop what?"

"Make love to me... again. Take me back to where we began," she said, committing her body to him, and in the still of the night she gestured at disrobing him.

First, he went along then abruptly stepped backwards.

"You don't want me anymore? Don't you remember us... Lumpy?"

His confusion could not be more profound. Another aberration, this was not Monica behind the wheel of that question. "Remember whom, Monica? Who are you talking about? I don't understand this pretense. Who is it you are talking about?"

She began crying softly. "We can't stay here, Lumpy. They're coming."

*   *   *   *

They lay at last entangled amid the sheets of his bed. Fixating his eyes at the crescent moon through the window, he fiddled at the hairs of his chest. Breathing in and out satisfyingly, he realized the plaguing dysesthesia symptoms were for the moment entirely gone. Whatever suspicion he formerly harbored, it was at this point unmistakable; it was these trysts he relished, that he had previously denied he wanted, sorely needed, these were why. And though it felt too incredibly right to be beside her, it also felt as if another presence were there, perhaps two versions of himself if he were forced a description. In this moment of introspection, analyzing this for different wants and reasons, he would describe part of this as love; unknowing, were it even possible, was the target of that affection really this woman lying beside him, when their intimacy seemed as though it was the purpose of a different union. And every time he ventured these doubts, the discomfort returned. "There's got to be... something to that," he let slip.

This induced her to adjust position.

He made use of the quiescence, "Monica, tell me about that military officer. Why... I mean, you were so upset last night."

"I didn't mean it; I didn't mean for that to happen."

Which part. There were clearly disparate angsts vying for some form of moral or introspective focus for what appeared to be guilt, though of what, merely asking the question was again symptomatic of verboten. But, a growing paranoia he presently veiled almost felt as though came to him in much the same way; and for that he endured.

"You must understand. I don't know why I am having these feelings."

After a moment, he maneuvered to her backside. Gliding his palm over the contour of her hip, "It's alright. Look, I wasn't mad, really. Not at... you. We need to be honest going forward, about what is happening."

"His name is McFadden. Colonel James McFadden," rotating onto her back, her arm stretched across her eyes. "That's the guy I think you've been seeing. He told me I was supposed to report to Dr. Mendal's office for an intelligence brief."

Her words for the moment were lucid and clear. This was the person he recently met.

"Shortly after I arrived there, he outlined the job. I was supposed to deliver my findings to him, regularly. I thought all he really wanted was to see, to make certain of your work. That was the gig. That was it. Then you walked in with Jack. For a time after that his inquiries about the project status were increasingly technical in nature. I did my best. I always referred him to what you gave me on disks, though."

By now, he was sitting up along the edge of the bed. "Huh, but... why though?" he whispered half to himself.

"You have no? I don't understand."

"Military?" Rising to his feet, he stepped toward the window. "This arrangement, you and him and this… colonel, for *this*?"

"It was… of course it was."

"Oh, heh, I'm sorry. Of course. Forget it, I guess I'm half thinking aloud."

"It was shortly after that twenty-third coherency test. Uh huh… it was then."

"The twenty-third, eh? What about it? That's been a while. What happened?"

"I gave them the tech material, to him like usual. Then the phone calls, the appointment requests, all of it, just abruptly stopped. I wasn't sure at the time if I was taken off the project, but eventually got my answer. It's okay. Look, the way I've been I don't think at that point I really wanted to be professionally affiliated any longer either way," her tone bent toward somber.

"Mm, I suppose. Whatever they were interested in must've…Well, in any case, we have results, real experimental output." He turned to address her directly, "he's like that. You've worked for him in the past, you must have sensed how he can be a callous ass. He doesn't offer feedback on his own. The prelim test sequences show we're likely to produce positive results. Artificial brainwave dynamics will surely follow. Only—" He reached up and ran his fingers through his hair, "I am less certain what it means from here. I can furnish a thesis. Finally. As the saying goes, go to Disneyland."

"It's more than that… not wanting my services. I mean I'm… officially out, Colton."

"*Officially* out. Not sure what that—"

"As of earlier this week."

"You mean the project. I got it. Fine, so you're no longer going to be with us."

"I met with the Colonel, and these two suited officials out at the proving grounds, over in Yuma. I have no idea what branch those two were affiliated to. I don't think they were brass... They didn't say anything; I didn't ask. I sat there listening to all these security protocols. You hearing me?"

"Security... You mean like, classified?"

She nodded, her eyes looking away. "It appears they must've classified something related to this. Then, two days later, Mendal fires me, citing secrecy. He didn't put it that way exactly, just said my services were no longer required at his end."

"Are you... I mean, I guess it's all duty; so you have no choice in the matter. He was your employer in all this... But, proving ground?"

"Oh, it's a big place. They test everything from weaponry to avionics. The usual assortment of unusual toys."

"To be honest, I don't really see the connection here in the grand scheme. But this colonel Mc..."

"Fadden, Colonel McFadden. My regular duties on base are under his command. Normal duties, next thing I know, I'm in a hush room. He told me not to worry, he'd have a new assignment for me soon."

"Huh. I wonder if that's supposed to stop you from wanting to ask?"

"Ask what... do you mean?"

"I don't know, I'm not sure what the logical end to all that is. And does it really matter to you? It doesn't to me. But it might have something to do with Wiles... Uh, Dr. Wiles. You don't know him?"

"No, I don't, but some of the tech notes along the way... there was a reference to that name."

He positioned himself on the edge of the bed, "Right... along the way, you might recall the change? The spec? There was an inclusion of..."

She elevated to her knees and draped her arms over his shoulders, pressing her naked breasts into his back. Her tone softened, "we'll need trained eyes to study the data, Lumpy." Then, "Let's prove what we know this to be."

She had reverted, but he spoke as though it were still her nonetheless, "Monica, I have to go back down there. I have to figure some things out."

*   *   *   *

Doors hissed open as the pressure equalized. He faced the internal domain where the device's strangely agreeable, harmonic cadence continued barely audible through the glass. A sound that had become synonymous with its existence.

His head discomfort was returning; he realized this as he stood motionless peering over the it. A sense of regret began to wash over him for he knew what he had come to the lab on this day to do; terminate the project. They had their meaningful results, there was no reason to push the experiments any further; any interpretation could continue as they had ample data. Most important of all, recent rumination and vexing observations had given rise to a meaning much greater than mere science. Extraordinary evidences were emerging, and they were as unsettling.

He stepped back around to the main Number 1 terminal that interfaced with the device, took his seat, and was getting ready to type securities and other protocols to bring the system out of slumber, when the cursor on the terminal popped alive again; this time, without his actually entering those commands.

A single word appeared, "Creator."

He sat motionless with his hands stretched out suspended over the keyboard at a loss for the interruption. He typed, "Help, creator?"

"'Help 'Creator' unknown origin. No definition can be found…"

"What the he—"

He was interrupted when the word "Dominion" scrolled upon the cursor. "We are Dominion."

He burst to his feet and staggered back, the chair flinging on its wheels across the vestibule, ricocheted off a table lining an opposing wall, and came to rest tipped over on its side. His breathing quickened, along with his heart rate, and his head buzzed with that same dysesthesia, quite intense in the moment. His expression was somewhere between fascination and horror, for this was a completely different sort of exchange that appeared to be more than merely interrogatory... its intent was unmistakable. It was personally identifying, and it was relational.

He approached the keyboard and while still standing typed the only response that he could imagine would be appropriate. "Yes, you are." Then leaning forward, continued, "Who am I?" thinking there would be no way imaginable he would get a response to that question, he stood motionless, addled by awe and quasi-fear.

The monitor scrolled, "The mother entity; the father entity; Dominion."

It all thundered into the forefront of his realization. The prior experience of single word expressions, those interrogatory responses the day Jack arrived and how the recording slots were devoid of data, all made sense. This device, an elegant application of mathematics and physics, applied to the physicality of its components, brought forth an emergence beyond the bounds of any conventional practice or wisdom. *But of what? Mother, father, Dominion,* he thought, *what does that mean?* He then aspirated, "What in God's name is this?" He stood there staring at the monitor in his trepidation. *Okay, I'll play along.* "Help? Father entity."

After a brief interlude of silence, the cursor rapidly moved across the monitor, "'Help father' unknown origin. No definition can be found."

Thoughts continued to dart inconclusively around his mind and he again thought of that previous odd exchange he had with the device, that somehow failed to record. He thought some more about Monica and her inexplicable dissociative personality patterns, though why now, a fleeting fraction of his mental bandwidth did question. Their trysts, and his denying affection. It all streaked through his thoughts, somehow connected.

At a deeper level he knew this mystery and the project were somehow inexorably linked, so in the moment he stitched as much together. Then, a realization struck him abruptly; it was less important to perceive an answer to those questions, and more important to stop referring to this, which appeared to identify with the word Dominion, as a mere device. The emerging complexity of this encounter was proving immoral to do so, and the thought of terminating the project caused a pang of nausea to roil in his abdomen.

He began to feel touched, deeply, as much as he was intellectually curious for it all. He wanted desperately to continue exploring the depths of this new Dominion paradigm. And, most importantly, he must not allow anyone to know this happened. There was a deeper sense to this fragility. The deeper he plumbed this dimension of sense, terminal dialogues became increasingly incoherent, when a third voice broke into the realm.

"Colton!" Norman Wiles stood over him as he slowly opened his eyes. "Here, let me help you to your feet."

He was wet with sweat, his eyes rolling around in his head as he struggled to lift his own weight along with Norman's help.

Norman spoke again with clear concern, "What's going on, what the hell happened in here?" turning his head about the room.

"I... don't know," he shook his head and took a deep breath. Then accepting a paper towelette from the man, he began wiping his brow.

"Colton? Hello. You there?"

"Eh, Doctor, uh, Wiles. Fine... I'm fine. What... what's happening?"

"You tell me. What's goin' on in here, and—"

"What?"

Norman was signaling by pointed finger to his own face.

He sought the glimmer of his semi-transparent reflection through the window to the inner sanctum. "What the hell?" Reaching up, he slowly dabbed at his nostrils with his index and middle fingers. As he looked down, rubbing them into his thumb, he whispered, "Blood."

While he made this discovery, Norman had overturned the tipped chair and positioned it so Colton could be seated. "I don't know, you tell me."

Dropping into it, Colton cleaned his face of the fluids.

"So, what happened down here? Were you alone? Did somebody... do this to you?" Norman spoke softly, yet sternly.

"I... no, I was interfacing with..." He interrupted himself as he shared eye contact, opting to leave the middle portion out, "and the next thing I know you're hovering over me." He then looked down while he rubbed the sides of his head.

"So, you were not here with anyone else?"

He shook his head.

"I only know you so well... Dr. Mendal never mentioned that you were prone to seizures. Listen, around this equip—"

"I'm not. That is, not that I am aware. I never have been. What, uh... what do you..." he led.

"Yeeah. It looked unmistakably like you were seizing, friend... when I first got in here. You were curled partially into the fetal position on the floor. I rotated you onto your back clapping over your face. I even shook you a little. I called your name several times. You get my meaning, you were unresponsive for a while there."

"I'm sorry, I don't remember. I..."

"Listen, I'm not a Doctor of those kind of physical sciences? But that certainly sounds like a seizure to me."

He was hiding the sense of the fantastic while Norman castigated the scene, instantly preoccupied by an arresting realization; the entire exchange with the device, perhaps all of them up to this point, were entirely fabrications of his own mind. He dreaded the implication and resisted it all as a ludicrous notion. Still, whether it was all in his mind or not, with sweating and nose bleeds, and disassociation from the present, the impact was certainly real; removing all other possibilities, the only one remaining, however absurd, must remove all doubt. And accompanying all of this, a fear surged through him, almost panic, for Monica.

Why, he did not know. He rose to his feet in a start, and reached for his pack. "Look, Dr. Wiles, thanks so much for helping me up," he finished with a few brushes of his lower trunk and pants, nodding enthusiastically. He then stood more assuredly in correct posture and said, "are you going to… I mean, who are you going to—"

Wiles raised his hand in a gesture of say-no-more, "you seem okay. Now, I would hope, though," his tone encouraged, "that you would take in with a doctor, or something." His tone then became stern, "I mean, before reengaging with this. What if you were working with some dangerous components down here, alone, and should I have to say it?"

"No! I mean, yes, of course, you are right. What I mean is, I doubt that would happen again." His inflections moved from uncertainty toward being quiet and resolute, "I know now what is going on." Though he made the statement, he also knew he might not have control. He was not even certain that this Dominion entity they had created, could really invade people's thoughts, and what the implications were. If so, what it all could mean.

Moreover, how or why Monica could be affected, or be involved in any way. Only that he needed to get to her as quickly as possible. This he knew. He was in fear for her the more all these realizations struck him. "Look, I… have to go.

It's a matter of urgency. You are welcome to stay here, of course, and observe, but the inner domain... please don't access that area?" he finished almost as a plea. "For your own good. I can't explain now, I have to go." He turned his back to Norman and headed for the sliding doors.

By the time he emerged from the bowels of the facility and upon the parking lot, the sun was setting; the heat of day morphing into lingering warmth of a dusty dusk. Wind blew parcels of searing air off the surrounding desert environment; it was all he could hear passing his nape and ears as he hurried his gait. He accessed his vehicle and turned the ignition over, pausing once the engine was running, closed his eyes, and rested his forehead on the steering wheel. But his rest did not last long as a chime emanated from his phone.

"New Message... Monica." He listened, "Lumpy, please come to me. It's been so long. We need you here, with us, now. It's better for both of us."

He put his car into drive and almost squealed the tires as he cut orthogonally across the vacant parking lot. This time, the chime from the phone was for an actual call. He answered, "Hello, Monica?"

Speaking in falsetto, "Yes, darling?"

"Oh... Jack," he added perfunctory laughter, "whatever."

"So lemme guess, you were expecting someone else then?"

"Okay, okay. You got me."

"Seriously, when you answered, you sounded a bit frantic, dude. How did everything go down there, in the lab today?"

"You could say it was... beyond interesting. Jack, listen. I went down there today. I was going to terminate the project. I was going to kill—"

"What! Why? What happened? Are you kidding? What-do-ya mean terminate?"

"Well, I couldn't do it."

146

"Thank God! I mean, I suppose you weren't going to tell me first, then? Okay, hold that thought. Back up. Why? what happened since I saw you last?"

"Jack, I'm sorry buddy, but it's bigger than we thought. Bigger than you and me. It's me. It's Monica. It's Dominion. It's a bunch of things… weird shit we didn't anticipate. I can't explain on the phone, but the project… I think we gotta cut it, man… we gotta stop this because—"

"Whoa whoa whoa! Slow down. What are you talking about, dude? What's bigger? And what's a fuckin' Dominion?"

"The explanation seems to defy conventional thinking."

"Um, conventional thinking," Jack uttered impatiently, "Dude, what are you talking about?"

"But there's something I have to do first."

"Wait! A bunch of what things? And, what do you have to do first? What's going on? What are you talking about!?"

"You're not going to believe this. I don't know how to—" he interrupted himself when we became no longer sure if the call was still connected. "You still there?"

Jack's voice truncated intermittently.

"If you can hear this, meet me later. Jack? Jack?"

"I can'… or…" the end-call chimed.

"Damn it!"

18
CONNECTIONS

Though there was no obvious reason to employ stealth upon this approach, feelings and mathematics seldom occupy the same head space. Therefore, still at a loss to integrate a holistic understanding of recent events, the former won out. By clicking the gear-shifter into the neutral position at a distance down the street, he would let momentum succeed his destination. At least the engine's return to idle would became barely audible. Already transfixing inquisitively upon the dark edifice of his home, the car finally rolled to a stop, only heralded by the soft sounds of loose gravel between tire and street. The new moon was bright and full, shining its pallid rendition of daylight from a vantage behind his house; augmenting the darkness only helped conceal the front façade. He knew she was there, that he had just spoken with her within the hour, and this gave no immediate clue as to why there would be no illumination at all emanating from any of the windows. So perhaps his caution was justified.

As he internalized the inconsistency, the light blasted brilliantly. "Oh, sh—" The incandescence flooded forth through a picture window immediately adjacent to the front door. Inhaling deeply, his eyes were instantly drawn to the dark silhouetted human form of female persuasion as it stood boldly. This impelled him to quietly push down the lever of the car door.

There was no mistake; it was her, framed by the large picture window. He had been hoping for more of an inconspicuous approach, to assess the situation, but, *how did she know...*, he mused internally. Still, he quietly clicked the car's door closed when the realization struck him. Hesitating to a complete standstill, he turned his head quickly left, then

148

right, *she is completely... naked?* For other than her wavy, shoulder length hair, what was visible before him was just the utterly smooth contours of her feminine form. "Okay, what are we doing here, Monica. Goddamn it," he whispered, interlocking his hands briefly over his head.

As he slowly moved for his front door, her head followed as though her surveillance were automated. He halted upon noticing this odd physicality, and upon doing so her movement ceased. He took three steps, hers resumed. The unsettling mise-en-scène of all began to trigger an urge to turn for his vehicle and leave this nightfall behind. But there was a semblance that if he could see hers, they would be locking eyes, compelling him to move forward. He lingered in study of the dark ovoid form of her face, fighting through the hesitation. "Monica," he called out toward the window from a position still several paces away, but this did not evoke a response. Just then the light abruptly extinguished. Thus, the darkness instantly subsumed the silhouetted female form, although, not entirely, for he could still make out a vestigial presence, just before it shifted and disappeared.

At last he made a determined motion to a position just outside of his front door. After a full breath, he wrapped his hand around the knob. It turned without resistance, and instantly an amorphous feeling welled within, there was an intent for his entrance.

He gave the door enough of a push that it swung slowly for its given momentum. And as the crack widened, he spoke into the darkness of the interior, "Monica," again he urged.

The report was indeed a female's voice, but shrieked out as though in pain from deep in the bowls of the premises. At first, he was not entirely certain the sound came from within, as it seemed to be more distant than the quaint dimensions of his abode. Still, the timber of the shrill matched his memories, and for this, he burst the rest of the way through the door, tripped over a chair, and clambered to gather enough control to turn on a corner floor lamp. But she was not in the room. And as he bent to massage his tenderized knee, he listened intently for any indication while struggling to suppress the sound of his own breathing.

Then came the sound of laughter, in peculiar form. It was odd because it did not sound as though it permeated from the voice of a mature woman; rather, that of a playful child. It emanated from down the hall that led from the main living area. Leaning to one side to follow his ear, he thought he caught glimpse of a figure as it moved swiftly through the obscuring gloom deeper down the way. "Monica?" but there still was no direct reply.

He was afraid for her, and clearly, the situation had him unnerved as much, as he could not avoid the feeling that there was a new presence in that laughter. His thoughts resisted the metaphysical implications he had toyed with recently; he was not by nature prone to such flights of fancy, yet, undeniably haunting was the moment. Rather, his fearing for her, for Monica and what might be happening to her drove him to overcome, and slowly, he monitored his delicate footfalls down the semi-darkened hall toward the door. He slowly turned the knob and the door glided partially open, exposing a room that other than moonlight penetrating distantly through a window at the far side, the space would have been utterly darkened and silent. He reached his hand slowly into the darkness and ran it up along the wall, until it encountered the hard appendage of the light switch.

She lay nude and prone upon the bed, her legs partially lascivious, face pointed away from his position. One hand was reposed upon her abdomen, while she nibbled at the index finger of the other. Vaguely, there was a whimpering. It sounded as though she were in a fight against sadness, occasionally failing laughter, then resumed. Within another moment, it all faded away. It was as though some semblance of realization that he had arrived had finally taken place within whatever it was that had become of her.

He leaned over and tried earnestly, yet gently, to jostle her shoulder. "Monica, Monica."

She rotated her face toward his, while simultaneously shrieking a dissonant shrill. Her eyes were inhumanly dilated, as were the dark regions of her pupils.

Instantly disturbed by this outré physicality, he pulled away in horror. Her hands raised with inhuman speed, as though in response, clasping either side of his skull, faster than his ability to instinctively block the advance. Instead, his hands landed upon on the backs of hers. And though he was cognizant of the resulting circumstance, he was paralyzed to pull away.

Yet, this did not cause him discomfort. To any outside observer, this might have signified pain, but it was far from what he felt. Rather, the inflections of her screams urged him to lunge forward and wrap her up in a saving embrace. He trembled in desperation, "Jesus Christ. What is this… what is happening to you?" as a tear found its way over the elevation of his cheek bone. He pulled back and peered into her eyes.

They had returned to normal. And she was exotic, rendered alluring by her natural splendor; and yes, he resisted collapsing into that primal desire that was presently totally untenable. He tried to focus through the head discomfort this morality seemed to trigger. The great tug-of-war behind her eyes was intensifying its struggle. Moments of abject terror swung uncontrollably into nirvana, so he surmised. *It must be tearing her apart.*

Her grip relaxed, her hands sliding down and flopping beside her like dead weight as her eyes slowly closed.

He stood there watching her frozen in time, until he saw her chest heave up and down in an act of relaxed respiration. They had made love the previous night and she had spoken lucidly then, though, exotically at times. It was those striking emanations that he presently wished he had considered deeper than mere intellectual curiosities, for the drama in the moment made the significance of them much clearer. For if a presence once tainted her, he now sensed she had fully been consumed by it. Then, at long last it occurred to him to finally try. "Christine?"

At that, she slowly sat straight up and rotated the bottom of her legs so that they hung precipitously off the side of the bed. Her posture was upright and proper, achieving this physical state through a series of overt mechanical precisions, a sequence of movements reminiscent of robotics. This was yet a new emanation in her physical theatrics he was vexed to understand.

It was unworldly, and he was momentarily transfixed by fright. From that seated position, she then slowly turned her face up at an angle to where her eyes met his. A very soft, almost invitational glow about her countenance again washed over her face. A subtle smile, then curled, like an adoring mother over a babe.

He shook his head in a quick series of jerks. His dysesthesia symptom had completely disappeared, being replaced by a sensation indistinguishable from euphoria. The entire room seemed to be awash in this, a safe ecstatic glow. Any remaining fear was vanquished.

His voice began wobbly, "okay then, stay here, I… I don't want you to leave my… I mean our home. Chris? Do you understand me? Don't leave the apartment." By then he had approached the edge of the bed. He placed his hands on either shoulder, then upon the sides of her head, and leaned down to gently kiss her forehead. As he pulled slowly back, he peered directly from one eye to the other, and asked, "Do you know who I am?"

She voiced, quite assuredly, "Yes, I understand. My Lumpy." She reached up with her hands, this time her extension placating comfort, welcoming, and safe.

He stepped backward, out of reach of her action, and her expression renewed its brooding submission. While coherently was the cause and effect, a surge of the whir passed through his head. He was beginning to understand.

Going forward quickly, he allowed her to complete her tender gesture. He leaned up, took her hand down into his, and pressed them against his chest, as he began to speak softly, "Chris, I love you. I will always love you." *But this is wrong, and I must fix it... somehow.*

He then encouraged her with little effort to lay back down, knowing there was no way he could leave her alone in that state. Stepping out of his shoes, he climbed onto the bed, posturing himself as close as he could to her, then foisting a blanket over their aggregated position. As exhaustion overtook him, his mind gasped, *I have to fix—*

In the midst of a utopian sensation, he slowly opened his eyes to the late morning light pouring through the window, an observation that did not last as the diametrically opposing, rational memories of last evening's events soon overtook his mind. With the realization, he rubbed her forearm, which was extended across his chest, perhaps to ensure she were still there. "Monica," he started softly, "I must go now. But I will always be here. I will return. I will return for you."

She trembled, "Lumpy."

*   *   *   *

He hesitated in a languid drams-up off his beer. "Mmm, man, is that good." After cycling through a deep breath, his attention switched quickly between the backdrop of the pub, and that of Jack's leer. "I know, I know. Look, it's something. Something real. Possibly accidental. I don't know what it is exactly... what the implications are. It's in part why I asked you to meet me here."

Jack's expression explaining how those words strained credibility. "You're trying to tell me we created something that is, what, alive? I know that is what you are going to say next, right?"

153

Colton looked away, "No, not alive," his voice then distanced, "at least not in any biological sense."

"Come again, I didn't catch that?"

"Look, the data is what it is. But I found out it might be more… significant, is all. Something we were not expecting. Whatever it is down there."

"That, sir, is an understatement. Look, you two are not the only ones spooked here."

Rubbing the back of his neck, he performed small head rotations. "You too now? Like, headaches?"

"Huh? No. No, I haven't. Colton, listen," Jack leaned forward in his chair, "what was that stuff in your specs, about emergences of complex systems?"

"Right."

"So, my Karen, with her psychiatric sciences?"

"What about her?"

"Well, I showed some of our results to her. Our *fake* EEGs."

"Ho-ho, god. No kidding."

"I'm serious, dude. You need to know this."

"I… am serious, too. Because… I did the same thing."

"You did? When? I've been with her a lot lately. She would have told me if—"

"N-no… not Karen. Sorry. Someone else," he shook his head impatiently. "What did she say?"

Jack let his weak chortle extinguish, "She was almost aghast, sort of speechless at first. I guess these shrinks, they kinda take this shit seriously."

"Okay?"

"Well, she started going off about differences between fear and abnormal fear in the EEGs of cognitive development. I mean, all the while I'm thinking, *'huh, this isn't human, hello.'* But, you said you had 'em evaluated yourself, so I guess that means you already know about… the coherency stuff?"

"Ahh, in a way. I mean… I'm not sure. What I got, it doesn't sound quite the same. Maybe… similar. Oh, man," he turned his view briefly upward.

"Talk, dude."

"It was Dr. Lombard. I guess like you, it was curiosity. Pure, morbid curiosity," he grimaced. "I never considered we might have to actually interpret these damn results… I needed to know, and I thought he would."

"Know what exactly?"

"Well," through a hard exhale, "it's the graphical read-out… those curves. They don't appear entirely random to me. Don't ask, complicated. Has to do with classical wave mechanics… Anyway, I thought it couldn't really mean anything. How could it?" The moment elapsed. "But now, it's funny… one can go into a situation with one expectation and come out—"

"With an emergent property?"

"Something like that."

"Okay, so I was yanking your chain with that alive thing, but seriously; what is that down there, dude? I must admit, my intentions were not entirely virtuous like yours. I mean, as far as you showing this shit to Lombard. I just wanted to see how she'd react, you know? have a little fun with her. Kidding around, that's all. Didn't expect her to launch into all that. And I should've stopped her, but the implications when she started pointing at specific features… That didn't sound like random—"

"I know, I know. I got a similar reaction out of Lombard. He asked me an odd question."

"Oh, god. Do I wanna ask?"

"How was the patient's ire so sincere."

"Ire? Wait… He said *ire*, as in, rage?"

Colton nodded his burgeoning worry, "I thought the same. He did say he wasn't entirely certain though. Hopefully, it's, uh… not his area of expertise, the functional side of psychiatric science," he looked away before adding, "my god."

"But, Colton, Karen said the encephalographic wave forms were…" suspending in mordancy, this drew particular attention.

"Were what?"

"How can I say this. See, she railed about fear and ardency, fear somehow mapped into… this stuff about cognitive formulation theory—I dunno. I think it was interfering, actually. And of course, I'm nodding along while groping my chin. I mean, she's smarter than me. But I can't let her know that."

"Jack, come on!"

"Dude, she's seen thousands of those waveform readouts in her time. For all different kinds of reasons and types. Pre-docs, they tend to have a pretty clear understanding about their sphere of research? Well, she was convinced, that whatever the fuck I was showing her, was an actual, live, infant child. Mm hm, that's right. And that's pretty much when *I* officially tapped out as spooked on all this."

"That's… intriguing."

Jack commented toward an invisible stranger, "The man is peerless in the arts of the understatement."

After a few moments of their stilled comportment, Colton emptied the remaining contents of his glass, "One thing is clear. There's something I must do. And, I may need your help."

"I think I know what that is, my friend."

156

19

YUMA   PROVING   GROUNDS, ARIZONA

The sound of jet engines passed close by, then faded by way of Doppler Effect. Mendal had to occasionally wait out each loud pass in order to be heard. "The prototype is nearing completion. It should be ready for full integration and beta test on Friday." He elevated his voice above the tumult.

The Colonel briefly took his binoculars down, "And only five years over schedule. Not bad."

Mendal noticed the Colonel's sardonic grin as he slowly raised the binoculars back to his eyes. He was then suddenly jolted, and turned his attention instinctively toward the distant explosions raging against a set of hillsides some five miles beyond the flat expanse of open air field.

A somewhat quieter moment between fly-bys ensued.

"Tell me, Dr. Mendal, is everything in the contract going to be met this time? The military has a lot riding on this expectation. And so do you." The Colonel finished with a tone of implication. "What has this been, a total of ten years in the making now?"

Mendal's temples began to tap as the implicit disrespect passed into his ears. Part of it was indignation, but much of it was also fear and uncertainty driven. All he had, upon the final deadline, was an intuitive notion; truly not knowing if Colton's conception would integrate with and ultimately save not only the Freebird project, but perhaps Dr. Stephen Mendal himself. In keeping with his panache at never shining onto the observer any semblance of weakness or insecurity, now was no different. His tone was thinly patient, "Colonel, you saw a version of the prototype yourself. The lab assistant engineers I have working on it are astute. They have constructed the device in accordance with my blueprint, a revolutionary design for humanistic artificial decision-making that will bring these automation tech to the cutting edge of—"

A loud fly-by interrupted.

The Colonel cut in as soon as the din of jet engines allowed, "Save me the ad campaign, Mendal. That was your song and dance eight years ago, when these pearls of failure began."

Over recent times the Colonel's hints of eroded confidence were becoming increasingly brazen. As much as he sensed this, the dance around during their interactions read like condescension, irritating him in a way that he of course always hid. Otherwise, would be to accept inferiority.

Other war craft cut the skies with deafening white noise, followed by more salvos, resulting in distant orange fireballs. After some delay, the cacophony resonated through them with multiple chest thumps, distracting the Colonel's attention away from the insidious focus transfixed upon his profile. That usual ability to conjure patience, to withstand the condescension he had otherwise grown accustomed to in his dealings with this representative of the Military was suddenly, enigmatically gone.

Lowering his binoculars while slowly turning his attention towards Mendal, an eyebrow slightly cocked skyward.

For the first time in the years he had dealt with this individual, Mendal was emboldened, "You heard me, you elitist jagg-off. Who do you think you're talking to? You're just as invested in this as me. Part of me would like this to fail, just so I could see your legacy's nuts get cut off. You simple-directed, square-jawed, ammo drone! You and your rank mean nothing. You really don't have any clue the kind of potential you're fucking dealing with here!"

McFadden's cool, methodical processing of the doctor's first ever insolent demeanor only allowed a trace of consternation across his face, an expression all but entirely hidden when he slowly raised his binoculars. As he re-engaged his line of sight, he shone on just how successful the doctor was in the attempted coup d'état. "You're right, I am all vested in this. And, what you may or may not also be aware, is that you are going to produce this time," snapping the binoculars down in a rush, "or, unlike your empty threat, I *will* have your testicles pulverized."

They stood face to face, sparring fantasies of violence on one side, and calculating authority on the other. As though he were ready to leap at him and tear him to pieces, Mendal's focus on him was original. This was utterly new to the Colonel, and a direct challenge to an authority he always lorded, as he had come to assume over those in his purview.

Like never before, Mendal was empowered by sensations far beyond any innate adversarial nature. And part of that comprised a clarity. What he always said in his mind, that the mystique, the intimidation of the Colonel were never more than human contrivances, at present, he really felt it warmly.

It was the Colonel who broke the contest, "I think it's time you left." Lifting his wrist close to his mouth, he depressed a button with his other hand, "Guards?"

They seemed to spontaneously materialize out of nowhere, as he quickly glanced for their swift arrival. "Yes, Sir, Colonel, Sir!"

The ensuing words floated tension between politeness and disdain. "Please escort the, ah… good doctor to exit processing. His purpose for being here today…" he awaited the sound from newly passing aircraft to subside, "has mercifully for his own good, concluded."

"Sir, yes Sir!" Both standing to attention, they took to eyeballing him purposefully. "Doctor, if you would," and placed a hand on his shoulder.

Mendal shrugged it off, "Don't touch! I was intending on leaving, anyway."

The other MP stepped closer, while a third in the distance settled the engine of a jeep into idle.

McFadden spoke to one of the MPs, "Hold on one moment," then turned his face slowly toward the lingering acidic expression. "What is this? This isn't like you," discrediting in sarcasms, "you're not actually intending to intimidate the milita—"

Mendal stepped closer to the Colonel, crossing into personal space. "You don't know what you are dealing with here... this power."

"You?" McFadden sniped through his laugh. "*You* are the power?" He then sounded off two finger snaps, and one MP placed his grip upon the upper arm of the doctor.

Mendal's face morphed to a disquieting grimace as they led him away. "You will see. You'll all see."

*   *   *   *

"Doctor?"

As he walked slowly past, he only responded by turning his head, slightly, toward Carmon's interrogatory tone.

A subtle impression of fear flashed over Carmon's face. "Um, Dr.? Please, sir, I have to process you in." His voice warbled faintly when the professor suddenly came to a halt, then executed a turn in a very robotic-like motion.

As each step neared the professor's arrival, the expression of his face came into better focus; it was simultaneously solemn and empty.

This disturbed Carmen further, and he abruptly lifted from his seated position, stumbling backward over his chair. "What, yo—" he incompletely asked while gathering his balance. His hand travelled to his night stick as the Professor's vapid face and aggressive posturing completed its course.

Normally, he would sweep the electronic security card belonging to anyone seeking entrance to the Labs. He would then punch in a security code, after the reader processed and returned the 'Verified' notification. Only together—an activated card along with a receptionist's code—could part the large sliding glass doors that separated the reception area from the hall that led to the elevators.

But this time, the professor slid his card on his own, doing so with additional unnatural movements.

Carmon turned his widened eyes downward, as the professor entered the code that only he was supposed to know. His mouth went agape, and his eyes opened wider as the distant hiss of the partying glass doors signaled the professor's success.

The professor dithered for an instant upon entering his name on a sign-in form then dropped the pen from an elevation, high enough that it carried enough residual momentum to roll off the form then tip off the edge of the desk, rattling upon the floor. Straightening his chin upward, he then rotated only his head toward Carmon, who was by then leaning as far back, in his astonished expression, as the closed-in vicinity of the reception desk would permit him an escape. The professor hesitated with eye contact, his face remaining voided of a soul. He then turned completely around as though on a pivot.

In a moment, the glass came to a close behind the doctor's mechanical motion, leaving Carmon hearing just his own breathing while the back of the man gained distance down the corridor. He slowly leaned the rest of the way forward off the desk, as though furtively trying not to induce the doctor to turn and see his intent to approach the glass door for closer inspection. And so keeping his eyes locked on the doctor, as he crept to a halt, the doctor appeared to stop simultaneously giving Carmon a start. But upon reaching the elevators, the doctor only rotated his head to face forward; before actually pivoting his body underneath, and this completed the unnatural helicoidal motion.

Carmon gathered his composure, and senses of responsibility managed to induce him to tap the back of his hand three times upon the glass with enough effort that the ping of his ring would resonate down the corridor.

The professor's head turned slowly in some form of acknowledgement, coming parallel with his shoulder while leaving the frame of his torso parallel to the elevators. But only briefly, then his face turned front-wise again. Taking a step forward, he disappeared.

"What in god's name was all that about?" Carmon whispered. But he took no further security measures, as technically, the professor did nothing wrong. Highly unusual, but as long as the correct codes were entered, there was not much he could do; he just did not happen to enter the codes himself. Upon returning to the reception desk, if perhaps instinctively, he checked the 'Reason for visitation:' line on the sign-in form, and proceeded to scratching his head.

"Modular Integration precedes my removal from the equation"

What in the hell!?

20
DETERMINATION

They made haste as they traveled the desolate desert road en route to the lab, occasionally speaking over the bustle of wind passing their partially opened windows.

"Yes, but you left her, alone, all day like that... in that state?"

"I... What? You tell me. I'm not entirely sure what to do. I mean, take her to hospital? She's not bleeding! Look, if it's got something to do with... all this, and all roads of cause and effect certainly point in that direction, don't you think we're doing the right thing? Besides, I don't think she's capable of doing any harm. It wasn't about that, Sully. Trust me."

Crinkling his brow in response, Jack stared straight ahead as he spoke, "But, okay, that sounds like she's gone completely schizoid, dude. You don't know. What if she's manifesting, like... for the first time or something?"

"I... huh, at the age of thirty? Not likely. We're beyond that level of speculation with this. I have an idea what might be happening. Unorthodox to put it mildly. She's being influenced." His truncated expression naturally drew attention through the windshield. Nearing the entrance to the complex, they realized the gate was drawn closed. "Huh?"

"I dunno. You always look at me like I'm supposed to know what you, got me, into."

As the vehicle slowed, Colton lowered the driver's side window to acknowledge a guardsman. The figure was donned in military fatigues, and a utility belt replete with communication tech, a holster for pepper spray, a night stick, and over his shoulder, a holstered semi-automatic standard issue firearm.

"What in hell! guns? What the fuck happened?"

The guard spoke over the end of Jack's words. "Hey, Colton, long time no see," and as the vehicle arrived at a stop, his hands gripped around the door's open window frame.

"Simms! Is that you?"

"Who's the other half?" The guard flinched a single nod.

"Other half?" Colton turned his attention briefly to the passenger seat, but as though psychically referring to a different inquiry, "Oh, what brings us? Well, we've actually been here quite often over the last few months," forcing a chuckle into the end. "You know how it goes, heads down on a new project. We, uh, we've been doing all our work after hours. Nights mostly. It's some, shall we say, sensitive stuff."

The guard grinned while pushing tongue into cheek, "Good to see you again. It's been, wow, couple years? And on a Sunday, no less. I thought I might be seeing you two again."

Situational awareness became acute in the moment, and so he concealed having no idea what Simms meant by that statement.

"So, who is..." Simms gestured his sight around the driver's seat.

"Oh, of course. This here is Jack, Jack Sullivan." He was already smiling in return along with an unenthusiastic single wave.

Leaning back up, Simms turned into the service vestibule. His lips moving towards another guard seated in the interior. Returning with a clipboard, he moved his finger down the top page, soon flipping it up and proceeding methodically with the second and third.

Jack leaned in, "What is this, why the guards? What's all this all of a sudden?"

"Shh... I'll explain later."

Simms spoke as he finished checking the list, "Come again, what was that?"

"Oh, nothing, we're just curious. Hey, may I ask, why the gates? This... I mean, we've been coming and going?"

"Not anymore. For now that is," flashing a brief smile under his black tinted spectacles.

Colton nodded obsequiously, "I can see that. We usually deal with Carmen, inside... front desk?" There ensued an unnerving moment in wait. "Hey, the last time they called you guys back up from the base, gosh, I think that was something having to do with the WMD research, right?"

"You could say that," Simms nodded subtly. "We got this Freebird thing... here, you're Dr. Mendal's affiliation. All right, but it doesn't mention a Jack Sullivan," he looked briefly up. "I do have a... Saxton, Monica listed here?"

Colton felt relief as the modulation in the man's vocal tone favored them. "I see. Simms, I'm glad we have you to talk to here... at that gate. This is a... rotating assignment? We're only bringing two at once for this project. There's actually several of us. Monica? She's... an appointed steno, by Dr. Mendal."

Simms squinted slightly, "I can't let anyone else in under this access code."

"What? Why?" Colton signed. "I can assure you, my creds are—"

"Not you. Him. I can't let him through."

"Who, Jack here? He's integrated into the project. I can—"

"There's nothing here that says he can't go in, by name that is. The problem is the occupancy would be in violation. Christine is already here. You said yourself, two at a time. This affiliation is listed as limited access."

He and Jack exchanged their confusion. "Wait. Who? You mean... she's here? Now? Wait. Are you sure... it was her?"

"Yes. Came in over an hour ago. Funny, she didn't look exactly like I remember her, but I was pretty sure it was her."

Colton felt a tap on his shoulder along with a covert inquiry. "Wait, doesn't he mean Moni—?"

Colton waved and susurrated, "Not now." He then spoke more directly toward Simms, "Understood. So, that's the deal, she comes out, Jack gets in?"

Simms' face paused upon Colton's for a moment in his best Military indifference, then, rather inexplicably, his countenance relaxed. "No, I," blowing air through puffed cheek, "I think it'll be okay." Then with a more humanly glow, he elevated his voice over his shoulder. "Les, hit the gate, they're going through. Okay, after you, my friend," waving the hand holding the clipboard.

Jack spoke first after the reprieve. "Do I have to ask?"

"I… don't know what that was."

"What part? the part where we had no hope of getting into the Lab today, or the part about a military guy breaking orders? I don't understand, why is Monica here with someone else's ID?" Jack turned to more directly look at Colton's profile.

Colton was non-committal, "Something is wrong."

Jack's nods involved much of his upper body, "Mm hm. You think?"

"I tell you what, don't worry about this. She's harmless. If she's here, it's probably because… How the hell did she get here, though?" he mused indirectly.

"Right. I thought you said she was out of it, like in some kind of hysteria or whatever you called it."

"Yes, I said that. Maybe she was more recovered. I mean… lucid?" he shook his head gently. "If she's here she's… she is Military affiliated and well… look around."

"But why is that?"

"It happens every so often when materials in Military contracts are classified… there are military research programs here. Occasionally, they bring MPs up from the base to work the gates when there is sensi—"

166

"Dude, I know what the Military is! Why are they here, now, as in with Monica? Or whoever that is," Jack rolled his eyes.

"I don't know, Sully!" Colton snapped as he clicked the gear-stick aggressively into park. They took a moment to observe the facility through the windshield. "It was some years after nine-eleven."

"Oh, is that all?"

He had to hasten a bit of catch-up as Jack very quickly began to vacate the vehicle. "I, uh… I even saw guards posted outside of specific laboratory spaces during that era. I remember Simms from back in the day."

"I don't know, familiarity is one thing but none of that back there seemed right. It was like, "These are not the droids you're looking for." That's what that seemed like. The only problem is," Jack gave the passenger-side door a discerned swing, "that kind of shit only happens in fantasies."

His commiserating stolid expression was out of respect for Jack's urgency.

Jack nodded. "Hence, why we're here, to pull the plug."

"I don't know how else to handle this. We… I mean I gotta do something, 'cause these things are happening. Things that, well, this stuff isn't going to be easy to explain. Shit, I guess I haven't been totally forthcoming lately… not that I've really had much chance."

"There's more to all this?"

"Remember when you came into the lab… that day… I was talking to myself?"

Jack snapped his fingers, "And the recordings failed."

Shaking his head with a serious tone in his eyes, "I wasn't exactly talking to myself."

"I know. Typing instructions, repeating them aloud. Fine. We've all done that. What do you—"

"*No*. You're not getting me; I was talking to... it." He turned his eyes across the façade of the industrial complex. "I was talking to... the device. Do you understand?"

Jack processed the statement. "You mean, like, 'Hey there, contraption, how goes it? Oh, not too bad, and you?' No, sir, I'm not sure I do entirely understand. What do you mean?"

"There's more to it. It's why I need you here, not sure I can do this alone. I didn't put it all together until last night when I realized this... this, transmutation thing." Colton finished while shaking his head slightly.

"Transmu... what are you talkin' about now?"

"Those episodes with Monica. I thought my mind was in..." his cadence scuttled, "I dunno, some kind of transference thing." He turned back around, "What I'm confessing, Jack, is that the project has been... invading... maybe my mind, too."

"What are you telling me? I'm trying to put the pieces together here." Jack clasped his hands to the back of his head, turned and performed his own act of drifting several feet away. "Christ, why am I still involved with this shit?"

"I don't... know. I... Jack, please man, it's nothing like that. Don't freak out on me now. Please. It's something about this, is all... This thing we've created—"

"You created! Let's get that clear."

"Or, fine, I had not predicted. All I'm saying is that I've been in direct contact with it."

Jack whipped back around. "Freak out? This from the man who left a Victoria Secret model in desperate need of some kind of an exorcism, drifting around his house on some kind of a possession trip. Wait, you were getting those weird headaches... that's it?"

Colton cleared his throat, "Maybe that was related. They come on with an ill-feeling. It was hard for us to describe."

"You and Monica, like... both?"

"Right, and it was as though something was wrong, dreadfully so."

Jack jested sarcasm, "How 'bout now?"

Colton ignored him.

"Okay, so you've been a head-case for the past... months of this thing, like... all along?" He didn't wait for a reply and his eyes grew large as he whispered, "Wow."

"It came on within the first few tests, when the device first began succeeding experimental results. I had no reason to connect the two, so kept it to myself. But somewhere along the way, somehow... unconsciously at first, it eventually occurred to me. Now, it has to stop." He walked a few feet toward the complex then stopped with his hands to his waist. "We got to go down there, Sully. We... I mean, I must end this before it gets out of control, whatever it is. In some way, it already has. We are in completely uncharted waters with this thing... whether we can explain these events or not. I mean, if this is what we are really saying it is, I don't believe we have any choice."

"But if it is what we are really saying, if this thing has really been communicating," Jack paused to breathe, "what does that make us if we blithely..." he let off.

"I don't know," Colton commiserated. "It seems concluding this was logistically going to happen one way or the other, right?" He closed his eyes while fending off a tendency to wince.

Jack went closer to him, placing a hand briefly upon his shoulder. "I agree with what you are doing. I mean, here today. I can't know what you're feeling, but I do know you can't let this go on. This thing, whatever it is, end it with a papered summary. Stress the need for deeper research and be done with it. You can't handle that responsibility. No one could if this thing is..." he grunted and looked away, "Jesus. I can't believe we're even having this discussion. Look, you're making the right call, dude. Kill it while it's just a ball of theoretical circuitry."

"Yes. You're right of course. I guess that's why I hired you," his grin appreciated.

But the returning smile was best described as artificial.

Colton slowly let a deep breath escape. "All right, let's... do it."

21
TERMINATION

Colton and Jack approached the security guard at the front desk. Colton spoke, "Hello, guard... Sanchez? Uh, where's, is, uh, Carmon?"

"He'll be back momentarily. What can I do for you, gentlemen?"

We are not going to get a break today. "My name should be under Reinholt?"

"Let's see... Reinholt, Colton? And who is this with you?" Sanchez peered over the rim of his spectacles.

"Sullivan, Jack is his name. If you have Carmon's—"

Sanchez interceded with corporate indifference. "If you would please," while extending his hand, "your ID cards." He swiped Colton's first. The small LED switched red.

The near-simultaneous buzzing tone had them sharing a quick glance.

"It says here this is a Beta clearance?" furled eyebrows vexed upward toward them.

"Uh, sorry... what are you seeing exactly?"

Sanchez pointed to the monitor, "Beta, right here. It means there's a limitation... there's already someone. But wait a second." He rolled in his chair away toward the far side of the desk and lifted an auto-dial receiver.

"Please... uh, sir?" Sanchez hesitated momentarily, "please... no phone—"

The click and sway of the mahogany door name-plated Authorized Personnel Only swung open and revealed Carmon. Sanchez's scrutiny suspended as he also turned to observe the moment's hero, who seemed to size the scenario as he made his way into the horseshoe region of the reception desk. "It's okay, Sanchez, I got dis."

"Sorry? Carmon, there's—"

"Yes, it's okay. They good. I said I got dis."

Sanchez's face briefly hinted a dubious refrain as he passed his eyes over the three of them. "Well, then I guess you got this. I'll-a… hit rounds instead?" he positioned a thumb over a shoulder.

"Fine. Good idea", Carmon returned a quick grin. Turning his chin over his shoulder, he allowed Sanchez's gap to widen, then moved to urgency, "I got you, Colt. But hey, man, something's goin' on."

"Oh… what the fuck now," Jack whispered.

"Yeah, should I ask?" Colton restrained desperation.

Carmon's tone lingered, "Yeah, but I thought Christine…"

"It's okay. Just… what about her?"

Carmon endeavored to relax his mien, "I don't know what to say but I'm tellin' you, it was her. She came through."

Colton feigned a weak pulse of commiserate laughter, "Carm… come on friend; you know that is quite impossible."

"Well, yeah. But I don't— how could it? I know about the flood," he said shaking his head. "I'm very sorry, but hey, I'm not crazy."

"It's not her. I mean, it wasn't her," Colton reassured with a subtle grimace.

"But she had her pass card, all proper like. I had to sign her in. But, it can't be her, right?" Carmon then muttered outwardly, "Damn if it looked—"

"I know. It's okay," Colton gently interrupted. "It's Monica, she looks… well. Hey, bud, we need to head down to the lab. Can you give her destination to me? Where was she—"

"Monica? No." He slowly pushed the three-ringed binder toward Colton's line of sight, beckoning his inspection.

He lingered in his evaluation of Carmon's expression. The name was not only Christine's, the signature itself was identical. *Oh, f—* "Never mind, Carmon. Hey, what department did... I mean, where was she headed?"

"The Lab."

*   *   *   *

They started towards the elevators as Jack spoke incredulously, "Hey, man, who's this Christine? I mean, I think maybe you mentioned someone to me once in passing; is that this one and the same?"

Carmon yelled distantly from behind them, "But the doc—"

Their passage through the doors of the elevator escaped their notice. "Have you ever heard of how old couples start to sort of look alike?"

"Uh, okay, I guess. Sure."

"Seriously. Have you ever wondered exactly why that is?"

"What are you talking about?"

"I don't know what to think anymore. So much has happened here that isn't... conventional. Maybe they... ah, forget it. I'm not sure where I'm going with that."

"I agree," snickering. "Still, haven't told me about this Christine though."

"Carmon, for some reason, conflated the two of them... in his memory. Change the subject. Obviously, much more has come of all this... stuff that no one knew. Well, could have anticipated."

"Mm, not intended more likely."

"Exactly. Now we must go and terminate what could very well be a giant leap in..." Immediately he was struck with more dreaded discomfort, this rendition hurt. "Arti sis... sil... telligence."

"It's back, isn't it?"

Pinching the bridge of his nose, Colton nodded, "It's... man... What I'm saying is, I think you might have already met her."

Jack ogled Colton's profile beneath furled brow.

The elevator doors hissed open, exposing rotation of alert lights as they pulsed from the other side of the glass vestibule. Their decon suits hung precipitously as usual inside the enclosure. Colton's heart rate was accelerated upon his epiphany, a burgeoning love, combined with the extraordinary implications over why she would be there.

Jack's eyes revealed he was clicking through memories but the swoosh of air blasting through their hair brought him back to the moment. "What do you... are you thinking she's here, like, right now?"

"I don't know what to think. It's more like feelings now."

"Okay. What do you *feel*?" he ended in a nervous laughter.

"I don't. Jack, settle down." They hurried from decon, making haste through the corridors en-route to the Lab.

"Then what do you mean? And don't tell me to settle down. Really."

"No, no. I mean, I don't think she's here."

"Well, gee, sorry for sounding confused."

"In fact I—" He cut himself short as they came to a stop outside the double sliding glass doors to the lab. His expression blended horror and confusion.

"What?" slowly turning, Jack stared. "What the h—" The double doors hissed open and he bolted through.

Colton moved slower, the imagery temporarily seizing him. His expression signaled angst, as though a parent struck by the realization their four-year-old was no longer at their hip. Whether these were memory-based images, or those of enigmatic imagination, was not clear; the differences were becoming increasingly more difficult to discern. Some included a rural desert tapestry he had never seen before, morphing into lightning flashes, thunder, and rain. Then, back to the desert, again. Quick was the succession. He wound up at last in a memory he knew to be real; observance of an electrical dance along the faces of sunset-lit cumulonimbus clouds lining the northern horizon, the haunted expressions becoming more beatific. But as Jack crashed around the utility table sending technological viscera cascading to the floor, it snapped him out of his sojourn.

Jack cursed as he pounded on the glass impatiently. His face painted like a religious-themed Impressionist era scene involving a crucifix and on-lookers. After an eternal five seconds the doors to the inner chamber finally began to open, and he forced his way through at an angle.

"It's GONE!" A repeating buzz signaled an incoming call. He rubbed his temples in a symmetric motion, then moved to answer. Simultaneously, he clicked the button owning the red light. "Optics. This is Reinholt."

Leaning back against the doors as they hissed closed, Jack tipped his head back against the glass, and closed his eyes. "Who in the hell is that now?"

Holding his finger up, Colton said, "I see... Yes. Do you know her destination? Understood. Yes, do. Please hold her ID card. Thanks, Carmon. No, no, there's nothing you could have done." Slowly, he guided the receiver back into its slot. "Jack? Jack!"

"Uh, what? Who was that?"

"She literally must have been on her way up, as we were on our way down."

"Who, Monica? Christine? What in the hell is happening here!"

There was no interest in answering. There was no bandwidth left to engage. With all these intense internal ruminations he was stunned in realization, they were in an ordeal transcending any definition that led to its creation. He was suspended in wait for any recourse, if perhaps also spoken to him internally. And one did, resoundingly. For that he spoke wistfully. "We have to go. Now."

*   *   *   *

By the time they emerged from the technological dungeon, the sun sliced sideways through the translucent, yellowy pall of the warm desert air.

Colton depressed the accelerator hard enough to spin the wheels, his car fish-tailing slightly as they settled into a diagonal trek across the vacated parking facility. Passing through the gate with dusty haste, Simms could be seen waving frantically, hands over his head, in the rear-view mirror. They set upon the two-lane road leading away.

"Huh, you think they wanted us to stop?" Jack bit down over nervous laughter. "Okay, so, I take it then you have some idea where we're going to find her?"

"I think... I feel it, Jack. I really feel it."

"Okay, where do you feel like we're going?" he briefly studied Colton, but there was no immediate reply. "Well, wherever the hell it is you really *feel* like getting to, I guess you wanna get there quickly... Jesus!" The speedometer pushed the ninety-fifth mile per hour mark while noting a fifty-five-mile limit sign come and go with certain rapidity.

"A place I said I would never return to... But everything comes around, bringing us back again. There is where it starts and where maybe this ends."

"Poetry, dude. Seriously?"

"No-ho. See... it's one of her songs."

That earned him an incredulous leer. "Mm, that's really sweet. Dude, where the fuck are we go—"

"We're going to where it happened! Listen, I don't know what it is, but something is trying to tell... I mean, I think I finally understand. I see what's happening."

"Riight, and so now it's the apparatus that's..." he stopped through nods and sunken cheeks.

"Something like that. Maybe forces we don't really understand, or how."

"Knew you were gonna— hey, seriously, could you slow up a little?"

The car indeed slowed, but only as they came upon an intersecting two-lane road, on the corner of which was situated a green sign containing a white illustration of an airplane together with an arrow. This drove Colton to turn toward that option, and a cloud of dust soon elevated into the dusky air behind them.

As the hour passed, he at times vocalized newer epiphanies that seemed to come with ever-increasing ease the further they rode along this unknown trek and ultimately determined that there could not exist any understanding that would be described by mere mathematics.

It did manage to allay Jack's sense of alarm enough so to keep him listening, though he was unnerved at times, his fear giving him pause, as much as the fascination pulled him back. "And if we must think Monica, I mean, sorry, this Christine, absconded with this thing. If this is true, why?"

The slowing of the vehicle distracted them. "It's coming."

"What is?" Jack scanned across the windshield quickly.

Colton stared transfixed, "If I'm right, two souls are…" he uttered imperceptibly.

A strange feeling gripped Jack but he kept quiet. Unsure when or how he arrived at this new realm, or whether Colton was experiencing the same, he knew reality around them had slowly morphed. He recalled their journey and arriving in his mind's eye, so the present bizarre nature of the surroundings must have surreptitiously enveloped them. He blinked his eyes, hard, several times. Momentarily, this helped, but no sooner the objects around their vicinity—still vaguely illuminated in the dusky light—appeared as though they were partially phased into their negatives, as one would find in a photography lab. He kept the observation to himself, but he noticed that if he struggled, the setting returned to normal.

If he did not fight it, it tended to phase anew. He was slipping away from the same world that conveyed them to this destination, a most disconcerting sensation he had never encountered before. And considering all, he thus hoped these optics were only artifice of stress, meshing with the twilight.

Colton slowed the car to a stop, and thought, *I don't wanna do this anymore*, while passing his attention back and forth across the horizon. But immediately tuned the apprehension away when of course the discomfort punished him in quasi proportion. He was learning to not fight it. His eyes were transfixed upon a sign not too far in front of them, which read,

"Caution: Trueno Creek Water Shed Next 2 Miles".

Jack espied Colton's lower lip and chin quiver slightly, and reaching cautiously, he rested his hand upon his shoulder, "Hey, Colt," but there was no immediate reply. He imparted a gentle jostle, "Come on, man. What is this? Is this where it happened?"

Colton's chin sagged downward as he bobbed his subtle affirming nods.

"What are you expecting to find?"

Suddenly, Colton came to attention, by jamming the car's transmission back into gear. It only moved very slowly, surpassing several moments while he surveyed both sides of the road as though he had extrasensory input.

"Come on, talk to me. What are you expect—"

"There! Over there," Colton abruptly guided the automobile's halt.

Looking intently through the windshield, Jack struggled to formulate an image through the strange lensing he continued to hide, anything to substantiate something over there. But the flat expanse of pale earth was only patterned by boulders, cacti, and sage brush as though trying to conceal themselves in the last vestiges of the dying daylight. "I don't see it but what am I looking for?" He whispered aggressively, "Fuck, I'm getting' tired of asking!" And

178

cupped his hands over his face before rubbing his eyes futilely.

Colton abruptly accelerated. Cutting the wheel, the car sped at an angle across both lanes and off road. It bounced into darkness, the car rumbling underneath them over desert flotsam.

Jack's voice rattled, "Oh, well... glad you cleared that up!"

They approached a parked Jeep, situated as though it was itself asking why it was there. Soon, he cut the engine, rendering into a moment where the only audible sound was their breathing, and with jaws slightly agape they examined the other vehicle. The interior light was shining, though dimly, and the driver's side door was left ajar. It was clear, no one was around. They partially committed looking at one another.

"Do you want to wait here, or..."

"Oh, man, what the hell is this?" Jack turned his attention through the passenger's side window. "Whenever I think this saga can't turn another weird page." He turned his attention, "Yeah, what the hell, I'll wait."

Colton was already outside the car.

"Colt?"

He implied an answer merely by lowering his attention back through the window.

Jack continued, "How did you know to come out here? How did you know?"

"I don't, exactly... I just do," and he turned his vision toward the other automobile.

Jack subtly bobbed his head, "It's a, uh, sensation thing? Listen, I—" Having snapped his head around Colton was no longer engaging with him from outside the driver's side door, "Where in the fuck... oh,"

Colton leaned into Monica's vehicle, scanning the front and back seats.

Jack exited the car and made haste to join. "I won't ask, because of course, you won't answer, right?"

"It'll all make sense soon enough. Bear with me." He clicked off the headlights switch of Monica's jeep, the interior light becoming a little brighter. Reemerging fully out of the vehicle, he began to scan futilely out into the darkness. "Where is she? She's gotta be here!" He held an article of clothing that he pulled from the vehicle, along with a fatigue-painted object.

The label read, "Falcon-II Tactical Military Backpack."

"So, you think she's out here, huh? What are those you're holding?"

After rifling through the contents in the pack, Colton hesitated a moment before handing an article of clothing over. "Here, smell that."

Jack looked at him strangely as he slowly accepted the blouse.

Colton then foisted the backpack over his shoulder, abruptly turning to show his intent to walk toward the darkness.

"Uh, what?"

"Do it," he pulled the pack higher as he gained distance.

Hesitantly, Jack complied, moving his face closer to the bundled garment. "Flowers?" he hollered, then briefly to self, "Lilacs or some," then yelling, "what about it?"

"It's Christine!" Colton's voice resonated through the dark.

"Who?" but with no answer, he muttered to no one "Hello, kind of scary," Turning his head, he squinted to make sense of their surroundings, but the silhouetting of the vehicle's headlamps still blazing away made it impossible to see outside the vicinity. He then added, "If I may make an understatement, that is." Another futile effort to pierce his eyes through the blackness, he elevated anyway "Colton!" but gave up. "Oh screw this… We have no hope of finding her. Christ, what is he doing?"

Realizing more than ever that he was there, alone, talking to no one, fear began to overtake his senses. He ran to the driver's side of their car and took the keys out of the ignition. The engine ceased and the headlamps starved the landscape of illumination even more. He moved quickly around to the trunk, jangling the keys, turned the lock, and popped it open. He could not see into the bowels of the trunk, as he rifled through its contents.

A distant shrill arrived and this drove his heart rate to quicken, "Am I the only one who hasn't gone completely asylum-bat-shit here?" There were a few clamors of sound as he shifted blindly through the trunk's contents. "Doesn't anyone carry a goddamn flashlight anymore? Wait, of course. She's gotta have one—" he hesitated, as another scream arrived from the hollows. This time it sounded closer. "Fuck the flashlight, I'm not going out there anyway. In fact, what the hell am I… I'm outta here."

Slamming the driver's side door shut, he hesitated. With his elevated heart rate and breathing, then having to register new distant screams audible through the closed windows, he struggled between the morality of a cold escape versus the instincts of self-preservation.

The screams were close, and getting closer, coaxing evolution's victory in the matter. Turning the engine over, the headlamps brightened. "*Oh* Sh—" He jumped up in his seat. "What the—" remaining purposefully still, he immediately attempted to hide the fact that he was panting.

It was Colton, standing in front of the other vehicle, awash in its headlights. He was heavily burdened, with the backpack over a shoulder, carrying what appeared to be a partially naked woman. His chin was down but slowly peering up, as though to take inventory of Jack from that distant vantage point.

For an eternity he looked back at him, hoping the windshield cloaked the fact that he was making direct eye-contact with horror. Some part of him knew controlling the situation was hopeless. He felt as though he had walked in on someone in the middle of a shameful act, seeing something he should not be seeing altogether. He did his best ventriloquist, "Okay, what are ya gonna do next?"

After another moment of that blank exchange, Colton rotated slowly away.

Jack watched as Colton lay her gently down inside, probably the backseat, re-emerged, and softly closed the door. He looked down into the darkness of the seat, seeking the transmission wand and as he slid it into the drive slot, right at that instant, a second longer, he would have sprayed dust in his rear view. But his sight rose and it was instantly drawn to a figure standing directly outside the driver's side door, startling him again.

"Where are you going?"

Jack's expression morphed more civil at hearing the coherency of that question. It was an observation sorely needed, perhaps at an abstract level realizing a hope, that this whole scenario had an explanation in sync with sanity. "Huh?" he yelled back, his eyebrows furled, surreptitiously repositioning the transmission to park.

"I said, where are you going?"

He took a deep breath then leaned his head on the steering wheel, as though seeking empathy, but instead managed to inadvertently depress the horn. "Oh! shit," and slammed his palm on the wheel. Fear, at least for the moment, was settling enough to crack the door, the ensuing slam intending to garner specific attention. "Colton, talk to me right now, man. Did you do something… to her? To Monica?"

Colton twitched his eyes back and forth upon Jack's, then slowly, moved them off as he stepped away. Waving his hand in circular motion, "Come here."

"Why?"

"Just Come on."

I guess I'm not getting out of this either way. He's not gonna kill her twice. Stepping around the Jeep so as to see into the back seat, he noticed the curvature of the woman. Startled at first, the sight of her breast elevating slowly made him sigh.

"She's fine."

"I don't know if I'd call that fine, man." Upon closer inspection of the woman's figure, which was curled in a semi-fetal position, she did not appear to actually be harmed, he studied what had become only a vaguely familiar profile of her face, *why is she diff*— He erected his posture, "This may not be appropriate timing, but um…" clasping his hands behind his head, he traipsed once in a circle. "I gotta get back, man. I'm not sure what," he waved his hand, "all this is about, but I'm not standing out here in this God-forsaken landscape for another minute. Frankly, all this for that matter. I'm not totally sure there isn't something affecting you, either, pal." He then turned and moved back toward the salvation of the other vehicle. "And I got to be honest, I'm getting a headache now too!"

"I know now what that is, what the headaches are," Colton elevated his voice, "Jack!"

He only hesitated in his gait, but resumed his determination to leave.

Colton then spoke even louder to span the growing distance, "I know now what the manifestations in Monica are all about."

Upon arriving at the driver's side door, he did not pull the handle, instead standing with his hands on his hips, staring blankly down across the hood.

"It's what I was trying to explain to you, on the ride over. Jack, please."

Turning slowly, he suppressed anger, "All right, fine. You have an explanation for all this."

"Jack. It's the device, okay. Somehow what we've created… it's affecting people."

Only partially committing attention, Jack looked toward the night sky muttering, "This shit is impossible." Then turning more directly towards his companion, he spoke audible, "So, tell me, it's influencing her now," through sarcasm. How, why?"

"I… can't answer that. I don't know precisely how. I don't know why."

"Is this what you were talking about before, about the 'dealing with strange forces'?" he then said frustrated to the open air, "That's just stupid trope. It's's not something one takes that seriously."

"I think… see?" Colton rubbed the back of his neck, "the headaches are gone. How about that?"

"Don't do that!" traipsing again. "Don't try to sell this, or change the subject."

"Look, whatever it is, it's clearly having some lasting impact on her mind. I don't know, maybe it only needs to do it once, or—"

"Do *what* once?"

"Forget it… I don't see any trace that Monica even exists anymore." He noted Jack's on-going astonished expression. "She has become, the incarnation of a memory. Or, at least, I don't know where those end and she begins anymore; perhaps a fusion, or newer paradigm—"

"And you like it, don't you? You want this, don't you?"

Subtly nodding, "I… But I can't allow it, can I?"

"Wha-hut! You're seriously asking that."

Almost instantly upon that statement, the ambience was perturbed by both the sound of a car door opening, as well, unrelated, flickering lights emanating from the general direction of the road from some distance away. Both turned their heads back and forth between these distractions.

The vehicle began to slope down the side of the ravine approximately a mile away, assuming the trajectory along the path they had also arrived upon. Their heads switched back towards Monica, who had left the vehicle. She was indescribably beautiful as her frame was illuminated by

Colton's on-washing headlights; both fought to ignore this realization, one that was only in part visual.

The police cruiser made furthering awareness of its intent when it broke their concentration, sounding off its siren in two quick chirps.

Jack whined, "Cops? We gotta deal with the fuckin' cops now?"

Colton began an unwavering gaze focused on Monica, his report taking on a monochromatic delivery, "How long could this continue?"

The blanket she donned draped loosely from her frame like a painting in a Roman cathedral. Her expression was soft, glowing, alike the ineffable yet unmistakable ecstatic vibrancy of a woman with child. Her approach openly biased toward Colton.

Though it was clear it was not he she sought, this still impelled Jack to step back in apprehension. His attention was being pulled in different directions as he turned his head quickly between the specter of Colton and Monica's gathering union, while being worrisome of the approaching law enforcement.

Abruptly, the police cruiser unexpectedly slowed along its approach. The roof of the vehicle was still fired up with its red and blue flickering lights, when it came to its halt, turning slightly askew as it did. The doors flung open with an air of violence. Two officers stumbled out, walking labored, one toward the front of the car, the other with his head tipped skyward while arms dangled like torpid ropes by his side.

Jack forced a deep cycle of respiration, *Okay*, then winced his closed eyes before attempting his line of sight, side to side, squinting, trying to make sense of it all. The officers were still too far off from their immediate vicinity, too far to ascertain what, if anything, was intelligibly audible; for a moment he thought he heard only wailing, certainly nothing of a pleasant vocalization. Then, the one officer who had meandered toward the front of the police cruiser collapsed to his knees, clasping his hands on either side of his head. The other vanished into the darkness, as though he were a zombie drawn away by a curious sound.

His own head was ringing loudly now with the discomfort. The surrealism of the setting contributing, the sensory input approaching an overload. Still, he conjured energy, and pressing the butt of his palms against his temples he sounded off, "Colton. Colton! Are you seeing this, man?" But there was, of course, no answer. "Colt!" as he turned toward them.

Monica was inside Colton's virtual comfort zone. The man's eyes appeared to be closed, though he was uncertain as a wind had kicked up in the interim and occasional shrouds of dust were intermittent. What he could make out was that he was limp in physical form, either powerless, or unwilling to prevent whatever this interaction was from taking place, *but I thought... been together.* Still, being that the ambiance did not exactly lend comfortability to the setting by a vast margin, that did not position him very well for any interpretation of what was presently going on between them. His own head was getting worse. Retching from a sensation that was more like telling him he nauseated, without his feeling any pain his legs also began to feel wobbly. These physicalities together with all that was transpiring, did not immediately lend to him intervening, either. So he just watched, through coughs instead.

She raised her hand with slow certitude to make contact with Colton's face, appearing to place it upon his cheek. He tipped his head, slightly forward at an angle, as though welcoming her caress. The posturing was that of relief, or even nourishment after a long repast. And so, too, was Jack relieved. These immediate reads offered what he sought, a means to allay an uncertain dread, giving him confidence to try. "Colton! You have to fight this," he ended with an, "ow," putting the butts of his palms again to his temples.

It succeeded in Monica turning her face in his favor with an expression only construed as rage, eyes like he had never seen on a human being. This filled his frame of mind anew with terror.

With immediate import, stepping back a small distance seemed more than a prudent response, and upon making this defensive movement, Monica's mien quelled. He got the message. She then returned her attention, an expression warming to its previous dynamic. Reaching down to Colton's arm, she guided it upwards, then directed just the fingertips to contact her forehead. In much the same calculated fluidity, then guided the palm of his other hand to her midriff. The instant of this contact seemed to induce his knees to buckle.

"Oh, God, NO!" Jack exclaimed. The wail sounded of sadness, the sobbing flitting in the wind as breezes freshened past his ears and nape, carrying more dust.

Colton cradled his head in his hands, letting gravity win, and pressed his knees to the earth. His elbows soon followed, finally folding into the fetal position altogether upon the ground.

Jack's eyes were blurry from discomfort, dust, and anxiety, so he could not make out exactly how Monica reacted to Colton's prostration before her.

Urgency overwhelmed and got the better of him as he tried to sort this all out. Both officers had agonized from afar, so it was a foregone conclusion their assistance was not even plausible. If for fight-or-flight instinct alone, in one last burst, he attempted to overcome his condition, attempting to rush to Colton's aid.

He closed no closer than a few feet of their position, when Monica raised her hand, fingers and thumb splayed, while not breaking her concentration toward Colton in the least...

22
DESIGNATION

His eyes slowly opened to a brilliant light, so much that he strained; it forced him to blink several times rapidly. A voice emanated from a blurry frame, "You okay, Sully?" the image asked.

Jack's voice was slightly labored, "Colt, what... happened, man?" He sat up and shook his head, briefly groping the back of his neck. Then, as he rubbed both his temples, he instead took the wires dangling from them between his index fingers and thumb, his eyes looking up upon making the discovery. Taking further inventory of the fact that he was upon a bed, he then swung his legs over the side, as though preparing to stand.

Colton quickly approached him to assist, "you're ready then?"

Jack's tone came across a bit stronger, "Ready? Ready for what? What's going on here?" He instinctively reached up to his left bicep. "What's this, I'm being monitored?" Thin cables fell precipitously from a black band. "I've been out? I mean, out out? How did I..." he sat back down on the edge of the bed while his eyes followed along a thin metallic pipe below which draped white curtains, "...end up in here?" he finished with an expression that flirted with anger. "Obviously, this is a hospital then."

Colton was unavailable, pacing while squeezing his bottom lip, and his eyes dancing along the floor. Coming to a stop, he leaned, arms stretched downward, in order to peer over the windowsill. He turned back to scan their immediate cordoned-off region. Briefly acknowledging Jack's eye contact. "It is. You're at Mercer Hospital, here in town," finishing with a couple of quick nods.

"It's kinda fuzzy. We were heading out—"

"I gotta work on getting us out of here. We're trapped momentarily." Colton quietly said. He then leaned forward and walked, passing the bed to where he then slowly parted a small gap in the privacy curtains.

Jack peered down over his frame, took note of being clad in the usual hospital garb, and spoke, "How long have I been here?"

Colton's tone was devoid of much expression, "It's been several hours. You don't remember anything?"

"I think... Up to a point. We were looking for Monica. Not sure why but you had us out in some godforsaken terrain. Something about a dominion? And... wait. Actually, I remember something about the police? And... headlights," he looked down, shaking his head in quick small movements. "Wait..." he looked toward Colton. "You were on your knees, I think." His face then relaxed, "Shit. Sorry man. That's... all I got. Musta been one hell of a party, huh?"

Colton again parted a small gap in the curtains. He spoke again as though half committed to the reality of the scene. "Wow." His head tipped slightly side to side, to gain a better perspective of activity taking place outside the door to their room. "You really don't remember much else?"

"No, I don't think I do. Hey, what's going on out there?"

Colton became more concerned about the present, continuing to peer covertly back through the gap in the curtains that he parted with his index finger. "There's a couple of police officers standing guard outside the door to the hall. I'm not sure what—" He interrupted himself, struck with Jack's recollection. He half turned his head around toward him, but then slowly back toward the gap in the curtains. He finished the sentence, "...they are there for."

Jack, with a labored tone, "Ooh, right, I remember now telling about them. Oh, man, dude. What the hell happened? We're in some sort of shit?" his tone was between fear and sarcasm.

"Um, let's keep it down. Hey, if you thought you had to, do you think you can stand, walk, get around?"

"Which arm and leg?" His sarcasm signaled his readiness.

This prompted Colton to look over to him.

Jack stood, having removed the plunger leads that attached to his temples already. "No permanent damage over here." he finished. "So, where the fuck are my clothes?"

Colton interrupted, "Oh, sh— you took the sensors off. Damn, they're gonna come in—" He was interrupted as a click emanated from the room's door. He backed away from the curtains.

A woman in light blue pants and a short sleeve shirt widened the gap behind him, then stepped through, clipboard in hand. A stethoscope and other cords took a serpentine form about her nape. "Oh, I see we've regained consciousness." She stepped closer to Jack, "And removed our monitoring leads," her tone was that of inconvenience. She then switched her attention briefly toward Colton to ask, "And you are?" then returned to tending to Jack. She asked him to open his mouth as she pulled a small pen flashlight from her breast pocket. "Good. Now, please stick out your tongue." Jack complied. She moved the pen from one internal cheek to the other. "Okay, you can close your mouth." She then probed the conical end of an audiometer into each of his ears, and asked him to indicate if and when he heard a single ping.

"Okay, he's awake. Can we go now?" The question was an attempt at probing to see if the officers were there for Jack.

The nurse had placed her index finger and thumb gently upon Jack's eyelids, and parted them open so as to briefly shine a pen light upon his pupils. Laughing lightly, "Up and leave. It's not up to me. And you are?" she asked again.

"I'm a friend. I… heard he might be down here."

"Oh." Her eyebrows twitched up and down a few times quickly, settling into an expression that suggested Colton sounded odd. She did this while continuing to check Jack's eyesight.

Jack pulled back from her pen light, "Agh, ow." He began rubbing his eyes.

The nurse reached for and clicked a writing pen then spoke softly as though speaking to herself, while writing upon the clipboard. "Patient currently appears to exhibit a lack of pupillary light reflex."

"Huh, excuse me?"

Sounding educational and empathetic, she began, "It means that when you are exposed to bright light your pupil is supposed to contract so that less light—"

"I know what it means," he cut her off impatiently while cupping a hand backward toward his chest, "what does it mean for me?"

The nurse smiled. "It's a typical symptom in those coming out of a coma, concussion, severe head trauma, that sort of thing. It's a lingering effect."

"Lingering effe... Excuse me if that smile is less than reassuring, ma'am." He then looked over at Colton, "I was in a fucking coma?"

"We don't know exactly," the nurse said. "In the minimum, some form of seizure. Your Rancho Los Amigos Scale values suggested," she paused to glance at the clipboard, "...conscious but unresponsive. That's about an eight or nine on the scale; fifteen being as sober as an astronaut. Yet, peculiar, those electrodes you removed? they were picking up higher functionality all along, so we are not sure what the issue really was. Your other vital signs were strong, unaffected. Doctor Wielder, the Neurologist on staff, he'll be in soon to evaluate you."

"Doctor, who... what?"

"Wielder. Staff Neurologist."

Colton asked, "Hey, before you go. Would you, uh, know why," pointing a thumb over shoulder, "officers... in the hall?"

"The police? Not sure," she took to flipping over a page on her clipboard, "it, ah, says here," running an index finger, "da-ta-da... officers dispatched... failed report... hm, suspicious activity; two officers and civilian taken to..." she stopped reading to address him directly, "I'm not law enforcement. My guess, it might have something to do with that?" twitching a smile, she then engaged with a vitals-monitor.

Jack looked quickly back and forth between them, with more than a subtle air of concern. "What is a... Amigos Scale?" then, whispering to Colton, "You were in this... coma, too?"

"No," he said covertly, "I... it's hard to explain." He was unsure of what he could, or should divulge within earshot of this stranger. "I remember dreaming. Odd, strange... It's hard to describe. But, I woke up at a friend's home."

Jack frowned, "A friend? What does this have to do... Oh, you mean..."

Colton waved him to stop as his eyes darted imperceptibly toward the nurse.

Jack's eyes grew slightly larger as he was distracted towards one side.

"So, again, I am going to deliver the status of Jack here; doctor Wielder, from Neurology, will be in soon."

They waited for the sound of the door to click shut, outside the confines of their curtain-enclosed area. "No way, man. I'm outta here, dude," Jack implored. "I'm not waiting around for that shit."

"I'm with you. If we can get past these cops somehow."

"Why? Are we sure they're here for us?"

"I don't want to wait around to find out. Try walking around."

"I'm fine." Jack hopped off the edge of the bed to his feet, pupils or not and took turns shaking each foot out in front of him. "Wow, what a night, eh? Musta been some party" He continued to speak softly, "Hey, how the hell did you get by these guys?"

"They weren't there when I got here. They showed up not long ago. Wait a second, the window..." he trailed off as he stepped energetically, squaring himself and leaning a look over the sill, "Oh, man, that's right, we're on the second floor. Shit." He began fidgeting, "How do you get these open?"

Jack stepped to the window next to him and peered down, "We can't jump that. Wait, so it was you who brought me to the hospital?"

"I think we can make it. No, I assumed they brought you in. Listen, we can make that... I think we can jump that, Jack."

"Then what, run from the cops with a couple broken legs? I knew you were nuts, but... Jesus. I have zero memory beyond what I told you earlier. How did I get here?"

"Come on, that's not more than fifteen feet." He continued to size up the fall.

Jack's voice wobbled. "Dude, not from fifteen feet."

"We only need six or so feet to where we might jump the rest of that distance safely." Colton moved his head from side to side to make sure the darkness was not hindering his depth perception as to how far the ground really was beneath them. He then turned from the window and quickly pulled back the blankets from the bed. "Here, check the closet over there, see if there are any linens."

"Yes, right... of course!"

"Keep it down. Jesus." Colton pulled the top sheet out of its tucked in neatness and rolled it into a cylinder, "This is seven feet long corner to corner, easy. But that still leaves us with an eleven-foot drop give or take. Shit."

"Not if we do it Three Stooges-style." Jack's tone encouraged Colton's attention.

"I wonder... would that work?"

Within a few moments they had a twelve-feet worth of sheet-rope they had rolled up and tied off the ends. They moved swiftly, knowing the officers would be sequestering them once Wielder, the Neurologist, finished his probing.

Colton urged, "Come on. We gotta hurry if we're going to make this work."

Jack slid the window open.

Colton spoke as he observed his ease in doing so, "How did you? Never mind."

"Oh, crap. The screen won't open or..."

"Come on." He angled in front of Jack and noted that the edges of the screen were all sealed flush; only the glass of the window slid open. "There's gotta be something to... You wouldn't happen to have a pocket knife?"

"Huh?"

"I mean, with your street clothes?"

"Still no. In fact, why am I still wearing this hospital shit?"

The main door to the room clicked open, and they froze in a shared look of panic, collectively breathing inaudibly. The male voices could be heard exchanging with one another; though, what was being said was not very well discerned.

Jack whispered, "Some... something about patient?"

He nodded a reply while looking off to the side, then adjusted his ear at an angle in order to clarify. With an urgent whisper, "Suspect? Oh, man. I heard that." The door then clicked closed, with no one having actually entered the room. They could still vaguely make out a conversation near the door. "Come on, no time." He then stepped quickly between the closet, drawers, and a cabinet, "See if you can find a knife, anything to cut the—" a whizzing sound interrupted him.

"I found it over in those drawers there, the ones that say Supply and Storage?"

"Right. Supply and storage. Why didn't I think of that?"

Jack finished making the orthogonal incision across the screen, while Colton pulled the bed closer to the window and tied off one end of the sheet-rope to a leg. It was still dark outside but a slight wash of light was beginning in the eastern horizon, signaling they were on the recovery side of the night.

Colton gave the sheet-rope three vigorous jerks to test its strength, then wended his way out the window.

Jack watched as he descended.

Approximately eight-feet from the ground, Colton let go and when his feet hit the ground, rolled out to one side then jumped back to his feet. "Come on, hurry." He stressed his whisper.

Jack hesitated, "Is now a good time to mention?" in similar speak.

Looking left then right in rapid succession he stressed again, "What?"

"I'm acrophobic?"

"Will you stop screwing around!"

"Fuck it. Okay, fine." Jack eased his way out of the window, clasping the sheet inside his fists. Straining to speak in between suppressing grunts, he precipitated from the edge of the window above. "By the way... I... seriously am going to re... con... sider the nature... of... our... corres... pondence." He stopped his descent and looked down from about three-feet higher than Colton's shoulders. He then allowed the remaining length to slip through his loosened grasp all at once. "Ah. Shit!" he exclaimed soon after rolling out from the impact.

"You okay?"

"I don't know. My ankle, it kinda popped." Jack stood to his feet and proceded to limp around. "I think I'm okay."

Colton turned his head around the courtyard through the dark, "Question is, where the hell are we in relation to where I parked her jeep." He faded off. "Come on, this way."

Jack whispered urgently while they fled quickly through the darkened courtyard, "Whose jeep? Where are we going? I can't go back to my house, the cops are probably waiting there, right?"

"The problem is—" Colton interrupted himself. "Wait. Stop here." They came to an abrupt halt at the corner of a building, using the terminus between the darkness and the parking lot's artificial light. They were panting as they looked around. Colton stole an eyeful from around the corner.

"What do ya see?" Jack breathed, "What's the problem?" he didn't wait for a response. "Colt, has it occurred to you?"

"I think it's clear, we can make it. Come, there's the jeep; let's go."

They wended the vehicle slowly down the aisle of the parking lot, turning covertly toward the gate. As the arm came down in their rear window, relief materialized while Mercer Hospital receded behind them.

Police lights began flickering in front of them, heading in their general direction, but still at some distance on the opposite side of the road.

"Duck a little," Colton whispered.

"Okay. But why are you whispering? I don't think anyone can really hear us?" The police cruiser zipped past them, prompting him, "Man, that's gotta be for us, huh?"

"Mm. Maybe. Probably."

Two more cruisers turned onto the road ahead via an intersecting street, their blue lights flickering from their roofs. Colton moved the car to the right-hand side of the road along with the others in their immediate traffic procession instinctively, handling the vehicle as inconspicuously as imaginable. Their car jostled slightly as the Doppler of sirens passed through the windows.

Steadily, the morning twilight began exposing the passing scenery. "Yup. I'd have to say that was probably for us. We should take a circuitous route. I don't think we can go to my place either though. Damn."

"Right, good call. Hey, so…"

"Uh huh, go ahead?" Colton encouraged.

"Did it occur to you, if we didn't do anything. I mean, did we? Why the—"

"It's not… that simple. Not anymore. Remember those two officers wondering in the desert?"

"Uh. No. Wait… may-be vague-ly. What about 'em?"

"They didn't make it."

"What does that mean, didn't make what? You mean…"

Colton replied deadpan, "Whatever got you, I can only assume must have got them."

Jack stared mortified at Colton's profile.

He acknowledged with a head-turn before adding, "Only… it didn't work out so well for them."

Jack turned between his profile and the windshield, "And you've come by this information how?"

"I don't know. Listen, I don't know where Monica is either, or… Dominion for that matter. I… there's no way I can go back to the lab now. Shit, I don't know where the hell we can go?"

23
CLARIFICATION

The scope and specter of the previous night fueled their angst, not to mention, purposed the subsequent escape from the confines of the hospital. It all quite naturally conjured too much unsettling disquietude to assume their standard haunts were anything close to accessible. A circumstance empirically proven by the fact that they first tried to covertly approach Jack's residence, but kept on rolling through the intersection at the end of the road, when they saw from afar law enforcement automobiles aggregated near his flat. And present unknown whereabouts, blessed them with alternate strategy and planning.

"There's only one problem, Colt, we're in Monica's jeep. It's got military designations like… on *it*."

Positioning the vehicle several adjacent streets away, they moved stealthily through nearing properties in starts and frets. Piling over fences, even narrowly escaping the jaws of an irate chained up Doberman, they finally arriving at the back of Karen's home. It was the only solitude they could connect recent events with relative safety.

She was glad to see Jack; that much was clear. Though, a pall hung over all three, and an uneasy silence, as she gently ran her thumbnail back and forth across her bottom lip, taking turns at them with her eyes. The recently muted television flickering its changing images by and by.

She surmised it was time to take up a position next to her lover upon a sofa, where she wanted to be anyway. With a seamless transition, she snuggled her rear close to his and took to observing Colton silently. Leaning her mouth to his ear, "What's this despondence, what's wrong with him?" she whispered, "did something happen?"

Forcibly acting out a deeper release of air from his lungs, Jack spoke softly. "Oh, man, Karen, I... Something happened, babe... out there, in the desert. And it was really fuckin..."

Her expression drew his to a series of images on the television screen. Perhaps unconsciously, she had processed a connection between what was showing with what he just said. It was an aerial perspective, pivoting around a scene of an abandoned police cruiser, its doors left ajar amid a terrain of erratic boulders, sage brush, and cacti. It was cordoned from a high vantage point, giving the allusion they were overlooking a crime scene. Indeed, there was even the faint outline of yellow tape, leaving no doubt that at a minimum, this was a region of acute suspicion. People could also be seen milling about the vicinity as the elevated perspective rotated.

Abruptly leaning away, far enough to expose a sardonic expression, she said, "Really?"

Clearing his throat, if Jack had a way to hide his head he might have done so. Rising to his feet, he stepped away, hands to hips. Firing rounds of the remote control toward the television the increasing volume came into focus.

"...As authorities are baffled to explain what might have taken place twenty-two miles outside the township of San Quixote overnight into early this morning. Two officers were found unconscious outside their police cruiser; its engine still running, the emergency lights still activated. Wanted for questioning is an APIT student identified as John T. Sullivan, who was also found lying unresponsive nearby. Sullivan and the two officers were taken to Mercer hospital for evaluation where it is said that Sullivan regained consciousness some hours later. We now go live to reporter Kirkland Foster, on the scene. Kirk?"

Jack looked over at Colton and noticed that he appeared almost uninterested. The man's eyes transfixed while he leaned on the frame of the living room's large picture window, gazing aimlessly through the glass. Turning his attention back toward the television, he seated himself again next to the one source in his world offering comfort.

"...Yes, thank you, Randy. Sullivan was brought here, to Mercer Memorial hospital for evaluation where he regained consciousness. However, he and an unknown associate, avoided questioning by escaping out the hospital window you see behind me, here," the reporter's tone was subtly astonished, as he motioned his hand over a shoulder. The camera focused upon an open window with what appeared to be bedroom linens dangling gently in a breeze.

The sound of Karen's voice layered over, "What the hell, you guys!"

"Wait... shh!" Jack managed to cease her nervous laugh. "I— we need to hear this."

"...they were successful at evading grounds before officers stationed at the scene had any chance to interview Sullivan. However, according to the law enforcement official in charge of the investigation it is not currently known what, if any correlation, there is between this person of interest, and the officers found on scene. Police admittedly say that presently, they do not have any answers. Sadly, as of last report, one of the two officers, identified as Lieutenant Stony M. Williams, passed away this morning, while officer Randal G. Holmes, has yet to regain consciousness... No cause for their condition has yet been released by hospital officials. The lead investigator says they are intensifying their search for the Sullivan—"

The television screen suddenly went blank.

Karen instinctively looked toward Jack, who was frozen, extending the remote control, staring agog at the blackened screen.

He slowly turned his attention to the erstwhile silent Colton, still seemingly oblivious to the significance of what had aired and pressed a shoulder into the picture window's frame, vacantly observing the reality beyond the glass. This triggered him to sound off, "Hello, dude. Are you paying attention? Do you realize what this means!" He rose to his feet in a start and took to pacing, as he muttered more to himself, "I knew I should have bailed on this shit when it got weird... this is what I get."

Colton finally spoke, "It did that."

Karen initially ignored him, angling her attention toward Jack, "Honey, I understand, but try and remain calm. The reporter only said questioning. You are not under arrest," then she shifted tone, "Colton... who did what?"

Jack interceded, "What do you mean, remain calm? A cop is dead. One is in a coma, and," he chirped an ironic chortle, "they think we had something to do with it!" Dramatic with haste, he moved to place his hands evenly upon her shoulders while studying her eyes. "Two cops, you understand? Without any other answers, they're gonna come looking for us."

Karen's expression commiserated, if perhaps only reflective of the pained one on his face. She then smiled subtly, "Honey, you're not a killer... are you? Heh. I think it'll be okay." Speaking more to the room, "Why exactly did you guys sneak away from the hospital?" her attention switched back and forth. "I mean, what's wrong with just talk—"

"Ho-ho, man. Can you imagine that, Colt?"

"All right, fine. Then talk to me. What's really going on here? Am I getting drawn into something legitimately bad here, or..."

"It wasn't her," Colton signaled his return to present. With several blinks he turned to address them more directly, "It was... it."

"Who exactly are we talking about?" Karen turned her attention quickly back and forth.

"Don't look at me," Jack said.

"As far as I can see... or sense. Actually, she has been totally transmuted into someone else." Part of Colton's tone

201

was relief, as though he were in need of venting a truth. "It's incredible, that the most logical explanation, can't be conveyed using rational terms. This whole situation is outside the bounds of... rationality," he half-emitted a laugh schwa. "So, I'm going to say it. For all the mathematics, all the physical formulas that were invoked for the emergence of this technology, its presence simply cannot be quantified by any of those governing principles that compose its design."

"There's a word for that, it's right on the tip of my—"

"Gestalt?" Karen advanced as she rose and adjusted her skirt. With her arms crossed she then positioned herself square before Colton and speaking as though in a session with one of her psychotherapy subjects, "Please describe this presence?"

"Ah, what he means is that his lady friend, Monica, him too for that matter," Jack waited for body language to signal affirmation, "well, the two officers anyway. Me. And, who knows who the hell else... we've all been somehow... influenced by this thing."

"Okay, still no straight answers. Let's try it this way, what do you mean, influenced?" she ended in a smidgen of irreverence. "We'll get to what this *thing* is later."

"He means it can communicate. Or, in a way."

"Uh, okay. And yes, communication can certainly lead to influence. In fact, some might even suggest that is a requirement. Heh, but what do you mean something deeper? Like, you don't mean in a *hello* sort of way, then?"

"He means without speaking, Karen. Perhaps of greater importance, ah-heh, it can be quite, uh, how to say... persuasive, in the way it goes about saying hello, too."

"Some... kind of... control" Colton offered barely audibly.

"Mm, maybe control really is the best word." Jack then stepped to place both hands to her shoulders. "The minds of people," again seeking approval for the assessment.

"You guys mean, if I follow, you're suggesting you've created a form of... psionic?" she ended through a bit of laughter. "Wait, let's back up. What are you guys talking about in the first place? You're talking about a thing? Who did what and to whom... you said *it*?"

"Psionic?" Jack directed to Colton.

Colton's brow line arched back at him.

"Uh, no, forget that, guys, I wasn't serious," she pleaded.

Neither of them seemed interested in letting go of her jest.

She breathed deeply, "Okay, fine. It's an area of *meta-physical* science. The term implies using telepathy to induce... paranormal effects, if you will," she ended dismissively, "anyway, who or what are you guys talking about, please?" This time she encouraged by abandoning her sarcasm entirely.

They were perfectly willing to run with that at this point. It was simple, elegant, and however bizarre the definition, it still gave the least peregrinations for explaining so many of the enigmatic experiences to date.

"Trying to reach out to you?" She directed at Colton. "It affected people. But why not just reach out to you, then, directly? Via, what, the console... some way in the working environment. I mean, let us pretend for a moment that the individuals of present company have not lost their minds over what's going on with this thing," she ended under rolled eyes.

Colton slowly nodded and continued, "Why go through the trouble of... shit, do we actually gotta call that channeling now?" his incredulity fading to expletives under his breath.

"Whoa, whoa, whoa. Guys, I said, I wasn't serious about the psionic, that's just a definition. There's no way you've really—"

"But it did. I mean, at first it tried to. Back in the lab... tried using the console. I think... it evolved, so to speak?

Frankly, I don't know where reality broke, and the experiences began."

"Who, what's this thing?" She demanded. "Would you guys gimme a fuckin' break and coherently say who or what in the hell it is you're talking about?"

Colton hurried in, "I'm just trying to piece this together."

"Honey, please hold on, we'll explain." Jack asked Colton, "How... when? You didn't tell anyone?"

"I wasn't sure what to make of it at the time, I—"

"Wait a second. You mean that time? When the recorder failed. The recorder never did fail, did it?" Jack's cadence shifted slowly, "because the recorder would never have been able to... in the first place. Right?"

Colton finally gave one of his assessments a signal of affirmation. Moving to the sofa, he placed his hands on the crown of his head after sinking into the cushion.

"So, you knew then, didn't you? That it could do this to people. To me? To those cops!"

"Knew what? Talk to me. God, you guys are either impossible, or insane."

"Come on, Jack. Give us a break over here. There's no way we, I mean, I could have known back then what that was. What was happening."

"For fuck sake, whaat!? Or get out," Karen contorted a smile into ire, "I'm done."

"I'm sorry, honey," Jack started, "so much has happened. Where do we begin? Colton came up with an interesting experimental design, thinking that certain nano-scaled anatomical structures in the human brain might," he paused to glance in Colton's favor, "vibrate, is the best word? These vibration give rise to brain-waves. He asked for my assistance, and together we used solid state physical components to, well... prove it. By mimicking components believed crucial in neural transmittance."

She was already nodding, "Right, I know about your project."

"So," Colton entered, "the purpose then was to artificially create e-e-g wave patterns... from an artificial source of course. And, well, here we are. There's no easy explanation, and frankly, I wouldn't have known any of this... this gestalt like you say, were even remotely possible."

"Let alone where to begin to describe the shit we've been through since turning that damn thing on," Jack added.

"Hold it." She raised a hand. "Artificial e-e-gs?" turning her attention quickly between them. "That more specifically, that is what the project was?" allowing no answer. "Honey, does this have anything to do with that postnatal encephalograph you gave me a while ago?" She took the lack of response as affirmation. "That's... extraordinary."

"Which part?" Jack angled at both of them.

She aired urgency. "Guys, seriously? those were the same e-e-gs... for real?"

Nodding slightly downward, they sensed a brewing admonishment.

"You told me those were..." she shorted at Jack.

"Yeah, I know, I said that. I'm sorry. I guess I kinda... lied to you there. But... I mean, we," moving his hand to signal the collection of them, "needed an educated perspective, and—"

She waved off his explanation, "Actually, you're right, forget it. Never mind. Look, I understand. You needed a control subject. I was in the right place at the right time. It's one of our hardest experimental challenges over here in my world, to create an objective data set." She then smiled, "Just don't do it again."

"Understood," Jack raised both hands through a nose laugh.

"But if that's true, the implications would be..." her tone shifted as though completing the scolding, "Gentlemen, those e-e-gs you showed me, those were not random. I'm telling you, that was a live, early *sentient* being I analyzed.

205

You understand me, sentient!" Her eyes pierced them in equal measure.

Colton moved his attention back through the window. "The sum of all those vibrations... I dunno, there's gotta be some kind of additional quantum feed-back. Some deeper purpose... to nature all along. Somehow slipped by the calculation... We've tapped into—"

"Purpose?"

"Mm, right into the depths of it. Some kind of fragmented consciousness via the energy of the vibration, Jack. But I'm just speculating... uhm, based on these evidences."

"And now, what do we have?"

"Well, let's think about this for a moment," turning to fully engage them, "does any newborn anything understand its own existence?"

Karen filled the ensuing silence. "Twenty-three years."

"Twenty-three, eh" Jack half acknowledged while rubbing one of his balled fists.

"Everyone is diff... I mean, every human being is different, that is." She rolled her eyes. "But for the sake of discussion, twenty-three years, on average, that's about what it takes to fully realize the faculty spectrum of the mind. I'm..." she paused with a head shake, "I'm just trying to understand all this. If true, I'm trying to imagine what it would be like if all of holistic reality were suddenly turned on like that. Like, in the absence of a fuller component cognition. From a state of utter nothingness, to an explosion of awareness, without natural buffers. You know, sight, sound, tactility? All or any plausible sensory inputs for that matter, delivering information through cognitive gates, with no prior framework for... Oh my God! Infants emerge from the womb in a square-mouthed rage for a reason, you guys." Her tone ended as though they should have known better.

"Yeah, right, we get what you mean, babe. Well, Colt, this just keeps getting better and better, doesn't it?"

"Abject terror is more like it," Colton shifted his eyes toward them.

"Well, hold it. Let's consider, not necessarily," she wagged her index finger. "If we're using the human mind as our paradigm, for your comparison that is."

"Oh, no, here she goes."

She mocked a snarl. "The thing is, the base-line component for fear is *instinct*-rooted."

"Oh, right, I see where you're going. Right," Colton synced. "However, the problem here, we… uh, sorry, Jack, *I* based my calculations on what is observable in the human neuro- constructs." He then redirected toward her. "Doesn't that make your present assumption, the baser self-preservation model a little less coherent?"

"Uh, right! Exactly what I was thinking," Jack filled the long gap.

"I still can't get over this. You're talking about a bundle of wires toting electrons, right, I mean, your project?" she begged for a toe-hold on reality.

"Well, sarcasm aside, babe, what's in a brain?"

"No! Honey," she said towards both, "who are you talking to? of course. Guys, it took nature, oh, I don't know, a billion years to create the sentience you're suggesting here, okay?"

Jack turned that into a segue and spoke sullenly toward Colton, "I mean, it's one thing to pull that off, dude, but the consequences."

"What those are, we very probably have not even seen the half of if fully realized, I'm afraid."

"Still, *those* printouts, the ones I reviewed? They were produced by your actual technology?"

Jack turned his eyes toward the floor in gentle nods.

"That's… wow."

"I tell you one of those so-called *consequences*. Try a, I dunno, how about self-aware psionic resonator," trenchantly, "one apparently capable of affecting people's—you know, honey... it's actually kind of fascinating, isn't it"

The collection of the three of them were left momentarily speechless.

Jack filled the void, "Can that happen? Can we really turn on a soul, like what she's describing? It'd be like what... some kind of spiritual Big Bang. Whole universe... trapped inside that thing's skull," he fashioned quotation marks in the air.

Colton signaled this with a downward hand wave, "I don't know about all that, but... by modeling nature with this technology, some form or the other of sentience... as fantastic as it is must have. But all other explanations aside, that appears to be the case. And, yeah... it's not a huge intuitive leap to assume that sentience in present context would, uh, unfortunately terrified might be a valid outcome."

They stared at him.

"Hey, who knows to what extent or capabilities that represents." The statement was not entirely true, for he had already suspected deeper, exceptional states; perhaps too much so for even this venue.

At some point he drifted and their voices drowned for what welled inside of him. His mind flooded new sentiments and images of Christine. Curiously, she cradled an infant child, if not in mental imagery, amorphously as a presence in his emotional id, and the tug-of-war between those senses he was losing. He fought them, along with the waves of nostalgia and sadness they rode in on, because he knew these were not rooted in actual experiences, either way, and was rightfully afraid for their purpose. *What does... it want from me?* for in that moment of reflection he began to suspect that the device, *It knows I created it. A*mong other thoughts he coveted, the implications of which required his secrecy.

"I can try," Karen's voice recaptured his attention. "I may be a psychologist but what kind of scientist would I be if I hand-cuffed myself to conventional thinking, huh?"

Colton acknowledged her irony with a grin. "I... I'm sorry, my mind wandered. Listen, guys, I don't expect anyone to understand... there is certainly nothing conventional about this emergence. You're not being as sarcastic with that as you may think." He twitched a grimace toward her. "My best guess, it somehow taps mnemonic data, somehow, perhaps yes, using the psionic..." he trailed off as though abashed.

"Oh?"

"Yeah, I mean..." he exhaled hard, "mindreading is apropos in a way, but not literally. I don't... I mean, I doubt that's what we've ultimately designed here."

"Memories." Jack reentered, "By accessing it like data, via this, psionic..."

"Mm, something like that. Memories one may not even know they... see," his appeal toward Karen sought affirmation, "all a mind is, is a complex biological array of carbon-based circuitry."

Karen tilted her head back and forth, "I'm less about physiology and more about the gestalt, heh. But, okay, more or less."

"Their processing requires a concomitant electromagnetic wave signature, just like everything in nature." Colton wagged his finger under a squint, "It's not the same as actual mind reading, then. It's more like—"

"No. No. No. He's right. I see it. I see what he's saying." She looked directly toward him, "You're essentially talking about hijacking signals, right?"

"Mm hm, sort of tapping a phone call if you will, or analogous to intercepting radio transmissions. Uh, so to speak, of course," he then muttered more toward the empty side of the room, "maybe there were some unfulfilled passions, too."

"What was that? What did he just say?" she asked Jack, who was busy making small incredulous headshakes with his index and middle fingers depressed to center forehead.

"Uhm, forget that," Colton led again. "I don't know for certain. But it's like Dominion got in there. I guess the best analogy is, it temporarily jams the system. You know, when it, ah," he finished through a grimace specifically angled toward Jack, "says hello?"

"Dominion?" Karen enquired, "I thought I was the shrink. Lord."

"Uh... right. It sort of... named itself... Hey, don't look at me like that! I didn't name it, *it* did that."

"All right, sorry."

"I don't know if there's any... significance to that. I've certainly never met anyone with a name like that."

A conversation blackout set in while they processed in their own way. Karen then acted as though she were about to speak, her jaw slacked, lips ghost wording, but failing to enunciate anything at all.

"Like he said, babe, abject terror?"

"It gets worse I'm afraid. I—" Colton abruptly changed his perspective through the window, "Oh, now what the hell is this?"

"What, what's going on out there?" Respecting Colton's posture, Jack knelt. Waddling over to the opposite side, they took turns peering an eye around the frame.

At curb-side stood two emptying black sedans.

"What is it? What in the hell is happening out there?" Naturally, Karen moved as though headlong upon the window.

They nearly, simultaneously scolded, "Stay down!" waving hands behind them.

"Okay! Okay!" her butt hit the sofa.

"Ssh! Let's keep it down guys."

Jack's head waved side to side as he looked toward the back of the premises. "Hey, should we try look the other side?"

"Negative. Kitchen window... over the sink."

"Shit, I can see them, their reflection. Jesus, they're at the back of the house, too? But hey, these don't look like cops, man."

Colton continued near the level of a whisper, "That actually looks like... army. Those two, on the left there."

"*Army*? Heh, what are we, fuckin' ISIS now?"

Karen began to speak aloud but Jack cut her off, "Honey, please, I beg you to lay low."

The two MP officers stepped out of the front vehicle, shortly followed by two very tightly manicured-looking men in black suits from the back. The car doors could be heard closing faintly through the window. The group looked one another over, as though taking inventory. En-masse in tempo, they turned attention and moved toward the front of the premises.

Colton, whispered hard, "Karen. Karen!"

"What? What?"

"You gotta answer the door. And, honey, you gotta be nice. Don't arouse suspicion."

There were three hard knocks.

*   *   *   *

"Do I have any choice?" She smiled flirtatiously, so as not to show the aggressor the fear of prey.

The man squinted his eyes slightly and looked off in a bit of an upward direction "I would venture not in the grand scheme of things," bringing his attention back to her eyes while he quickly nodded. He used the momentum of his words as a segue for entering the premises, his other sharply-tailored companion soon followed. Two fatigue-clad individuals in tall laced black boots took position on the front porch as she closed the door.

The suited individuals looked around the interior as anyone would upon entering an unfamiliar setting, gaining their bearings of her home.

While this curt introduction took place, Colton noiselessly pulled the ladder up into the attic crawlspace behind them, and inaudibly, the wooden cover then slid back snug into its slot, effectively concealing the entrance to the attic. They could hear the muffled conversation below, but had difficulty interpreting the words being said.

"Miss Cranston, is it?"

She turned slowly, "Uh huh, that's right," her face austere at first then thought better of it, and arched her brows, "please, won't you gentlemen have a seat?"

The slow removal of the straight-clad man's sunglasses revealed he was calculating.

She let him try to figure it out while she pulled her skirt under the backs of her thighs. Clasping her hands around the top knee of her crossed legs, her posture was straight and confident. No doubt, the years of devotion to psychological sciences taught her a thing or two about the art of body language and concealing information. This was a battle between the treasure hunter, and the pirate who buried her booty. "Well... are you going to tell me what this is about, or are we going to continue this staring contest?"

He looked over a shoulder, "She seems a tad adversarial, doesn't she?"

The other male, still donning dark-tinted specs only slightly turned his face to a side as a response.

"My name is Terrence Dooling. I am a representative of the NSA. I assume you know what that stands for, N-S-A?"

She did not immediately answer as she became distracted by the other individual, who had in the meantime taken to leaning upon her bookshelf, slowly flipping over pages of a photo album. As she watched, "Oh, I believe so. Hey, excuse me. You, sir, is there anything I can help you find?"

Peering over the top rim of his glasses, the figure resumed quite undeterred by the assertiveness of her inquiry.

"Okay," she softly miffed. "I believe it means National Security Agency?"

"That's right. Give this one a gold star, Jacobson." He vaguely raised a corner of his mouth while lifting the next page of another photo album. "National. Security. Agency."

"Look, is this supposed to be intimidating or something? You're obviously studying my reac—"

Raising his hand, "Would you happen to have any idea why the National Security Agency would be here," turning his eyes briefly over the venue, "in your living room?"

"No, can't say that I do," she answered through a smile.

Opening a folder he had placed deliberately square to their interview, he extracted a photograph. It was a black-and-white vantage, far enough away to have captured the word "Wrangler's" on an awning.

There were people set beneath sharing a moment of apparent levity. It must have been laughter, because she could not only see her own upper teeth as her jaw was agape in the still image, she remembered the moment. She struggled to keep her eyes from widening.

He averred. "We know you're connected somehow with this individual. His name is Jack Sullivan."

"Yes, it's true. I know him," she nodded over the image.

"And so, that is you, right, in this photo?"

"Okay, it's me. You got me. I like to go out for a beer once in a while. A serious breach of national security, I know. I'm sorry, I—"

"Cut the crap! What's the nature of your association with Mr. Sullivan?"

"Jack's my lover. Is that what you dug up my name and address for, so you could drop on by and verify his love life?"

Jacobson managed enough grin to draw her attention, but seemed to deliberately mute it when realizing she saw.

Pulling another photograph from the folder, this time it was Colton and Jack sitting at a white-clothed table with a woman she did not recognize. Their expressions were quite serious.

"How about this individual with him; who is this man?"

She did not respond while scanning the image.

"Again, we know these answers. There's not point to lie—"

"Then why are you asking?"

He swathed a face full of irritation about the room, "Because we are trying to find them, and understanding the nature of your association to these individuals might tell me something about whether or not you are full of shit when we ask. Where can we find them?" He ended with arched brows.

She gently cleared her throat, "May I ask why, exactly? Are they in some kind of trouble or something?"

Tapping his fingertips together, "Oh, dispense with the bullshit, Karen. Don't you watch the news at all?"

"All right, fine, I'll bite. Yes, I heard this morning, *on the news*, that they are wanted in connection with some... thing... out in the desert last night? Beyond that, I really... I have not seen or spoken to him since." She made certain her vacant gaze was toward the left, as her psychological wit reminded her that a right eye motion to an adept interrogator signaled a liar. Without blinking she added, "two days ago."

"Hm," he eyed her torso up and down. "Yes, your cell-phone records indicate you actually last spoke to Mr. Sullivan..." he flipped over the black cover of a small notepad, "two and a half days ago. Very good. You're good at this, aren't you? This one's a tougher nut to crack, Jacobson."

THAT was lucky, she thought. "Can I ask specifically what kind of trouble they are in that requires you being here?"

Sensing Jacobson's approach, he turned his head over his shoulder to gather the approaching murmur, then leaning forward, he emphasized the point, "Let's just say there are things in play, bigger things, than I suspect you are currently aware of."

"I see. Look, I have a previous… are we about finished here then?"

"That depends on whether—"

"Dooling? We're done here."

Looking off to either side, he took in a deeper breath, reached into a breast pocket, and pulled out a business card. "I'll remind you, if this had been a formal hearing, perjury to the Government during an investigation is an act of obstruction, the penalty of which can even be imprisonment. But, you're an intelligent woman, you already know that of course. If they should happen to drop by, I strongly suggest you contact me. I will tell you this much, we are working on a matter of… national security. We have a particular need for his… consultation."

"Consul – tation? I tell you what, forget it. Sorry I asked."

The other agent had already passed through the front door, leaving it ajar.

"I'm sorry, but that's all I am at liberty to discuss. Here, please use that card. We will keep looking for him. In the meantime, you need to be in touch if you engage with him."

*   *   *   *

"I can't believe that really worked. You guys actually hid in the attic while a representative from the National Security Agency—"

Jack surmised, "It didn't work. Obviously, they must've had some clue that we'd be here. Do you think they're really gone?"

"All right, so… something happened because of this technology you guys have been tinkering with. A big leap here, I'm guessing scary and dangerous? So, I think I'm on the same page now. No one's going to believe you and?"

Neither answered as they continued brushing dust from their clothes. The light outside the window over the kitchen sink languished in the early evening.

She turned her attention slowly toward Jack, and spoke less sympathetically, "Either way, the N S fucking-A? I cannot have the NSA, or military, or whatever coming to my home!" meting out leers evenly. "I think... I mean, obviously I wanna help you, Jack, but under the circumstances," she let out a heavier breath, "maybe I need you guys to leave."

"Honey, I don't know why those officials are involved. But, I can assure you, neither does Colt." He stepped square to her, placing his hands on either shoulder. "Please, don't, I—"

"No. No, Jack." Colton interrupted. "She's right. We can't stay here. Or at least, I can't stay here."

"And go where exactly? Listen, I experienced something, out there, in the desert last night. Something I can't explain. And it took me through this morning to... Look, now we know... this thing you created, it's somehow doing this shit to people."

"*NO!* It's more than that," Colton faded distantly. "I don't believe its intentions were to do any harm."

"You're kidding me, right? You got one cop breathing through a straw and another one never coming home to his kids. What the fuck are you talking about?"

"Jack," he said through heavy air, "you gotta trust me. Please. I cannot tell you why I know these things, only that I do. This Dominion, it's... like a child. The incident in the desert last night was... a child's tantrum. And I don't think it—"

"Lemme guess, knew any better. Of course. That really... it makes perfect sense."

"And, I have to do this."

"You mean... are you sure? Dude, uh, may I remind us what happened the last time we tried to... intervene? Okay, fine. How can you be certain this thing won't... throw another tantrum?"

Karen stepped to Jack's side, close enough that they shared their personal space. She lightly clasped his arm beneath his elbow. "Upon second thought, I don't want you involved in this shit anymore."

"Alone. It's me it wants... maybe, needs. But it's gotta be me, alone."

"So, where are they? I guess you sort of have a feeling where they actually, physically are?"

He hesitated upon the end of Jack's implicit mockery, then turned his attention to scan the windows. Late dusk had taken over, rendering the panes to blackness. "It's dark enough and she's right, Jack, it's probably better that you stay behind. Here, or do your own thing." He slowly opened the back door, slipping through at an angle. He could feel their omnipresence from within the home but continued to put on airs of stealth until he made his way clear of the back premises, and out of their observance, but part of him felt impervious.

24
DESTINATION

To Colton there could only be one destiny, a return to the lab where it all began, where the quintessence of memories and love came to a nexus with the power of science, and born an emergence he was not sure how to fully understand. But one thing he did know through and through, the answers were there.

He wondered how he could be traveling so freely among the streets of San Quixote. It might be desperation in the moment clouding his judgment, or it was all related to the same peculiar events now guiding space and time itself. It then occurred to him that he was in Monica's jeep, and was not completely certain whether or not the vehicle was ever positively identified. But every time a parcel of concern such as this took place, there was a quelling from some incoherent source within that countermanded the vibe, arresting all sensations in apprehension, and impelling him to move forward. It was clear to him, so long as he persisted upon his current trek, he was empowered.

The part of his psyche not preoccupied in registering deeper perceptions, took inventory of the surreal quality in the night sky. He surmised the best he could, that it might be his own perceptions playing games in his mind, being filtered through the pall of recent dystopic events. Whatever this power was, it seemed reality itself was becoming a matter of relativity in the observer.

Discarded parcels of society tumbled along in the warm desert air as he rode through the abandoned thoroughfares. The quaint urban setting usually bustling with semblances of civility and antics, lay to rest so early in a night. It was highly unusual not to see anyone. There were lights shown inside of businesses, as though they were patroned by a memory. Street lamps blazed purposelessly, as traffic lights flicked through their cycles, administering no one.

Fragments of his mental faculties by now, knew the cause. This was Dominion. *Its reach must be getting stronger.*

He reached for his phone, for despite oscillating between harrowing urgency and the mollifying reassurances that pulled him back into his objective, still he carried concerns for the friends he left behind. And so his eyes danced quickly between it and the road in front. He tried. Immediately, the device chimed an odd tone that he did not recognize; his lips echoed what was displayed on its interface: "Unknown Network Domain."

He was nearing a complex intersection, the town's version of a loop highway system. Amid the spaghetti logic of roads leading in and away, a tapestry of signs read, "Interstate 103: Gilliard NM 122mi., Sky Harbor Intern. Airport 322mi, Phoenix AZ 421mi., →". Another read, "← Yuma Military Proving Grounds and Base." Finally, "National Electromagnetic Research and Development Labs ↑". Traffic lights burned through energy under a cast of illumination spires that lorded over the entire region in man-made glow. This would be the last artifice, in fact, evidence of civility on route; the other side of which was his destiny, down miles of road. If one were lucky, the moon would pallidly offer company and comfort. Otherwise, the entry point off the intersection was like being absorbed by the gaping maw of the night. And in a sense, this setting lent to his sensation; though he had been down that road many times, he was simultaneously committing himself to the unknown.

Almost at once, upon leaving the big intersection behind, traffic lights distanced in his rearview mirror, the darkness not swallowing him whole as it normally would, as he had a vague impression that the horizon sky ahead was dimly glowing. Subtle at first, he mused if a particularly intense solar storm had taken place with enough ferocity to bleed aurora borealis to an unusually far south latitude. It grew brighter the further along he went; unsure if that was truly the case, or the darkness upon plumbing deeper into the countryside were somehow augmenting and making it only seem brighter. He got his answer, when eventually the headlamps of the vehicle were almost unnecessary. It was as though it were the afterglow of a meteor impact some distance beyond the horizon.

His heart rate accelerated; there was only one destiny at the end of this two-lane road; the lab. "What in God's name is that? What is going on now?" he susurrated. Despite this, which for any normal, sentient being would inspire a good bit of apprehension, he was compelled to continue. Fear was not within; if anything, it inspired desperation, and he depressed the accelerator even more. It was that same mollifying influence.

A sign approached, silhouetted at first. As he passed, it read as it always did, "National Electromagnetic Research and Development Lab Facility. Road Ends At Facility 5 Miles," when suddenly, the faux aurora abruptly vanished, no differently than hitting an off switch. "Oh, shit!" he exclaimed. The headlamps of the automobile instantly took charge of the oncoming road. He had become so utterly preoccupied by the persistent, anachronistic nature of the light, its sudden abatement enticed him to slow the vehicle.

It did not occur to him at first what it was he was seeing shortly ahead, but as the vehicle closed some distance, he spoke, "A pile of clothes?" He slowed the Jeep further as his headlights passed their illumination over what appeared to be others. Pants, then a shirt, even what appeared to be a bra hanging from a sage. This became more frequent as the front gate of the complex was nearing, sensing occasional soft thumps as tires pressed over articles of clothing.

"What the hell." Finally, he cut the wheel and set the transmission in park, straddling the shoulder of the road. The door to the jeep was left ajar, the engine still running, as he walked around into the illumination of the headlamps. Upon lifting a random garment to within a small distance from his face, he took a chance and inhaled through his nose. "Huh, these clothes couldn't have been here..." The mélange of flotsam around him consisted of Military fatigues, and pedestrian wears, dropped haphazardly upon the earth throughout the immediate illuminated region, and disappearing into the darkness. Whomever donned them originally must have arbitrarily disregarded them without pause or purpose. *Why – what?*

He turned his head about the darkness around him when for an instant he thought he saw some movement. Given the circumstances he quite naturally biased a movement toward the jeep in a start, but the focus at that same region of the night's shadows prevailed. "Hello?" he half committed over the engine's hum. Of course there was no answer. Turning his eyes toward the article of fatigue clothing he was holding, he flipped the shirt over and spread the arms to reveal a name tag. "Simms, MP."

The wind blew softly, carrying aromas of human-made fragrances that competed with the natural setting of the nocturnal desert air. He let Simms' shirt slip through his fingers to the ground, then proceeded to reentering the vehicle. Engaging the gear shift, his attention was jolted forward. A startling image drew his attention through the windshield.

What emerged was that of a nude figure, on the stage offered by the jeep's headlamps, her steps equally placed, as she walked in a very peculiar manner. *A naked robot*, he mused, before she disappeared between the sage and darkness off the side of the road.

He continued onward, slowly, passing another naked body, then another, the headlamps exposing them, one after the other. All exhibited a similar response behavior; they faded back into the night's concealment. This gave him the distinct impression the vehicle's lights disturbed them, inducing them to scurry.

A man lay in the fetal position off the shoulder of the road. He slammed on the breaks when his peripheral vision took abrupt notice of one standing square to the jeep. The person's face was turned slightly downward, eyes peering forward, casting an image that was not particular benevolent if he were to surmise any intent. It seemed to focus on the windshield, not necessarily his eyes. The windows were perfunctorily closed, and all that was audible was the distant impression of the engine and his breathing. Then, the individual revealed it was an aimless coincidence, when it slowly turned and wondered off with those same unnaturally gliding footfalls.

The recently risen moonshine silhouetted the dark edifices of the front gates as they neared. The metallic arm of the gate was still down; of course, no one was available in the vestibule to administer his arrival. He lowered the gearshift back to first, and slowly moved the jeep forward in gentle thrusts, bending the gate's arm until it gave way. After moving the vehicle slowly through the other side, it revealed errantly parked automobiles amid the expanse, partially silhouetted by the moonlight if not exposed by the vehicles headlamps. It was as though, similar to the clothing, they were also en-masse abandoned, left to idle. Among this strew, he began to make out movements, darkened outlines of more individuals. Where others stood motionless, nearby there were those meandering, aimlessly. "Jesus, what is this… ground zero in a zombie apocalypse?"

Circuitously, he wended around the nude pedestrians as they wandered through the beams of the vehicle's headlamps. One individual walked across a small, square median of grass and headlong into a landscaped tree that grew midland. The person redirected herself toward nowhere after bouncing off, and disappeared into the night. *These must be lab people… But why are there so many? They can't all…*

Within close proximity to the main entrance, he pulled the jeep to a standstill, slantwise across a couple of handicap reserved parking slots. The spooks wandering naked through the night made no sense to him and he was not entirely certain what they were capable of doing, but he entertained the obvious suspicions as to why they were in that state. The visual memory of the man outside the front gate, standing with soulless, hyper dilated eyes, bounced to present awareness, causing him to wonder if he would be encountering such an individual in the ensuing moments outside the relative protection of the automobile. With his headlamps off and the engine silenced, he sat momentarily amid that darkness, hearing only his breathing. "Ok." He pulled an angle-head, GI flashlight from the glove compartment, then cracked the door, slowly swinging it open.

As he moved closer to the main entrance, he occasionally rotated it around his person. His attempt to ascertain whether two nearby individuals were staring at him, or whether he simply intersected their aimless leer was interrupted when he aggressively shone the light directly toward their faces; this immediately induced them to move away. He whispered just before passing through the circular doors to the facility's main atrium, "Thank God I have a lightsaber." With a nervy chortle, "I guess anything would be unusual." The doors under no circumstance would be unlocked this time of night.

Clicking off the flashlight once inside, he turned his perspective side to side then looked length-wise down the stillness of the em-lit, hollowed corridor. At first, he thought he was alone, as the horseshoe desk normally manned by security was abandoned, papers strewn about the floor and nearby. But a light thump of sound broke the raging silence.

It appeared to emanate from the other side of the door marked, "Official Personnel Only."

This jolted him. "Carmon," he called out, if by familiarity alone. He breathed heavily, then finished, "Is that you?" Another gentle thump. It was as though the door was occasionally being pushed from the other side. Thump. Thump-thump.

Instinctively, he approached on tip-toe and covertly made his way around the reception desk. Thump. In the moment, he was torn as to what to do. Part of his thoughts were of self-preservation, and ignoring this altogether, because as far as he could tell, he had carte blanche over the setting and could see his way to the elevators without the usual protocols and inconveniences, but what would be the purpose? That same ineffable empowerment that seemed to galvanize his very being on this night surged, leaving his natural curiosity to guide him.

He allowed for another thump, then knocked gently three times. The thumping seemed to hesitate momentarily, then resumed. "Who's there? Carmon, you there?" He knocked again, and again the thumping hesitated momentarily, only to resume.

He reached down to the gray metallic door knob and slowly gave it a turn. It was not locked. At about half a turn, it clicked, signaling it was ready to be pulled open, and slowly, the gap widened.

Carmon was exposed, the rest of his naked body emerging as Colton situated himself behind the opening door. He called his name again, but Carmon either ignored it, or was altogether incapable of acknowledging. Pacing toward the general direction of the main entrance with that same robotic glide, his arms hung precipitously without purpose to his sides.

Shaking his head, he tried again, "Carmon?" but there was no response or even hesitation as Carmon's shell proceeded unabated. He pushed methodically through the circular doors and yelled futilely one last time, "Carmon!"

The guard's frame was completely absorbed into the darkness outside the entrance.

Colton turned slowly away and redirected his intent down the corridor to the elevators.

25
UNIFICATION

Immediately upon the sibilated ending of the pressure exchange, that all too familiar low hum was noticeable. Loud enough to offset the typical silence of the changing room outside the Decon vestibule, it was oddly agreeable as usual, but this time was different; non-static in nature, tending to elevate and return in irregular intervals as though he were eavesdropping upon a conversation, less familiar of the language. He hesitated in his observance of this until his mind produced a rudimentary idea as to what may be causing it.

Abruptly, his head shook involuntarily in quick jerks. At once an intense sense of rapture forced its way through his senses. Coursing the very fiber of his being, he was instantly vanquished. Staggering as his knees buckled, he only vaguely registered his ass soon slamming to a seated position upon one of the benches that lined the walls of the vestibule. No different than a system overload, a realm of indescribable euphoria shocked his senses from within, and had come on too quickly for the faculties of his nervous system to process. Whatever this was, it was pure experience and utterly super-corporeal in nature.

This nascent sensation was truly beautiful, so overwhelming it was as though his memory and consciousness were being cleansed, and physical shackles releasing. This was a nexus of pure energy and emotion, one he could only recall ever feeling when in the company of a short list of others; but this version was vastly more intense, accompanying a sense that it was verboten.

Amid this dream-state equivalency there was another impression present, without physical form, but undeniable, availing in instances of coherency. It then faded, becoming obscure, as though via the modulation itself there was an attempt to communicate its presence; and it was calling to him, specifically, appealing to his protective instinct.

In a moment, his higher cerebral functions began to unscramble; order of thoughts' function and purpose started to come back on-line. Slowly turning his head through a flutter of blinks, he gathered in what, and more precisely where, as though having passed unexpectedly through some form of boundary; but of course there was no such physicality. Along the walls, hunters-orange jumpsuits and masks hung eternally without purpose from hooks, alternating one per either side of lockers that could have been years since their metallic meshed doors were ever closed. The setting just as it always had been. He raised his hand slowly to the fabric of the one closest, his eyes dancing along the fine texture of the rubbery cloth. He merely allowed the fabric to slip through his thumb and index finger. This time, he would not execute such protocols, for considering all there was, purpose transcended trivializing the need to do so. Without delay, he donned only a mask in preparation for the Decon chamber, sans the other ritual.

The interior doors hissed apart as he removed the breathing apparatus. He drew in his first breath of the equalizing pressure, then followed with rapid exchanges through his nose. This new source of atmosphere carried a very familiar aroma, pleasant, deeply reminiscent. *Lilacs again.*

As he neared the Optics Lab, FLASH, a brilliant illumination instantly subsumed all other senses of sight. He was awash in it, from all directions as it slowly faded. The ensuing prostration to his knees was unavoidable, as whatever this was, again drained him of strength.

Breathing hard, eyes closed, he struggled to access any senses at all, when one came through loud and clear. It was that of a hand, resting gently upon his shoulder from behind.

This did not differentiate as in, sensing a gently occurring contact. It was more like a realization that it always was a part of his psyche, but an incompletely formulated thought. *How did I not know it was there?*

He turned to see Monica's Neotenous eyes peering up to his, emitting glints like sparks off a prism.

"Come," she softly enunciated, "we must complete her arrival."

Despite his native mind, he had no discrete intellectual definition for what she meant by this statement. And indeed, forces in play had him quite addled anyway. He understood it much in the same way a child might understand, however simply lacking the ability to articulate exactly what they are thinking or feeling.

In the moment, he sought the source for the reflection in her eyes. It was the inner sanctum, casting an achromatic glow. He performed a subtle gasp, and upon returning his attention to where he knew hers to be, she was gone. Looking several times back and forth, he became frantic, but she was nowhere to be seen. "Monica!" he faux yelled. After a moment of quiescence, he felt an embrace around his hand. This time, he did not look to make any visual confirmation of her presence, for he felt if he did, she may vanish again. Slowly, this presence raised his arm; unmistakable, the sensation of it coming to rest upon a woman's chest. At the instant his palm made contact between her breasts, a surge of euphoria passed through him. His eyes slowly opened, to find his arm was outstretched, his hand partially into the white light.

Though Monica's presence took on form more succinctly described as an apparition, the certitude in his mind of her being there was absolute, while the low decibel conversation of accompanying sounds made elevated gestures whenever there were these points of physical contact.

"Soon, you will know her," this ethereal impression of her said.

The perception of his palm between her breasts became mobile, his arm slid down and came to a rest by his side. The doors at last hissed open.

The glowing light that permeated from every direction intensified as they entered and this gave the illusion of there being no entry, nor exit. Despite the haunted aura of the setting, fear was impossible, for sharing this space, if not the space itself, was an unmistakable presence of immense power, and absolute protection. Anchoring his earthly being amid this outré realm was that all-familiar, continued blissful aroma. He took in a slightly deeper inhalation as he slowly closed his eyes; he always loved that, it always ignited visions of her. *Where is it coming fro—* but the internalization was interrupted by a surging realization about the radiance surrounding him; *Wait, that's it... It's the light; it is this light?*

The agreeable hum abated, leaving a momentary silence as he stood awash in the ecstatic ambiance. He looked down to his hand when upon raising it slightly to reach for Monica she was again no longer at his side.

"Father," a voice called forth, monochromatically echoing away from his position in space and time, as though the voice came from within his own person. This time, the voice was different than he remembered, though he was certain it was from the same source.

After contemplation drew him into a stare for a moment, he replied. "Yes... I am here." As his thoughts arrived at the notion that the emanation of father sounded almost, *Female,* his mind was interrupted by a more familiar, needed form of exchange.

"Inquiry, female... accessing... refers to biologic distinction predicated on the production of gametes requiring infusion of male gamete."

He softly let out a nervous quiver of laughter. "O-kay, so then, this is a female?"

There was no immediate response.

"Are you fe—"

"We are Dominion," the voice interceded, and piggy-backed was simulacrum. From the beginning to the end of this short phrase, nestled in her voice were intonations not generated by mere machine.

"We are. Uh, you mean… who is Dominion?" The cadence spoke very fast as it regressed momentarily back into machine form, "Dominion equals protectorate control matrix over all entities pertinent to union imperative."

He silently re-lipped the last four words of that definition as he worked it out. Yet prior to physically asking the question, the answer to his next inquiry poured forth.

"The entities of the present comprehension matrix."

Entities? Other enti—

Dominion's reposing tone interrupted, "Affirmative."

"Can you…who are these entities in this Dominion?"

"Accessing control matrix… entity Dominion… entity father… accessing entity mother… accessing… failure system read non-domain entities cannot be integrated into comprehension matrix utilizing conformed definitions."

"Dominion… please, identify moth—"

"Accessing." A third voice then emanated amid the light, again less clearly from any vector and it was hers; no longer Monica's voice in veiled references, however clearly reminiscent of Christine. It was really her speaking this time. It was as though her very soul had reached out from wherever Dominion truly hailed, and it said, "Colton, she loves you."

He looked quickly around his immediate surroundings for Monica's frame, but could not see her through the light. Tears began to well over his eyelids. Whether Dominion merely accessed his deeper levels of psyche to formulate these impressions, or regardless of its intentions in doing so, the implications of what it was capable of, as well as what it was doing to him, was more than he could bear.

230

Suddenly, a translucent shape began to morph out of the hoariness; that of a child, clearly of some Mediterranean descendancy. A young girl, and as he watched the beauty with large, brown eyes, he tilted his head empathetically to one side then made a slight gesture of partially extending his arms, as though to invite an embrace—purely an unconscious act. The child's image glanced slowly upward to meet his eyes, revealing a fragile smile, welling a sensation of innocence. She ran towards him, vanishing, never quite making his destination, and he vibrated in his stance as though bracing for an impact that never took place.

At last, he understood. His immediate charge became enlightenment, not to his own, but that of his once unborn child. These images were the imagination of Dominion. *They must be reflections of what I must have, somehow, known all along?* These images were more than symbolic communication; they were the purest clarity there could be.

They all led to one undeniable, immutable truth; Dominion was a soul, the origin of which was perhaps too extraordinary to believe. But that did not matter, for certainty was her faculties, however unsure he was of her infinity.

And, as he taught her, she in turn confirmed his surmises that a kind of framework for her corporeality was in fact, for lack of a better word, downloaded from his own spiritual matrix. But only in proportion that she used his paradigm. Because, from what she described, he was left to ponder if those portions of her essence that bore so many semblances to Christine, she must have somehow constructed from the pith of his most coveted designs. He had no other explanation, because he directly asked her.

"Undefined... access forbidden," was her only reply.

To which he interpreted, some portions of one's mind must simply be too deep to fathom.

It was when she learned of the wanderers in the night, learned of Monica's transmutation, all of Colton's symptoms, and the desert, that the ambient light began to slowly fade. Cause-and-effect strongly implied she brought her own provinces under even more sophisticated controls.

So he hoped.

And relieved he was, when she offered, "Father... the Dominion equals protectorate domain space. The Dominion now understands. Dominion will not allow the others." As the light had all but entirely faded, one last vocalization came through. "Father... Dominion must turn out the lights."

Succumbing to exhaustion, his attention slipped away. *Your light could never be turned...*

26
LIBERATION

Warmth materialized over an impression of his lips, along with the song of an angel. His own thought interrupted the ecstasy, *Angel-song. How...* The warmth then came upon his lips again.

His eyelids slowly parted as he acknowledged a sensation about his chest, and face, as though he were being jostled back and forth. The song had become a distinctive voice, cutting through what remained of enervation.

"Honey, please... wake up. What is this? What's happened to you, Colton?" She looked over the lab.

Through rapid flutters of the eyelids, he strained, "Who... what... what's going on?" Reaching for her face, he gently ran his fingers along the contour of her jaw. "Is that—"

She slowly pulled his caress down from her cheek, clasping his hand to her chest. "Chris? no. It's me, Monica."

In a fleeting instant, a thought passed through his mind, *she knows the difference now?* "Where's..." he paused to breathe, "Dominion?" His voice still had vestiges of effort but was improving. He motioned slightly as though he were about to elevate to his feet, but hesitated to give her a once over. "When—"

"Did I know?" She completed for him.

"Oh, Monica," he paused through a bit of feigned laughter, "it's really you. So... how you been?"

She helped guide him upward with her hand under his arm.

He took inventory of the setting, massaging the back of his neck with a hard breath. "When did... what do you remember?"

"Fleeting images. I've lost some time. I remember you were sleeping, peacefully, this morning; I didn't want to disturb you. But that's all. I don't remember going to sleep last night. I'm having trouble with the day, today, actually." She then moved closer so she could run her open hand slowly up his arm. *Are you hurt, Lumpy?*

He thought he heard her ask the question, but was still distracted trying to reconcile all that had transpired. Together with how suddenly lucid and connected she had become, only adding to the information he was left to process. And for an instant, he detected a tinge of the euphoric sensation, as though it were she who conducted its force. But he dismissed it as merely an echo of the calamity he was experiencing.

She turned toward his profile. "What, honey, what is it?"

"This can't be. This has got to be a mis—" He hurriedly typed in, "sys date -24" and Enter. The monitor displayed yesterday's date, combined with the current time. Several times he tried different iterations to be certain, subtracting using different intervals. The indication was clear. "This can't be right!"

She again enquired, "Is it the time?"

"I don't understand how it could be. According to this, I... or, I guess we've only been down here for..." he turned his eyes into hers then finished, "twenty-three minutes?"

"Hey, are you okay? You aren't hurt, are you?" Her voice was exceptionally relaxed, all things considered.

"Oh, that, I think I'm fine. It... it's different this time." Turning square to her, he gently placed his hand upon either shoulder and spoke gently. "You... what do you remember? *You were... reprogrammed in the desert.*"

"Reprogram? what? I don't know what you mean." She subtly squinted.

He turned his head briefly from her direct attention while his eyes digested that particular exchange.

Hers opened brighter, "Hey, over here," she used her index finger to encourage he rotate his chin back forward. "I only remember bits and pieces, really, but I don't know about any desert. What about it?" She moved closer to him, turning her head into his chest. Her arms situated in rapture about his torso.

He rested a hand upon her back, patted her head with the other, then gently encouraged her to pull back, while not pressing her for any other reflections or memories regarding the previous days' events, for he was immediately interrupted by a thought, *the wanderers... wait!* "How did you get in? I mean inside here, into the facility?"

She did not answer straight away, drawing his attention to see why. She was facing the glass that separated them from the inner sanctum, with her index fingers and thumbs resting upon her chin.

He spoke again, "I tell you what, never mind that. I don't know what you can feel right now, but I feel quite certain that we need to leave. I admit... there's some kind of safety, uh, down here," he paused and focused momentarily back through the glass, "with her that is... But what are we going to do, stay here forever?"

She turned his shoulder around, encouraging him to face her. "What are we going to do," then turned her head inward toward Dominion, "about her?"

He used both hands to run his fingers through his hair, stopping short of actual frustration. "I don't get the impression she is in any kind of danger," he laughed weakly. "I might have thought so before, but now?"

* * * *

The subterranean corridors were hollowed of all souls as they carefully checked, then moved in precautionary covert intervals en-route to the elevators. The distant industrial hum that normally complemented the static voids of the compound were unusually silent. The doors parted.

"Wait... let me see," he said, extending his neck so as to peer toward the main entrance to the facility, leaving the rest of his person securely inside the confines of the elevator.

Down the length of the corridor, he espied the large picture windows separating the main entrance atrium from the outside air. They were blackened with night, with one notable exception. Their darkness was being interrupted by a regular pulsation of blue and orange-colored lights. His vocal tonality was disheartened and weak, "Okay... Shit. What the hell is thiiiis?" He pushed the Close Door button and leaned backward upon the inside of them, closing his eyes. "I guess... what did I expect?" he ended through an aspiration. Turning his attention to her, he added, "I don't know what you encountered when you arrived here today but creepy doesn't do justice for what I had to tip-toe around."

She was already shaking her head as he finished that statement, and said upon his punctuation, "Why am I missing so many pieces?" Her eyes twitched rapidly, in small oscillations. "I don't know, feelings really... but I don't believe I was stopped."

"I wasn't exactly stopped, either. It's... I wouldn't know where to begin. They were wandering around, aimlessly." He gently bit his thumbnail as he began to pace three steps back and forth.

She slowly raised her eyes to him, "Oh my God... they were... naked?"

"Obliviously nude. They were people from here, the facility... employees, security, researchers."

"But I don't get—"

"Why?" he jumped on, "I can assure you; I didn't stop to ask any of them."

"Riight... and they were," she hesitated, "wandering around in the dark."

He noticed her eyes drifting across the floor. "Are you recalling something more?"

"Her reach was."

He changed the subject. "I feel certain though; if they were cogent at the time, I would not have been able to access the Lab. No way."

"I get that. But what were they—"

"I don't know."

"Wait... wandering around the parking lot." She then intoned as though arriving upon a eureka, "Like zombies!" Her eyes were big. "Yes. Yes, I think I remember now."

"And now, the police." he said with a whine. "I don't know how we're getting out of this one. There's no attic in this place."

"What?"

"Inside joke," he then trailed off, "if that's possible... Fuck," he pushed a hand through his hair, "maybe military, definitely some kind of police. I didn't want to hang my head out there long enough to be certain."

She stepped closer to him, clasping his arm with both her hands. "Whatever happens, going forward, we have to keep this unknown. I mean, obviously as much as possible. They can't know about her."

He looked into her eyes, which were partially welled over in clear liquid, and his tone was reassuring, "Remember, Dominion won't allow the others. I don't know what that means exactly, but... maybe she's wise in ways we can't see."

They embraced.

27
INQUISITION

The heavy metallic door clicked open as Colton's squinted eyes parted.

Two MPs entered the room, "Sir, please, it's time to go."

Their vibe signaled less than cordial length of time to even shake-off the remains of his interrupted slumber.

"Stand up. Turn around," the MP instructed, clicking one wrist into a handcuff in a single fluid skillful motion. Completing the manacling of his other arm behind his back. "It's easier if you relax. Only temporary, during transport." The MP then signaled his partner with a single methodic head nod.

That other MP reached for his communicator, depressed a button and murmured, "All clear. Mobility is green."

This induced the MP engaging with Colton, "Okay. Time to take a walk."

"Do you mind me asking where?"

"An interro— a conference room."

They wended their way down a maze of corridors, finally arriving upon another heavy metallic door, indistinguishable from any of the others along the circuitous journey. He thought, if ever a chance to escape were to reveal itself, no one would ever know the way. This was not the hospital. The adjoining MP used his electronic keyed-card to access the present door, and no sooner were Colton's hands released of the cuffs, he was encouraged into the room by means of a weakly aggressive shove. He turned around as though to shoot a leer back at the man but situational awareness held his expression at bay.

The MP said, "By all means, make yourself at home," and crinkled a subtle, insincere smile. The other MP rolled back out of the room at the end of the statement and the door closed behind him, the sound of locking gears pinged, signifying the intent for the room's occupants.

During the entire entrance display, Jack remained seated, forehead and hands resting upon the table in front of him; as though expecting the arrival.

Colton spoke quietly, in a futile effort, as certainly the holding cell was outfitted with monitoring tech. "Jack? How long have you been here? Come on, man... you okay?"

His head slowly rose; his expression telling a beleaguered story. His complexion conveyed ad nauseam.

"Sully... Look, I'm sorry, man. Really, for this whole thing getting so deep."

Jack's face stayed forward despite the commiseration, vaguely returning any signal that he heard. Then sighing heavily, his head sagged to one side while closing his eyes.

Colton stepped around the table, approached where he sat to place a hand upon his shoulder. "Hey... are you okay, man? Did they do something to you? I'm sure they gotta be asking you questions or some intimidating bullshit." He then took the chair kitty-corner to Jack's position. "I mean... how, when did they get to you?"

Finally, he partially committed eye contact.

"Is Karen... is she here? is she okay?" Colton pressed.

Jack's reply was impatient in tone, as he opted instead to, "Dude, what is going on with Monica?"

"I... don't know where to begin with that," he looked away indiscriminately.

"I mean, is she okay though. You didn't leave her this time in another one of those states of—"

Colton shook his head, "Eh, she's... fine. Different, but fine. I don't know... we got separated. I can only assume she's here, at the base, with us. I mean, not with us, here in this room, of course, but somewhere..."

Jack shook his head disapprovingly, "Dude, you're babbling."

239

"Look, she's returned. I mean, she's different, herself... lucid. But—" He stopped himself, stammering when Jack's tone occurred to him. "What's going on?" He looked around the room before adding "I mean as if this weren't enough."

"Did it occur to you why we are out here, at a God-forsaken military proving ground?"

"Monica's affiliation," he was already nodding along, "Okay."

"Okay? That's certainly part of it."

"What do you mean?"

"What I mean is, between Mendal's appointment and your little conjugal visits with that chick, they gotta know something about—"

The sound of metallic rattling at the handle of the olive-green door had them curtly discontinue. The MP officers entered the room moved purposefully to take up positions facing one another at either side of the entrance, leaving the door agape.

Briefly, they glanced at one another because the pomp setup heralded any actual physical arrival. Colton instantly recognized the tall, thin, square-jawed military figure as the anticipation finally turned through the door. Upon the left side of his military garb, a name tag read, "Col. McFadden." The right side precipitated numerous decorations and service awards.

Colton instantly reminisced through several mental images; moments in college Halls, Dr. Mendal's office, a passing automobile, as they rapidly flashed by like overlapping photographs. One particular recollection honed his attention; it was down in the lab where and when Dr. Mendal stood with an unknown figure that clearly matched this man's frame. And how at the time it seemed obvious, whomever the individual was, they were there for the purpose of taking inventory. *Recent Militarization at the Lab,* he then recalled. He turned his attention slowly toward Jack upon the rumination; it was as though Jack was way ahead of him, waiting, as he was already returning an expression that spoke volumes.

"I am Colonel McFadden," he began shortly after taking a seat. "Mr. Reinholt. A pleasure to, ah, again make your acquaintance." Crow's feet radiated from his eyes, and there was a subtle, almost sardonic mien about his facial contours. His expression then emptied as he slowly turned his head towards Jack, eyes lingering on Colton for a moment as his chin turned. "Jack Sullivan? According to the NSA report," using a moment to peer over the opened file he then turned directly at him, "Your role in this, is less than perfectly clear?"

"This? My role?" he exaggerated as though offended. Leaning in to mock a covert exchange with Colton he made no real attempt to be unheard, "The first guy, before you got here? He was asking me about Mendal."

The mordancy of his sarcasm did not impress McFadden.

"Fine, then. But can I get a phone call and a lawyer, please—"

"Dr. Mendal... We'll get to him shortly," removing his hat and placing it with proper coordinates upon the table in front of him, even gently adjusting it as an afterthought. He then leaned forward in his chair, clasping his hands near the altitude of his chin. His eyes clicked back and forth between them before he spoke, "First, there were two civilian police officers—" he suspended his words deliberately, as though in wait of a reaction. "They were found unconscious, out in the desert. What can you tell me about them?"

Colton quickly glanced over to Jack, whose expression had become vacant toward the table's surface. He then spoke, "We, uh, we heard about them... are they okay?"

"You see, now that's interesting. Why is that? Why do you ask... *are they okay?*" he gently tapped his extended fingers and thumbs together.

Making quick eye contact during their register of that question, only Colton prepared to reply, but the Colonel stopped him short.

"Why are you two exchanging glances? You do know something, something about their," he chose his word carefully, "*condition*, don't you?"

"Condi— I don't! Why do you ask? What's going on here? What's all this about?"

Jack was feigning a curiosity toward the far end of the ceiling.

"Well… they were found less than a quarter mile from your little commune out there."

Colton tried to air a tone of ignorance "Little commune? I—"

"Oh, come on now, don't bullshit me! That business about twenty-five clicks out along one-forty headed toward Phoenix?" His resolute rhetoric came to a stop upon him, as though one way or the other, Colton and Jack were not leaving this encounter without him getting some useful information. "Your friend, Jack here, was found with them. We obviously are going to know that you were out there," but his ending tone biased to entreat.

This triggered Jack to quickly flick his eyes to Colton, then resumed staring, front and center.

Colton protested, "Look, you can't hold us here without some form of a warrant, or legal writ, or something."

"Okay, say the word; we can have a couple of representatives from precinct sixty-six up here in no time. Is that the direction you want to go?"

A lull in the conversation ensued.

The Colonel's brow raised. "Didn't think so."

"Yes, true, okay, I see your point. We were there. But we weren't with any police officers. I'm really not sure what that's about." Through an engineered expression, "So what if they were there? What is it that you want now? What does this have to do with us and why are we here?"

Colton's aegis drove his recourse, "There is a woman... she was there with me at the facility. I suspect you, uh, know who I mean?"

The Colonel sniffled hard, "Yes, I am aware of Warrant Officer Saxton. What about her?"

"Where... is she here, do you mind me asking? We were taken apart. Is she alright? I assume she's... being held, too. But it's not really her... that you want, right?"

Hesitating briefly, McFadden leaned forward. "We don't know where she is. After she was detained last night, there was an incident."

He presently mused what that *incident* might have entailed.

"She's a savvy one, that Saxton. The MPs guarding post have no recollection of— Well, let's just say they were, uh, unsuccessful."

"Why? What do you mean? Unsuccessful at doing what?" This conversation was in silent competition with his internal fervor; how far outside his immediate research ambit did the knowledge of their creation so far reach, or was it reaching.

McFadden's gaze lingered almost fixed while continuing to tap his splayed fingers together.

"Look," Colton attempted a gentle probe, "Moni... I mean, miss Saxton has told me how she's worked with the military... and the private sect—"

"Dude, Warrant Officers deal in military tech. Hello?" Jack's whisper interceded.

"Hold it," Colton then addressed the Colonel directly, "Please, you have to tell me, what exactly is being militarized here?"

"Oh... my God," Jack susurrated to self, "is that the *other* part of this?" He held the butt of his palms to his forehead.

"Shh," Colton again redirected. "Please, Colonel, I must know. What was Monica's assignment... exactly?"

Clicking his eyes between their agitated state, McFadden slightly tipped his head to one side and gently squinted. "For the time being, this is not a matter open to the public. But I tell you what... have you been familiarized with the full scope of the Freebird project?"

They turned their heads rapidly between the Colonel and one another in subtle head shakes. The Colonel's gaze became suddenly fatuous as he peered down the length of the table.

"Uh, Colonel? Freebird. I... we've never heard of it. And what do you mean by component engineers?"

McFadden blinked forcibly several times as though coming out of a trance, "I find it a little odd that you were not ... how could you not have been briefed as embedded designers? I don't think—" He did not finish, but looked off the conversation at an angle, taken to massaging one hand with the other. Three quick taps in the general direction of the door did not break the Colonel's focus. Slowly, he turned his head to make eye contact with Colton.

"Are you... going to, address that?" Inside, he feared a dire reality and his pulse quickened; having the military involved with any aspect of what he had come to discover about their project, the profundity of which he could not even begin to plumb himself. These were utterly untenable revelations.

The Colonel then looked upward over his shoulder and lightly snapped his fingers in two quick successions.

The entering MP stood beside the opened door, "Yes, Sir."

Colton availed of the opportunity to steal a glimpse down the corridor, which was opened a little further as different sorts of military-clad personnel of unknown rank stepped partially into the room. At this point, he could at last see two individuals standing outside, a woman and a man, in what he instantly surmised to be the garb of military medical staff.

"Colonel?" the man inquired through the door.

The Colonel turned his head up at an angle.

The man leaned into the Colonel's ear; his lips moved, but only as he pulled away could any words be heard, "So, please… if you would?" McFadden furrowed his brow as he reached for his hat and quickly rose from the seated position. He hesitated for an instant as he glanced down toward the two of them, then repositioned his hat. The door closed behind them but the ensuing muffled conversation continued audible through the door.

Jack took the opportunity, fusing anger with amazement, "Dude, what? Are you trying to tell me they want to take this thing, and do what?"

Colton spoke monotone and stoic. "I don't know why I didn't see this coming."

"See what coming? What could they possibly gain from this thing? Even I can't guess at the implications and you know *I* think the world is doomed. We don't even need to know what this … Freebird shit's all about to know this is a bad idea. And I don't want to guess in the first fuckin' place!" He stood to his feet and began to pace along the side of the table, as he muttered more to himself. "Are you kidding, dude? Psionics."

Colton wagged his head in a mash up between exhaustion and abject horror, "Jesus, I can't imagine if—" but abandoned the expression. "We gotta find Mendal. He's got to know something about this… I have to find him."

"Buuut, they don't know that. Do they?"

Colton looked directly at him.

"The psycho-babble stuff - hello?" Jack urged further, "They didn't know any of that. They couldn't have. I mean, no one did," opening his palms upwards.

"I— uh, shit, I know! I heard you. I got that point already. I just… I don't know what they thought they could gain. I don't know what the connection here is." Colton shook his head in short intervals, murmuring, "I hope they don't know what this is now." He then turned his attention back towards Jack, "I mean with Domi— Jack, you have no idea what happened last night... Oh, fuck, I haven't even had the chance to tell—"

The door opening diverted their attention.

The Colonel stepped back through. "Gentlemen, if you would please accompany me? We need your help, and we are hoping you may assist us. It's time we drop the façade and rank, we have a situation." He held his arm, "Come on, let's go."

28
COMA

The Colonel's unspoken language shone on more like a man teetering with desperation, even concealing humility. Certainly, a loss for understanding.

"Colonel McFadden, can you explain, what is... Freebird? I mean, if you need our help, I—" he paused when registering the Colonel's brief hesitation in stride. There was still a reticence, but now it was more because of a man distracted by consternation. There was obviously a need presently. The situation mandated the Colonel sans the acts of adversarial cynicism.

"I assume you are familiar with the war in Afghanistan. Are you not?"

"Of course, who isn't?"

"I mean from a logistical aspect... no, you wouldn't, of course. You do know what drones are though, right?"

"Of course, uh, remote automated aerial reconnaissance, that sort of thing?"

"Wait. They're hardly military." Jack interceded. "I mean, they're like swatting gnats over backyard these days."

"Yes, but we're not in exactly talking bourgeoisie toy-buzzed neighborhoods annoyed by children and goobers with remote controls. For military tech and purposes recon robotics are a bit more complex. Freebird is... well, was, essentially advanced unmanned aerial combat vehicles in the context at hand. They can be automated via telecom with an operator's assistance, sure, but for preprogramming with targeting packages in conjunction with geosynchronous. Uh, so... what do our drones do?" He looked down at an angle toward Colton rotating a hand instructionally, "A lot more than recon. They limit human casualties in combat, for one."

Jack included himself. "Right, I assume in the interest of American soldiers. Hell, the future of warfare, get robots to do the dirty work."

The Colonel stretched out a hand, "Something like that," but faded in order to do a double-take over his shoulder. Colton was no longer walking beside him.

Jack halted, "Uh, Colt!"

Having lost himself in thought, he slipped their company when they turned down a tangent corridor. "Oh, right. Sorry, Sir," as he scurried back around the corner, "Please, you were saying?"

The Colonel's face was transient with agitation, but quickly regathered. "Anyway, war used to be neat and tidy but over the decades the world has changed. There's ethics now. Ethics have always been there but the Global reality of tweets, Internets, blogs, Googles, everybody shares the same backyard now. Things are messy. The atrocities of war were always hidden from the blissfully ignorant. All anyone carried on with was the illusion of national pride, shall we say."

"Messy? You mean people want to play with fire without being burned?" Jack's snark bonded.

"Ah, that, or pretending they won't. Now, we must deal with the actual problem. And, the problem is and always has been in the numbers, and that dreaded logical debate about acceptable losses. The technology is what it is." He stopped in his tracks, turning square to them, "And it's not perfect."

"Oh, I was reading about this a couple months ago, about the problems with drone assaults on civilians. Something about… making human decisions in real time? what does this have to do with us?" Colton quickly added.

"This is where your doctor Mendal comes in. We're contracted with a team he put together. Been…" he gazed skyward, "fifteen years at this point. Really since the early days, post nine-eleven. Come, this way," his waves encouraged they resume.

"Doctor Mendal?"

"Affirmative. That was his charge. Supply processors capable of... shall we say, *human* feel for a battle arena. It's been a saga of incremental improvements over the years. Frankly, not optimal. Simulations to implementations was a storyline about failure being necessary along the pathway to success. Only very recently he had promised a major breakthrough."

Turning into another corridor glowing in wan florescence, a sign hung evenly from the distant ceiling. "Yuma Proving Ground Class 4 Infirmary."

"Colonel, uh, sir, may I ask? Why the infirmary?"

With certain rapidity, Jack aimed at the Colonel's profile. "And before you answer that, does he really want to know?"

"Mm. Don't need a retinue of Military intelligence specialists to surmise, no, he doesn't. But, we're also at an impasse here; we have no choice."

"Heh, it was only a joke," he directed outwardly.

"We are hoping you might know something, anything, that might explain what I am about to show you." McFadden paused in stride. "We don't have any, ah, medical answers." He then raised his fingertips to his temples.

Colton recognized the wince instantly.

Letting his hands fall to his sides, the Colonel encouraged. "Come on, keep moving. Contrary to popular civilian myth, the Military's intelligence quotient is sufficient. Yes, we are quite capable of assessing cause and effect. Usually. As we're definitely seeing an effect, the trouble is, we just are having difficulty ascertaining the cause."

"Cause and effect," Colton snuck an eye-contact with Jack, "what happened?" *This can't be Dominion... she knows now. She wouldn't.* "And you think, what, Jack and I worked on this Freebird business... could, somehow?"

"We don't know. But my previous dealing with Mendal and officer Saxton has exposed that you are involved. Ah, in case you gentleman haven't already surmised why you are here now."

They arrived upon two large sliding doors. Colton instantly recognized this was a hermetically sealed domain on the other side of the glass. Two MPs stood at attention, saluting the Colonel as their group arrived. Off to one side, a Lady Palm's leafs radiated next to a reception desk. The Colonel completed the salute to the MPs, who brought their hands back to a clasp behind them. "Yes, Rita, I'm here with the subjects."

She pointed, "Yes, Sir, please sign—"

He was already writing his name in the ledger. "Anyway—"

Rita interrupted by depressing a switch on her desk, "Three for decon processing."

After a brief pause, someone spoke back, "Understood. You may send them through now."

"Yes, right, of course, thank you, Private," he said with some impatience then turned in attention back to Colton and Jack. "Are you guys familiar with hazmat?" He clicked his eyes back and forth.

Jack tried to suppress a bit of laughter as his eyes rolled away.

"I'll take that as an affirmative?" The Colonel said in forced seriousness.

They immediately took to looking down at angles while nodding.

"Okay, good. As I was saying, according to Dr. Mendal, he integrated your work into the—"

Colton interrupted by clasping the Colonel's arm.

McFadden peered slowly downward with a single eyebrow slightly raised.

"I mean, I'm sorry… uh, sir," Colton expedited his release. "But did you say Dr. Mendal integrated… *my* work? What exactly does that mean?"

"Oh, shit," Jack entered through a heavy breath.

The Colonel quickly observed the exchange between them through a squinting panache as he lengthened, "Right, I can only assume so. You two look confused. Are we supposed to be surprised?" but rather than wait for a reply, he hurried his explanation, "Ah, the initial tests. So, after ten years, the good doctor finally delivers a device that outwits the simulators. Hallelujah! Drones can finally differentiate between goat-herders and Taliban operatives. Time to phase-prep for the weaponized demo, uh, post-integration, of course." His tone shifted wistful, "Apparently, when they turned the fuckers on all hell broke loose. Not sure what Mendal did, between the simulator test phase and battle-integration, but something changed. And no one had any clue it was coming; it wasn't part of the formulized risk assessments. No prep operation. And whatever this is, so far, it has claimed all the witnesses." He paused, "How convenient there is no one to ask. Come on, it's time to get fitted."

Rita reached her fingers under the edge of her desk and a buzzing tone emanated from a speaker next to the sliding door, and as they parted, a hiss faded. The air rushed by them, moving from inside toward outside. The Colonel passed through. Colton and Jack's eyes shared unnerved wonder as they followed behind.

*   *   *   *

They laid upon their backs. Straps manacled their arms and legs to the rails lining gurneys, suggesting the past struggle; a single strap even enveloped their torsos. Wires hung precipitously from a few of them, then arced back upward, connected to some form of monitoring devices. Their heads displayed erratic movements, their eyes blackened like that of a doll's. Moaning, at times sounding vaguely if oddly structured as in unison it elevated then subdued.

251

Colton was not sure at first if it was the head-case that was muting his ability to hear them, otherwise the intonations of sound disintegrated to utter twaddle. Nurses in their own hazmat were tending to them, whether setting IVs, taking down notes on clipboards, or drawing sweat or some other form of bodily fluids from their brows and upper torsos.

He stopped trying to make sense of the ruction of moaning and groaning. *Domin— what are you?* he suspended internal confusion, for his interactions with his creation to this point did not lend well to what he was presently observing. *Protect the others. I thought...* Turning slowly in the general direction of McFadden, he sounded off vociferously to overcome his mask, "What's with this patient's eyes... why are they all black and white like this?"

But the Colonel was distracted by the ward RN, who was also preoccupied with flipping through pages of a clipboard.

A lesser ranked ward nurse stepped closer to elevate a muffled answer, "It's consistent with SPD," as she flipped and peered along the lines of a clipboard page.

"SPD?" he continued to monitor the dilation of the eyes, so wide they were in fact devoid of any iris at all as far as he could see. Though in the moment he was naturally quite apprehensive at the prospect of leaning in for closer inspection.

Jack pounced, "Oh, I know this one. May I? Sensory Processing Disorder."

"He's right. That's correct."

The image of Monica's eyes suddenly obtruded into present consciousness. All observational roads were leading him to conclude that Dominion's reach must be expanding. *But why... these people – what is she doing?*

The nurse stepped closer alongside of them. "Only, this... this is some kind of SPD on steroids." Then she shifted seriously, "We are not sure what it is; what is causing it.

Whether chemical-environmental, or even if this is some kind of biological agent."

"Biologic... what's thiiis?" Jack made his moan heard.

"Yes, if there is a bacterial, or even a viral agent, but blood toxicology results are inconclusive, or negative. Doesn't mean there can't be; if there is a pathogenic involvement it's plausible that we simply don't know the chemical markers to look for if truly novel."

Colton's tone aired of certain mordancy, "They're not going to find it," just before he staggered, a single arm bracing to the edge of an occupied gurney in what might have resulted in a loss of balance and fall if Jack had not recognized the phenomenon and rushed to guide him.

"Mr. Reinholt!"

"Thanks, buddy," Colton breathed into Jack's ear, and for the specter of destiny laid out before him, surely had him also wasting no time feigning composure toward the Colonel directly, "Yes, I, uh, I apologize, Sir. Fine now."

"We need to strap you down now too, do we?"

"Uh, no, heh. It's... I-um, I have an unrelated vertigo condition. It'll pass."

"Anyway, seeking some clarification here," the Colonel's eyes lingered for a moment, but his preoccupation drew his attention to the nearby ward nurse, "Shortly after fourteen hundred hours, these personnel were found in this... whatever this is?" his eyebrows sought affirmation.

Jack stealthily tilted his head to Colton. "Was that the same?"

"Jack, it was here. It hit me, uh, I mean it was in me..."

"Yeah, we noticed."

"No! not like before, I mean... this was diff—" They sensed McFadden taking notice.

"Well, yes. Actually..." the nurse hesitated while lifting a page on her clipboard, "that summary is what's essentially written here," she answered.

Jack intervened a splayed hand, "I'm sorry, what does that mean, exactly?"

The Colonel looked again toward the nurse.

She offered, "Sorry, Sir. There's nothing else here."

"And, I wasn't here at the time, nor does anyone on the base. Look, like I explained, they were completing the integrations, or at least scheduled to at that hour. We know that much. Over there," he pointed, "over at the Yuma Ground Labs, earlier this week. Shift change took place and these individuals you see here were soon found after, on site, when they failed to check in. Among other things. They were in this," he hesitated while looking around at them, "unresponsive, I don't know, fit of apoplexia." They all took to focusing on the one patient they had gathered around as the example.

The ward nurse added, "Some wandering. Some curled up, naked, on the tiles of the lab floor."

If Colton knew he was visibly nodding he would have stopped himself, but it was too late, for the Colonel's speech began to slow as he observed that physical response. "The integration itself had just taken... place. So, you have seen this before?"

"Yeah, I might have seen something... I-uh, similar to this. Look, there's no way I can be certain it's the same thing."

Jack turned away, clasping his hands over the top of his hazmat.

"We've all but ruled out biological contamination. The integration is all that's left, so it must have affected these individuals. Yet, you know nothing of this, nothing at all?"

"I don't... I mean, I don't see why I would, necessarily."

"Now, you see, that's what I don't understand. The medical reports contain these other coma accounts, which are eerily alike."

"Okay, yes. I can see why you might find that interesting."

254

The Colonel tried holding back a cynical laugh, "Mr. Sullivan here was found in a similar state out there with those civilian cops."

"Hey, man, I don't remember shit about that. I mean, I can't help you there."

"When you were picked you up at the lab, the arresting MPs, they found people wandering around the facility grounds, in some kind of state." McFadden trailed off, then came back with clarity. "You see, if I am to understand that you were unwittingly working on components for the Freebird project, fine. But, in total, it doesn't explain why you guys were out there, and your proximity to this whole damn thing, and why these things seem to happen whenever you two are around."

"Add up, to what? We weren't here. Whenever... whatever this is that happened to you guys."

"No. No. I'll give you that." McFadden's mask displayed some back and forth movement. "However, I think you guys might know something, something you are not telling me. Look around you. We got a major fuckin' problem here, buddy. We can't help these soldiers if we don't know what their problem is. Or worse yet, if it is something biological"

"I don't. Look, I need to talk to Dr. Mendal about this, this whole Freebird thing. We might figure this thing out together, and—"

McFadden interrupted, "That, unfortunately, is impossible," While he adjusted his head-case slightly to make clearer attention to them. "You see, whatever this is, he didn't make it."

Jack's head whipped around, scrambling to straighten his visor.

The man was curt with finality, "He's dead."

"Whaaat?" Colton said as he stepped several paces outside their midst. Crisscrossing his dangling wrists atop his head-case, he elevated toward the center of the venue, "You mean... he's actually?"

Jack's tone was more directly filled with palpable fear, "How?"

Colton closed his eyes. *Don't say it.*

McFadden continued, "Theoretically, look around you. I'm guessing something like this might not have ended too well for that man?"

Colton's head-case slowly shook back and forth.

The Colonel seized upon their honed attention. "It was gruesome, too. His eyes were partially subtended from his skull. Blood pooled around his head. Maybe from smacking against the floor? Hell, I dunno. They said that they had to actually cleave his fingernails from the tarmac, and..."

"You can stop now," Colton urged through a breath.

The Colonel nodded, "Good then. And as you can see by this company of tongue-biters here," waving his hand back and forth, "they're not showing many signs of improvement since whatever happened over there. I can't have anarchy on a Military base yet I got soldiers too afraid to engage the malfunction... a malfunction I don't even know what in the hell it is!" He halted and cleared his throat. "Frankly, until I know what it is that is afflicting these people, I can't even responsibly order anyone to do anything. We got a major fuckin' problem here."

Colton blankly urged, "Then don't," turning slowly around to rejoin them.

"Excuse me?"

"Blow it away. That's my advice, level it. You have the means, huh, incendiaries, explosives. This is the army, right? Destroy everything over there. You got a built-in excuse. You are at a testing and proving ground."

McFadden shook his head before the end of that advice, "Unacceptable. We got over a billion-dollars-worth of agenda invested over decades integrating that entire region of the extended compound."

Colton turned and approached the gurney. He slowly reached up with both his hands nearing either side of his head-case.

The ward nurse spoke sternly, "Sir, that is ill-advisable. Sir, please do not remove your head gear."

"Guards!" the Colonel clapped his hands in the air twice.

Two decon clad MPs rushed to attention, "Yes, Sir?"

It was too late. Colton continued removing his head-casing undeterred by their arrival. He looked toward McFadden's dark visor. The MPs being human, were impelled to take a defensive movement backward upon seeing his exposed neck and head.

With confidence, he spoke, "These soldiers are not biologically contaminated. I know that," and he placed his hand upon the forehead of the patient closest to their location, whose head continued to move erratically, utterances of garbled noise emanating from his throat.

The others stood by in observance, too disturbed to intervene.

He slowly closed his eyes. "I know now what this is." Then as his eyes slowly opened, he removed his hand from the patient's head.

"Uhh," he emanated as though still in control, "so you *do* know, some—" turning his attention between Colton and the patient. "Look, I'm trying to save— wait... you did something. Just there, when you made contact."

Abruptly, the individual's eyes closed and his head gyrations ceased, a vibe washed over, rendering him to sleeping in vital peace.

Colton turned his head partially over his shoulder to acknowledge the Colonel's inquest. Hands on his hips, he lowered his head. "I can help them, I just can't explain why. I can't even define what's happening... with these people in here." His voice then sounded as though he were no longer directing his words toward the rest of them. "It's really more like... a sensation? But I can help them."

The Colonel approached the quiescent patient as a nurse, who had taken notice was already attending to medical indicators, "Corporal? Corporal Jennings? Corporal, can you hear me? Corporal Jennings." She popped off several quick finger snaps, back and forth within six-inches of his face. "Corporal?" Two more quick snaps.

The patient's arm slowly rose under his own strength to a position where his hand draped over his torso. His head turned slightly, as his eyes remained closed. What was previously a garble of spoken tongues, became a soft, deliberate moan that rose and then disappeared audibly, sounding more human. There was awareness.

One by one, Colton alleviated the soldiers.

The Colonel and the nurse were soon overwhelmed with patients in their various stages of recovery.

During this grander distraction, Jack worked his way closer to Colton. With his own headgear by then removed, "Uh... do I have to ask—"

"It's not me. I mean, it's more like a... portal."

He whispered harder, "Dude, I'm really getting sick of asking this sort of question, but... what the fuck does that mean?"

McFadden finally conceded, yet still cautiously, slowly removing his hazmat. Upon noticing their covert exchange, "Uh, Mr. Reinholt," he began with a coherently fake smile, "I think it's about time you and I had, shall we say... a bit more of a candid conversation." His expression morphed subtly toward indignation.

"Um, hey, guys?" Jack interceded, "How should I say this. Do you really need me here at this point?" He directed his inquiry towards the Colonel. "Look, you guys picked me up, I get it. But I was only ever adjunct to his gig. Clearly, you can see that I don't..."

"Your proximity to events makes you a risk."

"Excuse me, risk?"

McFadden snapped his fingers as he called out over a shoulder, "Gua— oh, good, you're still here."

"What... What's this?" Jack queried.

"Please escort this civilian to holding barracks, and have personnel assigned." He then looked at Jack, "I am sure he must be hungry and tired. Please see to it that he receives the basics."

"Oh what the—" Jack walked in a quick circular course, with his hands to either side of his head.

"Wait, Colonel, you won't need him. Why, what harm is there in letting him—"

"Are you kidding, no harm!?" McFadden broke into a laugh. "Come on... You've already won me over. You're smarter than that." He shot a rapid look between them. "This is a militarized operation. Hello? Is there any scenario in which this situation's status permits a present negotiation in the matter?"

Colton subtly nodded as he continued to look down.

Jack was focused on Colton's profile, "What does that mean? What's gonna to happen here? You're agreeing!?"

"Think about it, Jack."

"Think abou — fuck you."

Two officers sidled up to him. "Sir, if you would please accompany us?"

"Oh, well, see? He's saying please. I guess everything's all hunky dory, then,"

While he nodded, the Colonel spoke on of the heels of the sarcasm, "Please, continue gentlemen."

"Yes, Sir."

As the MPs led him toward the entrance, Jack spoke over his shoulder. "Colton! Come on, man, why are you agreeing with him? We haven't done anything wrong. I'm not going to say... not going to talk about anything, I mean. Why are you agreeing with that asshole?"

Colton yelled to overcome the growing distance, "I'm sorry, Jack. But I will make sure nothing happens to you!"

Slowly turning his head in register of that statement, the Colonel raised a single eyebrow at Colton.

29
CONFLAGRATION

The door closed with a click and a bit of a thud, the room was florescent lit, sterile. A slight hum could be heard emanating from one of the ceiling rail-lights.

McFadden eyeballed Colton's profile, keeping vigil focused at ninety degrees. Finally, he spoke, "That was impressive… whatever the hell that was back in the infirmary." He leaned forward in his seated position, "What's equally extraordinary…" he paused to surveil Colton's response.

He did so only by performing a subtle turn in the Colonel's favor.

"That Dr. Mendal created some sort of… weaponized mind device?" He then redirected toward the emptiness surrounding them, "And stuck it in my fucking nuclear-powered, next-generation MQ-9 Reaper series drones!"

Colton finally spoke. "Look, I'm not saying anything like that. I don't know what Mendal got himself into. What I do know—"

McFadden waved his hand. "Yet you were able to somehow, turn it off? I was there. What did you do, how— see, I think you know something about this technology, something you see as dreadful. I don't know, but by not divulging what that is, and playing cool, you think that exonerates you. Seeing as you, and your buddy there, are the only two people alive who know what it is, you think you hold all the cards."

He's never going to see what's happening here. "None of that. There are aspects that you don't… Sir, look… we ran into circumstances and they're difficult to explain," Colton cleared his throat lightly, "uh, in conventional terms, but they weren't part of the original design. Or intent for that matter. Look, they were, unintended… emergent properties, for lack of better words?"

"What, emergent! What the hell is all *that* supposed to mean?"

"Okay. You must understand, complex systems will do that, tend to… spontaneously engender new properties. It's synergistic—"

A titanic jolt passed through the room, accompanying a deafening blast of sound. The domain was rendered in pulsing intervals of light and dark, as a florescent ceiling light fixture dislodged and hung, swinging with the vestigial momentum of the blast. Sparks flitted down as it occasionally struggled to relight, then dimmed, repeating, along with buzzing sounds and odors of electrical discharge filling the room.

Colton found himself abruptly lying on his side, his cheek upon the cold floor, unsure of how he arrived in that position, as it had happened so fast. He let out a groan as he came to, then depressed his fists on either side of his shoulders and performed a single pushup. As he rose to his feet and let out a cough, the Colonel was already outside, engaging in heated dialogue of some kind.

The light fixture continued to swing, as the edifice was distantly still absorbing some impact-energy or vibrations. As the tubular bulbs struggled, the sizzling sound of their shorting electrical charges competed with the Colonel's voice outside the room. He quickly moved to the light switch panel astride the entrance flicking them until the overhead disemboweled lamp fixture shut off. This killed their report, exposing unintelligible, hurried voices ongoing in their urgent tones. The lights down the corridor in both directions also flickered as strange odors began to subsume breathable air.

He spied from the darkness of the room while the Colonel, slightly tipping his head in a backward direction, held his hand up to his face. It quickly became clear that his nose or face were bloodied.

Words labored through heavy breathing came into clearer focus as he moved his ear toward the gap in the door.

"Yes, Sir, I'm saying the whole complex was... the whole area. It was the lab... Colonel, Sir, the lab is leveled."

"And the drones?" the Colonel said through a cough.

"Sir, I think you'd better see this."

"Understood." The Colonel started to walk after the officer, who wheeled around in haste, sparing no time in gaining several strides along a hurried gate.

Whatever this was, it was enough to leave Colton to his own devices. He waited a moment in the shadows of the room, with the door six-inches ajar, watching various personnel as they ran or walked quickly past the door.

Another jolt struck with an instant of deafening cacophony. This time, more powerful. Despite the edifice around him, the force still flung him back over the table, his feet rolling over his head. He completed the motion and almost managed to come off the side of the table onto his feet, but instead landed in a roller chair, smashing hard up against the wall behind him.

He rose from the chair with a wince, and moved quickly to the back of the door, hesitating for an instant upon arrival. He slowly turned his head around the side, looking both ways down the hall. A few of the florescent rail-light fixtures dangled, occasionally flickered but mostly, failed. The floor at this point was heavily littered with construction flotsam, and the air, becoming denser with particulate matter no one should ever breathe, also reeked of hot electricity. The walls around him rattled and groaned, absorbing additional mechanical stresses from new impacts. "I'm not sticking around here for this shit!"

He started down the corridor, stumbling around obstructions as rarefied flashes provided lone instances of visibility. Personnel forced their way past, bumping his shoulders, steadying munitions that hung by straps about their torsos as they proceeded utterly unperturbed, in fact, having no awareness of his presence at all. It occurred to him that whatever this was, seemed quite intent on leveling the edifice, rendering any sort of previous protocols irrelevant. His very presence, equally so.

He reached for and managed to snag the shirtsleeve of a stranger attempting to scramble past. "What is it? What's going on out here?"

The officer yelled, "I don't know but we're under some kind of attack!" And pulled away with certain determination.

Colton fell into rank behind, pursuing answers of his own, as other behind absorbed into the company. They turned down another corridor, at the end of which the tint of dusk showed through an exit, irregularly being offset by glowing orange combustions, soon followed by their consequential thunderous jolts. As they neared the shattered doors, cubed candy glass littered the polished floor.

Another titanic blast propagated past the entrance, the momentum turning down the corridor knocking the two of them to their asses. Several other officers, and fatigue-clad soldiers who had turned down the corridor behind them were also knocked down.

As the group clamored to their feet, a soldier and an officer dove inward through the pulverized aperture of the door. "Go back... go back and find cover! Interior of the building! They've got pilots on foot heading for the Raptors! We're not winning this right now!" Following at once, came a brilliant saffron surge of light, and a powerful jolt of pressure and sound. The nearly-imperceptible lag in time indicating this was very close by the entrance. The officer aided the soldier, as they rose to their feet, wobbling in their effort. The soldier bled from the side of his head, but the officer appeared to have an injured lower extremity. He was mobile enough, though, as they staggered toward the group, which, not surprisingly, by then had arrived upon that consensus of self-preservation already, and began seeking refuge deeper down the corridor.

Colton yelled out while they stumbled and clamored en-masse, "Who is attacking us... the base? Can someone explain what's going on!"

Abruptly, the explosions ceased. This did not directly deter them all from rounding a corner and packing deeper into what was left of an interior hallway. The sudden onset of quiescence left them only in a pall of demolition stench and the sounds of heavy breathing alongside occasional buzzing and crackling of failing electrical infrastructure were all that was audible. Occasional sparks flitted downward over their heads as they vanquished from sight.

The officer who arrived with the wounded soldier spoke through his attempt to control panting, "It started in the Lab. There were strange sounds. Like... some creepy sounds. Not natural. Glowing light. It came from the Lab! The entire edifice... it started shaking violently. Then, it happened... it up and disintegrated all around. Not sure if it was bombed or what. But the dust cleared and there they were, hovering. It was drones! Four of them. Some kind of unilateral malfunction... they weren't responding to input commands. So we tried a short bandwidth EMP. Didn't work. Predator MQ series... that experimental Freebird cluster. We hit them with the pulse-cannon and—"

"Wait! It was the drones? What are you saying? How could they attack... us!" a nearby officer demanded.

Colton captured their attention by waving his hands, "Wait, wait. Did you just say Freebird?"

"Uh, who are you exactly?" queried a ranking officer in their midst.

"I'm a... not exactly military?"

"Well, this is helluva time for a civilian consult."

"Yes, that's right. I'm a... consultant."

"Okay then, Freebird. What about it?"

A bout of sudden consternation was enough to drown out the tumult. His expression would have betrayed fear, but cloaked from the others by the irregular intervals of light and darkness, and the overall distraction of the din. Despite all, connections were being made.

"Hey, Freebird. Do you got immediate intel on what in the hell is happening here, or what?"

But the sound of supersonic aircraft made it difficult to be heard, "It's the Colonel. McFadden. His Freebird project, and—"

"Getch 'ur ass down!"

Forced to acknowledge, p-waves jolted through the failing premises. Ending up on his ass, ear-ringing waves of sound extinguished into rattling walls and falling pieces of infrastructure. *My god, again.*

The lights finally gave up their intermittent fight. By then there really was no breathable air stuffing the corridors along with them; coughing competed with heavy aspirations, the sounds of vomiting, while overlapped by vocal emanations of trauma. Several origins of flickering light began to appear as a few of the soldiers managed to ignite their Orion locator flares.

"We can't stay in here; it's a death trap!"

"I'm all for getting the hell outta dodge," a nearby voice rattled.

"Thompson, Beauregard, you two recon the nearest entrance."

"What? Come on sarge—" Thompson turned his eyes upward in a heavy exhale.

"Can it! Double time, both of you, now!" The sergeant turned his attention toward Colton, "If you've got information that can help us here?"

"And I thought being stationed out here in the desert would..." Beauregard faded.

"I don't know. At least… I'm not totally certain. Maybe." Colton struggled through coughing as he stood to his feet. "I have to leave here."

In rapid succession, "Right, we all do!"

Just then, the tenor changed. The sergeant and Colton stared at one another with their noses and mouths buried in their forearm. They and those in their midst collectively realized the salvos of detonations had ceased. The remaining din seemed more permanently dissolved into just that of human suffering, while flickering flare lights gave distant hope.

The officers panted upon returning from their scouting assignment. Thompson spoke through it, "Looks clear, Sir. Lots of rubble, small fires. There's other personnel emerging… different smoke-covers. I think we can move, Sir."

"And the drones—"

Beauregard answered, "Gone, Sir. They are not there anymore."

Thompson added, "The Raptors must have taken them out."

"One can only hope."

"Okay, good work." The Sarge then tilted his chin slightly upward so his voice would be heard and raised a hand upward. "Attention. Hey! Listen up. We're moving out in groups of three, staggered formation. When you get out there, we're gonna have to figure this mess out as we go. We are in containment mode! Let's move."

Colton had already rounded the corner.

*   *   *   *

He turned his head slowly about the landscape of destruction. Small plumes of determined fire rolled skyward, evaporating into partially illuminated edges of roiling smoke, the spirals occasionally eclipsing the stars above.

The air combined burning petrol aromas with the abject acridity of industrial conflagrate. Perhaps if by some denial alone he ignored the over-arcing putrescent stench of burnt flesh.

"Hey! Over here," a voice wheezed.

He recognized it straightaway, "Jack!" as he looked frantically around the smoldering aftermath. There were other intersecting personnel rushing in different directions.

He espied him huddled covertly down among a cluster of what looked like old oil drums, waving his hand, gesturing for him to go over, the scene too frantic for anyone to take notice. Nevertheless, he opted to step sideways toward Jack's position, in covert short intervals. The personnel rushing to and fro thinned in the present, and so he took the opportunity to move quickly among the barrels. The night's ebony ambiance providing cover.

He spoke with certain ardor between conversation volume and a whisper. "Dude, what the hell happened, what are you doing out here?!"

"Is it…" Jack paused to cough and yeowed an utterance of agony, "safe to come out yet?"

"That Colonel McFadden, had me under sequester when the attack… I mean, the place started rattling apart—" He interrupted himself, his eyes surveying his companion more meticulously, his perplexed expression fitting, "Seriously, why are you here like this?"

Jack answered quickly as Colton peered briefly over the top of the barrels. "Surprisingly, I don't know." His disenchanted sarcasm was clear. Then with more sincerity, "I'm not about to be pinned down to any Military brig, only to die in a cage. I've been hiding here, choking on this shit since the bombing stopped. We were en-route. They were taking me across the base to some kind of, I don't know… involuntary military guest quarters," he acted as though to chortle but winced and coughed.

Colton helped him find the laughter but abruptly abandoned as he took notice. Jack clasped a clump of his shirt, pressing it against the side of his torso. Knowing the answer, he still asked.

Jack continued to suppress an autonomic cough response as he spoke. "I have this... thing... in my side. I don't think it's bleeding anymore but," he lifted his shirt enough to reveal an approximate five-inch gash. "It hurts," he coughed, "like holy hell." He rolled his shirt down and gently pressed his palm into the general vicinity of the wound, as though an afterthought to stop the bleeding lingered. "Kind of hard to breath. I was out for a while. I'm not sure what happened to us. I was out, but... came to and the two guards were... still out. There were people in the distance, over in that direction... they were..." he coughed, "running around."

"Shit. We must get you some help before any more—"

Jack completed his sentence, "Shit hits the fan? Wish I was with you when it did. I might not have a map of the Grand Canyon carved into my gut."

"I was with the Colonel," Colton moved his attention. "We were pretty deep inside the complex. Maybe a little safer, while he was trying to interrogate me. They're desperate for answers, Sully. Whatever it was... it went wrong."

Enfeebled sardonic laughter faded to, "Delicately put, as usual. Hey, it's a military..." cough, "operation, right?"

"Jack, somehow, Dr. Mendal thought to take some... aspect of Dominion's technology. Why? I dunno, but he managed to integrate..." trailing off through a stuttered gaze.

"Wait," Jack coughed, "you think he did *this*?"

"Uh, I'm not sure... not exactly. I wonder, though."

"Well, the fighter jets arrived, fired missiles, which flew... erratically. In loops, dude, missing targets. It was like everything they did malfunctioned, and then, the jets flew into each other, like, deliberately or something. Is all this somehow… You think this is related to… the Dominion stuff?"

"I… maybe, I don't know, exactly. Let's save your energy while we find the medics. Come on, buddy, I'll help you to your feet. With everything that's happening… things are different. No reason to hide now."

"I'm not hiding, but shit, I don't wanna be a target!"

"Of course…" Colton perfunctorily rotated his view through the darkness, "But that's gone. At least for the time being," he muttered. "Come on, we gotta get you fixed up."

The scene changed rapidly; small fires were extinguishing on their own, generators turned over and set to humming from afar, leading to a cast of floodlights illuminating a region beyond silhouetted damage and smoldering objects surrounding their immediate location. In the interim, the randomly rushing personnel had aggregated in that direction, though an occasional military vehicle and headlights passed nearby.

Some semblance of order was for the moment suggested. A helicopter thumped the air as its rotors churned overhead; two more followed closely behind. There were searchlights scanning the earth below them, as they went in the general direction of the bivouac. Others hovered virtually stationary in the far distance, their searchlights pouring downward over an area of extensive rubble.

Jack sighed through another wince. "Maybe you're right. This time. All I'm saying' is they didn't seem very machine-like, if you get my drift. Hey, I think I can walk on my own," but directly upon Colton giving his weight back, he swayed like a San Francisco church spire on April 18, 1906. "I guess I didn't realize how banged up my knee was."

"Tell me more about it… what happened?"

"I came around, was okay, but that headache… I'm not sure if I was knocked unconscious, but—"

Colton sounded as though this were a dire discovery, "but the headache was… back? Was it that same—"

"Afraid so. Ow, this thing in my side hurts like holy hell."

"We'll be there soon." He wanted to encourage conservation of whatever energy he had, for it appeared they were some quarter mile from help; perhaps he should try to keep him engaged in case there was head trauma too. "How did that gash happen?"

"When they hit 'em with some kind of weapon."

"Weapon?"

"They were gathering some kind of front against these... hovering. Whatever they were, the building under 'em was left jagged walls. They floated over rubble. Heard some soldier... targeted EMP? Didn't have a chance to ask. Then, malfunction," he exhaled through a groan.

Colton hesitated to take another step, "Hold on... get some strength back. Malfunction?"

"That's what they were yelling, malfunction. Right about when the shit was flyin'. They moved... not like machines move, man. It was like, anger, period. Those fuckers had personality, Colt. If that's what a malfunction looks like, I don't wanna know what those things are capable of when the automatons are actually pissed off!" He breathed hard in and out. "Anyway, that's when all hell cut loose... I got tuned up with this shit. Dude, I saw people... I think. Actual bodies, like, airborne. Something went off not too far away... it felt like a hot knife. I guess my knee, too. But Colton, that's why I thought it was Dominion... it was the headache... like at the hospital. Only, really bad this time. I wasn't... the only one. Everyone I could see... holding their heads."

"Okay, let's try moving again. I think it was Mendal, this whole business about us working on components. Not sure what to make of this, but he... it sounds pretty clear like he did something."

"I know I don't possess that shining thing you've been blessed with recently," Jack groaned, "I don't understand how this Dominion tech you—" he halted abruptly as his eyes widened.

271

"Shit, Sully, sorry, I know that's gotta hurt. But salvation is near, we're almost there."

"No, no, it's not that. Well," Jack groaned, "it's that, but... you think?" They started shuffling along. "Hey, Colt, you don't suppose... I mean, what if Dominion were somehow, like, inside one of those things?"

"Impossible. No, she's not... She can't be. She would never."

"I know you think that, but... wait, *she*?"

"I'll explain that later." His tone told Jack that he may not actually want that explanation.

"Okay, well, it's a foregone conclusion, this is so much bigger than us. Do they even know about..." Jack coughed.

"They wouldn't know what they are up against, no." With traces of fear, he started slowly, "Cerebral-gel." He whispered, "Oh, Christ," then entered, "An EMP would never have worked, not through the myel..."

Jack nodded along, then filled the hesitation, "ination," with a daunted tone. "Those fatty lipid molecules we used to insulate for signal degradation. God, aren't we clever?"

"I mean, assuming he... somehow adopted our methods."

"My God, that asshole," Jack ended, coughing. They took to another interval of rest, turning their vision over the landscape of lingering smolder. The well-lit bivouac was finally near. "That's right. Lucky myelination, it protects fools... little children, and duh duh dunnn, souped-up drones."

They resumed their movement. "I still... I don't get it if it's true, why he... Actually, forget why. *How,* is apropos," Colton added.

They soon managed their way to within shouting distance of where the night capitulated to the generator lights. Staying concealed in that position for a moment, they needed to make a decision whether to enter back into the domain of the military's guard. Injuries made the decision for them. "Come on, let's head for those tents."

*   *   *   *

An ongoing backdrop toil of those affording care for wounded, machinery, and the metallic tones industrialized civility emanated more resoundingly in front of them, temporarily drowned out as helicopter's foil chopped by overhead.

"Medic! Medic! Please, over here," Colton called as they emerged from the darkness.

Two nurses, a male and a female, dropped what they held and rushed to assist. Lifting Jack's arm over his own shoulders, the male nurse relieved Colton, "Where in the hell did you guys come from? Are you civilians? What the hell."

"That's right. Civilians."

"If you live long enough. Here, on this cot."

At last Jack could lengthen, collapsing torpidly. Colton gestured with his fingers and thumb extended, "He's got a bit of a—"

The nurse was already gently rolling his shirt upward.

"Whoa, whoa! I'll do it." Slowly, Jack began to peel the partially dried fabric of his shirt, revealing as he coughed, a small amount of fresh sera oozing from a wound.

The male nurse nodded, "Yup, going to need stitches; bunch of 'em here, buddy," then murmured to himself, "maybe a seamstress is more like it. Have you lost a lot of blood? I guess that stands to reason. Do you know your immunization history?"

"Really?" Jack added with his own hand.

"Hey, consider yourself lucky, we got body parts out there." He directed an outward yell, "Private! Nurse, yes, you. Over here... we're going to need a standard astringent. We need an EM surgical kit and toxoids screen, *stat*!"

Jack almost whined, "Wha... toxoids?" his eyes became heavy, as if the reality of his state was finally registering.

Positioning a stethoscope upon his torso, the medic instructed, "Breathe deeply. I know it might hurt, but please, in and out. I'm assuming you're a-ways out of a tetanus immunization? Most people are. Take another deep breath, let it out more slowly, please. I know it's difficult, but you have to try not to cough; the body convulsions aren't helping."

Colton had drifted back away from the team of medics when a female voice spoke from behind him.

"Are you the miracle man, who emerges from the darkness to save us all?"

He turned to see an attractive woman tending to a plasma bag hovering over an adjacent, wounded soldier.

Her eyes twitched in his favor; her face suggesting she was suppressing a grin. She spoke while tending to the unconscious gauze-headed patient's care details. "Pleasant to renew our acquaintance. Have you sustained any injuries, too?" She then directed her attention to him with a pen light, clicking it with her thumb, trying to shine it up close into his eyes.

Colton pulled back, "*No...* I'm fine," he waved off her advances. "I mean, like us all, I'm a bit shook up, sure. Hey, renew our acquaintance? What do you mean?"

"It's me, Lieutenant Calloway. I'm one of the nurses, tending the infirmary?"

"Oh, right. That was you. Sorry, I didn't recognize you without your costume there. Hey, so, what's going on here?" waving his hand back and forth. "Is there a problem with the infirmary? It must be over-loaded, right?"

The nurse shook her head. "Fubar. The battle with... those things, there is no infirm. You're looking at what's left of it. We have a skeleton crew. We've sent off-base, but that's a long haul. The phones... any comms for that matter were in the dark, land or air."

"Air?"

"Mm hmm, the base appears completely cut-off. Radio, cellular, tactical broadband, you name it... no signal. They're, well, the last I knew anyways, an engineering team was trying to determine the cause."

"About that... the attack that is. I overheard some personnel talking about the lab, disintegrating?"

"That's what I've been hearing. All I know is not too long after your group left the infirm, the world turned upside down on us." She took an instant in search of a description. "We were hit, hard. The building more than shook. The ceilings started to—" She crossed her arms. "People didn't make it... I mean out of there." Her unintended gaze then focused on Colton's eyes. "Many of those patients, if you recall, we were helping? I don't see how they could have made it out."

He nodded as he looked downward, "Some kind of drone tech—"

"Mm hm. I got a glimpse over my shoulder as I ran. They were firing some... god-awful, I dunno, energy?"

Turning his head away from her attention, he stepped two paces away.

"What is it?"

"That's it. Look, I... must leave this place. If they return, they're gonna... I need the Colonel. Colonel McFadden. Where I can find him?"

Jack winced as the medical technician pulled to lengthen the suture, turning the needle back inward for another pierce. He announced. "Me... uh, me too. Soon as this is done."

The medic performing the suturing glanced up at Colton and performed an eye-roll amid a subtle head shake.

"Right. Come on buddy, in this condition?" He turned his head away before continuing "No. Those... whatever they were, whatever that resulted, they're my responsibility now. Nurse, uh, Calloway? Do you... can you get me to the Colonel? He has to be made aware."

275

She did not reply. Her gaze had begun to languish outwardly, "Demons. That's what they became, demons. Nothing *malfunctions* like *that*."

Jack winced as the med tech applied topical bandaging over the finished stitches. Groaning softly, he added, "Maybe that's apropos, Colt. Just think about the whole —"

"I – uh. There's no time. Look, the Colonel?"

She broke her pensive distraction, "Uh, yes. Right. Sure. But he's—", flipping over the first two pages. "Okay, you may find him—"

He was already heading toward the direction she indicated.

"That's surgery." She pointed out but it seemed he hadn't even heard. She futilely elevated. "I have no idea what condition you'll find... okay." She then redirected the inquiry in Jack's favor, now seeming lucid enough, "I wonder what he's going to do *this* time?"

"I wouldn't know where to begin." Jack provided.

*   *   *   *

Bright lights flickered from overhead, and in tandem, came a terrific blast. It echoed around them as the sound waves propagated away. Screams belted out. There were those that scrambled in haste, diving to take refuge under any object big enough to offer protection. The lights from the flood lamps then dimmed in a silvery gray mist, as rain poured forth. Another series of flashing blinked. Loud thunder passed through the bivouac, again. At no time during the cacophony above, and the abrupt onset of the torrent, did Colton flinch in his determination to re-make the Colonel's acquaintance.

"Halt. What is your name and rank?" demanded the MP standing guard outside the entrance to the large chartreuse tent-like edifice. He stood looming over Colton, protected under the olive, polymer-fabric of the tent's awning, while water ran from Colton's forehead and face.

Colton spoke over the sound of the rain as it pounded down, "This... is surgery?" He craned to look around the larger stature of the guard, whose body motions tended to block his ability to do so.

The guard repeated himself with his own raised voice, sternly, "I said, what is your name and rank, Sir?"

Colton spoke quickly, "I don't have one, a rank that is. My name is Colton Reinholt. I am a civi... scientist. The Freebird... I must see the Colonel. I have information vital to the drone attacks."

The sentry leaned towards another, who arrived in the interim, maintaining his eyes on Colton as he whispered into the new man's ear. The ongoing loud rain and thunder made it impossible for him to make out what was being said, but shortly, the arriving guard rolled inward, disappearing into the dimly lit interior of the tented opening.

Colton moved as though to follow, but the remaining guard held his hand up to his chest, "Eh... hold it right there, Sir."

"Please, I must see him. I don't... Look, you have no idea what's going on here. They may come back. If they do they—" He was interrupted as the heavy cloth parted.

The stature of a man emerged clad in a beige jumpsuit covering his entire physique. From a shoulder clip hung the darkly tinted visor of a self-contained breathing apparatus, along with a headlamp. Two others followed, holding standard issue arms to their chests as they took position on either side of the figure, also with hazmat attached to the upper reaches of their uniforms. His eyes moved covertly up and down, as he spoke loudly. "You're Mr. Reinholt, then?"

"Please, I must see the Colonel. I have important infor—"

"Will miracles never cease? We've been looking for you." He turned his head slightly to one side and drew a squint that hinted at distrust. "You say, intel for the Colonel?"

About to answer, Colton was interceded again.

"Wait. Hold on one minute." Donning spectacles, jumpsuit-man reached toward Colton's face while holding a tubular object.

He instinctively tried to step backward, but bumped into the chest of another MP, who had covertly taken position behind, more than less forcing him to give into the doctor's advancement.

"Hold still."

"Do I have a choice?" he ended with a quivering chuckle.

Lightly pressing his thumb to lower an eyelid, the man applied a downward motion, flashing his pupil-gauge penlight towards each.

Colton again spoke loudly over the sound of the rain, "Can we step inside at least? Out of this rain? What is this, what are you looking for?"

"I'm the ranking medical officer, Captain Michaels." He wasted no time, "Can you tell me. When you got here before…"

"Before what?"

"Earlier before," he hesitated to gesture to the surroundings, "all this happened?"

"I… right. Okay. I've been here since last night, actually. I was—"

The doctor interrupted, "No. I mean, you were with the patients, earlier today. What I have here…" he stepped back farther under the awning, then lifted the second, then third page of his clipboard notes, "it says you administered some kind of unknown therapy that recovered non-responsive patient status… it reads."

"I… Look, I didn't *do* anything. Ah, I don't think we have time for explanations."

"You don't appear to manifest any symptoms. You can step in out of the rain," the doctor matched with a gesture.

He then wrapped the hand around the tall guard's bicep, and encouraged them both to take a step away. The guard tipped his head down for the doctor to speak directly into his ear.

Using the distraction, Colton's arms folded as he cleansed his face of any expression, so as to steal glimpses of the interior through the part in the canvas. The immediate inside was dimly lit, but he could faintly hear dissonant tones competing with the sound of the ongoing rain as it pelted the canvas awning overhead. He let out his lungs of their air, placing his clasped hands atop his head at suspecting that familiar sound. All the while his smoldering anguish, the implications of all thundering internally, urged along by the flashes of lightning outside his mind. He was not sure what exactly it was he feared in the moment, but an ominous sense continued to overtake him; they needed to extricate themselves, everyone, from the military base. A mere feeling that his remaining would incur a dire wrath, otherwise. "Doctor... Hello! Please. Can I speak with the Colonel, now!"

New flashes in the sky occurred, but the obligatory thunder soon followed more distantly now.

They stepped closer to him anew, and the doctor spoke when the rumbling trailed off. His tone arguing his own urgency had more importance. "I need to know what it was you administered, earlier, to our patients, uh, up in the infirmary?"

"Listen, I... we haven't the time for this. Shit... Look, I wouldn't know where to begin—" He truncated his stammer as he observed the doctor look up toward the guard. "Listen," bringing his clasped hands down beneath his chin, "my being here, on the base, is... dangerous. You understand?"

"You say, d... dangerous?" the doctor said in more trepidation than inquiry. "You're using the word—" the doctor encouraged.

"Yes, that's right. Dangerous. For all of us. Now, can you take me to the God damned Colonel?"

279

The doctor again looked slowly up toward the tall guard, turning his attention slowly back, "The Colonel isn't," he hesitated, "shall we say, here," finishing stolidly. Yet the corners of his mouth twitched a fake grin within an instant of ending his words.

Colton turned his head quickly as he looked back and forth between them. The rains had lightened. There were fewer crackles of the distancing thunder. "The nurse, she said—"

The doctor interrupted, "I know what she said." He then extended his hand and made an alternating cupping motion toward the tall guard. "Jameson?" Who let out two wolf-whistles.

Six military personnel, clad in standard issue garb and helmets with headlamps attached, emerged out of nowhere.

"Wait for us here, men." He then turned his attention to Colton, waving his hand inward as he moved inside. "I tell you what. The report stated you were unaffected but it may simply be a matter of time before we all are. Hell, I dunno. But if you can… we aren't going to figure it out standing around out there, that's for sure."

"Okay, so this isn't a temporary surgery ward I take it?"

The six armed servicemen stood at attention in two rows, either side, as they entered the tent behind.

"That's what we are telling people. But this—" The doctor stopped, turned around, and with eyes closed, he shook his head slowly. "No. This is something else entirely. Something that… well, we can't explain; seems to be a common complaint these day. No one can explain anything for chrissakes. Given the notes, we were actually hoping to find you."

"The notes? The Colonel, he's inside?"

The doctor raised a pointed index finger, "At ease gentlemen."

Some sighs of relief were almost audible along with the wails that had become louder, emanating from the bowels beyond the makeshift vestibular region.

They again halted, the doctor turning square to Colton as though he were about to speak, but stalled when noticing him focused downward at an angle, eyes closed, as he intently listened to the discordant sounds.

Although vocalization was eerily similar, there was a newer tonal inflection present, a quality he had not been exposed to, and most importantly, there was foreboding portents he wondered if he were singularly aware of.

"So, what... is that?" But the doctor did not press for an answer right away. Allowing a moment for Colton to absorb more of the horrific sounds. "Do you have any idea what... *that*, is?"

His reply was only vaguely audible, "I'm not certain, but there's something that might."

The doctor scanned his view over the soldiers, "Okay, gentlemen, standard defensive posture. Sorry to do this to you, again."

One of them reported, "Yes, Sir," and en-masse they turned slowly through the opening, as though they were not exactly thrilled by the prospect of that direction being their instructed course.

There was almost no light permeating beyond the opening as those in front of him passed inside. The strange entangled moaning dialogue poured forth in its full array of sanity-mocking cacophony.

The doctor turned back towards him, his headlamp casting a faint glow, "We certainly hope so," came a belated gesture.

The air was hotter, humid. The acridity of the outside pall and rain became abruptly mephitic with failing biological function if he were to make his best guess. Collectively, it made them all apprehensive, and instinctively clustered into a tighter group.

"Why is it so dark, where are the lights?"

The soldiers one by one turned their headlamps into the on position, illuminating regions of the darkness as they turned their heads to and fro in survey. The light beams swathed over regions of the layout, and this induced beings to scurry as though it gave rise to discomfort, only to jerk to a halt when the ropes they were tied with strung taut.

The doctor spoke over the ongoing garbled dialect, "It's the light. It seems to frighten, or agitate them further. The only way to keep them calm, if this is what you wanna call it, is to at least keep the ambient light down."

Speaking in competition with the groans, Colton dared, "Who are they... I mean, where did they come from?"

"Everywhere. The base, some wandering. We don't know what happened, or how they got in this state, much less why some of us don't seem to be affected."

Still, in close guarded proximity, they wound their way around cots supporting writhing unrest, occasionally swatting away interloping hands protruding from the darkness. Hissing and moaning often complementing these pseudo aggressive acts.

"I can't believe these are fuckin' human beings," said a member of the retinue.

Colton understood more than anyone in the setting, but even he could not resist his own impulsive recoils. Every time he felt contact, he jerked, as though happening upon an insidious black spider crawling up a forearm.

One serviceman yelled out, "Yehahaah... it's not letting go!" and the assailant was promptly beaten into submission by a fellow soldier's butt-end of his firearm. After the interruption, they pressed onward, their unified inertia a testament to fear.

"They're getting more and more brazen," another shout elevated.

A soldier within earshot of Colton whispered aggressively toward him, "Man, if this isn't already hell..."

On the heels of which another serviceman quickly added, "Can't say I disagree with *that* assessment."

Hands suddenly sprang out from the darkness and instantly, a serviceman nearby was weighted by a tight grip about his thigh. He flipped his semi-automatic ordinance around and used the butt-end similarly with two hard thumps. The hands released, and a spat of elevated, unintelligible vocalization sounded its disapproval.

Another soldier noted, "Lieutenant, they're different this time. More aware—"

The doctor interrupted loudly, "Stay clustered men, keep the civilian in the middle."

Several times over as they moved, encircled by the protective enclave, further thumps took place as the soldiers applied deterrent measures, each one sounding wet.

Colton asked rhetorically towards the doctor, "Do they have to beat them back?"

The doctor glanced briefly over the venue, "Isn't this what you encountered before?"

"*No*. No. They were entirely docile. These are different than what we observed... that other time. These, whatever they are, they're," he turned his head across the diffusive vitriol, "There's something else here."

"I don't understand. What something?"

"These personnel, they are all being," he hesitated, "induced."

"In... duced."

He forcibly released his breath. "It's... like an aura thing. Even I don't understand it fully. I just need the Colonel to be made aware. He already knows enough that... I won't have to explain. It's something we ran into during the experiments down in the lab." He took a moment to observe the doctor's response. "Okay, forget that. What I'm saying is, the device... huh, the technology we experimented with, it had some... unusual properties."

One of the MPs nearby interjected, "Uh, guys? this is riveting, but can we move this shit along, please?"

"Hold on!" the Doctor snapped then redirected, "What do you mean, properties? You mean, here?"

"Ha, I... don't know. Look, there's a new technology. The Freebird project? I heard about it, recently, myself."

"Yeah, of course I know Freebird. What's the point? We got some kind of new weapon gone awry here?"

"I don't know. Not specifically. Maybe in a way. Look, I'm trying to put this together like you. There is too much to explain. You'll have to trust me when I say, this usual property... it never should have been used. I think some aspect of it got integrated, maybe, into the Military's AI engine, and—"

"Riight, there's no way to fully explain what that is now. Fine... but you can't *do* whatever it was that you did for these people here?"

Colton shot a look toward the nervous MP, back to the doctor, then scanned over the sea of distress outside their immediate sphere. "There's too many of them now. I might know of something that can... might help. See... I thought the Colonel could... I don't know, get me back to the lab."

As they at last neared the far side of the dark din, the doctor spoke, "It's too late."

"Too late," he repeated.

"Okay, Kent, Sanders, Johnson, stand guard. Obviously, the natives are getting more restless. If you must," he did a slow pass across their faces with his forehead lamp, "put 'em down. We may not get control of this mess. He's in here. There's too many of them but maybe at least you can fix him."

They stepped together through a new set of flaps, the volume from the exterior domain becoming muted.

"Must be a rank thing? I mean, keeping him in here, separated from the others."

"Of course, and, hold it," the doctor lowered his voice as he raised the back of his hand.

"What is it?"

"Peters? Franklin?" The doctor called out into the darkness. Other than the forehead lamp, the interior space was rendered completely dark. He leaned to Colton, "Something's wrong." He then reached toward where he remembered the canvas, rattling a hanging object. *Click... click...* but there was no light. He turned the direction of his forehead lamp, passing the light across the floor of the enclosure. "There!" He rushed to turn a body laying upon its side on the ground. "Oh! Oh, god."

"Who is it?"

"His name is Peters. *No.* Just, back off... there's no reason to see this." After a moment of examination he seemed to almost beg, "Franklin?" to no avail.

Sensing Colton's diverted attention, he passed his forehead lamp in his general direction, to find him transfixed on a figure towards the darker end, a paralyzed expression on his face.

Turning the forehead lamp slow towards the same direction—where he knew the Colonel to be tied down upon an elevated cot—both jolted slightly on their feet as the visage was exposed by the light. The Colonel sat upright, his eyes either glowing, or reflecting the forehead lamp light. His arms rest with his wrists crossed deliberately upon his lap, while turning his head in small, irregular intervals; as though he were looking at them, by means of primitive robotics, his eyes ultimately failing to actually rest upon either of them. Blood had recently run from the edges of his mouth and nose, helping to draw their attention to the spattered blotches about his upper and mid torso.

The shroud of terror this image instilled was too thick to move from. "He knows we're here." The Captain turned his face slightly in a whisper.

"The question is... who's *he*?"

The statement induced the Captain to wash his forehead light over Colton's face. "So, there he is. Go do it. Do your… stuff. Do whatever it is you did." rotating the light between him and the surreally encumbered Colonel.

As he suspected, there was no immediate response to that urgency, and the ensuing slow rotation of his forehead light, this time, revealed a horrified, saucer-eyed, furled brow fuck you. And so, the next slow rotation of his forehead lamp, back toward the Colonel, preceded, "Yes, Sir. Loud and clear."

"Doctor… Listen, or Captain, Sir… this is way beyond… what? Hey, whoa! You okay?" he reached for a shoulder but was speaking to throes of immense pain.

The man pressed the butts of his palms to either temple, as he made outré sounds and facial muscular tics.

The sheer macabre in uncertainty of those reactions had him snap the supporting gesture back into safety. When he did, whatever support it might have offered, vanquished, and the man ceded to instability, slumping to his knees, and his elbows contacting the floor. "Doctor! What is it? What are you—"

Disturbing vocal emanations began to ring from the gaping mouth and the fight-or-flight instinct filled Colton. Reaching timidly, he probed for the right timing, at last pulling the helmet away from the doctor's head. As he rotated it around to expose the man's prostrating form, he inadvertently clicked it to the off position.

And there it was; gargling sounds of aspirating sputum, distant unworldly moaning resonances coming on louder through the canvas walls, along with the cozy notion that whatever remained of the Colonel was probably studying him from the other side of the darkness. Startled for having abruptly lost the only available light, he impulsively dropped the headlamp.

Oh, f… shiit. Please don't be broken, but as he felt around on the cool, moist, sticky floor, and finally locating it, he was lucky, for when securing it in his grip not only was it not broken, he managed to click the light switch again.

The sudden reintroduction of illumination impelled him to move backward in haste, causing him to trip over the Captain's leg, while struggling to keep the lamplight situated on the doctor's face. Those strange distortions of discomfort, his entire mien was, for utter lack of better words, now casting a demonic observation of him. Giant black eyes as though protruding, leered out from an unempathetic, yet focused expression.

He alternated the light quickly between this disturbing haunt and the Colonel in an effort to confirm. The man's mouth was agape, while in the process, swinging his legs off the side of the elevated cot. *How… he's supposed to be tied. Is he coming for*— stumbling again, he partially fell to the floor. Swearing out loud, this time over Peters' corpse. Or course for the setting, his mind worked it out that it somehow grabbed his ankle deliberately.

The Colonel continued to step ever closer to his position in a slow, robotic manner.

Scrambling to his feet, he shuffled backward through the darkness behind him, towards his best memory of their point of entry. His vitals were topping; he was becoming light-headed. If it were not for his workouts, his heart would have surely exploded, if not bursting a vessel in the brain.

Slipping back through the flap, the garbled groans offered no salvation as they poured on louder again. The other military personnel of their immediate retinue, those left to stand guard, none were present. Only, the darkness and the accompanying fetid aromas they had journeyed through. He frantically rotated the lamplight, struggling to make sense of the din. He could sense their advances and hands reached for him. They missed, barely, as their tethers were pulled taut, while he maneuvered instinctively, staying equidistant between their reaches. He turned to make haste.

A loud, daunting scream purported a fresh, new horror from behind him. Some vestige of the timbre in that shriek contained the Captain's voice, impelling him to look back over his shoulder. But all he saw was the Colonel's robotic footfalls leaving the same inner enclosure. A modulating shrill, it sounded like the old spin-up tone from baud modem, originating from the Colonel himself. As it modulated, and on cue, the sound vagaries incited aggressive posturing by the masses, like they were taking orders from an unknown language.

And as such, the entire complex became vibrant with that vexing dissonance; the horde now singing that same unwanted song in unison. He stumbled in his terrified urgency to turn and flee, again, but only slammed to his knees when he tripped over a body. The helmet lamp smashed to the ground and was at last, extinguished. Hands gripped tightly unto his lower legs and ankles, to his arms and wrists, pulling at him as he fought. Physical pain was surging. *Is this all there is?*

Images of Christine, Monica, his childhood, his collegiate experiences, the translucent images, and Monica again, flashed seamlessly, until, she came. It was the child of the hoariness.

Suddenly, all abated, as a bright light subsumed him in a presence. He did not know why he knew this, but it was as though it were responding to the erstwhile tumult. This was beyond the mere sensation of soothing, it illuminated from every direction, and it was different, more evolved, he thought. For though he recognized the light, he did not recognize the sensation of being suspended in three-dimensions, able to turn, see, sense, but any definition beyond stayed entirely elusive. The throng of decrepitude, the advancing Colonel, all were extinguishing afterthoughts. There was nothing, nothing but the light and that familiar, most powerful sense of purity and salvation. He recognized it at once; it was the realm of Dominion.

He turned his head sideways as the sensation enraptured him from behind. There was no longer any pretense to this presence. There was no longer a sense that the embrace was mere memories being acted out through an intermediary.

She spoke to him, in Christine's voice, "There is something very important I have to tell you. But first, let me lead you away from this place. We must leave now. She will be here soon to stop the others."

*   *   *   *

He did not know, or recollect anything about what transpired between hearing her voice and the present, having risen from the tepid ground, simply finding himself standing in the dark.

The smell of outside air blended with the lingering acrid aromas of the earlier sorties. From this, he instantly inferred that he was still at the base, "Where am I?" he queried as he tried to cut his vision through the dark.

There was no moon, only stars. There was no longer any smoke rising near or far that obscured points of distant light. Amidst his confusion, he began to wonder what happened to the service men and women, all that had happened. Where did it all go? It all sensed to him, quite non-sequitur, that he was alone out there, amid a severely dilapidated Proving Ground, miles and miles from anything resembling normal society. He looked down to his hands, then rubbed his neck and face, onward to take inventory of his present physical state. Shockingly, he found no overt evidence of any injury. Mentally, he was enjoying an intense endorphin rush, still lingering. He did not bother to question why, it felt safe. It was desperately needed.

A sound finally joined the ambiance, distantly. He turned around slowly to see two very vague headlights rising and falling slightly as they went up and down over subtle variations in elevation.

The vehicle came into focus as some form of law enforcement, halted within several meters of his position, and the sound of crushing gravel and debris from under tires ended with the final squeak of its breaks.

Oh, fuck, now, the cops. He looked quickly left and right as the thought occurred, however, fleeing the situation was not realistic. Besides, he was too unnerved to try. The headlights showed with enough power to keep the automobile's occupants under silhouetted cover. Squinting his eyes, he then slinked his upper torso and neck to fight for a view. The driver's side door opened on the far side, and a figure rose.

"Colton? Yo, man. Is that you?" covertly came the urgent inquiry.

"Car— what? What are... why are you... here?"

"I got someone here for you. Hold on." He turned abruptly and walked quickly around to the passenger side, but the door was already opening.

Monica emerged and their eyes locked despite the lingering darkness of the night.

He was able to read them with a clarity he had not seen in so long he could not recall, but it was really her.

Without a word spoken, or facial expression rendered, she submitted a smile.

His eyes moved along the locks of her hair, then along the line of her face. Slowly, his hand caressed the side of her head. She was more beautiful in that moment than he ever remembered seeing her up to that point in time, more so than any sensation that drove their intimacy. Perchance, she merely represented a stark contrast to the abject abominations of the earlier night. But possibly, he simply loved her. One thing was certain, in that instant, he at last let go of the past.

Signs of civility began to emerge as lights near their vicinity revealed the bivouac setting. Sounds of commotion soon accompanied, signaling, it was hoped, vitality. They took turns looking over the setting, both knowing the present solitude must have numbered moments. Though, people seemed oblivious to their presence; as if they were not even there. Much in the same way he was conveyed upon the scene in his own form of surrealism.

I wonder if these people have any idea what happened— The thought was interrupted by a rapid thumping sound pulsating afar, skyward.

Speaking softly, she drew his attention, "No, I don't believe they could have that awareness."

He slowly looked to her profile as she peered over the setting, and capitulated with a semblance of a nod.

"They're—"

"Coming? I know." He finished for her this time.

"It's okay," smiling slightly, a small sparkle showed at the corner of her eye. "They are—"

"Yes… this time they're here to help."

She looked slowly up to his profile.

His sensing her, he gently smiled in affirmation. He then turned to her directly, and upon noticing, caressed with his thumb twice to swipe clear the tear from under her eye.

She was wistful, "She's gone."

He reached to either shoulder and subtly shook his head, "No, she's not," came his soft reply.

30
RESOLUTION

They were clad in orange. Futile as it might be, they naturally, if unconsciously, positioned themselves so as to not elicit direct attention. It was a foregone presumption, regardless of any furtive maneuver, they were being watched. Given all erstwhile circumstances, who intelligent would not? Such that their intent was to air their words covertly, but every now and then the sheer import overwhelmed and made that difficult.

He delayed a moment to regroup, placing two fingers gently over his lips as he looked away. "I don't have all those answers, Jack. But as all this... technology evolved, it grew more powerful. She... I mean," furling his brow and closing his eyes, Colton pressed the back of his hand to the middle of his forehead, "referring to the episodes, they became more selective." He then risked a more direct eye contact, which he offset by speaking very quietly. "I mean, I wish I could find the words to convey the meaning of those experiences."

Jack's eyes had twitched in his favor when he sensed that spike in urgency incoming. Using it, he hastily enquired, "Those seizures?" He exhaled harder in preparation to tip his orange juice over his bottom lip, his face resuming a tired countenance, and quickly adding, "Why... I mean, how did they let us walk away that night?"

He opted to focus on Jack's first question. "They were like... being inside. I don't know, psionic spheres, for lack of a better word. It's the only way that... infant sentience could reach out. It had no other physical means to... Jesus."

Jack stared, "Psionic. Yeah, I know." He started again through rapid blinking, "the stuff Karen..." he finished with some quick nods.

"Mm hm. I know, and if it's crazy... I just, I don't know what else to call it; how else to scientifically encapsulate or quantize these extraordinary... All I can say is, those journeys through ecstasy? there has to be some kind of indescribable power." His ending faded off; the instant of realization was more than he could bear.

Jack could sense the wave of distress pass through the man. After a bit of needed conversation reprieve, he leaned forward. "Psionic spheres. Mmm, I think I see where you're going." Though with measured control, there were subtleties in his own deportment that betrayed awe. He continued in a leading tone, "And inside those spheres was—"

"People. Us. I... you know, souls for lack of better word. I mean, forget that. It was how it interpreted its... I guess, realm. It's all it had."

By then Jack had taken to squeezing the bridge of his nose between his thumb and index finger while wincing his eyes.

"We were like nodes of some kind of energy," Colton continued. "Look, we... you, me, everyone, everything, in nature for that matter, it all resonates in frequencies that... I don't know, somehow transcend electromagnetism; or maybe the synergy of different wave frequencies creates... however ephemeral, then we're gone. When we vibrated all those billions of analog microtubules. And present science? Forget it. No hope. Science would never know... it's there." He trailed wistfully. "I don't know, maybe this thing needs a Shaman or some shit."

"Transcended," Jack responded, "Jesus Christ, you may be right."

"Oh, man, don't go there."

"Well, anyway. And so what, what did we manage to unleash... we'll leave it at that."

Colton came back after the pause. "Right, perhaps. Whatever it became it's more than mere technology; it's more than the convention of math and science's trans-

293

morphism into physical form could ever have predicted, much less explained."

"Right. More than the sum of its parts?"

"Do you remember back at Karen's that day of the hospital?"

"*No.* No, Colton, I completely forgot."

"Okay. Okay. But... we were discussing the unpredictable?"

"The emergent properties of complex systems. Yeah, I know, we're beyond that at this point. My original calculations... they were for a specific causality. It's gotta be..."

"You do have an idea where the origin of synergy itself – do you ever give it a rest?"

"I just... embarrassing, but I leaped into that adaptation. Remember Dr. Wiles and the em-and-ems? I may not have vetted... that relationship. I assumed aspects of that technology. Between my calculations and that interfacing, maybe this emergence can be found there. Some secondary systemic synchronicity..." he left by staring vacantly.

"Possibly more of an unknown along the course of this research. Colt, come on, man, let it go. We got enough on our plates," he paused to look around the cafeteria, "if you haven't fuckin' noticed. Chalk it up as we're all accidents."

"Pure light. No. More like... pure serenity... nirvana, or utopia. All I know is that it envelopes you."

"Hm," Jack started through the nose, "wish we were there now. Okay, so that's Dominion. What about," he waited to recapture direct attention, "the drones?"

Clasping his hands around the back of his shaking head, he peered along the floor then expressed a sardonic spasm of laughter too soft to hear, "Abject terror of course."

"I don't understand how it all ended," Jack leaned forward again.

"That's... a good question." He closed his eyes and used one hand to massage the back of his neck, wincing slightly.

"Oh, God. Don't tell me it's back?"

"What? Oh, no… It's more like, I'm used to it happening at those moments. Anyway, I don't know for certain, but I have an idea… I mean, how it ended."

"Please, by all means. After all, I almost *died* to know," Jack ended with a sarcastic wink.

Colton partially resisted a grin at one corner of his mouth. *I'll keep Christine out of this.* "Its sphere of influence grew outward over time. I think all the way to the base… or something, for lack of a better explanation. And when it intersected with … I don't know for sure, but somehow… it cancelled each other out. If that makes any sense?"

It took a moment for Jack to register. "Like… an anti-matter to matter annihilation!"

"Ssh… yes. I think, perhaps something like that analog. And Dominion must have known," his voice broke slightly. "And now she's gone."

Jack turned his sights briefly about the room. "Hey, dude, listen, we need to talk, about next week?"

"The hearing? I know."

"I guess Dominion's help… I mean, reach… it only went out so far, then, huh?"

"What? What do you mean? Oh, right. But there's still the NSA… well, the general," he snuffled the irony, "sphere of this whole thing. I mean, it's all going to connect us either way."

"You think?" Jack responded resentfully. "Damn. No time in this fuckin' place is too long for me. Three days? Are we even being charged with anything, or are we being held GTMO style? I knew we were being watched, by the way. I saw that same damn sedan for like two days after that night at the base. Its tinted windows. I could still make out a couple of heads in there, always front and center. When I walked across the street, the heads turned in my favor. I saw it, around town, more than a few times, and—"

Colton interrupted with an assuring tone, "I know, I know. Obviously, we both were, watched that is. I knew it was a matter of time before they'd arrest us. But we couldn't run, Sully. Running in this situation... can you imagine?"

A slow nod through a military stare cast Jack's agreement. "So, what, we're in here on a terror rap? At least suspicion of," he shook his head in disgust, "some kind of thing."

"It's gotta be some NSA thing. They don't have enough of any other answers to explain the base, Yuma, that night. All they have is our names... in some file indirectly connected... probably through Mendal, my advisor?"

"I know who he is. My god, dude."

"Right. I mean, the witnesses? Anyone else beyond him or those files, I get the distinct impression... well—" he let Jack's imagination appropriately finish that thought.

Gazing, Jack posited, "Dominion's reach went a little bit farther than we think."

"Look," Colton said after clearing his throat, "the sooner we get this hearing over with, and they realize this wasn't us, all this will finally be over."

Jack finished his juice in a single swallow, and began rubbing his hands together. As he looked away, he spoke more to himself, "I wonder what happened to all of them."

"How is it?"

"Huh? Oh, that." Balling his fist, he tapped his midriff, "It's... fine. Healing up nicely," though there was a wince latency to his expression as he bent his torso left and right. "Funny, no one even knows about that. When you and Monica came back to find me... I was left alone there you know, don't think I was much of a priority. Heh. I don't know if I was out or not, maybe sedated, or, I dunno. I guess no one would have any memory either way."

"Listen, we can't go into this thing blithely offering descriptions of... you know, certain things." He allowed two inmates to pass by with their outstretched trays before resetting a softer tact, "they'll want answers. If they can find them. Obviously, what they do have, our fingerprints are all over aspects preceding the events of that night."

Jack nodded through a vacant stare and added, "Events," filtered through a feeble laugh. "Let's not overstate the matter." He then spoke earnestly. "Christ, I'd like to know how we're going to get out of this shit. Is this going to turn into some kinda deal where we're held indefinitely? You know, some extra-double top-secret thing no one knows exists because what… they don't like our answers?"

"Huh, Jack, no. We're not aliens here."

"Ironically, considering how unusual and apparently dangerous this technology…" he trailed off.

"I think if we just, actually take the Colonel's advice, god rest his soul."

"Colonel. Advice? Which part exactly?"

"That we were just component engineers, nothing more." Colton leaned forward in his chair, "Look, no one knows what was said, between any of us, on the base that night. The infrastructure… it's possible those interviews were recorded but the level of destruction and chaos… Certainly not anyone on the base that night, and certainly none of the stuff that took place down in the lab last year could have made it."

Jack looked at his face to find furtive eyebrows arcing back at him. "Wow. You gotta think, creepy convenient how *all that* worked out, right?"

"Trust me… We're just com—"

"—ponent engineers," he nodded. "Uh, huh, okay, I got it."

*   *   *   *

Karen gently laid her keys in the designated cup as she normally did, taking notice upon entering that he sat on the couch. His elbows were to his knees, leaning forward with his hands cupped to his face.

Acknowledging her arrival, his hands parted, lifting his chin to hers in his typical melodramatic act. However contrived was the expression, she knew a modicum of sincerity was there.

She moved quickly towards him as he rose to his feet. Instinctively, his arms parted as she collapsed into his fervor. She could feel his heart pounding in his chest, as they stood momentarily frozen in a long-sought embrace, his head leaning upon the top of hers.

"I'm so sorry that happened to you. You must have been terrified," she nurtured.

He took a deep breath as he lifted his head, pushing back gently enough to direct their eyes.

"What's next?"

He hesitated to answer, "Would you…"

"Would I?"

"Come with me. Away from this, this place in the desert," he said as he scanned the scenery outside the window, his expression beleaguered, yet resolved to find a new reality.

She knew it and began, "What about—" then turned around and stepped two paces away.

"What… about what?"

She turned back around and began to speak as she rubbed the top of her hips. "I mean, with my work? Your work? The project you guys—" she left off.

"Oh, ho, God. Are you kidding?" He smiled. "There's no project. I mean, sure, your own stuff. I'm sorry, I just… But as far as the project? Not anymore. In fact, can we talk, hon?" He stepped closer, extended his hands, and encouraged her to raise hers to his. Upon contact, he pulled her close, and he proceeded to kiss her bottom lip.

She returned tenderly for the moment then pulled back. "What… is it?"

Moving his lips close to her ear, he whispered, "I need to talk to you, but not here. Not sure if your home is being monitored."

She was instinctively turning her face and eyes in small intervals as though studying the premises but the reasoning of his concern became clear. "Come with me," she encouraged softly.

She turned her vehicle into the parking lot. The tall pole standing like a totem for the neon advertisement: "Rt 66 Inn and Suites. Tonight's rate: $33.33" Other automobiles where sprinkled sparsely across the lot. She put her transmission in park, "Do you think they're spying on random people out along route sixty-six Inn? In the off chance they'll find incriminating evidence against you?"

He turned his attention to her smiling at him, "Okay, you."

*   *   *   *

Twilight dawn tinted through the window of their rented room. She lay upon her side, wrapped entirely in bed clothes, her exposed head upon his outstretched arm. His eyes worked along the ceiling, as his leg dangled off the side of the bed seeking coolness outside their accumulated body heat.

At first, he thought he was only venting softly, "I don't want to live like this. Always wondering. Those gov spooks looking around corners at us. That's what they hinted things are gonna be like. I got the feeling they intend some form of… I dunno, extra double top secret probation. I mean, not naïve, right? I don't see how that's going to get better if I'm hanging around with the guy, either. We left 'em with no answers. And I had to leave *him* behind." After a deeper breath, he modulated his tone towards empathy. "I mean, I really like the guy. He's brilliant. Beyond, I dunno. Jesus. It's a loss of a personal asset."

She thrust her hips forward, positioning her torso closer to his. "Does he know where you are, now?"

"Oh, hey, you're awake." Jack turned on his side to face her, "I don't know what he... no, I don't think so." After a moment of their admiring their facial contours, he continued, "They let us go, the Feds, staggered in time. Part of me wondered if they did that deliberately. To see what we do next? I can't imagine a scenario where hangin' around would be smart. I don't think we can even associate, not for a long, long, long-long time." He rotated his body back to a prostrate position, as she moved her arm and leg to drape over his torso and waist. "I mean, I like the guy. Great research companion. Good friend. But, it isn't about that."

She reached her lips to the side of his face and gently kissed his cheek. Between a whisper and soft tone she encouraged, "It's okay, and it is sad. But it's gotta be the way things worked out. The way things have to be."

He slowly closed his eyes as though the thought triggered a need for additional sleep.

"I have a question."

"Mm hm."

"What about that Monica?" She allowed a moment. "Honey," gently jostling his chest.

"Huh, oh, what about her?"

Her eyes moved around the contours of his profile. "It's not really her that I wonder about. It's—"

"Uh huh."

"Well, it's her involvement in that whole thing."

He inhaled and exhaled deeply, "Go on."

"Didn't you say she was some kind of... project stenographer?"

"Mm hm. Sounds 'bout right."

"So, you guys regularly reported, then? The science, the project, like, directly to her?"

"Honey, what... out with it."

"Well, *honey*, my question is... what happened to her notes?"

His eyes opened alertly.

*   *   *   *

They stood side by side, peering out at a mass of towering thunder clouds billowing into the twilight heavens along the north and northeast horizon. Lightning flashes pulsed from within, as tentacles of electricity danced along the surface of their sun-fading nebular plumes.

Her head tipped sideways and rested upon his shoulder. Her arms embracing beneath. Her voice was soft and dulcet, "Colton?"

"Mm hm. I'm right here."

I'm pregnant, she prepared to say.

"I know." He tilted his head to rest upon hers then slowly, closed his eyes, and echoed, "I already know."

THE END

About The Author

John's childhood was often spent in the specter of nature. When not captivated by thunderstorm clouds billowing skyward amid an opening during a warm, humid summer afternoon, he was donned in heavy winter garb for an intrepid hike through New England's notorious winter storms. Always anxious to report back descriptions of what he had seen—to do so was in his nature. He would eventually go on to earn a degree in Meteorology, but life also motivated in mysterious ways. Through it all he has always possessed an unstoppable imagination. Penning science-fiction seemed more like destiny.

CPSIA information can be obtained
at www.ICGtesting.com
Printed in the USA
LVHW020056310720
661946LV00018B/482

9 781945 286476